SEASONS OF CHANGE

Seasons of Change

Richard J. Moeller

The Pentland Press Limited
Edinburgh · Cambridge · Durham · USA

First published in 2001 by
The Pentland Press Ltd.
1 Hutton Close
South Church
Bishop Auckland
Durham

British Library Cataloguing in Publication Data.
A catalogue record for this book is available
from the British Library.

ISBN 1 85821 894 2

Typeset by George Wishart & Associates, Whitley Bay.
Printed and bound by Antony Rowe Ltd., Chippenham.

Poor naked wretches, wheresoe'er you are,
That bide the pelting of this pitiless storm,
How shall your houseless heads and unfed sides,
Your looped and windowed raggedness, defend you
From seasons such as these?

(*King Lear*, Act II, Scene 4)

*For Rosemary, my wife
and infinitely patient
proof-reader who offered
continuous encouragement.*

Chapter I

Most of the time the only movement was in the Watcher's eyes. Eyes the colour of a deep lake hidden behind glare specs and in the shadow of the hood that covered the head. Eyes almost unblinking, swinging slowly but unceasingly back and forth across the valley. Very occasionally a small section of the rock face seemed to flow and move as the Watcher stretched his neck and swung his arms for a few brief moments beneath the grey-green mottled cloak. The Watcher had been there since shortly after dawn when the great red ball of the sun exploded out of the smoky hills, a difficult time to see anyone coming out of the rugged and ridged terrain. Aside from occasional sips of water and some food extracted from a Kevlar pouch beneath the cloak, there was no movement perceptible to anyone more than a few metres away. The search pattern had long since become automatic, but none the less effective for that, for while the mind behind the eyes was busy with series after series of complex mental exercises, a portion of the brain registered and noted any and every change, the flight of a hawk, the movement of some startled animal in the bushes, the falling of old, cracked rocks, even the changing of the shadows as the sun traversed its route. The valley stretched off to the east before turning north-east, a great bent and broken 'U' shape. Sparse vegetation dotted the better areas of the central floor where it fought the age-old battle for survival, seeking out what little water was available deep in the tired earth. Both sides of the valley were deceptively smooth, but there were lethal scree slopes over which any sort of progress was practically impossible and any speed unthinkable. Despite this, or perhaps because of it, the careful scan took in the slopes as well, sure in the knowledge that some day the precaution would pay for itself, even though nothing had ever come over the top on foot. The overall colour scheme was one of sandy tans and greys with sparse patches of olive green to indicate the presence of the hardy thick-leafed plants that somehow still clung tenaciously to life in this barren land.

As the day wore on the sun's now dull orange globe passed overhead and the hollow in which the Watcher sat receded into deep shadow, thereby allowing some limited use of the binoculars which could be used without fear of a stray reflection revealing the position. Early morning and mid-afternoon were as always the times for the Watcher to be extra vigilant, for these were the slots the Outsiders preferred to creep up and try to outflank any guards before attacking. So far the Hold itself had been lucky, lucky in the skill of the Watchers who had done their jobs well, for no intruder had ever come any closer than the outfields some three klicks from the main gate. Every now and then, and less frequently now than a ten cycle ago, some traveller brought news from outside, sometimes tales about towns overrun and burnt out, sometimes of Outsider attacks beaten off. In the Hold communications centre, a continuous watch was kept over a wide spectrum of both audio and video frequencies. Time was when frequent transmissions had been received and sometimes, but only very occasionally, replied to. Calls for assistance, calls of hatred, almost gone now, for of late it had become rare even to hear the hiss of a carrier wave. Overhead and to the north the clouds began to thicken forming indefinitely threatening shapes that dipped ever lower promising to engulf the peaks of the higher mountains before the day was done. Scan, pause, scan, pause, an eight-second rhythm from start to finish, unceasing, as rebel gusts of wind tugged at the ends of the cloak, a finely loomed piece the richness of which even the fine coating of sand and dust could not hide. As the wind gusted stronger, the Watcher snorted to keep the nose plugs free and he tightened the straps on the glare specs where dust particles threatened to seep through. Glare specs. Damn them. At best they were a necessary evil to combat the still high levels of uvee, less now than in the Old Days before the Fall when the Hold had been set up, but still strong enough to damage a man's retinas after a few hours.

How often had he sat here? wondered Brendt, for such was the Watcher's name. Too often even to consider counting was the easy answer, with duty shifts covering the daylight hours every day for a sevenday, followed by a sevenday without watch duties. Duty provided ample time for thought, sometimes too much, when ideas that challenge conventional wisdom slipped from the subconscious to the surface. Why was it that the Record Keepers were so reticent about admitting that the Hold had fallen into a decaying cycle? To be sure, food production from the 'ponics was up, and even some surface farms were showing increasing output. It had been almost a whole cycle since the last Outsider attack. The truth, as Brendt saw it, was that the technology that had kept the Hold running strong for fifty-two cycles was slowly beginning to fail. Even the equipment used by the Watchers had begun to fail with depressing regularity. Sooner or later they would run out of spares or cannibalizable parts for the beepers that the Watchers carried with them to warn of any approaching enemy, and then only if the remaining batteries didn't fail first. Gone were the old days of portable comm and video linkup, the remaining units being too valuable to be used for the everyday activities of the Watch. The more sophisticated production technologies had even begun to assume an aura of mystery as the background know how became more basic with the passing of the cycles, despite every effort made by the Techs to the contrary. Inside the Hold all sorts of devices, machines and assorted equipment continued to run smoothly, performing their functions flawlessly, for this was the cream of the old technology. The official answer to any such queries was that the Elders, while sharing the worries about any possibility of decline, were adamant that all this had been foreseen by the Founders who had set up the Hold as a bulwark against the inevitable fall of night. Therefore, they stated, no problems were to be expected. Brendt knew, of course, that he was regarded as something of a crank on this particular subject and he was therefore careful about sounding off in public. All the same though, there was no denying that the subject worried him deeply.

Sometimes his thoughts drifted to more pleasant matters, Ania's raven hair and pale face leaning over him sleepily in the morning, small pointed breasts more felt than seen in the dim light of the glow bulb built into the ceiling. A soft brushing kiss building up to a slow climax, a warm wet welcome where all other thought was temporarily suspended. Soon, within the next cycle probably, they would register as a permanent couple, and, if the geneticists permitted, make babies to contribute to the continuity of the Hold. Yes, he mused, life sure had some nice rewards if one was lucky.

With the first moments of the falling twilight Brendt rose stiffly to his feet and climbed the short chimney to the top of the cliff, moving slowly but easily, using the hand and footholds cut into the rock long ago. Stretching luxuriously, savouring the regained freedom of movement, Brendt stood for a few minutes to watch the swollen belly of the sun touch the mountains off to the west, seemingly spreading and flowing outwards as it slipped out of the

3

hazy sky, spreading its deep purple-red light across the landscape, hiding the few remaining colours. The coming chill of the autumn night nipped rapidly at his back, for once the sun was gone temperatures would drop quickly to a couple of degrees above freezing. This of course was the basic reason why no watch was maintained at night, the chill factor added by the night-time westerly winds made any serious attack out of the question. Some Watchers had even found freshly fallen snow in the early morning, although given the lack of water vapour this was rare. Off towards the coast, which no one had seen since the Long Days, the cold was less intense as the land dropped downwards to meet the sea, but three thousand metres above sea level in the thin night air was no place to be.

The five-klick march back to the Hold over some moderately rough territory took Brendt just over an hour measured by the hands of the old mechanical timepiece on the leather thong round his neck. Some Watchers used the so-called 'quartz' watches, but these were falling victim to the declining manufacturing capabilities. To be sure, batteries could still be produced in the automatic machines, but the mechanisms themselves had reached their limits. The mechanicals on the other hand were manufactured in the Hold and could be replaced without difficulty. The last part of the journey was made in almost complete darkness along a well-defined but cleverly concealed track, a track which was heavily defended and watched over by electronic sentinels that sent ahead notice of Brendt's coming as the smart chip in his wrist strap announced him. Any stranger coming up this way would have had to possess a very sharp pair of eyes indeed to follow the track over the bare rock, even in daylight.

The sight of the Hold, as always, surprised one by seeming to spring out of nothing as one came out of a shallow canyon and looked up to the south face of a rock face towering upwards almost vertically over four hundred metres out of the foothills through which Brendt had come up. This mountain in its turn was dwarfed by larger and taller cousins, stretching westwards like row upon row of teeth, up to the final ridge, once known as Mount Fitz Roy, now a dimly lit silhouette in the dying afterglow. A few entrances and windows of varying sizes carved into the rugged rock face hid the Hold away from the outside world. No Outsider seeing the approaches could have guessed that the Hold totalled over 290,000 square metres of construction in six levels. Rooms, passages, halls, tunnels – all cut from the rock long ago. All outward signs of the vast undertaking had been carefully obscured, leaving only a few disguised openings and some ramshackle buildings. And yet here in the mountain more than 8,600 souls lived, worked, played and planned for the better times that they were sure lay ahead. Not necessarily for themselves, for there were only a few of the original survivors still living, and the poisons in the world outside would not yet be fully cleansed for some cycles, but for their children and for those to come. These were the remnants of the great scientific cultural industrial society that had spanned the Earth. These were the survivors who owed so much to those who had seen the coming collapse, the famines and the diebacks, and not only seen, but also taken action before the Fall. Little war after little war, dragging in neighbours in a deadly frenzy of fire and pestilence, had finally reduced the cities and towns to rotting lairs for rats and savages, anti-technology groups run riot, destroying everything in their path in the belief that they did their God's will, while in the Hold the flame of civilization was protected and still burned. The Hold, and maybe others like it, hidden from view and waiting.

The sensors took note of the approach and at fifty paces or so Brendt was suddenly bathed in the bright actinic glare of the spots while the traditional challenge issued forth from a small slit high above the pathway.

'Who comes out of the darkness?' and the response, equally familiar and traditional rolling off Brendt's lips: 'Brendt Maxon of the First Watch, with all quiet.' A few seconds of silence were followed by the distant whine of the hydraulics swinging back the entry port, a rectangular hatch two metres high by one broad, a handspan thick, made of hardened alloy plasteel. Brendt passed through, stepping over the slightly raised frame. Behind him the door swung back and settled on its seals with a barely audible thump. Eyes tightly closed, he raised his hands and stepped onto the grid that occupied most of the left side of the airlock room between the two doors. After a few moments the sensor chimed softly, having admitted to itself that he was clean enough in the radiological and biological sense to enter the Hold. The twin of the door through which he had entered chuffed, and once again the whine of hydraulics admitted him into the complex.

The other Watchers, for there were sixteen manned posts in all, were already in, for the eastern point where Brendt had been on duty was the farthest out. The Watch system had not been part of the original plan, at least so the Record Keepers told. In the beginning the Hold had often sent out parties to assist others, sometimes in vehicles and sometimes on foot, occasionally by air in the small helicopter. But as the Outside became more and more unfriendly, and after a number of unpleasant encounters, the easy tracks and roads had been closed off or concealed. Additionally, the Watch system had been set up to supplement the automatic sensors, which were reliable but could not offer a full guarantee. The sensors, both passive IR, sound and active camera sites, still operated, at least most of them did for most of the time, but the Watch system guaranteed a rapid and accurate analysis of any incoming traffic. The Watch also served as the nearest thing to a formal fighting group the Hold possessed, having taken over from the first guards and soldiers. Members of the Watch were chosen in a rigorous selection procedure, one overseen by the Elders themselves, to ensure that only the most balanced and stable characters were accepted. All this before even considering the physical and intellectual attributes of the candidates, where the highest standards were also applied. To be chosen was an honour, and there was never any shortage of applicants. Time served in the Watch was normally short, an initial training period of a cycle, a programme designed, in the words of the ancients, to 'separate the men from the boys.' This was followed by a period of three cycles at the most after which the Watcher returned to the Hold as a normal citizen, unless chosen to be one of the six Watch Leaders who served for another three cycles. Apart from formal Watch duties, the Watchers escorted expeditions to the Outside, kept and repaired surveillance equipment, weapons, transports, etc. and acted as guards and fire wardens, as well as performing any other civic function that called for their specialized abilities. The Watch totalled between 110 and 130 members, depending on how many recruits were in training at a particular moment, with around forty percent being female.

In the guardroom where the Watchers changed, cleaned up and stored their equipment, the usual light banter flowed easily, the camaraderie of an élite group. The guardroom was a copy of any other that could have been found down through centuries of history in dozens of lands. The locker and shower rooms were shared regardless of sex, although in practice the furniture was placed such that the men had half of the area and the women the other.

'And so,' Davis was saying as Brendt arrived, 'I saw young Matthew here making eyes at old Zeeb's daughter,' pausing for effect. 'In fact I'd go as far as to say that something pretty interesting is going to happen soon, eh my boy?' nudging his victim in the ribs.

The younger man, with a long mane of red hair dangling almost down to his shoulders, shrugged. 'Well old man, I'm better off than you, all you're going to get a chance at is Clementine, if she'll have you that is.' The accompanying burst of spontaneous laughter drowned out all other sounds, for not every day did the biter get so well bitten. Clementine, loved by one and all, was the distant descent of the chimpanzees that had originally been intended for research but had long ago passed from being experimental subjects to being pets, tended by the staff of the Hold. Davis, a senior in his last year of the Watch, accepted defeat gracefully and having completed his change made his way out of the guardroom. Brendt stood in the shower enjoying the prickle of the hot water jets on his body, washing away the dust and the tiredness. His thoughts on decay passed into the background, held in abeyance, as though they too could be washed away with the water sluicing down the drain, taking all the impurities with it to be filtered and recycled.

Leaving the guardroom, which was on the lowest of the six levels in the Hold, Brendt used the moving ramps to pass up through Levels B and C, where the power reactor and much of the industrial operations were housed, to Level D. At each level he passed through another set of airlock-type safety doors, all of which had been designed to seal off the area in the event of any threat. He arrived at the refectory, a hall some thirty metres in diameter with a ceiling three metres high set with lighting fixtures that illuminated the table booths without seeming to be either too bright or too dull. Climbing and hanging plants decorated the area, two of the walls appeared to be picture windows looking out onto the mountains, but were in fact high-definition vid-screens fed off remote cameras set into the mountain some distance away. After collecting his food tray, Brendt sat down next to Matthew who had arrived a few minutes ahead of him. They had the table to themselves, the hall being only half full as most people tended to eat early in the evening before going to one of the recreation centres up on Level E. It was difficult to imagine that this hall, and indeed most of the Hold, had been cut out of the living rock, and that the ceiling over their heads weighed several million tons, supported only by the smooth columns which arched up into the roof. To those of them who had been born in the Hold there was nothing surprising about its construction, but to some of the older people the place was a miracle, a monument to the power of man over inanimate matter.

'So then Matt, what's new with you?' asked Brendt as he began to sort out his food, 'anything interesting today outside?'

'Nah, about as exciting as sucking a rusty nail' replied his younger friend, busily spooning soup into his mouth, 'I found myself half wondering if all the Watch makes sense.' He stopped suddenly, turning bright red, not altogether an easy task for a man with flaming red hair. 'I mean,' he stammered, 'I mean, I'm not ... ahem ... questioning the Watch, or the need for vigilance, I mean I know the history, it's just that ...' he trailed off helplessly, then tried again. 'We should be ... the Watch I mean, we should be more active, not just waiting for others to come to us, but going out further and further like they did in the Old Days.' This was a new side to the young man that Brendt had not seen before, for Matthew was still embarrassed at the thought that his ideas might be interpreted wrongly, perhaps taken as some sort of treason. But he did not back down from his statements by attempting to cover them with some excuse. 'Look, I'm not saying we're out there for nothing, I mean look at that fellow whom Bob Cantor caught last week. You'd not believe some of the stories he told Bob, he actually claimed he had been a spaceman, it's ridiculous, I mean no one's been up since the Old Days, but still, all this effort to catch the occasional wanderer, it doesn't make sense any more ...'

'Relax fella, relax, we all question the sense of it all at some point, I know I did,' pausing, and then carefully going on. 'And to be honest I still do, though in a different way from you. Look, do you know the vid-radios we carry when there's a mission to the Outside, not the Watch, but a real outing?' Seeing the assenting nod, accompanied by a puzzled frown, Brendt continued his line of thought. 'In the Old Days, everyone who went out carried one, now it's only one per group.'

'But why? What happened to all the other radios, I mean the maintenance people fix them if they go wrong, don't they?'

'Ah, that's where you've hit the nail right on the head,' Brendt replied, pushing his plate away, using the time to gather his thoughts, 'I've been talking to the maintenance boys, and to the lab people come to that. You know of course that the Hold was built during our parents' and in some cases grandparents' time. Well, they had all the technological resources of the Old Times available, and they set this place up with as much of it as they could. But somehow, I don't think they realized that we would be here for so long.' His companion sat still absorbing this concept, his food unfinished and growing cold.

'But then what did they think? I mean how do you know that they weren't thinking in terms of a fifty or sixty cycles?

'I can't prove a thing, but for a start the Record Keepers are very reluctant to let anyone see the transcripts related to the construction of the Hold, but what little I have found out indicates that their most pessimistic scenarios were in terms of twenty to twenty-five cycles, and we've been here twice that long already!' Taking a deep breath Brendt launched into the theme that had slowly grown from idle speculation to a near certainty, at least in his mind, although he had never spoken so openly before. 'Look, all the machinery and equipment here has incredibly sophisticated diagnostic maintenance and self-repair routines in their systems. We can manufacture an enormous variety of things, from transistors to nuts and bolts.' Pausing for emphasis, and then softly, almost sadly. 'And yet, we are fighting a losing battle. Look at the radios for example, maintenance fixes them, but the repaired parts are never quite as good as the originals, perhaps the germanium isn't so pure so the transistors burn out sooner, perhaps the cases aren't so ductile because each time we use more and more recycled materials, with the result that they break at the slightest knock. At the end of the day what it means to you and me is that we carry a basic signalling device out on Watch duty, but no radios because they are kept for major expeditions.'

Matt shook his head slowly. 'Not good enough, I mean sure, some things have broken down but others are coming into use. Look at the microvee detector they've developed to check the uvee levels. They launch it by balloon and it sends back gigabytes of data from hundreds of klicks away until it finally goes out of range. And another example, Tellman and his team have gone further and further into machine intelligence, I mean I saw that thing working and I swear that if I had been blindfolded I would have been convinced that I was talking to a human being.'

'OK, OK,' said Brendt, gathering up the remains of the cutlery, and they continued to talk as they made their way through the now almost empty hall to the recycle bins. 'I grant you that in certain fields we have continued to progress. But look at it this way, most of

9

the new stuff is inwards looking. We talk of the long-term; we talk about reclaiming our heritage Outside. We talk about helping bring back the best of the old civilization. We talk, and talk, and talk about the future waiting Outside, but who actually goes out? The scientists, no way, they just take measurements and plug the information into giant databases; the medics, no, they're too busy looking after our health on the inside of the Hold.' He stopped, interrupting his own train of thought, 'I don't mean to criticize the medics, they do a great job. So, where does that leave us? The farmers, yes, just, they've turned the soil and added nutrients and managed to get a few things to grow, and the new genetically disease- and uvee-resistant crops are doing well, but never more than half a dozen clicks from here. Let me tell you who goes out,' Brendt went on, jabbing his finger in the air for effect. 'You and I, the Watchers! And every time we ask about mounting a serious expedition we get fobbed off. And the excuses are reasonable I can't deny it, we need to perfect this or that which is still under development, the meteopredictor says that the next two moons will bring higher than usual winds, whatever. The point is we're not going anywhere, and in the long run not to go anywhere is to die. No,' shaking his head, 'I'm convinced the founders were thinking in terms of a decade, two at the most.'

Leaving the refectory, still talking, they walked out of the hall and took the elevator to Level E where many of the personnel quarters were situated. They parted, Brendt somehow feeling lighter for having shared his thoughts with his young partner, and Matthew with much to think about. In his bachelor quarters, a sitting-dining room with a kitchenette off to one side, and bedroom leading onto a small bathroom, Brendt tossed himself down in an easy chair and whistled at his message machine. The thing hiccuped, hummed to itself for a minute and then spoke, its electronic voice soft and soothing.

'Messages two, first, received twenty twenty-eight, reads,' and the voice changed to that of the caller. 'Brendt, this is Ania. What happened to you? We were supposed to meet after dinner, I suppose you forgot again.' Resignedly, 'never mind catch you tomorrow, Bye.' Brendt swore softly to himself, thought about calling his wife to be, but then, glancing at his watch, realized that it would be too late and that Ania's parents would definitely not enjoy being woken up. The machine continued unloading its memory. 'Second, received twenty-one oh six, reads,' again a change of voice, this time to a deep bass rumble. 'Brendt Maxon, please report to Elder Fernan in his office at oh nine hundred. The duty roster has already been changed.' Once again the machine's voice. 'No further messages. Ends.'

Brendt sat still, the stillness only a trained Watcher can find within himself, face expressionless, but his mind raced, analysing and discarding ideas. What did a summons like this to a junior Watcher mean? The Elders didn't call the likes of him for a social chat, that was for sure. He tracked back over his activities of the past few days to see if he had done or seen anything that could have called an Elder's attention. And came up with nothing, absolutely nothing. Around him the quiet noises of the Hold told him that all was well, the faint murmur of the air flow, the distant kliks as sensors switched devices on and off, the occasional distant sound of people talking as they passed his door. After a while he sat back in the chair, eyes closed, breathing easily, relaxing as the Silva exercises took over. Around him the room was quiet and warm, the cheerful colours and décor hiding the fact that it was buried inside the mountain, surrounded by rock. When the sequence was complete, he rose and undressed, throwing his clothes into the laundry machine, then crossed into the small brightly lit and cheerful bathroom where he brushed his teeth, used the toilet, and returned to the bedroom and slipped into bed. He turned off the lights and then dimmed the vid-wall that showed a computer-generated view of a moonlit lake, waves rippling in the silver light. In a few moments his eyes closed and Brendt slipped without effort from wakefulness to sleep. Tomorrow could bring what it wanted. Now he was tired, and it was time to sleep.

Chapter II

Herbert Kramer II was fed up. Not to put too fine a point on it, he was absolutely and totally cheesed off. What was the good of planning to study, analyse, repair if necessary, test and eventually learn to handle a perfectly good piece of equipment if the stuffy old Elders had placed a block on its use? He and David had built up their hopes of being able to use the Gevcars since they had discovered them a fortnight ago in an abandoned tunnel at the western end of Level A behind a sealed off passage. And worse, they were not even allowed to talk to anyone about it. He lay on his back fuming. He had been awake since the early hours turning the matter over in his mind. The ceiling above his bed remained the same, its soft peach-off-white colour that had been chosen specifically to soothe troubled minds failing miserably in its task. The longer he stared at it the more convinced he became that he had been unfairly dealt with. In the end he got up, a series of rapid jerky movements elevating his long, lean frame to a vertical position. Pacing back and forth like a caged tiger, although the phrase was both archaic and meaningless as there were in all probability no more tigers to be found anywhere on Earth, he worried the problem with his mind. He paid no attention to his living quarters around him. The tinkle of a mountain stream that played in the background, the aroma of fresh coffee from the tastefully decorated kitchenette where the cooker had produced his breakfast as programmed, the hum of the air-conditioning system, it all faded away, meaning nothing. Finally, taking a deep breath, he stopped, having at last reached a conclusion. He rubbed his hands over his short-cropped iron grey hair, massaging his scalp to ease the tension. Yes, he would ask to see. ... No! He would demand to see the Council again to explain clearly why the Gevcar should be put into service and why the decision banning its use should be reversed. And if David wasn't interested in coming along, well, he'd go it alone.

It had been a fluke, of course. He and David had been assigned by the lead Tech to trace a problem in one of the main trunks of the habitat control unit. They had often worked together and enjoyed each other's company. Seemingly a pair of opposites, for David bar

Delf was short and plump with a severe case of verbosity to which he gave full rein in the face of Herb's occasional laconic comments. Not only that, at twenty-three he was half the other man's age, and nevertheless they worked well as a team. On that particular morning when they had been sharing a duty roster, the monitoring system had detected an apparently random interference pulse that exceeded the specified acceptance level and had printed a report out to the maintenance terminal. David, bored with the book he was reading while Herb worked on the programming of an elaborate scale model of a nineteenth-century ship, had been only too happy with the interruption. After isolating the possible source to one of three terminal cabinets at the far end of Level A, they gathered up their tools and left the workshops, riding the elevator to the lower level.

There, in the depths of Level A, no effort had been made to go beyond the utilitarian. Grey slightly rough concrete walls rolled directly into the roof. Lighting fixtures threw diffuse light every five or six metres giving an even, almost shadowless light that gave their faces an unnatural green-yellow tinge. The walk to the storeroom where they began the trace had been short, not more than ten minutes. The first terminal cabinet tested normal, each i/o test and diagnostic took around two minutes as a series of signals was sent out to the main system, checked and resent back to their portable. At just over 250 i/o's on this particular trunk the day was done by the time they completed the sequence. The second day brought them no joy, but being highly trained Techs they soldiered on obstinately, confident that the problem would not elude them for long. The second cabinet also came through the test with flying colours, so they packed up again and moved on to the final one. This last terminal cabinet was mounted on the wall in a long passage, almost a tunnel really, leading off to the water recycling plant. They worked steadily for the first two hours, chatting inconsequentially while their hands flew over the keyboard of the portable as they linked up to the terminals. Their toolboxes lay open on the grey concrete floor, equipment and tools laid out within easy reach. The three-metre wide elliptically shaped passage curved off into the distance, allowing only thirty metres or so of visibility either way. The echoes of their voices seemed to hang in the air before fading, almost as though the concrete structure was parroting their statements. It took them until mid-afternoon to find the fault, which as they had half expected turned out to be a corroded terminal connection. Even the use of top-quality materials in the building of the Hold and the dry constant temperature environment had not been guarantee enough to avoid all problems. There was no way of knowing what had triggered the problem, possibly a spot of grease off the installation Tech's fingers, a drop of sweat or any number of other variables could have been enough to set the long, slow process off. This was not the first time that such things had cropped up, and it would be unlikely to be the last. A few moons ago someone in the maintenance section had called up stats from the database and they had shown a slow but steady increase in the frequency of circuit integrity problems. Not alarming in absolute terms, but nonetheless twice as many as ten cycles back, indicative of something perhaps, or there again, of nothing at all. In less than ten minutes the repair was complete and the cover screwed tightly down again.

Herb stood up, groaning as he stretched his back for he had been crouching over the open terminal cabinet while David handled the portable. He stood up, stepped back and promptly fell sideways over his toolbox. He attempted to recover his balance but events were already moving much faster than the speed of his reactions, his leg buckled under him and he went down, slamming into the curved wall with a loud thud which he accompanied with a yelp. Holding his shoulder he slid down the wall until he reached an uncomfortable sitting position and emitted a loud groan. David almost dropped the portable in his hurry to reach his partner.

'Bloody fool! Are you OK? What a bang! Here, let me see you, move your hand, have you broken anything? Sit still, put your head between your knees.' Comments and questions were spewed without pause as if David was afraid they were going out of style.

'Oh, shit,' groaned the other man. 'Oh that hurt. Ouch! Watch it David, watch it. I'll be OK, just give me a minute,' the last as David started to pull his shoulder back and forth to see if anything was broken. After a few more minutes of sitting with his head resting on the hard, cold wall he got up slowly, still holding the wall for support and with a final push straightened up, and forgot all about the pain in his shoulder. Not believing the message his hand had delivered to his brain, he turned to confirm the evidence with his eyes. David stood, puzzled, misinterpreting his friend's silence, reaching out to hold him.

Herb was now oblivious to anything else. 'Look! Do you see it? There man, there!' pointing to the wall, where the previously rough and unbroken surface had split, where a segment about a handspan square had slid a few millimetres inwards. 'Look, that's no plastered over rock cut, that's a concrete block! Give me a screwdriver. I must have loosened it when I fell against it. Ahg!' The last torn from him as he attempted to gesticulate in his excitement.

'Move over,' said David, 'I'm in better shape than you after the knock you gave yourself.' He set to work on the crack, using the screwdriver as a chisel, as he chipped away, lumps of mortar began to come loose, confirming that the loosened section was definitely of artificial origin. After a few minutes of rapid work, David tossed down the screwdriver and began to bang on the block with a small hammer he had taken from a toolbox. On the third blow the block shifted slightly, and then propelled by successive blows it slid inwards until it suddenly dropped out of sight and with a muffled bang hit the floor behind the wall. Both men stood silent, staring at the dark hole now revealed. Finally David, for once speechless, reached for the pocket torch on his belt and aimed it into the hole. Crouching slightly to see better he placed his head near the opening, smelling the cold, vaguely musty scent of places long closed. The beam of light, designed to help in close-up work reached but a short way into the darkness. In the background he could see a series of large, shapeless objects cocooned under coverings, and what appeared to be steel beams and pipes stacked in classified piles. In the tenuous beam of light dust motes danced, but the shapes, dim in the background, remained tantalizingly unclear.

'Wait a bit,' said Herb, beginning to get his thoughts together for the first time since his meeting with the wall, 'David, wait a bit, we're going about this the wrong way. First, let's tidy everything up, we've done the job we came to do, all that's missing is the report. We'll cover this up for the moment. I want to look into this more closely before we tell anyone about this find, and we must check the layout drawings to see if this is simply the back of a storeroom, although somehow I don't think so.' Pausing, then holding up his hand for silence as David made to counter his suggestion. 'My dear young friend, I hate to disappoint you, but this is not the time, I fear that my shoulder is beginning to feel uncomfortable so I want to pass by the Medcentre to get it seen to ASAP.'

'But we have to tell people' came back David. 'We can't keep this to ourselves, it's much too big. Look, there could be anything behind that wall.'

15

'Yes, anything including absolutely nothing, we could have been looking at heaps of rubble for all we know, it's impossible to be certain until we break a bit more of the wall and go in ...'

'But we can't just leave it ...'

'Oh yes we can! Listen David, what we have to do is leave a temporary cover tonight and then we'll come back when we're not on duty. If it turns out to be important, then we'll bring in whoever we need, an Elder if necessary. Look, the place has obviously been there for a long time, in all probability for the fifty cycles since the Hold was built.'

But David did not want to be put off. 'Well, ... maybe, but what if someone else finds it now?'

'Somehow I don't think that's very likely, us Techs are the only ones who come down here, and that doesn't happen very frequently.'

Finally he managed to convince his younger partner that their discovery would be perfectly safe without them. They stuck a temporary patch on the hole left by the block using a plasteel sheet from the toolkit. The patch was clearly visible, but this particular passage was so rarely used that Herb was not particularly worried about someone stumbling across it. Just to be on the safe side, they left a note pinned to the wall giving their contact numbers in case anyone should stumble across the hole. All the way back to the workshop on Level C, David chattered on about their discovery. Even burdened with both toolkits he managed to keep an incessant flow of words coming, a flow which Herb as usual was happy to encourage with the occasional nod or mumble, just to show he was paying attention, even though he wasn't really.

After leaving their equipment and filing the job finished report, they rode up to the Medcentre on F Level. There, in a warmly decorated consulting room, with walls picturing scenes of long-vanished beaches, Herb's shoulder was X-rayed and declared sound, his bruises sprayed with Neocain and ably bandaged by a cheerful young nurse who was only too glad to interrupt a boring afternoon duty shift to attend a real live patient. After chiding him about his clumsiness, she issued him with a three-day pass and, after chatting inconsequentially for ten minutes, reluctantly ushered both men out of the Medcentre.

'Give me a day to work on my shoulder' said Herb as they finally parted ways, 'I'll put in some time tomorrow at the Fitness Hall, and then we'll meet the day after tomorrow and have a go at the wall.'

With this agreed upon, each man retired to his rooms with plenty to think about.

The sledgehammer thudded into the wall for the eleventh time and four more blocks fell inwards. The hole, now half a metre wide and twice as tall, seemed to beckon to them, a place of mystery, a place of treasures yet to be discovered. The air was thick with dust, despite the efforts of the portable vacuum unit that moaned lustily as it sucked in and filtered the particle-burdened air. David, sweating slightly from the effort, laid down the hammer and wiped his face leaving a streaky smear of dust across his forehead.

'That should do it for the moment, plug in the lamp and let's go in and have a look,' a touch of excitement in his voice revealing the excitement within. David turned again to the opening while Herb unreeled the lantern cable and walked a few dozen steps down the passage to the nearest power socket. He plugged in the lantern, did a quick on–off to test the connection and walked back to the hole, laying out the cable to be sure to avoid any knots. Both men stood for an instant, their minds on what lay on the other side of the wall, the first exploration ever to have taken place since the Hold was built. Their eyes met for a brief moment, David's mouth twitching upwards at one corner, the only indication of his inner excitement, and with a slow nod to each other and with Herb leading they clambered through the hole. They had checked the layout drawings carefully, very carefully, but had been quite unable to find any indication about the mysterious room they had uncovered. David had even queried the central archives regarding temporary construction storerooms abandoned after the building of the Hold was completed, but had drawn a complete blank.

The lantern beam swept out a tunnel of light through the stygian darkness within, revealing a cave rather than a tunnel, for the walls were rough and unfinished. Turning the beam back the way they had come in, it was possible to see that the block wall against which Herb had stumbled a couple of days earlier was only three metres or so wide and about the same in height, covering a hole which had been blasted into the rock face.

'Just look at that,' marvelled David, 'the chances of you doing that again are so small that it's not even worth thinking about, I mean with all that wall and you hit just the right place ...,' he trailed off, still lost in thought.

'Yeah, but I sure don't feel like trying to find another hole, at least not using the same method' replied Herb with a rueful grin, 'my shoulder's still stiff, even with all the stuff the Meds put on it.' He spun the beam upward onto the rock roof at least twice their height above their heads, and then back into the cave. Ahead of them and slightly off to the left were the piles of pipes they had seen from the outside, and beyond these the piles of something under what appeared to be plastic cover sheets. Their footsteps made very little noise as they advanced across the slightly uneven floor, each step raising a little puff of dust that billowed out like a miniature fountain before settling again. The bobbing light showed them that the cave was at least sixty metres long by forty wide, but whether it was natural or man-made was difficult to tell. They walked alongside the lengths of different diameter piping, where Herb stopped and ran his finger across a card that hung from one bunch allowing him to read the discoloured writing, simply technical specs, not a material they were personally familiar with, but somehow reassuring in the strangeness that surrounded them. Far more interesting was the inspection date given on the tag, 5 July 2025, halfway through the final construction period. Leaving the packets of piping and construction beams they moved on past other assorted piles of materials, until they reached the first of what they could now see were three separate covered objects. The size of each object was larger than they had first thought, taller by a metre and a half than Herb and about twelve or even more metres long by five and a half to six wide.

Putting the lantern on the floor with the setting on wide beam they started to work at removing the covering. The material was simply polyethylene sheeting or some similar material laid over the object in overlapping strips. The covering had obviously been done carefully with clips at regular intervals along the bottom, which they popped open one by one as they moved down the length round the back into the shadowy darkness and round again to the front.

'OK, here we go,' David practically beside himself with excitement, he stepped forward picking up one corner of the sheeting.

'Hold it, hold it, I'm not quite done.' Herb had retreated a few metres to set up a vid-unit, for they had agreed to record their activities just in case something should happen to them. He completed the job, pressed the record button and moved over to join his partner.

'Let battle commence!' announced David facetiously as they pulled together at the cover. After a brief initial resistance the first section of the cover slid towards them releasing a cloud of fine dust, no doubt the result of decades of settling particles. They retreated pulling the sheet with them, coughing as the man-made dust storm flowed downward off the top, pulled by the suction of their passage, enveloping them in their own private cloud. After a few seconds it became obvious that the mystery object was a vehicle of some sort. A vehicle, but unlike anything else in the Hold, unlike even anything either of them had seen on the films about the Old Days which were always available in the Library, although they drew less and less interest as time passed. Slowly the dust settled, leaving only a thin dissipating cloud of fine matter, and both men had without conscious thought stopped pulling and they stood gazing open-mouthed at their find. Squat was a good description, squat and almost threatening it sat there. It was painted in a grey-green mottle camouflaged pattern, at least so it appeared in the light from the lantern that tended to distort colours. At the bottom folds of a flexible black substance surrounded it, much like a short skirt. There were dark windows at the sides of the uncovered part, with a large sloped windscreen at what was presumably the front of the vehicle. Glancing at each other, they started pulling off the remaining covers, releasing with each fall new clouds of dust that hung in the air, particles swirling in the glow of the lantern. Once the vehicle was uncovered they retrieved the lantern and walked round it – twice. There were doors on each side, and a large hatch at the back, the whole aspect being one of utilitarian ruggedness and power. There was no identification of any sort other than a five-digit serial number painted on each door and the legend 'SITE 3' on the nose. A number of covers and protuberances in the rough metal sides of the vehicle were also identified by their functions: hydrogen, air, water, 380 V 50 Hz, oxygen, etc., others were obviously handholds, while some were unidentified and meaningless.

'So what now,' queried David.

'Well, I guess it's time to take a look' replied Herb. 'Let's see if the doors are unlocked,' reaching up for the handle as he spoke. The door handle, recessed into an opening, remained unmoving for a few seconds, and then yielded with a slight scrape as he applied more pressure, moving down and releasing the door which opened slowly outwards in response to Herb's pull. Both men stood still, staring at the open door, probably an armoured construction for it was at least ten centimetres thick, through which they could see a slightly curved stairway leading up to what was obviously the pilot's seat with the control panel in front of it. Both men peered into the vehicle, and then at each other.

'I don't think anyone is going to be getting out after all this time' joked David, a comment that earned him a grunt from his older partner. Herb cautiously climbed the stairs and pulled himself up into the cabin. He sat in the pilot's seat for a moment breathing the slightly musty air and then slid across allowing David to follow him into the vehicle. The controls were for the most unfamiliar as neither of them had ever driven any sort of vehicle other than the electric carts inside the Hold. They sat together pointing out this and that detail, until they noticed a large envelope on the floor in front of them. The envelope had been hanging from one side of a length of what had obviously once been adhesive tape, long since dried out, a fact confirmed by the presence of a matching stain on the windshield in front of them.

'Instructions to whoever finds this envelope' read David. 'Read this before proceeding any further. Justin Cooper, August 2026.' With a glance at Herb, he slit open the envelope and pulled out a folder with fifteen or twenty sheets of closely typed data. Together, in the yellow light of the lantern, they read with increasing wonder the story of why the vehicle had been hidden in the cave. The Hold, as they knew from the history lessons, had been conceived as a contingency plan against the fall of civilization. This vehicle was, on an infinitely smaller scale and in its own way, a contingency plan within the plan, in case the Hold was unable to fulfil or was delayed in the fulfilment of its Prime Directive.

Every person now resident in the Hold without any exceptions, from the few oldsters who could still remember life in the Old Days to the new generations who had never lived outside, knew with absolute certainly that the one and only reason for the Hold's existence was to maintain a basis for the reconstruction of civilization when the troubles ended. Of late there had been some discussion as to the time period this waiting phase should take, but there was no doubt that at some moment they would be going out into the world to help rebuild. Yet, here in black and white was the proof that someone among the far-sighted men and women who had organized and built this safe haven had also envisaged that the time might come when fresh input might be required. They read through the sheets in silence and without pause, in awe at this message sent down through time to them. The hard core was that two very advanced Gevcars (or Ground Effect Vehicles) along with a number of parts and spares, had been placed in an unmarked tunnel along with a quantity of supplies, without the knowledge of the majority of the inhabitants in the Hold. These vehicles were so secret that not more than a couple of hundred people knew of their existence, and when the advancing waves of chaos had threatened to wipe out the industrial plant where they had been built, they had been spirited away. There were, the two Techs read, always supposed to be two Elders on the Council who would be informed by their predecessors about the existence of the cave and its contents. The decision about their use or the continued secrecy regarding their existence had been left exclusively in the hands of the two Elders. When the Hold had been set up, its founders had foreseen a period of not more than thirty cycles until it would be safe to go out again, therefore a clause had been set into the instructions to be handed down, that if this time limit was exceeded, then the knowledge was to be shared with the Council. The documents also made reference to a pack of computer discs containing more detailed information on the construction, operation and maintenance of the Gevcars, as well as locations of supply drops on the outside.

'Wow, something somewhere got screwed up, don't you think?' muttered David, 'we've been running for fifty-two cycles, and no one talks much about going out yet.'

Herb, who had been sitting staring into space, spoke at last. He spoke forcefully. 'You've missed the point, no, that's not fair, you've only understood part of it. Look, do you realize what this document is telling us? We're not alone, the Hold was set up as Site 3.' Pausing for breath and then delivering the clincher. 'That means there are or at least were two other Holds! This is amazing, why haven't we heard from them in all this time? Look, I don't know what went wrong, but we'd better get this information back to the Council as soon as possible.'

'And we'd better not say anything to anyone until we've spoken to them,' ventured David, 'I mean this is going to be big, big news ... wow, you'd better believe it!'

They descended from the vehicle, the Gevcar, for the name sounded right somehow, as though familiar. They turned off the vid,

21

which was still recording, gathered up their belongings and climbed back out to the passage taking with them the computer disc pack which they had found where the notes had indicated. As they left the tunnel they were invaded with a sense of unease about their discovery, an event which had appeared from nowhere to threaten their comfortable and routine existence. Once again they covered the now enlarged hole, this time using a flexcloth which they had brought with them all rolled up, and made their way back to the maintenance workshops. After washing up and putting everything away as their training demanded, Herb sent off a request for an immediate audience to the Council, which was as usual answered by the automatic appointments system giving them a slot the following morning. They had called up the general layout drawings on the maintenance terminal only to find that there was no record of any sort of blocked off tunnel. The only conclusion they reached after estimating the position and size of the tunnel was that the far end would be fairly near the outside rock face, so it was even conceivable that there might in fact be a hidden exit in existence. They had queried the archives about Gevcars and Ground Effect Vehicles, but all that came back was general information on the concept as well as some vid-film showing practical applications constructed in the twentieth century. Having resigned themselves to this dead end, there was nothing further to do except wile away the time until dinner and afterwards bed.

The meeting with the Elders had not gone as they had expected. Definitely not. They had received no commendation for their albeit accidental discovery. The Elders had shown considerable interest but no visible surprise at the news. They had questioned Herbert and David at length on the state of everything found in the tunnel, their opinions on the operability of the vehicle and on how the vehicle could be moved were discussed at considerable length. The notes and discs retrieved from the Gevcar however had been rather rudely confiscated, as had the vid-recording. Elders Koslowski and Sandre had cautioned them against telling anyone about the affair as well as against pursuing any further investigation. After a brief consultation the Elders present had declared the matter closed and had formally dismissed them.

'We thank you Herbert Kramer and David bar Delf for bringing this matter to our attention. The Council will discuss the correct actions to be taken and in due course the Hold will be informed.

Meanwhile you are reminded that any and all information pertaining to the issue is reserved information.' Herbert standing on his dignity had attempted to make the Elders see the benefits of further investigation, specially as a result of the possibility of there being other Holds. He was rapidly dissuaded from this approach, less by his partner pulling on his arm than by the very cold stares given him by the members of the Council.

And so it was that Herb found himself deciding to go back to the Council. Having taken the decision he suddenly felt much relieved, he finished his breakfast rapidly and then went for his shower. He was just getting ready to leave when he realized that a message had come in while he had been in the shower. He flicked the switch and the machine gave up its message in its lilting electronic voice.

'Messages, one, received oh seven twenty-one, reads,' and the voice changed to a deep bass rumble. 'Herbert Kramer, please report to Elder Fernan in his office at oh nine hundred. Your supervisor has already been advised.' Herb slumped back in his chair feeling slightly deflated. Here he was all steamed up about demanding an interview and now he had it. Assuming of course that this call was related to their discovery. He was reaching for the phone with the intention of calling David when it went off under his hand and his friend's voice came over the speaker.

'Hey Herb. You'll not believe it, I've just had a call ...'

'From Elder Fernan,' completed Herb, 'so have I my friend, now we'll see what the Council has come up with, see you there pal.'

[Extract – 2019]

(The following reports are excerpts from the minutes of the Site 3 Steering Committee meeting held on 19 December 2019. It is to be noted that all records related to 1 January 2018 to 31 December 2025 have been classified as restricted and can only be accessed with the authorization of the Council of Elders.)

The removal of any documents from the Records Hall or the copying of any information relating to this period is strictly forbidden.

Phase II Construction Contract Report: Four construction companies have now been preselected to tender the Phase II construction from a total of seven possibles: Betchel Brown Corp., Daniel International Construction, Takyama Heavy Industries and Techint Worldwide, Inc. All these companies have ample experience in heavy rock construction above and below ground. All are now fully under the impression that the Owners have located an extremely rich bauxite field and wish to keep the information secret for as long as possible in order to avoid any sudden share revaluation. Information supporting this has been allowed to leak in such a way that it has been seen as genuine. No further investigative activities by or on behalf of the participating companies have been detected since August last. It has been decided to subdivide the construction activities between the two winning bidders. This will permit us to supply technical specifications edited in such a way to confuse any interested party further about the final destination of Site 3. Tender specifications are currently being completed and will be handed out at the end of this month. The time limit for the delivery of the technical bids has been set at a maximum of ninety days after this date, and commercial offers a further thirty days beyond this date. The date for awarding the contract will be kept at 1 June 2020 in accordance with the Site 3 Masterplan Time Schedule, with on site activities to start within twenty days after this date.

Attachments:

- Shareholders Reports on Preselected Companies
- Technical Evaluation Reports on Preselected Companies
- Preliminary Phase I Layouts

Phase I Time Schedule (Preliminary): Power Subcommittee Report:
Continuing with the status report presented two months ago we are
pleased to report that a decision regarding power generation for Site 3
has now been taken. The tests carried out at the CERN facility during
the past weeks have shown that the new ceramic coupling system has
reduced plasma instability in the reactor core to well within
manageable levels. The liquid sodium fission reactor option has
therefore been abandoned in favour of the CERN double-core toroidal
fusion reactor (TFR). Although the prototype at CERN is not strictly
speaking a power reactor, it has provided sufficient data on power
performance to proceed onwards with the building of the 30 MW
reactor necessary for Site 3. The confidentiality of the Site 3 TFR unit
has been guaranteed by CERN, which is also initiating the construction of four other power reactors for the EC Grid. No press releases of
any sort will be made throughout the construction period other than
those relating to the EC Grid units. These commercial units are
expected to be ready for installation within three years of P/O receipt.
Shipping, installation and commissioning will be carried out by Site 3
teams with CERN supervision. A cold start-up date has been set for 15
March 2024; this date has been integrated into the Masterplan Time
Schedule and has resulted in an improvement on the originally
planned completion date for the power services. It is of special
interest to note that the use of the TFR has eliminated the need for
the fissile materials lager and the associated cooling equipment. These
savings to the budget will be applied to additional redundancy
systems and an additional remote control and monitoring system for
the TFR. The design of auxiliary and ancillary systems is proceeding as
scheduled, with the tender specifications for the central control expert
system expected to be completed by mid-2020.

Attachments:

- Abstract: Fission Reactors – The New Generation
- Basic TFR Schematics
- Preliminary Layout Site 3 Power Installations
- TFR Construction Time Schedule
- TFR Installation and Commissioning Time Schedule
- Cost Control

Hydrogeological Report: After completion of the additional hydrogeological survey, water adequate for human and animal consump-

tion has now been confirmed at a depth of four hundred metres below the surface at this point. A borehole site has been chosen on the edge of the N2 seismic survey zone on the basis of this study plus the site security parameters stated in the specifications. A series of six shots were executed on each of five lines covering an area of approximately five hundred hectares. All these showed multiple reflecting layers at depths varying between 250 and 620 metres. Analysis of the results showed that in areas N1 and N2 a third impervious layer some two metres thick is present. Above this area is a layer of water-bearing limestone some sixty metres thick with enough feed to ensure a low-pressure artesian supply. This area is limited on its eastern side when the second and third granite layers merge. Core samples also confirmed the seismic results. The site chosen is in a large natural cave reached through a tunnel some thirty metres long opened by the exploration team. Water samples from the test bore show a medium hardness, slightly alkaline, non-carbonated water. Sediment levels are extremely low and will be non-existent once the final bore is drilled and a filter installed. Water analysis shows no harmful constituents and no signs of any contamination have been found. Temperature has remained steady at sixteen degrees Celsius, and it is estimated that given the depth of the bore there will be no seasonal variations. The permeability of the aquifer is exceptionally good with dynamic levels falling only two metres during the extended pumping tests. When the definite pump and bore are completed it is recommended that continuous pumping rates should not exceed twenty-five cubic metres per hour. A second borehole site has also been established in the N1 zone approximately 570 metres from the first bore. Work will commence there once the first bore has been completed, with an early start date having been set at 2 February.

Attachments:

- Survey Map 1:20,000
- Seismic Data Summary Printouts
- Core Sample Reports
- Water Analysis

News Item Summary: Israel yesterday launched a retaliatory attack on Tehran after the attack by Hamas suicide bombers last Saturday in Jerusalem where the entire city centre was sprayed with radioactive dust from a low-flying helicopter which destroyed itself before the airforce could arrive. Two Israeli two kiloton warheads carried by Galahad missiles spaced twenty minutes and fifteen miles apart were detonated five hundred feet over Tehran. The death toll is expected to be close to one million. The UN has issued a strongly worded warning to both parties to stand down or face the consequences of direct action by the UN Defence Forces currently on exercise in the Mediterranean.

Wo Chang Lee the new Premier of China has issued a statement refusing to withdraw his troops from Taiwan. It is believed that all organized resistance to the Chinese invasion has now ceased although resistance groups are still operating in the mountains. Unconfirmed reports tell of an entire Chinese division put out of service after drinking water contaminated with an unknown and highly virulent poison which attacks the central nervous system. All communication links out of Taiwan are in the hands of the invading forces, any official news is therefore considered unreliable at best.

Protesters using hand grenades forced the temporary closure of Frankfurt Airport last Tuesday claiming that heavier-than-air machines are the works of the devil. This is the third time this year that anti-technology terrorists have struck at airports in Europe. Six demonstrators were killed by one of their own grenades and two members of the security staff were seriously injured. Two aircraft including a Boeing 787 were slightly damaged. Over five hundred of the demonstrators were arrested and are being held pending appearance before the magistrates.

A report released yesterday shows that desertification in the Amazon basin is advancing at a rapid rate. Despite efforts by the Brazilian government and an international aid programme the tropical rainforest is being reduced at 3.7 percent per year due to excessive burn-offs. This is already resulting in significant climatic changes including the destruction of large tracts of arable land due to almost permanent rainfall, particularly in Southern Europe. So far the US has made up for crop shortfalls, but the report warns of hard times ahead.

Chapter III

'Here's to you old pal, and many happy returns,' Karel Houseman, seventy-six years old, late of the ESC, raised his glass to the face that stared back at him out of the mirror and took a gulp from the tall glass of ale. A face with a lifetime of experience, wrinkled and burnt, with a thin, pale scar running down one cheek from near the bridge of the great hooked nose to the base of the left ear, bright blue eyes that seemed capable of boring clean through anything they might choose to focus on and a shock of white hair tied back into a ponytail, held with a multicoloured strip of cloth.

He turned from the mirror and ambled over to the desk on the other side of the room, back straight and head held high, his walk that of a man forty years younger. Karel Houseman, one time Captain in the now long defunct European Space Corps, one of the last surviving men on the planet who had orbited the Earth and stared down on the green and blue cloud-spattered globe, closed his eyes in thought, a small smile tugging at the corners of his mouth. It was amazing when you thought about it. He had spent the better part of a lifetime wandering in the wilderness, where just staying alive from day to day was enough of a task to occupy any man. And now here he was, a luxury guest in one of the Survival Centres he had heard about all those years ago, and had searched for far and wide across the continent.

When he had been chosen at the age of twenty-three to join the ESC Copernicus mission he had not hesitated for a moment, even knowing the degree of resentment that the continuing space research programme was generating among dissident groups could not dim the thrill and honour of being chosen to occupy the right-hand seat in the cockpit. The mission had the prime objective of monitoring changes to the ozone layer using a new space-borne imaging technique, as well as half a dozen other less important scientific studies. The scheduled duration of the flight had been planned as two months with a relief science crew to come up halfway through the mission. When they heard the news about the take-over of the ESA space centre halfway through the second month, the five men and four women aboard Copernicus were only half surprised. The planning included contingency telemetry centres and alternate landing sites that the planners had never expected would be necessary. In any event, they knew they could stay up for several months until things were put back in order again. Unfortunately things were not put back in order, the anti-technology fanatics, led by the group calling itself the Luddite Revival, systematically targeted space launch and control centres across the planet, making it impossible to maintain communications for any length of time. Despite their rejection of all things technical, the Luddites had no compunction about using jamming devices and even stolen radar-guided missiles to destroy the tracking stations.

In the end they were limited to contacts with independent short wave radio stations from whom they heard over eleven months all about the seemingly endless series of pogroms, social disorders, civil wars, diseases, police actions and, of course, diebacks. At first it was in the back of beyond, in the so-called Third World nations, where the old diseases emerged again, tuberculosis, bubonic plague of the airborne variety, all helped nicely along by mass starvation, ethnic cleansing, surgical nuclear strikes, disease seeding and the use of Nogrow, once hailed as the cheap birth control solution, and so on, a seemingly endless litany of man-made disasters, complementing the usual crop of natural events, earthquakes, typhoons, tsunamis, etc. By the end of the first half of 2024 it was clear that the old world order was on the way out, Africa, much of Asia, as well as parts of Central America had begun to vanish into the twilight world of war and pestilence, diebacks and decay. The cost, a mere three-quarters of a billion or so lives, in the end body counts were meaningless, just lost statistics. The major remaining power blocks began their own journey inwards, their objective now being simply to protect their own, for there was no longer any way they could prevent the fall of the poorer nations without destroying themselves in the process.

Up in Copernicus the crew had got on with the job, working and studying, and waiting for things to get better, which was a forlorn hope. Finally, they had decided by majority vote to take the shuttle down, and after endless discussions had agreed on the choice of landing site, opting for Edwards Air Force Base, which they knew was still operating and where they would be welcomed. After carefully programming the re-entry parameters, checking and double checking the data with their on-board computers, they were ready.

Unfortunately it is in the nature of things to go awry, and the final decision on the landing site was made for them by the failure of a chip the size of a pin head and costing no more than a couple of Euro's, which led to a misfiring re-entry engine, which burned on long after the signal to stop the burn had been sent, ignoring the manual cut-out as well, bringing them down in a much steeper than intended path. Karel and shuttle commander Pete Thorson had done what they could to save the situation, bringing into play the hundreds of hours of rigorous training which had been drummed into them. In the very short time available they selected an alternate site from way down on the contingency lists, fighting for control all the way. They had put the graceful bird-shaped lifting body down more or less in one piece in South America, on a far too short military field in Mendoza, on the eastern foothills of the Andes mountains.

The landing run had been rough. A real pig of a run, Karel had dumped every fuse on the fuel system in order to shut off the runaway engine while Pete fought to adjust the re-entry attitude by hand to avoid burning up. Together they had ridden the beast down, the intense vibration had seemed to threaten to shake the instruments right out of the panel and the roar of ionizing gas on the outer skin had been heard through the shuttle. As the air thickened, the control surfaces had begun to take effect and they were able to stretch the glide path far enough to make it into the field, one that was listed as an alternate to the alternate, in other words, pretty far down the list. The runway had definitely not been designed for a shuttle landing, too narrow and too short, and even at maximum brake pressure they overran the end of the runway by some two hundred metres ending up with a crumpled belly in the rough desert beyond the field. The damage was such that even to the untrained eye it was obvious that the shuttle would never fly again. Bits of the undercarriage and other sundries littered the track the shuttle had plowed into the rugged ground, enough, as Pete said afterwards, to give the bean counters a good headache as they worked out how much it had all cost. But, as the old saying goes, 'if you can walk away from it, it's a landing.'

Karel had sometimes tried to estimate how far he had travelled since that last hair-raising landing fifty odd years ago, thirty, forty or even fifty thousand klicks? Who knows? Certainly he had seen a good deal of the southern half of South America, practically

everything below the Equator in fact. The nine crewmembers of
Copernicus had been made welcome on the arid slopes below the
towering height of the Aconcagua. The town of Mendoza, once a
thriving industrial centre and an even more famous wine-growing
area, had also decayed since its heyday at the end of the twentieth
century. Social unrest, local rebellions and squabbling political
warlords had all taken their toll, leaving a partly empty city with a
loose social structure and some working industry. It was a small and
still civilized outpost, lost in the dry, stony desert that had once
bloomed under the watchful eye of man but now was reverting to its
original status. The crew of the Copernicus had stayed on for almost
five years, the locals being only too happy to add nine very highly
skilled workers to their number. Some of them settled in on a
permanent basis, finding partners among the local residents and
producing children, a hope for the future. The world around them
continued to self-destruct, a behemoth out of control, though no
single event could in itself have been taken as earth shattering.
Sometimes things seemed to improve for a few months with new
alliances pledged and trade picking up, but in the end this or that
political faction or terrorist splinter group would commit some
atrocity plunging yet another fragment of the globe into conflict. For
the first decade since the turn of the century food production
declined even faster than the world population. The old bogey man
of population explosion had long since vanished back in 2017 when
Roche Labs first marketed a workable airborne contraceptive virus,
the Nogrow virus as it came to be known, which inhibited ovulation
for eighteen to twenty months after inhalation. The use of Nogrow
hailed at first as a boon to civilization soon became its nemesis as
rival states used it on each other, and the world population having
peaked at something over five billion soon began to drop back. Even
so, starvation spread its hand at an ever increasing speed over vast
areas of the planet, there being no longer mountains of butter and
grain to fall back on as there had been fifty years earlier. Quietly and
without too much fuss another two and a half billion souls vanished
in the short space of five years.

While some of the new arrivals from space settled in well, others
continued to feel a sense of unease at the way time was passing them
by. Four members of the Copernicus team in particular had never
managed to feel quite at home in Mendoza. Chief scientist Jose
Marlont and biophysicist Susanne Polk were two, the third being

telemetry officer Sandy Cook with whom Karel had maintained a close affective relationship since before the flight. Karel smiled to himself, he and Sandy had been casual acquaintances at the academy, but had not had much to do with each other until at one of the postgraduation parties, when after being formally introduced by a mutual friend they suddenly sensed something between them, pheromones, magic, empathy, call it what you will. The friend, proving that he was indeed a friend, had had enough good sense to realize what he had done, and had vanished into the noise of the ongoing party leaving them to themselves. Out in the garden they had talked until the early dawn began to lighten the sky, they had returned to Karel's room and before the sun was clear of the horizon had become lovers. And so it had remained between them, a bond neither of alikes nor of opposites, but of complementary parts, as solid as a rock.

As the days and then the weeks passed in Mendoza, they had at first kept in touch by short wave with the few remaining ESC communication centres in Europe, but these contacts became less and less frequent until finally they ceased altogether. Eventually the day came when they made up their minds to leave Mendoza, a difficult decision, slow in the making, triggered in the end by a piece of information which Jose had extracted from some computer discs he found by accident in the archives of the engineering company where he was employed. While searching the files for some data on a previous job order, Jose had come across a lot of references on jobs related to equipment for a large and apparently secret mining project. As he delved deeper into the files, driven simply by a scientist's innate curiosity and the urge to get to the bottom of things, he began to realize that much of the equipment ordered had very little to do with mining. Inevitably, he had shared his discovery with his colleagues, a discovery which had turned out to be the point of inflection in their lives, a discovery which was to send them out on a trek which was to last most of their lives.

The information Jose had found on the discs was between two and four years old, yet it had been disguised with work order numbers to appear to be ten years old. Much of the equipment delivered had appeared to be related to a very large and complex life support and air-conditioning system equipped with multiple redundancies and failsafe accessories. The delivery address given was for a mining conglomerate in southern Brazil. Between them they had tracked

32

down as much information as they could, fabrication schedules, subcontracts, invoicing and payments, all of it available but disguised in such a way as to make it seem other than what it was. The price paid for the equipment had seemed exorbitant to them, even in a period of inflation and financial uncertainty, 30 million Eurocredits paid through Geneva was a very large sum. It had been Susanne who had first proposed two ideas that could be used to explain the equipment supplied. The first was that it was for an underground secret Survival Centre, a sort of equivalent to the twentieth-century bomb shelter, but on a vastly greater scale. The second was that it was for a space habitat, possibly even a long-term venture with the idea of travelling to nearby stars. After some discussion the first idea was accepted as the most likely because none of them had ever heard anything about a space habitat and given the easy relationships between astronauts of different nations it wouldn't have been possible to build such a ship undetected.

Karel interrupting his reverie lowered himself into the chair in front of the desk. Here at last in this place they had searched so assiduously for, here where he had arrived after being spotted by the scout, the Watchers as they called themselves. Truth was, he mused, if the boy hadn't seen him he would probably have missed the place altogether. All the information he had gathered over the years hadn't given him an exact location, just an area of some one hundred hectares. Yes, he had been lucky there. The place, this so-called Hold, though his information had referred to it as Site 3, had been an amazing surprise. After so many years of primitive living with the assistance of ever more decayed technology, the Hold was like finding a miracle. What little he had seen as he had been escorted here, and later as he had been very professionally debriefed, had confirmed beyond any doubt that Susanne's first suspicions that someone or some group had been setting up Survival Centres were correct. Jose, now long dead, would have been pleased about that, definitely pleased. And Sandy and Susanne as well, God willing he would see them before too long if these Hold people believed him about the other sites and allowed him out. The women had remained at a small town they had come across, on the shores of a blue-grey lake some five or six hundred klicks to the north. This was not the first time he had gone out alone in order to move faster, but it was a shame they couldn't have been with him to share the moment, that and the almost forgotten luxury of soft beds and hot showers.

So far Karel had seen only a small part of what was obviously a vast underground complex. Apart from the guardhouse area round the airlock where he had been brought in, he had seen workshops in what was obviously a maintenance area, what appeared to be a production line for small plasteel components (question: where does the power necessary to run that come from?), a glimpse of what had seemed to be a computer assembly room, and a little of this floor called Level C where he had been housed and where he had been interviewed by members of the Council. Certainly everyone he had been in contact with had been very friendly. Especially once it became obvious that he had no intention of harming anyone, but equally it was clear that he was something less than a guest, not quite a prisoner, but not a free man either.

Once again Karel Houseman, seventy-six years old, late of the ESC, raised his glass to his lips and took a swallow.

'Here's to you as well Jose, you were right as usual, and now it's up to me to make sense of it all.' He placed the glass carefully down on the desk and leaned back, the chair automatically adjusting its angle to his movement. The picture window in front of him showed the peaks of the mountains to the west, gleaming in the afternoon sun, which had not yet gone behind them. Karel let his eyes wander over the scene as he sat there, eyes which looked at but did not see the mountains as past memories swept in. Memories of a life more adventurous and exciting than he had ever dreamed of as a young boy, school, college, space and the endless wandering across a burned and barren land.

Never for a moment imagining the years and distance that lay ahead of them, the small group of four ex-astronauts had set out from Mendoza early in June 2029. The weather was already bitingly cold, though no snow had fallen so far that year. All the information they had gathered on the mysterious Site 3 pointed to a location some 500 klicks to the north of Santa Catarina in what had once been Brazil, and they had planned a roundabout route to get there so as to avoid large population centres where such a small group would be likely to be attacked and possibly killed by vigilante groups.

They travelled on modified electrobikes that they had been able to salvage and repair, these all-terrain three-wheel bikes being a practical form of transport as the old road system was in a poor state of repair after almost a decade of negligence. Long-distance travel on a planned basis had to all intents and purposes ceased to exist, and even then had become something of an adventure. To be sure there were a few quasi-regular bus services still running, but these were few and far between. It was also possible to get a ride with truck convoys carrying goods between towns, but these ran at irregular intervals to say the least, and destinations were in any event decided by the loads offered. As they moved along the empty road, in places not much more than an overgrown track, they looked for all the world like a collection of beings from outer space with their helmets with darkened visors to reduce the glare to a minimum, an impression heightened by the face masks they used to protect themselves from the all pervasive dust and smoke, the by-products of years of fires and explosions which had flung dust and soot particles right up into the stratosphere. With the high uvee radiation levels it was essential to avoid direct exposure to the sun whenever possible, at least during the middle of the day. Either that or run the risk of early cataract development and skin cancers of varying lethality.

The first fifteen or so years of the twenty-first century had seen more man-induced changes in the world climate system than all the previous centuries combined. The most pronounced of these was a steep increase in the carbon dioxide content of the atmosphere, which by trapping heat within the atmosphere led to an overall increase of the average temperatures by a couple of degrees. This resulted in the melting of a part of the ice caps with the consequent increase in average sea level by something between fifty and seventy centimetres. Most of the coastal cities of the world had been ill prepared for such an event despite the fact that scientists had been predicting such a catastrophe for many years. Although many of the cities were still standing and were still inhabited, the years of chaos had reduced their population to a mere fraction of what they had been. A secondary aspect affecting climatic changes was the result of the ground level detonations of a significant number of tactical nuclear devices over a period of years as the political situation became more and more uncontrollable. These explosions had flung vast quantities of dust into the upper atmosphere, radioactive particles which reflected and absorbed some light and heat thereby cancelling out a part but not all of the greenhouse effect. The only marginally positive effect of the dust was spectacular sunrises and sunsets, the like of which had rarely if ever been seen before. The high uvee levels were a result of the previous century's excessive use of the so-called CFC gases, and although by the middle of the first decade of the twenty-first century these gases had been phased out, the recovery of the uvee levels would take several decades at best.

The group journeyed south-eastwards, following wherever possible the old roads. Each village or town was an adventure on its own, in some places they were welcomed and stayed for a few days or even weeks to recover from the rigours of the journey. In other towns they barely got out with their lives. Suspicion and hatred of strangers had become in many places the order of the day, and it was better to attack and kill anyone rather than wait and see if they were likely to be friendly. Sometimes in order to avoid passing through or near one of the larger towns they were forced to make detours of several hundred klicks. Speed was not an important factor in their planning; even so they despaired of the days when conditions were so bad that they barely covered a dozen klicks or so.

Whenever they stopped for more than a night Sandy would set up the communications unit and listen in to whatever radio traffic was on the air. Since their arrival back on Earth they had established a fairly regular listening in pattern. At first they had kept contact with some of the remaining ESC station officers up in Guyana who had managed to get their equipment running again, but one day they vanished and were never on the air again. It was something of a paradox that the anti-technology groups continued to hit out at the very technology that could have been used to help the world pull itself together, but on the whole they were by now little more than mobs of fanatics, unable to understand any rational argument. The decline in the number of stations on the air over the months was noticeable, and the remaining ones were small stations a long way from any of the old population centres where the Luddite Revival or any of its clones were happily destroying generating stations and cutting down power lines. News, news in the old sense that is, politics, economy, technology and sport was as such sparse. Mainly it was a way in which small groups of survivors kept in touch, sharing a sort of hope that the world might be able to pull out of the suicidal dive it had got into. From Namibia they heard of entire tribes being wiped out, from Iceland of the return of half-starved polar bears filled with hate for man, from the Australian Outback stories of drought and death, from a small town in Kansas pleas for help against radiation-induced diseases, and from a few, words of encouragement for their search. The were even able to speak on occasions to a radio operator a couple of hundred klicks from their objective. This contact knew nothing about the mining company they were searching for, but was able to give them the heartening news that the area itself was peaceful and that farms and small industries were still running.

By the end of the year they had reached a point where, after several attempts, they were forced to conclude that it would not be possible to find their way by land across the vast swampy flood plain produced by the rise in sea level. After consulting their maps, they turned northwards and followed the western shore of the new wetlands. Another month passed before they reached the end of the vast flood plain, well to the north of where the city of Parana had once stood, and were able to begin the search for a means of crossing the river that still lay in their path. The problem of course was that the existing bridges had either been destroyed or were in the hands of some local political bigwig who all too often had no compunction about confiscating any property he found interesting. The group therefore chose to stay well away from any confrontational situations that could lead to the loss of the electrobikes. In the end they found and repaired an old pontoon raft and floated themselves across. This story was repeated at the next big river, after which they were into higher lying land and were able to continue north-eastwards. Finally, fourteen months after they had set out they arrived at their planned destination, tired and somewhat thinner than when they started, but in high spirits for all that.

As was common in places that had escaped the worst of the turmoil, they were, after a cautious reception, made welcome in the town that served as the local centre for most of the area. Somewhere between thirty and fifty thousand inhabitants still lived in or around the town, and unlike many other places that had succumbed to military power in a fruitless effort to impose order, here the military garrison had placed itself at the orders of the civilian authorities and had been deployed to protect the area which had remained essentially free from outside attacks. The four astronauts were interviewed at length by the governor and by the military commander as to their experiences during their travels. After telling their tale, they in turn obtained considerable information about the mining operation that had basically ceased operation the previous year, although a small smelting and rolling mill was still in use for local supplies. Jose and Karel had made the thirty-click trip to the headquarters and had begun to try to trace any information relating to the secret project. Inevitably, this turned out to be a longer and harder job than expected, and their research went on for seven months at weekends, while during the week they worked at tasks assigned to them in accordance with their specialties.

The Survival Centres had been given no names. In the documentation they were referred to only as Sites 1, 2 and 3. Underground Survival Centres being built in secret over a period of eight years in different parts of the world, and all staffed with chosen specialists. A project so large and ambitious as to be mind-boggling. Organized and funded by a group of very wealthy men and women using discretionary funds from the hundreds of companies they ran through holding shells. A project whose organization was filled with cut-outs and firewalls so as to avoid too much information being in the hands of any one person or groups of persons. A project where components were purchased and transported from one place to another, and then again, leaving a paper trail so misleading that it was almost impossible to trace. The mining company had been but one of the nexus points in the routing, this much was clear once the basic set-up had been discovered. The locations of the Sites, however, remained tantalizingly elusive. At the end of seven months Jose and Karel believed, although there was no hard evidence, that two of the sites were on the American continent, one in the north and one in the south, both on the eastern side of the mountains, and that a third was in Australia, somewhere in the Northwestern Territories. Exact locations had not been recorded anywhere, either on paper or on discs. What did come to light however were references to the participation of two major engineering construction companies, one with its corporate offices in Manaos and the other in Buenos Aires.

Disappointed by the lack of more concrete results after their trek from Mendoza, neither of the two women were anxious to set out on what could turn out to be wild goose chase. In the end Karel and Jose compromised and sat out the winter months planning and preparing. After a long discussion they discarded the possibility of finding anything in Buenos Aires, which according to reports had been half covered by the rising waters, setting their objective on Manaos. As Susanne said, they had all the time in the world, and if Manaos proved to be a dead end, then they could always come back southwards to Buenos Aires. They planned their route carefully, trying to avoid the larger towns, as well as any place where there were reports of major trouble. They had headed eastwards to the coast, a distance of some three hundred klicks, and then by boat up the coast to the mouth of the Amazon, and from there upriver, emulating the explorers of long ago. The idea of travelling by boat had seemed simple and obvious to them, but in truth had been an adventure all of its own, where finding a suitable vessel had been by far the easiest part.

It was hard now for Karel to keep things in the right order after so long, they had travelled from clue to clue, sometimes just the four of them, sometimes with other companions. From Manaos to Trelew, from Campinhas to Neuquen, they adapted and grew tougher as the years succeeded each other. To their extensive technical skills they had added new knowledge about survival, about fighting and about courage. Sometimes they settled in for several years at some place along the way, once for almost seven years in a small town north of Santos, but in the end their own personal Holy Grail beckoned, and they moved on, adding at each stop more detail to the information they already had on the Sites. Jose had been killed in December 2046 in an accidental explosion in a generating station they had been trying to repair. They had buried him there in the grounds of the power station in the shade of a group of stunted grey trees that struggled to survive the latest drought. A small, lonely funeral attended by less than a dozen people, for they hadn't been there all that long. After that the journey had turned from being a personal quest for each of them into an obligation to a lost friend, perhaps they might even have called it an obsession if they had stopped to think about it. By the time Karel was finally picked up and brought back to the Hold by Bob Cantor, he had gathered enough data to place the Holds to within ten square klicks, a day or two's work for a surveillance aircraft, but several months work for a man on foot, but it was not in his nature to be daunted by such formidable odds.

The quiet knock on the door brought Karel rushing back to the present with the sensation of having been in some sort of distorting warp which left the past seemingly more real than the room around him.

'Come,' he stood and moved towards the door which swung open to reveal the presence of a short totally bald man of indeterminate age.

'I am Elder Fernan, Jock Fernan. You may remember me from our previous meeting,' the deep rumbling voice coming as a surprise from such a small man, who seeing Karel's assenting nod continued.

'I fear you may think us impolite to have kept you here on your own over these last few days, however there was much to be done. May I sit? I won't keep you long,' and without waiting for an answer sat carefully down in the armchair. Karel also sat, unwilling to lose what he felt was the upper hand by asking a question, although inside he was burning to do so. This Elder obviously carried considerable clout in the Hold, for although at the debriefing where he had been present he had hardly said a word, the others had always looked to him for approval when talking or asking specific questions.

'You arrival has been some sort of a trigger for us here at the Hold, Pilot Houseman.' Giving Karel his almost forgotten formal title. 'We have lived isolated for a long time, and some of us have been pushing for this to change. You are the catalyst in our equation.' Pausing, as though lost in thought for a moment, 'I would be grateful if you could join us in a meeting tomorrow morning, I believe that you will learn something of interest, in fact, I am sure of it. I will send for you at oh eight forty-five.' He nodded, rising to his feet. 'You should get some sleep now.'

After he had left, Karel lay back, satisfied that at last things were on the move again. He did not reflect long on what Elder Fernan had said, if nothing else the decades of searching had taught him the art of being patient. Yes, tomorrow would be soon enough to find out what the next step in the game was to be. Soon he was asleep, quite relaxed, his breathing deep and easy.

Chapter IV

The room on Level E was the one used by the Elders whenever there were important meetings with a reduced number of people. To anyone coming in, the first impression was one of tranquil richness without the least hint of opulence. Here one felt at home, a part of the room, not diminished because it was part of the Council reserved area. The deep burgundy and ochre colours of the enormous Bokhara carpet contrasted with the pale off-white tones of the walls and ceiling. In the centre of the room, shaped like a flattened ellipse, the surface of the long table gleamed in the subtle indirect lighting. The polished surface of the lignum vitae, the holy wood, shone with greenish brown depth, a tribute to the master carpenter who had made it five long decades ago. There were only twelve chairs set round the edge of the table although at least twice that number could have been seated. The sound system in the room had been set to just above the audible threshold, but four centuries after his death the tinkling melodies of Johann Sebastian Bach brought peace into a place its author could not even have dreamed of.

The two people present at twenty-five to nine worked smoothly and without speaking, long since accustomed to each other, preparing for the meeting to come, laying out the briefing folders, loading the projector, programming the refreshments dispenser, and setting the air-conditioning sensor to the desired level. Finishing his task, Jock Fernan let his eyes sweep round the room and then to where his companion completed the projector load. As though sensing his eyes on her, Janice Jennifer Jackson returned his look, her pale eyes contrasting with her almost coal black face.

'Don't tell me Jock, you're still not sure you can convince them, and you with all that Irish blarney to back you up,' she said smiling to remove any malice from the statement. 'Jock, we've convinced the Council at last, and thank heavens for Houseman's arrival, it was providential to say the least.'

'Mmm, I'm afraid the only Irish thing about me was my grandfather. No, we should do all right if we present it correctly, I'm not worried about the boys from the Watch, they'll go for sure, the

Outside holds no fear for them. The two Techs probably will as well, the little fat one, what's his name? Danny Bardel? No, that's the technician down in 'ponics, mmm, David, yes, David bar Delf, that's it, he's the weaker of the two, but he'll follow Kramer's lead. Kramer, now there's a tough one, once he's set on his way there's not much will stop him. Houseman of course will be OK, he knows more than all of us in the Hold put together about what it's really like out there and we need him. We'll need him, make no mistake about that, if he refuses then the whole enterprise will be that much more difficult. Erik will also agree, not because he's my half brother, but because he's an adventurer at heart, and also a damn fine doctor I might add, but you know that of course. No, it's the three scientists who worry me.'

'But they've all expressed clearly their opinions that we've sat here for too long, that it's time to go back outside and pay the debt to the Founders.'

'Aye, but from there to being willing to go out on such a trip,' the deep bass rumble stopped as he gathered his thoughts. 'Putting one's mouth where one's money is, that's an archaic expression from the Old Days by the way, but the meaning is more than clear, eh Threejays?'

Before the handsome black woman who towered a head over her bald companion could reply the door swung open and Karel Houseman walked in, his easy, confident walk conveying a sense of concealed power.

'Good morning to you Karel, welcome, may I call you Karel?' Threejays smiled, 'I'm Janice, but everyone calls me Threejays. Can I get you a coffee?'

'Coffee, yes, a much appreciated luxury,' Karel smiled back, looking around the room, seeing all, missing nothing, 'I've the feeling I'm going to need it to keep well alert while listening to what you people are going to spring on me.'

'Spring on you?,' the deep rumbling voice floated across the room.

'Come, come Elder Fernan, I may not be part of this or any other government, but give me credit for being a good judge of people.'

'My apologies, of course you're quite right.' Jock Fernan's reply conveyed none of the surprise he felt inside at the accuracy of the big man's perception. 'I was underestimating you, I'm sure your travels have provided you with much more experience on human behaviour than we here in the Hold acquire. Yes, I have a proposal for you and the others who will gather at this table today. It is a proposal I have had to fight hard for at the Council, and now at last I have a go ahead on it.' Seeing that Karel was about to speak, he held up his hand before continuing. 'Please bear with me for the moment, I will explain when we are all gathered. But seeing we are having this conversation, I would be grateful for your help.'

'Please go on, you've made me welcome here, If I can be of assistance to you ...'

'When the meeting is over, please stay behind for a few moments, I would very much appreciate your opinion on the others' reactions to the proposal.'

Karel nodded his assent and would have added more, but the others began to arrive, Brendt Maxon with the red headed Matthew Wilton in tow, followed almost immediately by Bob Cantor and Pico Farrel, all obviously Outdoorsmen despite being dressed in the traditional loose shirt and trousers which in varying colours was the unofficial uniform in the Hold. Erik Fernan, the doctor, was a neat man with combed back hair and a goatee beard in which the first traces of grey were beginning to show. The two Techs: Herbert was tall and serious, David being plump with a glint of laughter in his eyes, which not even the seriousness of a call from the Elders could suppress. And the three scientists, researchers would have been a better word, Kord Warten, the astrophysicist, and a frustrated one from having to do most of his work underground instead of up a mountain with an optical telescope. Lee Sun Yan, a petite woman of mixed race whose specialty was cell bioregeneration and cloning, and lastly Miguel Pardo, whose research work had led to the replanting of the vegetable fields near the Hold with new disease- and climate-resistant strains of many traditional vegetables.

As soon as everyone was present and seated, Elder Fernan made the introductions, giving a brief summary of each of their specialties or areas of expertise, the presence of the ex-astronaut giving rise to several murmurs of surprise and some admiring and envious glances.

'No doubt you are wondering why you have been invited to this meeting. Let me begin by reviewing some history, not only for the benefit of Karel who is new here, but also for the rest of you, as not everything I am about to say is public knowledge. This Hold was set up for the express purpose of conserving a nucleus of civilization on which eventually to rebuild the world that was then entering a period of self-destructive and chaotic decay. The men and women behind the idea had become convinced that it was no longer possible to save society as a whole, but that with much effort a small, reduced number of highly specialized and motivated people could be saved in order to give the eventual rebuilding a head start.' He paused in his speech, taking a sip of water while eleven pairs of eyes remained fixed on him.

'We have been here for fifty-two cycles. We have gathered information, we have carried forward extensive scientific research in a number of fields, we exist as a harmonious society, we prepare for the day when we go out to fulfil our prime function,' voice rising to a shout as he struck the table with the flat of his hand. 'And we have failed!'

His hand shot up at once to quell the incipient buzz of comment that ran round the table. Without haste he surveyed the gathering, making eye contact one by one with all those present.

'Please, hear me out! We have reached a moment in the history of the Hold where a number of seemingly unconnected events that have occurred over the past half cycle have made it clear to those of us who are in a position to see the broad view that we can no longer sit passively waiting. Some of us have long held the opinion that we are beginning to stagnate here despite our advances in certain fields. It is only now however that the Council has voted to proceed with this meeting. I will lay before you some points that later will be backed up with concrete data. Firstly, many among you have noticed that in certain areas our technical expertise is slipping slightly, not perhaps in major items, but in the details, things which no longer function correctly, spares which are no longer in stock, and so on. Some of you have even dared to voice such opinions, more often than not to be met with the scorn of your superiors.' Pausing for breath Fernan noted that two of the Watch members were nodding assent, as were Threejays and Lee Sun Yan. 'A second point, in all the records which our founders left for us they were vague about very few matters, one of these was the expected duration of our stay in the Hold. We have always supposed that this was simply because there was no way for them to predict the future accurately. Now thanks to Herbert Kramer and David bar Delf sitting here with us today, we know differently. These two colleagues discovered a hidden area here in the Hold in which was stored information relating to the mission of the Hold as well as to the duration of the mission. This information was supposed to be passed down by certain Elders and shared after a particular period of time had expired. This did not occur. We have been here for fifty-two cycles. Our Founders foresaw a maximum of thirty cycles.'

Once again Fernan surveyed the table, taking in the shock in the eyes that stared back at him before carrying on. 'Point three. The last one, but certainly not the least. Contained in this same information stack was another item, an item which has now been confirmed by our new friend Karel Houseman. We have always supposed that we alone carried the torch of knowledge into the future. It will shock you to know that this is not so, because this Hold was once known as Site 3.' Pausing to deliver the clincher, 'we are not alone.'

Fernan allowed the hubbub to wash over him and the discussion to go on for several minutes before calling the meeting to order.

'You will immediately understand the implications of this. We have sat passively on the sideline while the game of history played on, we have been at best observers, waiting, planning, even willing to go out and help. And while we waited, billions died. I will show you a graph, which in part has been prepared with data supplied by Karel.' Jock turned and nodded to Threejays. The wall at one end of the room changed to show a graph scaled in millions on the vertical and years on the horizontal. Starting at something over five thousand a thin red line curved downwards, at first steeply and then less so reaching four hundred by the end of 2077.

Although he had not expected to be an active participant, Karel rose and walked round to the end of the table, near the projection. 'This is what is left.' Sadness pervaded the flat statement that issued from his lips. 'I have been outside for the last five decades, fifty years, cycles as you call them here. I have covered a lot of territory in that time. By rights I should be long dead, but here I am. The data of course are not really accurate, I've put them together from all sorts of sources, with much guesswork where hard data were lacking. Added to your own information, the result is this graph. Still, I believe it to be essentially correct, our world today numbers somewhere around four hundred million people, give or take ten percent, of which perhaps ten million still live in some semblance of civilization. The rest exist on the verge of starvation, a life where most of them are just waiting to die. Some, a few, are part of the many roving bands of savages, still scavenging off the carcass of civilization, happy to destroy anything they find in their path.' He stopped speaking, looking around the room, eyes were focused on sights only he could see, and then turned to Jock. 'My apologies, I didn't intend to interrupt you.'

The Elder nodded. 'We have in our power the ability to stop the trend,' his words catching the attention of the gathering. 'We have the technology we were given, we have our own developments, particularly in the field of new disease- and drought-resistant food crops. Now, we also have the equipment to take us out into the world again, and,' turning to look at Karel, 'we have someone to lead us.'

The meeting ran on, its participants interested, shocked or anxious in turn, as the two Elders presented fact after fact and answered to the best of their ability the flood of questions. They broke up for a light lunch served in the meeting room, and then continued with the discussions

What had happened to the Elders who were supposed to carry and pass on that knowledge? Why had the knowledge of the Gevcars been kept secret in first place? What good could the Hold do on a world scale and in the short run with their limited resources? Why should an Outsider lead them when everyone knew the abilities of the Watch? What did a few minor failures mean to the Hold in the long run? What was the planned duration of the first expedition and where would it go? If this Hold had escaped detection for so long, what guarantees were there of finding the others? Why had no message of any sort ever been received from the other two Holds? Do the other Holds in fact still exist? Why had the participants been selected over others? All these and many more were thrown on the table and discussed.

Finally, towards the end of the afternoon the participants ran out of questions, or perhaps simply became unable to formulate more until they digested the vast amount of information that had been dropped into their laps. Jock finished up by announcing that the Council would continue to review matters and that those considered suitable as participants would be contacted in the near future. After the rest of them had left Karel swung his chair round and looked thoughtfully at Jock who stared back equally calmly.

'Well then Karel, I think we can consider ourselves on a first-name basis, don't you? 'A slight smile twitched on Fernan's lips, and without waiting for an answer he went on, 'what did you make of our little group of volunteers then?'

'Volunteers?' Now it was Karel's turn to smile. 'I don't know if that description quite fits the case, you run an apparently easy-going outfit here, but it's still a tight ship. Don't get me wrong, I think you've done a good job to survive and grow here for over half a century, even more than that, an incredible job. Given the intellect of the people gathered here I am filled with admiration for how well everyone meshes together, but at the end of the day the Council runs a benign dictatorship, in other words, a tight ship. So, volunteers? Perhaps not, although several of them almost certainly would have been if they had been asked first.'

'You are very perceptive, again you surprise me,' Jock's deep voice rumbled across the room, a smile taking any offence out of the words, 'all the more reason to ask your opinion about the other participants.'

'I'll start with the easy ones, the members of your Watch, Maxon is a natural Outdoorsman, he'll do well, so will the redhead, Matthew Wilton. The lad who brought me in, Bob Cantor I think, as well, he showed good judgement when he found me, and his comments today reinforced my good opinion of him. The fourth one as far as I'm concerned is a no-no. My opinion is that while he may be superficially competent he lacks the balance necessary to participate in this sort of venture where a poor decision taken in a hurry could endanger the rest of the team. The doctor I liked, I gather you're related to him? A calm man, a quality that will be much in need if we are ever in a tight spot. The scientists are an odd kettle of fish, perhaps you are familiar with the old saying? The woman Lee Sun Yan is acceptable, so is Miguel Pardo, both of them work in areas where their expertise will be useful and appreciated.' Karel paused, his lips twisting slightly. 'As for the astrophysicist, he should stay home, his interests are so far away from the reality of a trek across half the world that he would at best be a simple burden on the team. Lastly, the two technicians who I liked and at first sight would certainly seem solid enough. I would however like to interview them sometime, I have a feeling that this could be important as our lives may at some point depend on their know how.

'Thank you Karel, your opinions on the whole confirm my own, the only surprise as far as I am concerned is Farrel, but certainly I will accept your judgement. I will make arrangements for you to meet the Techs, and I will also try to pick out a couple more, ah ... volunteers.' A genuine grin spread across Jock's face sweeping years of seriousness away.

Karel paused for a moment gazing at the evening scene that filled the viewscreen now that the projector had been switched off, the towering peaks still dimly seen through the purple haze of the coming evening. On the sound system the distant echoes of a piece of music Geoffrey Chaucer would have felt at home with softly played, a melody unchanged in seven hundred years. Reaching a decision Karel swung round to face Jock again.

'Elder Fernan, sorry, Jock, applying some reciprocity. There is one other matter that must be settled before we, and basically I mean myself, go on with this venture. You said you had found someone to lead you, I am flattered that on such a short acquaintance you should consider me so highly. In my time it was common practice to discuss such things prior to any public announcement, I can accept the fact that you may have felt it was better not to, but there is something which must be made absolutely clear. You as an Elder in this community must be aware that leadership is much more than a matter of honorifics. Know then that I am willing to lead you, but I am not willing to be a figurehead for you or anyone else. If I am to lead you then I will need and demand the allegiance of every member of the group. When in an emergency or difficult situation I give an order it is to be obeyed immediately and unconditionally, for you may rest assured that there will be a very sound reason for giving that order. There will be no time for discussions on the merits of the order, nor for holding a meeting to look for alternatives. I will make sure that everyone is aware of my plans, I will ask opinions and expect suggestions from each and every member of the team, but, when the moment comes, my orders will be obeyed. Do I make myself absolutely clear?'

'Karel, I hope you will believe me when I say that I am not looking for a figurehead.' Jock leaned forward, elbows on the table hands loosely clasped in front of him. 'If I required a dummy leader I could find one a lot easier than by asking you. I am an Elder on the Council, as is Threejays, and I like to think that the Elders govern here with the support of the people. I also believe that we have done and are doing a good job within the charter laid down by the founders. Now however we are faced with a situation where we know what must be done, but if we are honest we also know that we are not the best people to lead this next stage. Oh, if you had not arrived, then in all probability I would have been the leader of any expedition, and as I told you earlier I personally have been pushing this for some time but it is only now that we have the full backing of

48

the Council. But, I do not believe that I could lead as well as you will, and now that you are here I do not wish to. I offer you my full support.' He stood up and walked round the table until he was facing Karel who had also risen towering over the Elder. The two men shook hands and then stepped back, both aware that a bond had been forged. Karel cleared his throat and spoke quietly.

'Thank you. I imagine that there may be reservations in the group about giving such power into the hands of one man, and an Outsider at that. I am not interested in being a dictator, therefore I will offer you a solution I have used several times over the many years I have travelled. You must set their mind at rest by making it clear that if at a moment when no danger threatens a total of two-thirds of the group, in a public vote, feels that I am unfit to lead, then I will step down. No hard feelings.'

'An interesting solution,' murmured the shorter man, 'a very interesting concept. Have you ever been called on it?'

'Twice. On both occasions I myself called such a vote, and in both cases I remained as leader,' Karel replied, 'the secret of course is not to let oneself be pushed into a corner where such an event happens.'

'Hmm, but no doubt in any group there is always someone who thinks he or she could do a better job?' Jock smiled, 'I suppose that that is an inevitable part of human nature. Still, I will back you in your decisions, and if I have anything to say, I will say it privately.'

'Very well, I accept your proposal, nomination, call it what you will. There is much to be done on the planning side, and it will not be easy. We must choose the order in which the supposed sites are to be visited, we must set a departure date based on that order with a view to avoiding winter wherever possible. We have to do a lot of mapwork in planning the route. We ...'

'Why the problem with winter?' interrupted Jock. 'I don't see a problem there.'

'Not a problem as such, but in these latitudes the additional daylight hours will help a lot,' seeing the other man nod in understanding, Karel continued. 'We must determine the size of the team, and choose them. We need to check out your Gevcars and see if they really are the best means of transport, we may have to look around for alternatives. Supplies, we have to set up a minimum list and a maximum list according to what the means of transport is to be.' Karel paused, thought for a moment and then went on. 'It's a long time since I set up anything this big, the past few years have been in five- or six-person teams, more often than not on horseback. Look, give me a few days, say until next ... what do you people call the days?'

'We settled that a long time ago, but with people of so many different origins each sevenday simply kept the old Anglic terms, Sunday, Monday and so on. Today is Tuesday by the way.'

'Right, then give me until next Monday morning and I will present a preliminary proposal for the expedition. If you approve, then we can move ahead and start involving other people directly. What I'll need is a complete briefing on the Hold as well your permission to move freely about and talk to people,' he paused looking at the Elder.

'You have my full backing to go anywhere and ask any questions you feel like, by tomorrow morning all Department heads in the Hold will have been so informed. I also apologize for having confined you to a limited part of the Hold, I hope you will appreciate that we had no choice but to be cautious. It is very seldom that anyone such as yourself comes our way, and we had to be sure you were not something other than you stated. You will not be surprised to learn that our Records System gave you a clean bill of health, nor that our people are now convinced that you are who you claim to be. So, Karel, I think we should call it a day for now, we have made a start at long last, that is the most important thing. Call me whenever you need anything, otherwise I look forward to seeing you again here on Monday, say the same time as today. I will arrange to have a guide waiting tomorrow morning, one of Threejays' assistants.' Holding out his hand again, Jock said 'Good Luck, we'll need it if we are to see this thing through.'

Over the next five days Karel toured the Hold, his tall lank frame and flowing hair tied back in a ponytail as well as his brilliantly blue eyes became familiar to many of the Hold's inhabitants. He spent time with the Records' people checking through satellite photos, the last of which had been received as recently as four cycles ago, although most of the satellites had ceased to transmit on a regular basis. He also requested a review of the communications register, a task that would take several weeks to complete.

He had a long meeting with Kramer, and together they visited the Gevcars in the now well-lit tunnel. Not surprisingly, Herb himself had been anything but idle, for despite the Council injunction on secrecy, he had worked out how the tunnel fitted in with the existing layout and was now firmly convinced that the far end of the tunnel contained a hidden airlock to the outside which would bring them out slightly higher up the valley from the main entrance at a point hidden behind a boulder field. Karel, seeing at once that the matter was in competent hands, left him with instructions to pursue the matter and to demand any assistance needed, including a trip to the Outside if necessary. He pored over the downloads from the discs found in the Gevcars and was amazed to find that much of the preliminary work had been done for him fifty years earlier by the unknown Justin Cooper, who had apparently been a specialist attached to the Founders. As he read, his admiration for the now long dead psychologist grew, for here was a man who had looked at his fellows and foreseen the stagnation of the soul that would keep the inhabitants of the Hold from action, and had done what he could to tip the balance in the favour of civilization.

The Gevcars it was clear were the ace up the Hold's sleeve. Powered by advanced fuel cells supplying enough energy to light a small town, these massively armoured vehicles were supposedly capable of skimming over land or water at a height of up to two metres if the terrain permitted and at speeds of up to 180 knots. Totally self-sufficient, using the same technology as a submarine, they were capable of travelling through toxic or radioactive areas without problems, at least for limited periods. Having originally been developed for military operations by the North American Federation, the two prototypes had been transferred to the Hold before the collapse of the military industrial complex. The records stated that no additional vehicles had ever been built and that all records relating to their construction had been destroyed. The most amazing thing was that the discs contained the full specifications and schematics for the building of new Gevcars. These Karel handed over to Jock, with a strong suggestion that the technical people begin working on how to build some new Gevcars. Cooper had certainly done them proud, for with the Gevcars they had the reach and the power to return knowledge and civilization to the world.

He also asked for, and after some delay received, access to the earlier records covering the period of the construction of the Hold. These did not add very much to the knowledge he already possessed on the exact location of the other two Holds, but at least it served further to confirm their existence. In the case of the second American site he was able to narrow the area by half an order of magnitude thanks to some rather obscure geological references that, coupled to information he had obtained years before in Manaos, allowed the Hold geophysics specialists to pinpoint the area more precisely, within a range of ten to fifteen klicks.

He visited the fabrication facilities installed in the Hold, plasteel production units, synthetic fibre plants, semiconductor plants, fully automatic metal foundries and workshops good for the production of pieces from a few grams up to five tons. The power reactor, the so-called TFR about which Karel vaguely remembered being briefed, was still running smoothly and problem-free long past its original design life. The intense energy of the nuclear fusion reactor heart was safely contained in intense magnetic pinch fields, a solution which bypassed the necessity of advanced shielding materials. All in all it was a truly incredible installation considering the short seven years in which it had all been designed and assembled, more so in view of the secrecy in which it had been done.

In the Personnel Department he reviewed personal files normally accessible only to the Elders, and began to assemble, at least in his head, the team that would be needed, a balance of technical skills and all-round general knowledge, coupled with a capacity for pragmatic thinking. Of those originally present at the meeting, he kept Brendt Maxon, Matthew Wilton and Bob Cantor, the three Watch members he considered reliable, Erik Fernan, the doctor, Herb Kramer and David bar Delf, the two Techs, and the scientists Lee Sun Yan and Miguel Pardo. To this list he added himself and the two Elders, giving a total of eleven. He thought long and hard about his own companions who would be waiting for him at the town on the lake shore, now just a few hours north of the Hold by Gevcar. Suzanne, still healthy despite her seventy-eight years, but now slower than in earlier times, would he decided be better off remaining in the Hold. Sandy, a year younger than himself, was still as tough as ever, and her communications skills probably outstripped anyone the Hold could put in the field. That left him with another twelve spots to be filled as he calculated that a crew of twelve per Gevcar would be reasonable, with as many skills as possible being duplicated.

The amount of jobs to be done seemed endless. He began listing essential supplies for eight months, which he reckoned was the longest time they would need. This he calculated on the basis of five months' exploration and a month on site followed by two months to get back to the Hold taking the shortest possible route. After a while he found himself getting side-tracked into analysing the relative merits of four hundred-metre coils of carbon fibre rope with a breaking load of seventy tonnes against an additional electrostatic water purifier. Realizing that this sort of task could be easily delegated after the next meeting, Karel left it aside and got on with setting up a draft schedule for the preparation of the expedition. There was no point in leaving before the spring, not only for the longer days as he had explained to Jock, but also because they would need several months, moons as they called them in the Hold, to train the team. Karel became more and more convinced that training would be the key to success. They had to train as though this were a space mission, every specialist would have to know his own job perfectly and would also have to do at least one other job adequately if it came to the crunch.

The choice of what to aim for was almost academic, to attempt to reach the Australian site would involve long stretches over water, which added considerable danger to an already risky enterprise. They would definitely aim for the North American site to start with. According to Karel's analysis of the latest data, which had been supplied from the Hold records and added to all the previous information, the location of the site had been narrowed down to an area of some forty hectares, located some one hundred klicks to the west of where the town of Calgary had once been. Although none of the Hold reports made any mention that the town had been nuked from an unknown submarine late in 2024, Karel had seen this with his own eyes a couple of months before the Copernicus shuttle was nudged into re-entry. If that site could not be found, or if it had been destroyed, then they would have to look seriously at the Australian option. They would have to head for the Pacific coast, and then the risks of a long over-water stretch versus a trip up north to Alaska, the Aleutians and back southwards past the Kamchatka peninsula would have to be analysed. That, Karel decided privately, was a bridge he would cross when he came to it. Meanwhile there was a whole expedition to mount.

[Extract – 2023]

(The following reports are excerpts from the minutes of the Site 3 Steering Committee meeting held on 12 November 2023. It is to be noted that all records related to 1 January 2018 to 31 December 2025 have been classified as restricted and can only be accessed with the authorization of the Council of Elders.)

The removal of any documents from the Records Hall or the copying of any information relating to this period is strictly forbidden.

Phase IV Construction Contract Report: Building work on the Site is now nearing completion, Betchel Brown Corp. has already begun reducing its on-site staff, with work on Levels A to C expected to be completed by May 2024, still three months behind the original Masterplan Time Schedule as a result of last years sabotage attempt. Plant and machinery for installation on these two levels is being stored in the outside sheds under camouflage netting until such time as the construction work is ready. Overflights at ten, twenty and fifty thousand feet show no visible trace of the storage sheds. Installation work on Levels D to F has now entered the final stage. All ventilation and life-support systems have been completed and certified. All power, signal and lighting cabling have been installed and are currently being tested, no major faults have been detected to date. Techint Worldwide, Inc. has met the agreed upon dates for these systems and has submitted invoices including the two percent bonus payment as per the original contract. Arrangements are being made to transfer the required funds. Furnishing on Levels E and F is estimated at seventy-eight percent complete although most of the living quarters are in fact already habitable. Major items of equipment for the bio and chem laboratories are expected to be delivered at the end of this month and will be installed within 120 days. The hydroponics test rig (Unit 1) has successfully produced a first crop of assorted vegetables, and assembly of the remaining four units will begin within two weeks.

Attachments:

- Shareholders Reports on Financial Position
- Technical Status Reports on All Systems

- Bio Report: Hydroponics
- Phase IV Layouts
- Phase IV Time Schedule (Adjusted)

Staffing Report: Site 3 staffing planning is now into its eighth month. To date 1,348 specialists have been carefully vetted and of these 1,065 have been contacted with a preliminary proposal of participation. All have indicated a willingness to be interviewed and subjected to further testing despite the vaguely worded explanation as to the nature of the project. Basic training and indoctrination courses for department heads and research scientists is proceeding as planned in Albuquerque, New Mexico, with a dropout rate of 6.85 percent, which is well below the expected level. Relocation logistics studies will be beginning at the end of the year when the construction teams complete their work. It is estimated that the first staff members should be able to move in as of the end of June 2024, leaving over a year to complete the on-Site training programme.

Attachments:

- Site 3 T/O
- Staffing Situation Update
- Masterplan Time Schedule (Staffing)

Power Subcommittee Report: The Site 3 TFR installation is ahead of schedule with a number of secondary and redundancy systems already installed. All main equipment construction is expected to be completed at the end of the first quarter of next year. So far the strict security measures taken have continued to avoid outside awareness as to the identity of the final user of the Site 3 TFR. Criticality test results on the reactor core have been completed with all parameters within acceptable limits. Further MCA simulation scenarios will be tested over the next sixty days and a special report prepared for the Steering Committee.

Attachments:

- Layout Site 3 Power Installations
- TFR Installation Time Schedule
- Delivery Schedule for Outstanding Items

News Item Summaries: The typhoid epidemic situation in Bombay has become critical. The UN has declared an area of two hundred klicks round the city as a disaster area and has promised assistance at the earliest possible date. So far it is estimated that the death count stands at twelve million. Medical studies are still not conclusive on the origin of the typhoid outbreak, but it now seems increasingly likely that a genetically altered variety was released on purpose. So far no group or agency has claimed responsibility.

The European Space Agency facility in Free Guyana has been overrun and destroyed by rebels claiming to be the Luddite Revival, a group that has become increasingly radical in its attacks on centres of technology. Most of the staff were allowed to leave freely. However, the mission director and his assistant were crucified in a public ceremony. In addition, the ESA headquarters in Brussels has been occupied and all communication to the ESA network has been put out of action, and all telemetry stations are off-line. ... This leaves the Copernicus shuttle mission in a four hundred klick polar orbit. This mission has been studying the alterations in the ozone decay rate over the poles. Contact with the shuttle has been maintained and the crew are all in good health thanks to the new centrifugal gravity chamber installed after the problems encountered during last year's mission. The mission has oxygen and supplies for at least six, and possibly eight, months, after which a manual entry approach will be necessary if the ESA cannot bring its facilities back on line in sufficient time.

No further news is available on conditions inside the ex-Russian Republics since the Russian Federation annexed them. Satellite photos indicate that at least seven low-yield thermonuclear devices were exploded at or near ground level. The resulting radioactive dust cloud has effectively eliminated the possibility of obtaining further information by satellite. The cloud has been drifting eastwards into Russia leading to panic-stricken evacuations in a number of cities. A steady stream of refugees, many suffering from radiation sickness as well as semi-starvation, has been reaching the West. The NATO-aligned states have already issued directives to limit the amount of refugees to be admitted, with priority being given to highly skilled and healthy workers.

Chapter V

The ice-cold water stream numbed her face, the splashes and spray forming a halo around her, rainbow colours inside each droplet glistening and sparkling in the early morning sun, vanishing away as they fell into the shadow, hitting the rocks and racing off to rejoin the stream. Janine Saleh stretched back and upwards her arms held above her head, hands clasped together, her reddish gold hair swept back and gathered at the nape of her neck. She shivered involuntarily as the cold bit deep into her and she stepped out from under the waterfall. They had arrived late the previous night after a long day's drive, a day of slow advance over the roughest of terrain, the roughest so far, where even the tough versatile Gevcars had trouble averaging more than thirty or forty klicks per hour. Picking up her towel she walked over to the rock where she had dumped her clothes, breasts moving rhythmically to her long strides, nipples hard and erect from the cold, goose bumps coating her body like a rough carpet.

Dressing quickly after a brisk rub down, she made her way back to where the Gevcar was parked in a hollow that concealed its presence from anyone looking up the hill. Most of the others had slept inside the car, cocooned within its shelter. So far, only the Watch people had adapted to life on the move, the others despite hours of training still missed the safety offered by the thick rock shell of the Hold. Bob Cantor glanced up at her from where he crouched over the little electric burner on which a pot of coffee bubbled gently, its aroma reaching out across the clearing to welcome her back to the glade in which they were parked surrounded by miles of dark grey spindly thorn bushes. Dropping her belt, which had been slung over her shoulder, she reached gratefully for the mug he offered, still shivering slightly from the effect of the early morning bath.

'Lo Jan, you're looking wide awake and in the pink,' he grinned, 'at least what I can see of you looks pretty pink.' He laughed, stepping back and easily avoiding the damp towel she playfully swung at him, accepting the comment with a wide grin. Janine, originally chosen as a communications specialist to assist Sandy, had soon become the logistics officer. Blessed with what bordered on an eidetic memory she had shown an unexpected talent for organization, a fact that soon drew the attention of both Karel and Jock who promptly reassigned her communications job to Jean Klock, a short rather overweight man, leaving much of the planning in her hands. Janine, who with never failing good humour chivvied them all into getting things done as they should be, forgetting nothing and leaving very little to chance. Janine, at first rather shy and aloof, was now slipping into a growing relationship with Bob, two people feeling their way towards each other in easy stages.

On the other side of the clearing an ill-defined mound rippled, resolving itself into a cloak-covered body that had lain so still on an inflatable mattress that it could have been mistaken for part of the natural rocky soil. The shape stirred sleepily, and then and in a smooth flowing motion rose to its feet, the hood falling back to reveal Karel Houseman's craggy face, eyes as blue and piercing as ever. Smiling, Cantor poured a second mug and walked across to hand it to him, knowing how much the spaceman enjoyed his coffee after so many years without any.

'These Hold cloaks are a bloody marvel,' said Karel sipping the piping hot coffee, 'I know I've said it before,' holding up his hand to forestall comments. 'They're so amazingly light, incredibly warm but never stifling, and the colours are perfect for this sort of terrain,' holding up the cloak, which by turns seemed brown-green and slate grey according to how the early morning light caught it. 'Well, today we should make better time once we reach the flatter land, perhaps we might even find the remains of the road that figures on the Hold maps.' He grimaced, for the old maps had so far proven to be little more use than as a general guide. In many places the roads had vanished altogether and in others the surface was so decayed as to be useless to ground vehicles, although this fact bothered the Gevcars little as they skimmed along a metre or so above the ground. Also, roads tended to be places where traps and roadblocks could be set, although so far they had met nothing like that.

One by one the others began emerging from the Gevcar where they had chosen to sleep. After a week and a half on the road the morning activities had become routine: wash, breakfast, a short review of the previous day and a planning session which usually took them through to the time when it became necessary to put on glare specs, after which they got moving again. The briefings were informal to a degree that at first had startled Jock and Threejays, used as they were to the more formal Council proceedings, but Karel's natural authority made this unimportant.

'We'll head north-east again and see if we can't pick up the old road going north. If that works, then according to the old satellite photos we should have a clear run up to around the eighteenth parallel where we can turn west to the Pacific across the desert. According to Threejays' map readings we shouldn't have to go much higher than three thousand metres, which is just fine for my old lungs.'

'Come on Grandpa, it's not as bad as that, you're not a total cripple yet,' Janine said, unable to repress her usual good humour, drawing a laugh from them all.

'OK, OK, but if it's not so bad, how come I beat you hollow on the forced march test we did last moon?' Smiling to show he was just kidding, while Janine who had prided herself on her fitness looked sheepish remembering how she had been unable to keep up with a man three times her age. 'I was speaking with Sandy and Jean earlier, I think today we'll give the GPS another shot around midday, the printout they sent us from the Hold shows that should be well within range of one of the Sentry satellites by then.'

'So what's the guarantee it'll be working?' This from Brendt Maxon.

Sandy chipped in to the conversation. 'Well, they were one of the last launches before Vandenberg closed down for good back in 2024. These birds were both solar- and nuclear-powered, and a geo-synchronous orbit won't have declined. The only unknown is how well the components have stood up to solar radiation, vacuum, micrometeorites and so on. Anyway, even if we don't make contact today we'll keep trying as we get nearer the orbital path further north. It would be really good if we could make that contact, not only the GPS for navigation purposes, but also we should be able to use the Sentry for communication relays if we can get through the code barriers.'

Karel stood up and looked around. 'OK people, let's make a move,' nodding to Jock, he started towards the nearest Gevcar. The Elder picked up the map case from the rock where it had rested and set off towards the second car parked a few dozen paces down the valley, followed by his crew including Sandy Cook who had been assigned to communications in the second car and who waved at Karel as she left the clearing.

Once inside and seated, Karel checked to see that the others were all at their stations, David bar Delf in the co-pilot's seat, Jean Klock at the communications console, Bob Cantor and Jules Borman on the defence systems control panel, and the remaining ten members of the crew strapping into their seats, Threejays as usual was already engrossed in dictating her journal. Karel thought, not for the first time either, that he hoped to God the processing software back in the Hold would be up to the task of transcribing all the tapes she was storing away. With a last look around he pressed the door control switch and having made sure that the door was properly settled on its seals stretched up flipped the power up toggles to start the Gevcar engine.

The car shuddered slightly and as the power came up the whine from the power unit grew in tone and pitch until all of a sudden it became a barely audible hum as the engine reached its operating level. Together with David they ran through the short checklist, more akin to what Karel remembered of a small aircraft than for such a sophisticated vehicle, although of course the on-board computer took many of the routine chores out of the crew's hands. David glanced at his Captain, and receiving an affirmative nod nudged the joystick yoke mounted on an extension of the left armrest. The nineteen-ton Gevcar rose slowly, spun round on its axis apparently without effort, and in a cloud of dust and small gravel moved out of the clearing heading down the gully up which they had come the previous evening.

The handling of the Gevcars had now become almost routine. Karel smiled to himself, remembering the first supposedly short trial run when they had set out to pick up Sandy and Susanne. In spite of his skills as a shuttle pilot he had twice lost control of the Gevcar, fortunately at fairly low speeds, so the only damage had been to his pride. In the end he adapted his half forgotten space skills in the handling of vector velocities to a two-dimensional operation and after that things got better. Really, of course, the first journey had involved getting the first Gevcar out of the Hold. Kramer's first suspicion as to the existence of an alternative way out had been confirmed, for after a brief search they had found the hidden exit with its own airlock and blast doors which had been concealed inside a loose rock field. The clearing of the fallen rocks, some over two

metres in diameter, had taken almost three weeks, but at the end
they had a serviceable track from the newly found lock round to the
main entrance, a distance of some two klicks.

On that first run it had taken them all of three days to cover the
five hundred or so klicks to the town where he had left the two
women. Not only did he have to keep the speed down to compensate
for their lack of experience as first he, then Kramer and finally David
tried their hands at the controls, but the rough broken landscape
with its sudden gorges, drop-offs and loose rubble made higher
speeds inadvisable. For the most part they had attempted to follow
the remains of the old road which at one time had run up the
backbone of the country, winding through the dusty foothills of the
Andes, but at a number of points it had ceased to exist so they were
forced to find their own way.

The reunion with the women, though Karel still thought of them
as the girls, had been an emotional one, they had come skimming in
over lake Buenos Aires from the east, moving at thirty knots, leaving
a cloud of spray behind them, slowing down only for the last two or
three klicks before coming to rest on the gently sloping beach on a
field of multicoloured pebbles of varying sizes just outside the town,
a town once known as Los Antiguos, with a stable population of a
couple of thousand. The local people, after some moments of caution
and seeing that the newcomers carried no visible weapons, emerged
from behind their walls. As soon as Karel was recognized as their
visitor from a couple of months earlier, the greetings grew warmer by
several degrees. Susanne and Sandy, unable to believe what they were
seeing, were overcome with joy at seeing Karel back, safe and sound,
and in such style.

'You've found them! You've found them!' was all they could say,
tears running down their faces. 'Oh, God, but it's been so long Karel,
and now we've found them!' Karel, had held them both tightly, his
own anxieties at last put to rest at being reunited again with his
companions of a lifetime of wandering. The townspeople, most of
whom had never seen any vehicle other than those which could be
pulled by a horse or by oxen, crowded round the newcomers, and
even the older ones who remembered the now vanished time of cars
and trucks, helicopters and aircraft were amazed by the size of the
Gevcar. Karel introduced Sandy and Susanne to his new friends from
the Hold, who were somewhat in awe of the fact that they were
meeting people who had survived so many years on the Outside, that

mysterious place beyond the safety of the Hold. Both the Techs, as well as Jock Fernan and Maria Sanches, a psychologist from the Hold, were taken aback by the sight of all the people, healthy enough to be sure, but so withered and old looking by Hold standards.

That meeting lay four moons in the past now, and Los Antiguos had taken on a new breath of life, for with the arrival of specialists from the Hold the generating station was running once more, and in the fields the first of the genetically enhanced Hold crops were sprouting up from the stony soil with the promise of a good crop of vegetables to come. A radio and video link station had been installed and the town was rapidly becoming a formal outpost, a new start for the old town. In the Hold itself the feeling of change and optimism had also taken root quickly as a sense of purpose gripped a generation getting ready to fulfil its prime directive.

The next Gevcar trial run had been to one of the supply dumps mentioned in the discs found with the cars, but all they had been able to find were the remains the scavengers had left behind when they had wrecked anything that had been too large to carry off. They had continued on north-eastwards, almost as far as the Atlantic coast, to the next dump which proved to be intact although the passage of time had taken its toll of a number of items. The cache had included several weapons canisters, a reminder of the origin of the Gevcar, and at Karel's insistence these were loaded into the cargo bay. Afterwards, and from high up on the plateau, they had looked out towards the ocean, an ocean no one in the car except for Karel and Sandy had ever seen, where the remains of the town of San Julian rose out of the waters some hundreds of metres off the shore line. The few half submerged buildings which still stood, battered by the unceasing winter storms of many years, were so decayed that in some cases it was even difficult to be sure they were man-made. The coastline was totally deserted, and apart from the ruins of the town and the remains of a paved road leading down into the grey blue sea the works of man had been swallowed back into the earth as if they had never existed. The second Gevcar had been made ready by the time they returned to the Hold, so after that they got down to the job of training in earnest. Communication procedures, survival techniques, Gevcar maintenance and operation, map reading, even some old-fashioned traditional stellar navigation using the sextant the Techs had built using information supplied by the Hold records, all this and more as the days slipped by ever faster as the planned departure date approached. As the world swept forward into spring, the Gevcar teams begun to camp out, living off concentrated rations, and doing forced marches by day. Asked by Jock why he thought this sort of training was necessary, Karel had replied that it was to teach them the value of hardship, and that if the time came when they had to survive on their own, then there was some small chance that they might not perish.

The expedition to search for the other survival habitat had finally left the Hold on 1 January 2077 by the old reckoning. A new year with new hopes, and new roads to travel. With the summer well underway, the shrubland around the Hold that had sprouted anew in spring was already beginning to turn brown, burned by the high uvee dosages thrown out by the sun. The farewells had been low key, almost muted, with only fifty or sixty people who had made their way down to the exit hangar on Level A. Most of the personal goodbyes had been said the night before, Brendt sat at his post in the upper turret of the second Gevcar, feeling the emptiness which he knew would remain with him until he returned. Ania had reluctantly accepted his need to participate in the expedition, but parting with her had been hard. Erik held the little paper flower handed to him by his three-year-old daughter as he left his apartment. Miguel patted the scented handkerchief in his breast pocket, the lavender scent might be synthetic, but the thought of his wife Tilly was real and comforting. Married or single, each and every member of the Gevcar crews felt their pulses quickening as the moment approached. Susanne Polk had said her goodbyes to Karel and Sandy the evening before, understanding why she could not go with them, but still holding within her a trace of resentment. Down in the bay several of the Elders talked over last-minute things with Karel and Jock, and then finally it was time to leave, just as the sun's first rays slipped over the horizon colouring everything in a deep red-orange, pushing aside the haze.

Once down the valley, the Gevcars travelled parallel to each other wherever possible, separated by half a klick or so, a procedure Karel had designed to avoid both cars falling into the same trap or problem. They ran eastwards for half a day, coming down from the higher foothills before turning north, travelling through the deserted, stony countryside, a place where man had passed through often but had never really stayed. The second day their route detoured westwards again, stopping briefly at Los Antiguos to drop off supplies and mail, exchange news, and stay the night before travelling onwards. As they journeyed northwards, they encountered two more isolated townships, neither over a thousand strong, and in each they left a comm unit and the word that help was on the way. Their reception in general was one of awe and no little fear, a fear undoubtedly generated by the stories handed down from fathers to sons about the brutal raids of previous generations. In the second of these two places they found the bare bones of technology still operating, for the place had once been the Balseiro Nuclear Research Facility, not far from the shores of Nahuel Huapi, the lake of the lion. For the most part they had planned a route that gave the larger towns a wide berth in order to avoid any unpleasantness with local leaders who, as Karel knew from his own experience, would be only too glad to lay their hands on the Gevcars. Mendoza was different, and special. Karel had looked forward to calling at Mendoza in the hope that some of his old companions from the Copernicus might yet be alive.

Karel kept his eye on the crewmembers, knowing full well from his own experience that all the training in the world was different from the real thing. Over the last few weeks the sense of being a team had strengthened as they meshed together, each with his own skill and character, each a part of the intangible whole. But now at last they were underway on a journey half way round the world, and it would be many moons before they returned to the Hold. People would change during this journey, some would open up, others would retreat into their shells. They had been carefully selected, interviewed and tested, but as Karel said to Jock Fernan, how does one know how a person who has spent most of their life indoors will react to extended periods in the open.

As things turned out, their proposed visit to Mendoza never came to be, for the car's sensors began detecting a significant increase in the level of radioactivity about fifty klicks south after passing the remains of the town of Tunuyan, still overshadowed by the almost perfectly conical crater of the Tupungato volcano, which despite the haze they could see quite clearly. Giving up the direct route they had planned, they had turned away to the east, passing through long dried out vineyards and fruit farms, where, without the watchful eye of man, the desert had returned to take back what it had lost. Behind them the plume of dust hung, a beacon to mark their track, until slowly the winds blew it apart. They wasted half a day and circled round for a second attempt after getting halfway to San Juan, coming back towards Mendoza from the north, but they met with the same problem and once again they were forced to accept defeat. The science team took a number of samples for testing, but finally recommended against trying to proceed further, for although in theory the Gevcars' decontamination systems could have handled the load, there was no possibility of finding anyone alive with such a high background count. They tried unsuccessfully to raise an answer on the radio until with the approaching dusk they gave up and drove northwards until they reached an area where the count though high would not be harmful for a short stay. The rest of that evening, their sixth since leaving the Hold, Karel had sat shrouded in gloom, wondering what had put an end to the place where he had spent the early years after the crash landing.

Karel's breakfast forecast proved to be correct, and by the end of the morning they were racing along the floor of a valley, crossing and recrossing the small stream that meandered down its length. The hills that lined the valley on either side climbed steeply, sometimes precipitously, upwards to ridges at least eight or nine hundred metres above the valley floor, their multicoloured flanks and heavily eroded formations offering the passing viewers a bewildering array of illusions. Giant faces, leaning towers, crouching animals, ships crashing through waves, mutating as the angle of vision and the shadows changed, all contained in the eye of the beholder, and then lost as the two cars swept onwards. As with most of the country through which they had been travelling, what little vegetation there was tended to be sparse with a predominance of thorn bushes, cacti and other hardy plants. Only occasionally had they found groves of trees growing near springs or on the shores of small lakes. On six or seven occasions they slowed to examine what had once been small primitive villages, sometimes they saw small packs of wild dogs, sometimes groups of half-buried white weathered skeletons, lying where they had fallen decades earlier, bleached by the action of sun and wind. Of the living there were no signs, no half smoking fires, no tracks in the sand, simply nothing. In itself this was not entirely surprising as the area through which they were travelling had been, even in better times, an arid one, where without complex irrigation systems very little grew. The valley climbed steadily as they drove north, 2,500 metres, then 3,000, reaching a maximum of 3,200 metres before they levelled off. The most prevalent impression was one of dryness, as they pushed northwards, great plumes of choking greyish brown dust billowing out from their passing, adding to the ever-present haze. By midday when they stopped for a break they had covered well over 350 klicks, which was their best so far.

At the insistence of Maria Sanches, backed up by Jock, they had taken to stopping for an hour for lunch, not because it couldn't have been eaten while on the move, but to give everyone a break and a chance to stretch their legs. Most of the members of the two crews sat around in the limited shade offered by the Gevcars, except as usual for the Watch members along with Karel and Jock who shrouded in their protective cloaks and glare specs wandered off to look at anything that might be of interest. Repeating the previous days practice, Sandy and Jean Klock set up a small dish aerial, made the connection to the GPS unit and began to crank the tripod handle to scan the sky, keeping to the sector where, according to the information they had, the satellite should be located, poised forever above the Earth.

'No luck, eh?' Matthew Wilton, his red hair obscured by the hood of his cloak, wandered over to where the two comm specialists were working. 'I wonder if you'll ever find anything, Brendt thinks that the satellite's dead.'

'Well, Brendt is always pessimistic about the state of our technology, so there's hope yet,' Jean replied with a smile, trying as usual and without much success to tuck his shirt back into his trousers. 'We'll just have to keep trying, won't we?' Getting no answer to his metaphorical question he turned back to cranking slowly at the tripod mechanism. Sandy, taking pity on the young man's curiosity, turned with a smile to explain.

'Look Matt, the Sentry satellites were very special, they were designed for military use so the band they operate in was very narrow and was coded. The GPS unit we put together with the Techs can in theory receive the signal, always supposing the satellite is still active, but we still have to try a number of frequencies as we do the tracking, and that's a long, slow job. In theory we could even have reached them from the Hold although it's right on the edge of the footprint. In practice it will get better as we get further north. At least the Sentries were EMP shielded so there's still a chance. First we need to find the bird with the GPS signal, after that we can move into communications if we can crack the code, then we can begin to access the Sentry command computer which hopefully will open a whole lot of new doors for us.' Brushing back a lock of her grey hair that had slipped out from under the wide-brimmed hat she was wearing, she turned again to the GPS and switched to the next band. Matt smiled his thanks and was turning away when the unit gave a sharp beep and a set of incomprehensible figures appeared on the small display screen.

'Yes,' shouted Jean, echoed almost instantaneously by Sandy. The others within immediate hearing range came running over, excitement spreading through them like wildfire. On the small flat screen of the GPS unit incomprehensible symbols appeared, vanished and appeared once more.

'Sandy, love,' said Karel as he arrived at a trot, 'have you got it? Is that a clear signal?'

'No, the signal is still coded, but we're in, amazing that the bird is still active after all these years,' Sandy's fingers danced over the input keys. 'I'm loading up the old EMT code, I'm hoping that at least I can get a reaction, then maybe if I can identify the answering system I can get at the access code.'

The gibberish on the screen cleared, vanishing for an instant, and was immediately replaced by three lines of code, unreadable, but clearly no longer just random symbols:

WRPT67 GOVV25 ZSQP98 LHOI77 VBUE41 NBOZ09 SXCE86 RGYH44 HVPP82 OLLG56 RBBM38 WWHH11 UYBF72 LFEJ15 GBRP86 QWIP03 ERAK88 NTPE47

'Ah, that code format looks familiar, it's very like the one the UNDEF service used to use for their tracking stations,' Sandy said, talking more to herself than to her audience. 'Jean, give me a quarter degree more elevation, would you?' She typed in a new set of instructions and was rewarded with a blank screen followed by a message, this time clear:

**Surveillance Entry Numerical Tracking & Retrieving Unit
RESTRICTED ACCESS – AF COMMAND –
ENTER PASSWORD**

'Right on, here we go,' she typed in another instruction sequence and was rewarded with a repeat of the previous message. She tried again with a third set of access instructions with a similar lack of success, then with a fourth set, appending her old ESC serial number. The screen cleared, but instead of producing a message it stayed blank for several seconds during which sighs of frustration and disappointment flowed through the group. Sandy sat still, waiting, leaning forward slightly, her hands resting gently on the little keyboard, and then the screen flickered and came up again:

POSITION READING: S 22° 14' 33"
W 66° 12' 45"
RELATIVE VELOCITY: 0.000 KNOTS
SIGNAL STRENGTH: 48%
CHANNEL: 244

'Got you!' said Sandy.

'You're as good as ever!' said Karel exultantly, picking her up and kissing her quickly on the lips. 'I'm so glad you're with us,' smiling, a sharing of past events in a few seconds contact.

'I don't believe it!' said Jean Klock, quite forgetting in his excitement to tuck his errant shirt in again. 'We're in! This is great.'

'Marvellous, Sandy, well done!' said Jock Fernan, a grin spreading from ear to ear beneath the glare spec-protected eyes.

'It'll get better as we go further north, meanwhile I'll try to improve on the signal strength by changing the pulse scan rate. Now that we're linked up I can alter some of the telemetry functions by remote. We'll pass the data back to the Hold, with their phased array system they should be able to contact the bird even though they're so much farther south. If it works, then we'll be able to keep them posted really exactly as to our position, and they'll be able to feed us data from the Records mainframe, this is looking better and better.' Sandy rose to her feet and walked over to Karel, who in a movement automatic as it was familiar, massaged her shoulders, easing the strain of having been crouched over the GPS without moving for almost twenty-five minutes.

By the time they tidied up, their normal midday stop having extended itself to two hours as a result of Sandy's success with the GPS, the signal strength had increased to sixty-seven percent, and Sandy had been able to download a status report which they had radioed back to the Hold for further analysis, although between Karel and herself they had been able to understand most of it.

They continued northwards for the next three days, up through what had once been northern Argentina and southern Bolivia. They bypassed all the larger towns that figured on the Hold maps, Tucuman, once the commercial centre of the area, Salta and then San Salvador de Jujuy, long ago an outpost and way house for the conquistadors of the sixteenth and seventeenth centuries on their way down to Buenos Aires loaded with Inca gold and stones. The average speed was relatively low, both as a result of the rough conditions and because they were cautious. Each day they carefully planned their route and stops, reporting back to the Hold morning, noon and evening. La Quiaca, Potosi, Sucre, all dead names on the map, they moved onwards across the Altiplano, seeing no one, neither man nor beast. Turning westwards down across the Uyuni salt flats, where muted greys and whites contrasted oddly with the outcroppings of brown and red rock. Meeting up with the old railway route and following it down towards the Pacific, emerging finally from the mountains late in the afternoon of the twenty-second day since leaving the Hold.

High on a barren ridge some fifteen klicks from the coast, the two Gevcars came to a halt, doors hissing open to allow the crews to emerge. As though through a dirty reddish mottled glass the crumbling remains of a largish town could be seen. A town which according to their maps had once been the port of Arica. Originally a couple of klicks from the coast, the town itself now perched right on the edge of the great Pacific Ocean whose rolling swells ebbed and flowed through what had once been a posh residential district. In the reddish orange haze of the dying afternoon, the town appeared to waver to and fro in the rising thermals. Even when looking through the powerful scopes that formed part of the Gevcar's equipment, no sign of any human activity could be seen, only decaying buildings and littered streets. This being the largest town they had come close to since passing Mendoza eight days earlier, they discussed the viability of going down to investigate immediately, but eventually decided that the risks outweighed the benefits, and that it would be better to wait until the following morning. They drove on for a couple of klicks, eventually finding a place that offered both shelter and a view of the town, and there settled for the night. As the sun slid away to its deep purple-red death in the ocean, the shadows behind their backs lengthening and flowing up the hillside, they watched eagerly for any sign of life in the form of fires or lights that could indicate the presence of humans. Soon, however, the ruined town was absorbed by the darkness, quiet and impenetrable, with no sign of any lights. The Watch members needed no instructions on setting up the surveillance and defence perimeter, with a duty rota that had three Watchers on duty at any one time. Just because they had seen nothing did not necessarily mean that no one was there, a lesson Karel had learned early on in his travels, and had never forgotten.

The next morning, after the usual meeting, they drove slowly onwards, down a winding valley towards the town, drawn by the invisible magnet of having to know what might have become of the inhabitants of the once thriving town. Passing the long-abandoned airfield, the Gevcars threaded their way through the debris of the dead streets, accompanied by their private dust storm swirling out from under the skirts. Moving over many of the abandoned wrecks, bulldozing larger obstacles aside, occasionally scraping the sides of buildings, the two cars advanced steadily, the hardened armour absorbing punishment that would have destroyed lesser vehicles within minutes. In places there were still signs of long past fighting, shell-holes in building fronts, craters in the roads, gutted buildings with caved in roofs, broken vehicles thrown up into positions in which they resembled abstract sculptures, all gave evidence as to the savagery of the fighting. In what was left of what had once been a hospital, the scene that came to their eyes was the thing nightmares are made of. Dressed in full biohazard kit they emerged through the airlock built in to the rear of each of the cars. On foot and in a group led by Brendt, they searched through several buildings including the hospital and what had apparently been the municipal or civil centre. To those who remained in the Gevcars the scenes were bad enough, but at least they retained some sense of unreality, like scenes from a bad film. For the eight out on foot it was worse, much worse. In the ruins, mutilated remains of corpses still lay, for the most part picked clean, if not by scavengers then by the elements. Whitened bones, pitted and broken revealed the violence of many the deaths, others were simply laid out in the passages, row upon row, empty sockets and lipless grins, a grim reminder of the horror long past. The passage of the seasons with their wind and rain had taken care of most of the contents of the buildings, furnishings, papers and computers, all gone. The one thing they did find, sealed in a carefully hidden cracked plastic box, which crumbled almost to dust when touched, were the remains of a report, all substance now faded away, except for the date which had remained, for some obscure reason, perfectly legible, 15 October 2038. The municipal building had obviously served as a command post against the invading forces, the remains of hastily erected sandbag barricades still blocked doorways and windows, rusting weapons lay around clutched in the skeletal hands of long dead soldiers.

Eventually they had had enough, with hardly a spoken word they returned to the Gevcars, appalled at the sight of so much destruction, yet aware that this small town represented only a microscopic fraction of what had taken place in the megacities of the world, the world of the Old Times, now dust forever. In the evening, twenty klicks further up along the coast, most of the usual small talk was absent as they ate their evening meal. Jock talking quietly to a solemn and withdrawn Threejays, Bob Cantor held a still shocked Janine's hand. Jock's gravel voice seemingly deeper than ever, and in his eyes the knowledge that this day's sights were in all probability the first of many similar ones to come as they advanced on their journey.

Chapter VI

'Maria, I don't like it, there's no way of knowing whether they'll let us back out or not,' Matthew Wilton said, sliding down from the top of the ridge to where his colleague waited squatting in the shade of a rock, cloak draped loosely over her head. A few loose pebbles dislodged by his movement rolled on past where they sat just below the top or the ridge, bouncing their way down the uneven slope to vanish in the undergrowth below them. Overhead, clouds which had been absent earlier on had begun to drift in from the sea some five klicks over to their left, first the high cirrostratus, and then the lower and thicker altocumulus, occasionally obscuring the hazy sun, taking away the midday warmth. Matt shivered slightly pulling the binocular strap over his head and setting them down, waiting for an answer from his partner and senior.

'Look Matt, we're up here for a reason, remember? Karel doesn't want to bring the cars any nearer until he's certain that the locals are friendly or at least provide no threat to us.' Seeing the lack of confidence in his partner's face, Maria Sanches continued. 'I know you think that it would be simple to come shooting in along the beach, but if there's someone there with any heavy artillery they can still damage us, even the Gevcars aren't totally invulnerable you know.'

'Well, then I don't see why we can't turn inland and avoid the place altogether.'

'Come on Matt, that's not a solution, we've not spoken with anyone since that place two days out of Antiguos. We haven't even gone near any towns since Arica, and that was over a week ago. We need to have some idea of the set-up in this area, what the threats are, how far afield these people go out, who they trade with and so on. So far what we've seen looks peaceful ...'

'Peaceful!' interrupted Matt. 'What about the watchtowers over there? They're bristling with guns, and we've seen the guard shifts coming and going.'

'Well, what did you expect? The Hold has the Watch, these people have their guards in those towers. Just because you're not warlike doesn't mean you have to be naïve to the point of stupidity. We've watched them part of yesterday afternoon and again all this morning and almost all of the activity we've seen is moving goods back and forth, some building repair work, farming those fields just outside the wall, and so on. They're not savages, they've got machinery working there, so someone has enough know how to keep the generating station going, the buildings look cared for, and the streets we can see into are clean. They've managed to keep some vehicles going, and that implies a serious education effort.' She stopped, pausing to gather her thoughts before continuing. 'The people that designed, built and serviced those tractors have been dead for quite a while you know. I do realize that what we can see is still only a part of the town, and that they could easily have an enormous military camp just over that hill,' Maria smiled ruefully, 'but there's no way of knowing unless we spend a lot more time than we have surveying the place from outside. And it doesn't make sense, you don't just militarize part of the encampment, it's all or nothing. Look, we found them by chance because of the smoke from that large building, so they're making no effort to hide. No, Matt, I reckon we're just going to have to go on in, we don't have time to sit around for days on end. All the basic conditions for continuing on have been met, and besides, from a professional point of view, it's quite fascinating, I mean surviving as a working society in the Hold is one thing, out here ...'

'Yeah, yeah, but I can't help thinking we're sticking our necks out' returned the younger man shaking his head, his long red hair dancing on his shoulders in sympathy with his movements. 'But, I suppose we've not much choice, so we better get going.'

The two gathered up their packs, a large one for Matt and a smaller one for the psychologist, and returned back down the way they had come for half a klick of so, scrambling round the larger boulders that dotted the hill they had used as a viewpoint. After calling the Gevcars on the comm unit to tell them that they had decided to go in as agreed, they set off down back the way they had come. They reached the old track they had seen earlier and followed it round the hill to the east, towards the small town they had spent the morning watching. As they trudged along the obviously seldom used track, packs bobbing on their backs outside their cloaks, they kept a sharp lookout for any sort of activity. The landscape that had once been subtropical was a lot drier now, but there were still areas of trees and heavy undergrowth. Every now and then they passed some decaying indication of man's passage, fallen fences and tumbled stone walls separating patches of what had once been farmed fields, now overgrown with weeds and bushes. By the time they had covered about half the distance towards the town gates, passing a few outlying and long-abandoned buildings, they heard the distant ringing of a bell, which they took to be the warning that strangers had been spotted on the road. Half a klick further on, just past the remains of what had once been a large tower building and where the track ran between two low man-made embankments, probably earthworks left over from some forgotten highway scheme, they were stopped by the local militia. A hastily thrown up roadblock, really just a pole on two tripods, more symbolic than effective had been placed across the track. Behind it two armed men waited, and on either side of the track and some metres behind the pair more heads appeared, probably a dozen in all, a classic outflanking manoeuvre, which, had they wished to, they could easily have avoided. Maria and Matt came to a halt, slowly holding out their hands to show that they were unarmed.

'A quick reaction time, well done.' said Maria in Anglic the language most likely to be understood. 'We're peaceful citizens passing through northwards and we'd be glad of any advice you can give us.'

'That's as maybe' came the reply from the grizzled veteran who stood behind the barrier, 'meanwhile, you'll be laying down your packs and stepping back, slowly. Leave your hands where we can seen them, we don't want to make a mistake.' The voice was neither friendly nor unfriendly, but a trace of nervousness could be read into the well-rehearsed speech. The two Hold members did as they were told, without speaking, and making sure that they kept their hands in view. When the packs were on the ground Maria also opened her cloak to show that no weapons were hidden on her person, and on her nod Matthew followed suit. They were given a rather perfunctory body search, more of a pat down than anything else, applied equally to both of them. Matt stood quietly, apparently at ease his hands hanging loosely in front of his body. Inside he was coiled like a tightly wound spring, right hand just a fraction of a second away from the small flat needle gun strapped inside his left sleeve, prepared to counter any unpleasantness that might arise because Maria was a woman.

SEASONS OF CHANGE

There had been much discussion on who and how many members should be a part of the group going into town. This was the first time in the eight days since they left Arica behind that they had decided to head by a medium-sized town in the hope of picking up fresh information. They had basically followed the coastline up the bulge of South America, keeping between ten and fifty klicks inland, well away from most of the larger towns. A number of voices had been raised to propose that the party be limited to male members of the Watch, but in the end Maria's argument that making contact with a new society demanded a person trained to analyse and interpret reactions, body language and nuances of speech had convinced Jock and Karel. Karel had in fact supported the decision from the start, a fact that had done much to convince the doubters. He had stated that with the exception of the early years after the collapse, men and women had shared almost all the roles available in any surviving groups, a simple matter of need as normally there weren't enough able-bodied adults to go round. The final decision had been left to the two members of the party as a function of what they were able to see through the binoculars, with the proviso that if the locals looked threatening or if the town turned out to be a military encampment, they were to turn back at once. As the two locals who had patted them down stepped back, Maria spoke again.

'We've come from the south, and we're on our way up to the NAF territory, whatever may be left of it anyway.'

'Heard of it,' the speaker spat, hesitated and then continued, his curiosity at meeting strangers finally outweighing his caution. 'Don't believe it exists any longer, my father used to know something about that.' He shrugged, then remembering what he was there for said, 'follow us, your stuff will be taken care of, and if the Captain likes what he sees, you'll get it back, we're honest folk here.' So saying he turned and set off along the road, while some of the rest of the guards scrambled down from the embankment and stood a few metres away, waiting for their two captives to follow, which, after a look over their shoulders, they did.

'Tell me again, why is it you're going to try to find these other ... Holds you call them?' The speaker, a tall cadaverously thin man, to whom the others were all very respectful towards, stared at the two Watchers, his dark unblinking eyes giving nothing away. The man sat in a high straight-backed chair, at the end of a large hall, lit now as

75

the evening wore on by the dim glow of electric light bulbs. Situated at strategic points stood his staff, all in positions from which they could gun down the two visitors should they be so foolish as to try to attack the so-called Captain. Maria, tired after the two-hour wait which had preceded the interrogation sessions of which this was the third, straightened up in her chair, gazed back at the man in front of her, eyes steady, but allowing a fraction of impatience to show.

'Captain, as your subordinates have already told you, unless they're even more incompetent than they've led us to believe after the two previous interrogations, we are part of an exploration team from a Survival Centre we call the Hold. It is located well to the south and east of here, several moons on horse and foot. We are on our way up to what used to be the North American Federation Territory because we believe that a second Hold was set up at the same time as ours. We don't know the exact location, unfortunately these two Holds were left in the dark as to each other's existence, and it is only by chance that we found out that they might exist.'

'And why wouldn't these two groups have been told about each other?' retorted the speaker. 'It seems to me that two together would be stronger than one, isn't that so?'

'Captain, I wasn't even born at the time these things were decided, but I have read the history.' At Matt's reply the dark eyes swung round to watch him. 'I imagine you have as well, so I don't need to tell you about the extremists who played such a large role in the destruction of all the technology that helped hold things together.'

'Hmm,' said the Captain, adroitly changing the subject. 'And if you are part of a team as you claim, why did you came sneaking in here, why not come openly?'

'Captain,' Maria took over the conversation again, 'if walking down the road without weapons other than light handguns for personal defence isn't open, then I think someone has got the wrong end of the stick. We could have come here bristling with weapons, however we are not soldiers, we are not conquerors, we are simply an exploration team, a fact which I have been at pains to explain to your people.'

'And if this is true, where are the rest of your team?'

'Well, you will appreciate that as we could not be certain as to the reception that awaited us, we were sent out to have a look. If and when we decide that the situation warrants it, we will call our friends down. Please understand Captain, we have every right to be as suspicious of you as you are of us, and there's a lot more of you than there are of us.'

'And what's your guarantee that you will in fact be allowed to call your friends, after all you could be an advance team for some group trying to take over our town. It wouldn't be the first time that sort of thing has been tried. We could have you executed just as a precautionary measure.'

'We understand your worries, and we ask you to believe that we too accepted some degree of risk in coming down here. Obviously we watched you for some time before coming down, if we had felt that this place had fallen back into savagery, we wouldn't be having this conversation.' Maria looked around the room, taking in the guards who had remained there, unobtrusive but still vigilant. 'You must know there is no real way we can prove to you that we are who we say we are, at some point you will have to reach a decision, either you will have to dispose of us as you see fit, or you will allow us to call our companions.'

'And you would do that with the devices we found in your pack, I take it?'

'The communicators, yes. But I must tell you that as far as today is concerned it's already too late. I can speak to them of course, but there's no way they'll come down tonight, so I'm afraid tomorrow morning will have to do. You might say that the uncertainties prevail by weight of volume, a night trip is out of the question.'

The Captain sat, apparently lost in thought, and then looked up, and for the first time smiled.

'My people trust my judgement, that is why I am allowed to lead them. I do not as such give orders, I make suggestions which are acted upon.' Again a brief smile escaped as the Captain sat back in his chair and rubbed his hands across his eyes. 'I have watched you since you arrived. You are wary but not frightened, you were not in the least impressed with the electric lights, you carry communication devices the likes of which we no longer have, though there are pictures and explanations in the library. You are dressed in a strange fashion, certainly no one within several days riding has cloaks like yours. You,' indicating Matthew, 'are clearly an Outdoorsman but not I judge a soldier, yet your level of education is as good as that of our teachers. And you,' looking now at Maria, 'have I think been carefully trained to handle people, not once have I seen you lose control of the conversation, nor show any fear in what could have been a dangerous situation for you. Surprising, very surprising, we must talk some more. Here in this small town which once went by the name of Tumbes in the north of the old Republic of Peru, we have struggled to remain civilized. I believe that may also be true in your Hold. I will accept your story, and I bid you welcome, tomorrow we will meet with your friends, now I will invite you to dine and you can tell me about this Hold of yours.'

With this, the Captain rose from his chair and indicating that Maria and Matthew should follow, he led the way out of one of the doors. The men who had acted as guards followed as well, pausing to leave their weapons in a rack, though Matthew noted that several of them still kept their hand weapons. They came out of the building into a walled courtyard and continued through a gateway which opened on to a dimly lit street, along which they went some two hundred metres before entering a low building which turned out to be an eating hall. The visitors noted that all the buildings appeared to be in a good state of repair and that the streets were clean, all of which indicated that their earlier fears had been groundless. Many of the buildings were obviously old, but a few newer structures were also to be seen. Inside the hall they were escorted to a table where plates of food and glasses of what turned out to be a sort of beer were brought. Throughout the meal they were questioned at length on the Hold, questions which they both answered as openly and as fully as they could, for this was what they had agreed with Karel and Jock. There was amazement at the news that the Hold had managed to keep all the technology of the Old Days, and in some cases even improve on it. Fission reactors as a power source lay beyond the wildest dreams of the town leaders, genetically modified plants and vegetables and hydroponically grown fruits bordered on science fiction. Most amazing of all, was the news that a spaceman would be among them the next morning. Maria could have created no greater sensation had she said that tomorrow someone would wave a magic wand and return the world to what it had been. A spaceman. Two generations after the last flaming lift-off this was the thing legends are made of. Even the news that after so many long years of fighting for themselves, someone was now offering to help had less impact than the coming presence of a spaceman.

In comparison, the town where they were seemed to the visitors to be part of another era, where although much of the old technology had survived and was still in use, the more sophisticated machines and systems had failed and their replacement had proved impossible. With a population of just over thirty-eight thousand, they had managed to survive numerous outside attacks over the first few years after the final collapse of the central government in the first part of the fourth decade. They had kept the two oil-fired generating stations running and at a cost of several thousand men had secured the wells that fed them the vital fuel. Many of them had become farmers and raisers of small tough and scrawny goats and sheep. Cattle, although they had started out with some stock, had proved almost impossible to breed, probably a result of sterility or at least lack of fertility induced by the radioactive dustings that had drifted around during the early years. The level of live normal births had fallen alarmingly before recovering enough for them to guarantee at least a stable population. For a number of cycles they had striven to avoid outside contact, knowing that their safety depended to some degree on remaining undetected. Most creditable of all, successive Captains, as the leaders in the town were invariably called, had kept an education system going. They had produced no great scientists or thinkers, but they kept the old technology alive, and almost everyone could read and write, no small thing in the face of such a tough survival situation.

Having finished the meal, Brendt called the Gevcars on the comm, obtaining an immediate answer, interspersed with occasional bursts of static.

'Maria, is everything alright? You've been off the air for over six hours!' The strain of keeping the radio watch was clearly audible in Jean Klock's voice. Maria answered in the affirmative using the verbal code they had prepared in case she was speaking under duress.

'Hi Jean, tell Karel that both his babies are doing just fine,' she said, knowing that any other statement such as 'we're OK' or 'everything is fine' or 'no problems here' would have meant that they were in trouble and needed to be rescued. 'We've been in a meeting with the leader of the community here. As we had expected, it took some time to convince him that we really are interested in helping out in any way possible, so we'll look forward to you coming in tomorrow.' She was answered by Jock Fernan's deep rumble.

'Well done Maria and Matthew, I knew you were a good choice for the mission. Karel tells me that we'll be ready to go in as soon as it's light, so we'll see you then. Are you with the leader of the community? Perhaps I should exchange a few words with him.'

'Yes sir, he's here beside me.' Turning to the Captain she spoke so that her voice could still be picked up by the comm. 'Captain, the person at the other end is Elder Jock Fernan who is a member of our Council. If you speak normally in the general direction of the unit he'll hear everything you say.'

The two men exchanged formal pleasantries over the air for a few minutes, agreeing to continue their talk in the morning, after which Maria signed off for the night.

The next morning, after a frugal breakfast, the two visitors, escorted by the Captain and some of the community leaders, walked down to the edge of the town and out through the gateway under which they had been marched in as prisoners the day before. In the early morning light the town had looked washed out, colours muted and flowing into one another. Close up observation as they walked the few hundred metres to the gate had confirmed the impression they had obtained through the binoculars and briefly the evening before. The place was in a good state of repair, most of the buildings inside were low house-type constructions, but there were also one or two taller buildings in every block, some six or seven stories high. In general most had seemed to be occupied, other than those which were clearly community buildings, stores, eating houses, workshops and so on. Outside the wall it was clear that many constructions had been bulldozed away, destroyed they assumed to give the town a clear perimeter some three hundred metres wide at its narrowest. Matt asked one of the group they were in about this, and received an affirmative reply, with the information that it had been done at the time of a typhoid plague some thirty-five cycles ago.

Word of the event had obviously got out for they were soon joined by a group of a hundred or so curious onlookers, who stood around aimlessly in little groups, unsure as to why they were there. Maria and Matthew had tried to explain the Gevcars to the locals, but even so the sight of the two vehicles coming over the hill and down towards them sent a wave of unease rippling through the crowd. While still half a klick away the cars slowed down even more and drifted in the last few hundred metres, the whine of the power units muted but still penetrating.

The two cars came to a halt a few dozen paces away from the group, and as the engines whined down to nothingness, the doors hissed open, the short stepladder extending automatically from the underside of the door to the ground. Karel was first out, followed by

Jock from the second car which had stopped a few metres further away. He walked across to where Maria and Matthew waited, and as always he seemed to flow effortlessly than to walk, his long grey mane giving him a leonine appearance.

'I bid you good day, my name is Karel Houseman, I am the leader of our expedition. Thank you for coming to meet us.'

'Welcome to Tumbes, I am the Captain here, on behalf of my people I welcome you. From what your scouts have been able to tell us I believe we can perhaps help you with some information, and of course I look forward to establishing a solid relationship with your Hold.' At this point Jock Fernan joined in the conversation and soon most the rest of the Hold group had descended and were being introduced in turn to the leaders of the town. After a brief conversation with Maria, Karel looked over at the Gevcars and with a quick but complex hand gesture indicated that the weapons crew could stand down, for being a cautious man he had wanted to make sure that they had not been tricked into walking into an ambush.

Jock Fernan, with a keen sense of good politics, invited the local leaders to climb into the Gevcars, and this gesture more than anything else caused the last barriers of reserve to crumble. The cars were a source of wonder, for although many of the visitors were familiar with basic engineering and scientific theory, the industrial base necessary to build such machines no longer existed. They climbed in and out of the various compartments, marvelling at the optimized usage of every bit of useable space which allowed twelve people to live and travel over extended periods without getting on each others nerves or going round the bend. After half an hour or so, with a number of the locals including the Captain still on board, the Gevcars were powered up again, and expertly handled, advanced into the town, their great width only just scraping in through the gateway. The arrival of the two Gevcars seemed to be taken as an excuse for a day off, and if not every member of the population came to see them during the rest of the day while they stood parked in an open plaza, then the number was not far short. The speed at which the Hold team was accepted was little short of amazing, the two doctors, Erik Fernan and Sanjay Dever were spirited away to the local hospital almost at once, while Miguel Pardo and his assistant Samantha Alessi went off to investigate the town's seed production facility. The two Hold leaders, Karel and Jock, accompanied by the communications team retired for talks with the local council, Herb

Kramer along with the other three Techs remained with the Gevcars, taking advantage of the unexpected break to carry out routine servicing and maintenance activities. The only people with little to do were the Watch members, who after setting up their duty rotas to cover the cars, went off to offer their services to Miguel and Samantha.

Having originally planned to stay only long enough to find out whether the locals had any information about conditions further to the north, the exploration team stayed on for two weeks at Tumbes, mainly because as the days passed, their technical skills became more and more in demand. After consulting with Karel, Sandy and Jean Klock set up a full comm link with the Hold using the same scrambled frequency as their own, using one of the spare sets they had carried with them. The rest of the team worked with the local inhabitants, helping wherever they could, happy to be doing something positive. On two occasions, one of Gevcars made a trip out to some of the outlying towns that traded with Tumbes, towns with populations of only a couple of thousand, but nevertheless important trading partners for the town.

They continued to exchange news with the Hold every day, with the added advantage that as they had no travel schedule to stick to while they were in the town, the contact time could be extended allowing everyone time for personal talks with friend and family. One particular item of news coming in from the Hold over the radio link was extremely encouraging. The Tech department had completed their study of all the Gevcar design specs and drawings which Herb and David had found along with the cars themselves, and the general opinion was that it would be feasible to build a basic transport Gevcar in less than half a cycle. It was to be unarmed, unarmoured and with minimum comforts, nevertheless it would enable renewed and frequent contact with the town of Antiguos to be established.

A further item of good news was the presence of a young couple who had arrived in the town three cycles earlier, having trekked down from two thousand klicks further north, from what once had been central Mexico. The couple was then subjected to a friendly but intensive debriefing, returning over and over every point to ensure that no valuable information was missed out. With this new information a new route was mapped out, a route that would take them inland some fifty klicks, away from the coastal plains where a number of non-friendly settlements were still supposed to exist, emerging on the coast again at around latitude twelve degrees north, some hundred klicks south-west from where the South American continent narrowed down to the isthmus. From this point the plan was to make a short run over the water so as to avoid the heavily contaminated badlands where radiation levels from the bombs targeted on the Panama Canal remained high, even after more than forty years. It proved impossible to choose a fully safe point at which to come ashore again, but Karel's feeling was that any stretch of coast more than 250 klicks away from the ground zero on the canal, even allowing for inaccurate targeting, should be safe enough with the shielding afforded them by the Gevcar hulls. After this the plan was to follow the old coast road up the west coast, and then aim to turn slightly east to avoid the old megacity that had spread eastwards from the Elay/Sandee urban sprawl. Beyond this they would have no choice but to play it by ear, as the old satellite photos from the Hold were long out of date.

They finally departed the town mid-morning fifteen days since their arrival under a grey leaden sky that held the promise of later drizzles. They left behind the start of many new ideas for helping Tumbes to grow, and not least they left behind a full communication link to themselves and to the Hold. Despite having planned an early start the two cars were practically besieged by well-wishers including the Captain and his advisers from the town, and it was only after a couple of hours that they were able to set out. Once clear of the town, they swung eastwards away from the ocean and began climbing up the winding valley leading into the foothills of the Andes. The slopes, despite the generally dry climate, showed many areas of new growth as a result of the return of the rains after many years of absence. Most of the growth consisted of low wind-twisted fir trees that had obviously been of hardy enough stock to resist the years of poisons, droughts and radioactivity. In sheltered spots bunches of succulent spiny plants grew, with little red berries decorating the dull green growth, adding a splash of colour in an otherwise pastel coloured landscape. As they drove onwards, they passed abandoned villages and houses, sometimes they even saw the remains of stone citadels dating back thousands of years to the time of the older civilizations, but it was all the same, for everything was deserted with no signs of life to be found anywhere.

By the time evening arrived they had reached the undulating

plateau at around two thousand metres above sea level, having covered a good two hundred klicks since leaving Tumbes. They stopped as usual before darkness fell leaving enough time to and set up their camp and prepare the evening meal. While several members of the team grumbled good naturedly about the return to eating concentrated rations, Karel sat quietly in the doorway of the Gevcar, lost in thought, secretly pleased to be on the road again. Sensing someone watching, he glanced up meeting Sandy's eyes as she helped serve the food, knowing then that she shared the feeling.

[Extract – 2018]

(The following reports are excerpts from the minutes of the Site 3 Steering Committee meeting held on 5 January 2018. It is to be noted that all records related to 1 January 2018 to 31 December 2025 have been classified as restricted and can only be accessed with the authorization of the Council of Elders.)

The removal of any documents from the Records Hall or the copying of any information relating to this period is strictly forbidden.

STEERING COMMITTEE MEETING #1
Summary/Excerpts of Presentation Speech by John C. Mulder, FRS, Chairman of the Steering Committee, CEO of GE Advanced Technologies, Inc.

Ladies and gentlemen,

Today we meet for the first time as the Steering Committee for the construction of a survival habitat for a maximum of ten thousand people.

Before I go on to talk about the organization as well as about some of the technical aspects for this Site, I would ask you to bear with me while I expound on the meaning of this endeavour. All of you here today have been chosen on the basis of your drive, your achievements, you knowledge, and above all for the opinions you have expressed publicly regarding the state of the society in which we live. All of you are convinced that unless action is taken, civilization as we understand it today is doomed to self-destruct or at best to decay to a point where it is no longer functional. You have been offered a chance to be a part of just such an action. All of you have committed yourselves and your families to this great project, in the hope that we will be able to guarantee a new and better world for our descendants. We will call on that commitment to its limit. We will ask much of you, your time, your know how, your absolute discretion outside these four walls, and in the end perhaps even your lives.

Our sponsors in this venture are many, captains of industry and commerce, military officers of many nations, and simple ordinary people who believe in the future. We enjoy their trust and confidence. It is up to us to live up to that.

There is a special topic that I wish to touch upon now, and which we will not talk about again unless an emergency arises. It is that this habitat we are to build over the next seven years will not be the only one, it will be one of three. The building of each of these sites has been entrusted to separate committees, the only contact between these committees will be through the Chairmen and via our principals. The decision to run the three projects independently of each other rather than to take advantage of the synergy offered by a group effort has been a hard one, but due to the uncertainty of the world situation it was felt that this would offer more security from attacks by anti-technology extremists. The locations for the habitats have been chosen after an extensive survey that has been carried out over the past eighteen months. Our project will be known henceforth and in this room as Site 3 and will be built in southern Patagonia. To the people who will eventually work, live and play in this habitat, it will be the only such habitat. Only one or two members of the governing body will be aware of the existence of the sister habitats.

Each of you has in front of you a folder containing the basic specifications for Site 3. All the information in this folder has been prepared by a specialized technical team, which will be reporting to this committee. It is little more than an outline, a concept document if you will, nevertheless it contains all that we as the Steering Committee need to know at this stage. To fix these basic concepts in our minds I propose briefly to run through the main points, which for convenience have been separated into six distinct project phases:

Phase 0 – already completed
- Feasibility studies
- Area search
- Basic habitat concept/general databook
- Preliminary layouts
- Geological/hydrogeological surveys
- Site confirmation
- Preliminary Masterplan Time Schedule

Phase I – 1 January 2018 to 30 September 2019
- Layout development
- Basic engineering

- Heavy construction specifications
- Complementary geological/hydrogeological studies
- Power reactor definition

Phase II – 1 October 2019 to 30 September 2021
- Power reactor design
- Building and accessory system specifications
- Heavy construction work start
- General building work start

Phase III – 1 October 2021 to 30 June 2023
- Heavy construction work end
- Power reactor construction start
- General building work
- Accessory systems construction
- Detail finishing specification
- Personnel search and selection

Phase IV – 1 July 2023 to 30 June 2025
- Power reactor installation
- Accessory systems installation
- Detail finishing work
- Personnel induction/training
- Power reactor checks

Commissioning and start-up – 1 July to 31 December 2025
- Reactor criticality
- System checks

For each of the above points a summary folder will be made available after this meeting, I ask that over the next three weeks you jointly review this information and submit any changes you see fit at the next meeting. Members of the technical staff will be available to brief you on specific topics as required.

Before we begin work, a final thought. This is the single most important project the world has ever seen. The fact that we cannot share it with the world at large is distressing to all of us, unfortunately it must be so. Ladies and gentlemen, I ask you to pray for God's guidance, as you may perceive Him to be, for the task that lies ahead of us. We must not fail.

News Item Summaries: The indefinite closure of the New York Stock Exchange has caused widespread panic selling in world markets. All precious metals quotations are being withheld for the time being, however reports indicate that most of them have at least trebled in price since the beginning of the year. The EU Joint Stockmarket Commission has so far held off major price drops with the aid of the EU central banks.

The Panamanian Independence Army has placed explosives on several of the canal locks thus denying passage to any shipping. This will result in higher commodity costs for many items. Experts estimate that world inflation due to this fact alone will run to 2.25 percent unless negotiating teams can break the existing deadlock by the end of March.

In Brasilia striking municipal workers took over the water treatment works with the intention of closing off the mains in order to apply pressure to the State Legislature in their request for wage increases. The authorities reacted with unexpected firmness calling in troops to squash the strikers, in the resulting fighting over two hundred people including at least sixty soldiers have been killed. Sporadic shooting can still be heard throughout the city which is now entering its fourth day without water and where food is becoming scarce.

A group of terrorists has hijacked a 350,000 ton supertanker in the Indian Ocean and is threatening to blow it up causing a massive spillage of oil which will destroy sea life over an estimated twenty-five thousand square kilometres. So far the demands of the group have not been made public but are believed to include the immediate release of Pyotr Kosawoski, the leader of the New Brigade captured in Poland last month, as well as payment of an undisclosed sum. Special forces are being rushed to the area in an effort to neutralize the threat, but past history shows that such efforts usually arrive too late.

Chapter VII

As the sun slipped out from behind the thinning cloud front which had been drifting westwards across the sky since before dawn, the wavelets on the otherwise smooth water of the bay seemed to sparkle like rapidly blinking little reddish orange signal lights. The Gevcar, with David bar Delf sitting relaxed at the controls, cruised just above the water at a steady thirty-five knots, raising a light wake, leaving behind a cloud of spray particles drifting in the morning air. Jean Klock as ever sat at his communications console speaking with Sandy in the second car, now running five klicks away and inland from the coast. The coastline off on their right remained hidden in a sort of shadow, colours washed out as they looked in the direction of the still climbing sun now beginning to lose its deep early morning red as it crept upwards. As they reached a point just over half way across the small bay, a circular patch of water ahead of them suddenly seemed to become grey and frothy, and then in a split second begin to climb into the sky. It was only David's quick reactions that saved them. Without conscious thought, and before the waterspout had reached its maximum height he jammed the joystick over, reversing the starboard lateral thrusters on the Gevcar. The car seemed to run into a brick wall, tilting crazily for an instant while water from the explosion cascaded across the hull, and then with a body-crushing acceleration leap sideways as the next shell exploded where they would have been had they continued on their original course. The crew, many of whom had been relaxing, were thrown from their bunks and chairs into untidy heaps of struggling arms and legs, shouts and screams of pain and confusion echoed through the car.

'They're on the beach, left end near the headland, on the beach!' yelled Jules Borman, one of the few who had been strapped into his seat and had seen the muzzle flashes.

'Take stations! Jules, Sara, get the cannon on line, this is an emergency,' shouted Karel from the floor where the unexpected turn had thrown him. The two Watch members threw themselves across the still-bucking floor towards the ladder leading to the upper turret, while David continued to take random evasive action, the Gevcar practically hidden in the clouds of spray coming off the water. The next shell burst some seventy-five metres away from them, the range finders working the attacking cannon obviously thrown off by the car's unexpectedly rapid reaction. David reversed course again and shot through the still falling water from the second explosion, and then turned towards the attackers still zigzagging violently. Up in the turret where the control system of the twin electric cannons seemed to be taking an agonizingly long time to clear for firing, Sara Mesada worked the range computer frantically, fingers a blur as she fed in the solution parameters. Her Watch partner Jules Borman, sitting at the main board, waited patiently with the head-up display screen in front of his eyes counting slowly down.

'Locked, I have a confirmed lock on point of origin,' Sara's voice, strained still but calm as she wiped the trickle of blood from the gash in her forehead which she had acquired when she was thrown into the table.

'Nearly charged, come on ... come on!' and then a deep rumble as the gun fired, a one-second pause and another rumble. 'Christ!, will you look at that,' involuntarily torn from Jules' lips as the Gevcars anti-glare screens came up to full power, again a pause, another rumble, pause, another rumble, 'I can't ... the light, unbelievable, what a flash, ... yeow! ... Now the whole cliff's going down! What a sight! Are there any more targets on your screen?' And then as he watched a line of froth sweep outwards at incredible speed from where the canon shells had struck. 'Watch out! Shockwave! Shockwave! Hang on!' The Gevcar shuddered suddenly and then bounced as if struck by a giant hand as the shockwave from the multiple explosions reached them, David fighting for control as the heavy vehicle was tossed aside like a feather.

'No more targets, no targets ... I don't know for sure what else there was, ... I'm scanning for any more heavy pieces, need a couple of minutes more. ... Ask David to slow down, we'll be in range of any small stuff before I've finished.'

'Got you Sara,' from David over the intercom, now back in control of the car again. 'I'm swinging round to the left, we'll make a full circle.' And the Gevcar, once more under control swung round in a tight sliding loop at over 120 knots a metre above the surface of the still turbulent water surface, leaving a wake well over a hundred metres long which rode up into the air some three metres. With the end of the evasive manoeuvres the rest of the crew picked themselves up and scrambled to their action stations. Karel slid into the pilot's seat beside David, grimacing from the pain in his side where he had fallen against something or other.

'Good work David, bear off to the right a bit. Jean, get Sandy on the radio and warn them! Tell them to go inland a bit and then come back in from the North. Reports please, anyone hurt?'

'You sure as heck scared me.' Petra Zimber, third pilot strapping herself into the chair behind David and jamming her headphones onto her head.

Unfortunately there was also bad news. 'Oh God, Patric's unconscious with an enormous cut on his head, he was thrown onto the floor. He's bleeding a lot, I don't know if I should move him or not. I need Erik back here fast!' said Lee Sun Yan from the samples storeroom aft, voice high with anxiety.

'Maria's fine, I've collected a couple of cuts but no big deal. Karel, I'm on my way to take care of Patric. Maria can take over the sick bay if anyone else needs any help.' Erik Fernan as efficient as ever.

'Communications here, I'm fine.' Jean Klock

'Watch team, a couple of bruises and some cuts but we're all OK. We're ready with the sockets if you need them. Jules is checking the shore to see if there's any more hostile activity.' Bob Cantor as head of the Watch.

'I wish you wouldn't do that while I'm in the toilet David, I nearly tore my arm off trying to hang on.' Janine Saleh, her irrepressible good humour taking over as usual, even in moments of crisis.

The car slowed its headlong rush and cruised towards the beach where the dust cloud from the collapsed cliff, now half a klick in diameter and still growing, billowed in the air, forming strange multicoloured patterns in the sunlight. As they approached closer they could see that the four shells from the electric cannons had torn out a huge section of the cliff face which had fallen onto the attackers below, burying them under thousands and thousands of tons of yellowish grey rock. The new face, now exposed to daylight for the first time in uncounted aeons was a different colour, even through the dust it was possible to see that the rocks were paler, not yet oxidized and burnt by the sun, a scar that only time would cover.

The electric cannons that formed a part of the Gevcars' defensive weaponry were a derivative of the old rail gun concept, the theory of which had been around for at least fifty or sixty years before the collapse. Take a series of stationary accelerator coils arranged in a tube and successively energize them thus creating a travelling magnetic field which induces a frequency in the projectile coil. The magnetic field resulting from this interaction generates an accelerating force. Place the coils in two parallel rails and use a projectile as a moving electrical bridge allowing current to flow from one rail to the projectile and through its base, with the armature consisting of plasma-generating material, to the other rail that acts as a return lead. The magnetic field surrounding the rails and the charge carriers flowing through the electrically conducive plasma generates the Lorentz forces that accelerate the projectile along the rails. The theory was simple, but it had taken a long time to develop the compact energy supply systems needed to power the guns. In the end of course it got done, and the Gevcars, still on the top secret list, received the first of the new compact rail guns, each capable of throwing a projectile out at speeds in excess of five thousand metres per second, over fifteen times the speed of sound.

For the crew from the Hold, this was the first time the Gevcar's cannons had been fired, though Karel and Jock had drilled the gun teams until they were sick of the sight of the gun controls. The destructive results had exceeded anything they had expected, for not all the theory in the world could describe the effect of the high-velocity projectile striking a target, transferred its immense kinetic energy, vaporizing everything in the immediate area, with a shock wave enough to flatten any nearby structures. They came to a halt on the beach just outside the cloud which was beginning to dissipate as the heavier particles settled and the wind blew the rest out to sea. For a few long moments no one spoke, the only sound being the changing note of the power unit as it wound its way down to idle speed. No one even felt much like talking with the adrenaline shock now wearing off leaving them feeling flat, wasted and perhaps a little bit scared at the destructive power they had unleashed.

'Jean, do you read? This is Sandy, do you copy?'

'Loud and clear Sandy. Go to action stations, we've been attacked from the shore, no damage. We took them out with the electric cannon.

'Give me the coordinates, we'll circle round.

'We're at the northern end of the bay at the top of Chart 265. ... We're coming ashore now, stopping on the beach just short of where the headland used to be. No sign of any activity here. What is your status?'

'Patric's hurt, don't know how badly, Erik's with him now, otherwise we're just shaken.'

'We're coming in just offshore about ten klicks north, we can see the cloud from here. You people have been having some fun. ... We confirm no further activity ... coming round now. ... Herb says he can see you now, we'll be up to you in a couple of minutes.'

The second Gevcar sailed in from the north, trailing a wake that diminished as they turned to come ashore, sliding up the beach and coming to a halt fifty or sixty metres away. Karel and Jock conferred briefly on the radio, after which the second car discharged Jock, Threejays, and four Watchers, and then lifted, spun round and drifted back along the curved beach to a position half a klick away from where they were able to keep the whole bay in view and if necessary provide covering fire. Janine and some of the Watch from the other car also descended, and began to walk towards where the enemy had been earlier. Under their feet the coarse grey sand grated with a slight squeaking sound, their feet sinking in, leaving clear lines of footprints behind them. Reaching the edge of the fresh rockfall they began to clamber up and over, trying not to dislodge the still unstable pieces.

Back in the Gevcar Erik laboured over the still form of Patric who still lay on the floor where he had been flung by the explosion. The blood that had poured from a gash on the side of his head had been stopped by the application of a pad, but the real problem lay with the ugly looking wound on the upper back of his skull which had been pushed in when his head met the edge of the doorframe. Karel watched anxiously, seeing the depressed area on his skull, knowing that such a terrible wound boded ill. Working with the limited equipment at his disposal and aided by Maria, Erik worked frantically, attempting to lift out the crushed pieces to relieve the pressure on the brain, while Maria hooked up a portable plasma drip, hoping to reduce the shock to his system.

'What a mess, I don't know if I can get this fixed in time. Pulse?'

'Uneven and dropping, the shock is setting in.' Can't we move him to the sick bay?'

'Not at the moment, this is more important, give him a full unit of plasma, maybe that will buy us some time. If I can get this splinter lifted we have a fighting chance, otherwise ...'

Down on the beach, fifteen minutes of searching the gigantic jumbled pile of rubble had revealed, not too surprisingly, very little of interest. Most of whatever or whoever there had been on that part of the beach was now buried under tons of rock. Among the items they found were several packs containing some rather battered automatic rifles as well as some foodstuffs, all of which had been left behind a large boulder. Other than those there were few other indications of human action to be seen, no bodies, no vehicles, just a few unidentifiable pieces of equipment, some of it scorched by the short-lived fireball. The weapons were a mismatch of different calibres, as though gathered from the battlefield where six or seven armies had fought, each with different equipment. The food consisted mostly of dried rations of the sort that could be kept almost indefinitely if the original containers were undamaged. Not wishing to stay in the area for too long in case the late but unlamented attackers had any friends who might be coming in to see what had happened, attracted by the explosions and the dust cloud, they gathered up all they could find, including a very battered old leather briefcase which had survived unscathed apart from getting covered in dust.

As Jock accompanied by Bob Cantor and Jules Boreman reached the car, Erik emerged, face strained, hands and clothes bloodstained, still holding a set of surgical tweezers in his hand. Stepping down to the sand, he looked at Karel who had emerged from the Gevcar behind him and shook his head mutely. The older man stopped by his side, resting a hand on his shoulder, knowing that if Erik hadn't been able to save him, then none of the others would have been able to do any better.

'Couldn't save him ... he just went straight into shock ... I couldn't get him stabilized quickly enough.' He blinked, pushing back the tears of desperation that threatened to come. 'What a stupid bloody waste ...'

They buried Patric on the top of the headland just before midday. The whole group stood in a circle, cloaks flapping softly in the wind, hoods pulled close round the glare specs. For a headstone they had taken a flat stone on which Herb Kramer, using a small power chisel had cut Patric's name and the date, nothing else, just his name and the date, 21 February 2077.

'We have lost a friend,' Karel's voice was low, sometimes almost lost in the wind blowing across the headland. 'Patric was one of us, he knew that this journey might be dangerous, but it didn't deter him. He was here because of a sense of duty, not to any particular person, but to all humanity. He was born in the Hold, he was taught to know that his mission was to bring help to others. He did that. Now we have to go on, Patric's body may lie in this lonely grave, but his spirit lives on in our memories. We must continue with our mission if we wish to honour him.' He pushed back his hood, and his ponytail blew round in the wind. With a ramrod straight back, Karel Houseman executed a perfect salute. 'Patric, we will remember you, your death will not be in vain.' He stood for a moment, head low, then spun round and headed back down to the beach. The others followed after him, some stopping to say a few words over the small mound of earth and stones on the lonely headland, some just leaving silently, until all that was left was the gentle moan of the wind.

The Gevcars powered up and headed back the way they had come, turning eastwards and inland up a valley they had passed the day before. The two cars climbed to the top of the first ridge, and then, as they had planned, came to a halt in a slight dip in the plateau, hidden from casual view by a grove of low bushes. Karel, who knew that half of any battle was good intelligence, sent Bob and Matt out on foot each leading a scout team, with instructions to report back every quarter of an hour, and then gathered the remaining crew members together.

'We have two options,' he said as he sat in the hatchway of one of the cars, hair loose and blowing in the wind, sometimes whipping over the glare specs which he wore on his forehead, a medieval knight with his visor lifted. 'We can resume our route northwards, keeping further out to sea this time, say a minimum distance of four klicks from the shore. Or we can scout around and see where those people came from, maybe even find out why they opened fire on us though I rather doubt that will be possible.' He smiled, but there was no humour behind the ice blue eyes. 'I've seen this sort of thing before, destruction for the sake of destruction, show your power and watch people cringe.' Pausing, 'I'm afraid the only way to deal with it is an even greater show of power.'

Threejays interrupted before he could continue. 'But that would delay our search, we already lost a lot of time at Tumbes.' She held up her hand to forestall comments. 'And that's not a complaint, just a statement of fact. Besides which, we didn't come out here to fight a war, we're supposed to be helping people to recover the civilization they've lost, not destroying what little they have left,' she said, her hands spread open as if to emphasize the point. 'We're only likely to run into even more trouble.'

'In principle I tend to agree with your point of view,' Jock Fernan chipped in, his low rumble seemingly amplified rather than dispersed by the sighing of the wind. 'We definitely didn't come out on this trip to act as a conquering army, and we also have a clear objective to achieve.' He stopped as though gathering his thoughts. 'On the other hand it might be better to try and find out what we're up against. It could be just a few bandits, but it could be something big. I'd like to know if we can expect to meet up again with them. We have to be prepared for any eventuality.' He pushed back his cap and scratched his bald crown, now turned a tanned brown colour, even though they wore headgear most of the time they were outside.

Brendt Maxon looked around. 'Yeah, we beat them this time, but what if there had been five or six gun emplacements, even with the cannons we'd have been in trouble.' His weathered forehead wrinkling like a ploughed field: 'I for one would prefer to lose some time and find out what we're up against, maybe next time we won't be so lucky.' Karel looked around, noting that this point of view got a unanimous nods of approval from the other members of the Watch who had not been assigned to the scout teams. Yes, he mused, the Watch were too well trained to leave an unknown enemy force behind their backs.

'I'm not sure I would welcome another fight,' said Alice Folsom, 'I'm a co-pilot, but back at the Hold I worked in the science labs, my specialty is hydrogeological modelling. Threejays is right, I didn't come with you to start fighting with those we're supposed to be helping.'

'I fired that cannon, I know I was replying to an unwarranted attack, I don't regret what I did, but it still goes against the grain to kill people, and now he,' said Jules pointing at Karel, 'is proposing going out and attacking them. I don't like it.'

Karel sat quietly and let the arguments roll back and forth for a few more minutes and then, after exchanging a look with Jock, stood up and waited for silence to fall.

'There are points in favour of both possible courses of action. I've been out here before, I've seen this sort of thing, all too often. Today these people failed in their attempt to wipe us out, but we lost a good friend, a valuable member of our team. Tomorrow maybe they might have more luck, and if it isn't us, then surely it will be someone else.' He looked around, 'we'll wait for the reports from the scouts, if there's nothing we'll move on. But if there is any sort of positive indication, we'll stay around until we know what sort of opposition we're up against.' He paused again, and then added quietly, 'and if possible we'll take them out. We didn't come out to help vermin, and believe me we'll be helping everyone by stamping them out. This is my decision and mine alone.' Jules opened his mouth as if to reply, but then snapped it shut, and looking grim walked away from the group.

While they waited for the scouts to report, the scientists turned their attention to the booty salvaged from the beach, searching for a clue as to whom their attackers might have been. Some of the equipment carried markings dating back fifty or sixty years, markings from armies belonging to nations that had long since disappeared, some of it was obviously newer and had markings unfamiliar to the Hold team, a depressing thought really as it showed that even with society collapsing around them the armament manufacturers had been unable to stop their production lines from rolling. Justifications were always easy to find, a threat to our way of life, pacification of the border area, ethnic cleansing, even lebensraum, though with the rapidly declining populations that one took a bit of swallowing, all too easy, far too easy. The briefcase which they had picked up was unlocked and proved to be a disappointment as it contained only an unloaded and rather rusty revolver and a few incomprehensible notes apparently relating to foodstuffs. In the end they had learnt very little, other than what had been obvious from the beginning, which was that the attackers had long since lost any capacity to produce their own weapons, and in all probability anything else requiring an industrial power base.

While they waited they ate a quick lunch, reconstituted foods washed down with water, healthy, filled with vitamins, minerals and trace elements, but hardly appetizing, less so with the state of tension in the cars. The midday radio contact with the Hold was made as usual, this being the first time they hadn't stopped specifically for a midday break. They passed on their news and signed off, there being nothing much the far off Hold could do other than to warn them to keep a sharp lookout. It was an hour and a half before Bob called in that they had spotted smoke in the distance to the north. Karel told them to stay put and then moved up the cars, keeping off the ridges wherever possible. The terrain was fairly rugged with low hills and abundant low brush that afforded them reasonable cover although of course the dust cloud was a clear give away for anyone watching closely. Having picked up Matt's team on the way, they advanced on until finally they pulled up on the edge of a group of heavy branched grey leafed trees where Bob Cantor who had been waiting with his team, stepped out from behind a rock and waved them down, eyes gleaming with excitement.

'We're at least four klicks away from the smoke, but if they have any sort of patrol or lookouts, the Gevcars will be too noisy to bring in close, at least if we want to maintain any reasonable speed. If you agree, I'll take up a party of five, we still have about five and a half hours of daylight. I'll need over an hour and a half of that to get there. The terrain isn't too rough so we should be able to keep up a good pace.' Bob said, obviously enthusiastic about his proposal, and glad to be doing something active after so many days cooped up in the Gevcar.

'OK,' said Karel finally, nodding but obviously not entirely happy. 'But no rash moves without calling us, with this terrain it'll take us at least ten minutes to get up to you even if we come in fast, and much more if we creep in on low power. So Bob, be sure to keep your head down.'

While the patrol team set about gathering up their supplies and equipment, Karel and Bob laid out the few satellite photos they had of the area, unfortunately all taken over five decades earlier and of a not very high quality as the area had not been of any particular interest to the Sentry System. When they were ready, Karel moved the cars up a further half klick which was as far as they were able to go and still remain concealed in the woods, and then the team set out on foot, leaving the rest of the crew in a state of high anxiety.

They kept up a careful scan of all the surroundings as they moved up towards the distant smoke. They advanced as fast as they reasonably could, using the old ten minutes trot, five minutes quickstep and two minutes rest pattern. Their Hold cloaks, greyish green with ends taped down to stop the them flapping in the wind, helped them to blend into the background as they slipped from cover to cover, only the noise of their boots on the loose soil giving them away. At every stop they checked the area carefully with the binoculars looking for signs of unusual movement or other non-natural activity. At Karel's suggestion they all kept their mine detectors turned on at full strength, despite the drain on the batteries which would be dead after a couple of hours, but so far the route appeared to be free of mines or other booby traps. The hand-held detectors had been one of the items they had salvaged from one of the supply dumps and worked on both a metal detection system and on a sophisticated ionization sniffer which supposedly would warn them if any explosive material was in the scan area. As they moved up, Bob kept the patrol strung out in a loose line with a distance of around ten or twelve metres between each member making them a more difficult target. The landscape consisted mostly of rolling grassy hills with occasional wooded areas, all natural growths, for there were no patterns in the positions of the trees. After the sixth stop the smoke appeared to be coming from just over the next low hill so they spread out and approached slowly keeping in the shelter of every available hollow or bush.

At last they reached the top, most of them breathing heavily from their exertions and were able to look down, taking great care not to show themselves on the skyline for more than a few seconds, for nothing is so revealing as movement against the sky should anyone be watching. The source of the smoke was revealed as an open fireplace constructed against the wall of what had once been a large shed. Below them and some four hundred metres away in what had once been a small village or perhaps just a group of houses, some forty or forty-five people, mostly men, sat around, apparently just eating and drinking. They were mostly dressed in random mixes of army uniforms, men and women alike, and many of them carried weapons strapped to their belts or across their backs. A number of field artillery pieces had been lined up beside one of the buildings and five or six people were working on them, other than that there was no sign of anything resembling productive activity. With the wind blowing slightly towards the watchers on the hill it was occasionally possible to pick up random sounds of talking and occasional banging. Most of the buildings appeared to be dirty and in a poor state of repair, and several were obviously ruined beyond recovery, some having been burned out at some point. None of the activities indicated any degree of worry about the explosion off to the west, so presumably the event had passed unnoticed, and the group from the coast wasn't expected back for the moment. Behind the largest building, a two-storey affair with a water tower, it was possible to see some battered-looking military transport vehicles, though whether these were operational was anyone's guess. Certainly the whole place looked like a more or less permanent base rather than a temporary camp.

It was only after a quarter of an hour or so that Sarah Mesada who was out on the left flank noticed a wired-off enclosure some five hundred metres away. Only a part of it could be seen as the rest was hidden from view behind another small hill, but the mere fact that it was guarded was enough to make it worth while investigating. After calling the others attention to it with a low whistle and with hand signals, they all edged over until more of the enclosure came into view. Seen through the binoculars, the enclosure appeared to be only a few dozen paces away, and the despair on the faces of the people inside the enclosure, some twenty or so in all, was obvious to any watcher. Most were thin to the point of emaciation, ribs outlined against parchment-like skin, chests and backs covered in running sores, scabs and dirt, they lay or sat around, barely moving on the hard packed earth. Men, women and the occasional child were dispirited to the point where their fate had obviously ceased to matter to them. Their clothing was in rags, and in some cases practically non-existent, revealing that several of them were cursed with deformities, bent and twisted limbs, grossly misshapen heads, hunched backs, the end product of years of exposure to radiation and chemicals. The wire fence that appeared to be around three metres high, although it was difficult to accurately estimate heights from their vantage point up on the hill, was patrolled by two armed guards who wandered up and down, obviously bored with their job. Inside the compound were four sheds, mostly roofed except where parts had fallen in, with makeshift walls made out of bits of tin and wood. For the most the ground inside the fence was quite barren, but in the lee of the sheds some effort had obviously been made to grow something, a pitifully small patch protected by sticks with little bits of coloured cloth attached, waving fitfully in the occasional breeze. As they lay watching, trying not to be sickened at the sight that confronted them, a second group of prisoners appeared from behind some trees off to the right, heading for the compound accompanied by several more guards. As they watched, a man near the rear of the column stumbled and dropped to his knees, clearly so exhausted that no further threats could touch him. A woman turned back to try to assist him, but by then two of the guards were up to him and began to poke him with the bayonets mounted on the rifles they carried. The man's thin screams reached up, blown on errant gusts of wind. As the woman reached the man and bent to help him she was clubbed to the ground by the guards, one of whom then grabbed her by her hair and began dragging her away, back towards the rest of the prisoners. The other guard turned back to the man lying on the ground and slinging his rifle over his shoulder, the bloodied bayonet tip pointing like an accusing finger up into the sky, drew the handgun from the holster on his belt and shot the man twice through the back of the head.

The shock of seeing this barbaric act of murder was too much for one of the Watch who rolled over pulling out his needle gun and starting to aim it down at the guard, adjusting the sights for maximum range. Before he could fire, Bob Cantor had somehow covered the distance between them and pushed the barrel down into the earth.

'You bloody fool!' he hissed. 'What are you thinking about, how much good do you think you can do by shooting at that animal, you couldn't even be sure of hitting him at this range with that!' The anger on his face was clear for Peter Whade, one of the youngest Watch members on the expedition, to see, and he immediately realized what he had almost done.

'Sorry, I'm sorry … I lost control, I couldn't stand it, I mean he just shot him where he lay. I'm sorry, Bob.' Tears began to roll down the young man's almost beardless face, rolling out from underneath the glare specs.

Bob signalled them all to pull back, and they retreated away to a small copse of stunted trees where they stopped again. After a brief talk, three of the group, Bob, Sara and Matt, crawled back to where they had been while the other two, with Peter looking suitable subdued, set off back toward the Gevcars.

In the dim red glow of the infrared screen the figures round the house looked almost ghostly as they ate and drank their evening meal. They were being served by several women prisoners, slaves would probably have been a better description, who were subjected to all sorts of abuse, physical and verbal. Karel sat at the screen, his face a grim mask, headphones on his head listening to whatever the directional microphone which they had set up was able to capture. Bob Cantor, having finished his report to Karel and Jock some hours before, sat slumped, gazing into space. At his side Janine held his hand, offering the comfort of physical presence, though the sight of the fountain of blood that had spouted up from the back of the man's shattered head would remain in his mind for a long time yet. Save for the six or seven unwilling servants who had not yet finished their duties, and from the look of things would not do so until the following morning, all the group save for three guards who remained at the compound had gathered in or around the large shed at one end of the village. There was no indication that they were worried by the absence of their colleagues on the beach, so presumably they hadn't been expected back at all, and for some reason the explosions from the beach had not been detected, possibly due to the wind blowing off the land.

Darkness had fallen shortly after the Gevcars had arrived and stopped as near as they could to the village, further east up the valley from where the scout team had watched the execution. Using minimum power, the two cars had crept up with barely a muted whisper to disturb the gathering darkness. Even the dust devils from their passing had seemed to be subdued and had vanished into the gathering haze of the purple evening.

The lights in the house, oil lamps for the most part, began to go out shortly after midnight, and by the end of the first hour the place lay in darkness. In the Gevcars most of the crew dozed uneasily while one or two members of the crew kept watch. There was nothing else to do now but wait, the discussions on how to handle the affair had lasted a long time. At times the discussion had become quite heated as each member expounded on his or her point of view. In the end of course Karel's decision had prevailed. The people from the Hold long used to living under the direction of the Elders had tended to side with Jock Fernan who was of the opinion that the group presented no danger and that they should move on. By the end of the discussion, however, the sheer force of Karel's personality had swung most of them over to his side. His argument had been a simple one: evil should be dealt with before it got worse. In the end the matter had been settled when Jock, honouring their agreement, had with considerable grace accepted defeat. They would, they decided, wait until an hour before dawn, and then take out the whole building using their small bore conventional solid fuel-propelled short-range attack missiles with chemical incendiary warheads. The multi-barrel missile launcher had been built into the side of the Gevcar in a hinged pod which opened when in use, allowing up to eighteen of the small missiles to be fired before a manual reload was needed. The kicker in Karel's decision was that this would be done even if there were prisoners still in the building. The second Gevcar would be withdrawn to the other side of the hill, but would also be on full alert in order to back up the attack if things started to go wrong.

The hands of Brendt Maxon's timepiece seemed to creep slower and slower round the quadrant as the time approached. He dropped the watch which swung back and forth from the cord round his neck as he leaned in to check the sights of the launcher once more, as if they could somehow have moved off the target on their own. He was the only member from the second Gevcar with them, but as senior Watch Officer he had insisted on taking the responsibility for the firing of the missile. The air in the Gevcar had grown thick with tension. No one had needed waking, now they sat quietly at their stations, nervousness displayed only by the clearing of throats and the shuffling of positions as they sought to ease the stiffness in their bodies, a stiffness that only the coming action would release. Five minutes before the deadline the glow of a low-powered lamp became visible in the shed, and after a minute or so four figures emerged, carrying what appeared to be buckets, heading towards the well seventy or eighty metres away.

'Three minutes,' came Jean Klock's quiet voice over the speaker. From the surveillance microphone came the sound of a somehow muffled scream and then of something falling, followed by a raised voice. Then the door of the shed opened again and two more figures came out hurriedly, the second one stumbling heavily and then falling as if propelled from behind. The first figure helped the second to its feet and they both turned off towards the lane leading down to what were apparently storage buildings, the one leaning on the other for support. Petra Zimber at the screen clenched her fists and bit the inside of her lip to stop from shouting out loud.

'Two minutes.' The sound of bolts on the automatic rifles carried by the Watch assault team led again by Bob Cantor seemed thunderous in the confined silence of the Gevcar. Karel sat impassively, a statue carved in reddish sandstone weathered by endless storms. Inside his head the uncertainties grew ever larger. Have I taken the right decision? What if there is still another prisoner inside? Have I the right to do this? Unconsciously he rubbed the scar on his face, a reaction which to Sandy alone would have betrayed his nerves.

'One minute.' The water party had reached the well and the members were beginning to fill their buckets before returning to the shed. Brendt looked once more at the hands of his old mechanical timepiece, then leaned back swinging his neck back and forth and shrugging his shoulders. Ania, why couldn't I be safely back in bed with you? What possessed me to come on this crazy trip anyway? He carefully lifted the protective covers on the missile firing toggles, positioning his fingers just beside them.

'Thirty seconds.' The assault team slipped on their glare specs which would protect them from the flash of the explosions and slipped out of the car through the rear hatch, dropping quietly onto the night-cooled stones. Dressed in black, it was as if they ceased to exist the moment they cleared the doorway, and their weapons cocked and ready, carefully wrapped in cloth, made no sound at all.

'Twenty seconds.' Now at least time seemed to be running at its normal speed as Brendt checked the firing coordinates for the last time.

'Ten seconds.' Everything was racing down now to the moment of decision. I could still stop it thought Karel. I could.

'Three … two … fire!' With an oddly muffled whumph, the first missile's fiery breath lit up the night like some demon's breath as it exited the launcher and streaked towards its target, accelerating to its top speed in less than one and a half seconds, already past the halfway mark to the target. The second missile followed a second behind adding to the fiery light. The shrieking roar of their passing was surely enough to paralyse anything and anyone with fright. For one brief unholy moment after the missiles went in through the door, the whole building seemed to glow with a powerful inner light. Then it bowed outwards as though expanding to accommodate its new tenant, and vanished in the orange-yellow fireball of the exploding missiles.

Having left the coast which soon began to lead off towards the east, and given the good weather conditions, they decided to push on and do the over water stretch they had been leaving for the following day, heading for a point some 530 klicks away as the crow flies, across on Coiba Island, itself still a further fifty klicks off the isthmus coastline. The cars rode smoothly over the lazy Pacific swells rolling in from the east, at first the movement, a sort of extended yaw and pitch resulting in a sort of slow corkscrew motion, had produced some discomfort, but after a while this vanished and the movement became almost hypnotic.

They were all glad to be on the move again after staying on to help in the village. The doctors had done what they could to help the released prisoners during the ten days they had stayed there, but in truth it hadn't been that much. How does one rebuild the shattered minds of those who have lost friends and loved ones? Physically most of them would heal, the other wounds would take longer. Of the building the missile had struck, nothing had remained, the four water carriers seventy metres away had been scorched by the fireball but had survived, the other two women had been protected by the bulk of the stores building and were unharmed. The assault team had raced to the compound to make sure that the guards didn't try to exact revenge on their captives, but as it turned out they had vanished without trace, leaving their weapons behind. Bob had wanted to go in pursuit but the idea had been vetoed by Jock.

They didn't even find out much about the gang they had destroyed other than that they had terrorized villages up and down the coast for several years. They had lived only to destroy, burning, raping, looting, and taking prisoners to act as slaves for work and pleasure. Sometimes the younger prisoners were offered a chance to become members. The price of admittance was simple, they had to kill and eat their parents. Sometimes the gang had grown in strength until it had numbered several hundred, but internal bickering had kept it from going much beyond that number. The current low size had in fact been the result of a split into two groups several moons earlier, but none of the prisoners had been able to shed any light on the whereabouts of the second group.

Using one of the recently opened communication channels on the Sentry satellite, they had talked with the Captain, 565 klicks away down the coast in Tumbes, and he had promised to gather up a group to come and fetch the survivors. This, of course, would take time, for such a trip was not to be undertaken lightly or when ill prepared. Meanwhile, the survivors would have to depend on the food supplies in the village, which would take care of them for several months. The most important thing was the feeling that the process of helping rebuild lost society had begun, only in a small way, but it was a start.

Taking advantage of the prolonged stay, Miguel Pardo had carried out a number of atmosphere studies and had reached the conclusion that the uvee levels were within acceptable levels up until around half an hour before noon, and that the danger period lasted only two and a half to three hours. He had as a consequence authorized the team to take off their glare specs for the rest of the day, much to everyone's delight, but had cautioned that they must still carry the specs with them. The explanation he offered, apart from hypothesizing that the upper ozone level was showing signs of recovery, was that the old studies showing that at equatorial latitudes there had been less reduction were still valid. More conclusions could not be drawn from the existing data he said, after all, this had been Patric's special field of study, not his.

As they sped over the ocean, their speed already up to just over eighty-five knots as the pilots gained confidence, the sun continued to shine fitfully through the high-level haze, an orange and yellow sphere shrouded occasionally behind passing clouds. The coast already a hundred klicks off to the east was no longer visible, lost behind the indefinite point where the sky and the sea met in the haze. The surface of the ocean over which they moved took on a grey-green almost oily look, disturbed only by the occasional breeze which rippled the surface, allowing the transparency of the water to be appreciated. They saw regretfully few indications of life, a flock of high-flying seagulls heading east, a couple of porpoises jumping in the distance and the occasional silvery sheen of a shoal of fish, lost almost immediately in the rush of their passing. Behind them the wakes from the two speeding cars frothed wildly, boiling up into a long tail and then spreading out for a long way before being absorbed finally to leave no record of their passing, no trace at all.

Chapter VIII

The smoke from the fire swirled slowly around driven by the light breeze, spreading outwards and upwards, thinning out before losing itself against the dark night sky. The smell of the roasting meat was appetizing almost to the point of agony. Twenty-five pairs of eyes focused on the slowly turning spit with the gutted carcass of the wild pig Sarah and Jules had brought in. Twenty-five mouths salivated at the thought of the delicious meal that was to come, caught in some atavistic need that required freshly caught and cooked meat, before it could be laid to rest. Twenty-seven minds, all grateful that they weren't one of the three unfortunates chosen for the first watch, all sitting around the fire gazing into the leaping flames and sparks that born in the heat shot skywards dimming to nothing, brief bright lives in the darkness. The pig dripped its fat and each falling drop hissed to a fiery end on the white hot coals below. Around them the shadows from the columns seemed to waver, giving the illusion of constant movement on the old stone wall against which most of the crew sat.

The temple was old, not a remnant of the civilization which had given birth to the Hold, but much, much older. It too served to remind them all that theirs was not the only victim of history, for the origins of the Mayan Temple of Tulum on the north-eastern coast of the Yucatan Peninsula were a mystery that years of archaeological research had failed to reveal, and now never would. No logical explanation as to the why the Mayan civilization, which had spanned five centuries, should in the short span of a few decades have decayed and vanished, had ever been offered. But vanish it did, its end simply hastened by the coming of the European conquerors in the sixteenth century. Across the open area from where they sat, the main temple with its wide and steep stairway faced them, weathered stones, greyish white where the moss hadn't been able to take hold. Beyond the temple and the various smaller buildings, invisible now in the dark, the land fell precipitously down to the seething waters of the Caribbean Sea. On the ceiling above their heads, lit by the slightly eerie glow from the lanterns, friezes painted by long-dead masters, mostly ochre on a pale background, stared down at them, geometrical representations of gods and of people, of hunts and of feasts, and of things and places, all made meaningless by the passage of time to the eyes that now gazed up at them, but none the less beautiful for that.

They could have chosen to stop at any number of the abandoned tourist resorts that had sprouted like mushrooms on the east coast of the peninsula during the halcyon days of the final decades of the twentieth century. Ornate buildings in glass and concrete, low stuccoed villas, modern split-level bungalows, homes to the very rich and to the package tourist, now long closed up and decayed, all up for the taking. In the end and without much discussion they had chosen to make camp at the old Mayan ruins, a place that held no memories or connections to the recent past.

'Come on then Matt, surely it must be ready by now,' the speaker, tiny Lee Sun Yan whose slightly oriental features seemed to blend in with the place as though she had always belonged there, smiled gently as she needled the red headed Matt Wilton.

'You scientists! Patience dear lady, patience, I was under the impression that that was one of the great virtues of scientific research. Never rush to a conclusion and all that ...' replied Matt, always happy take part in the friendly banter that had become a sort of game with the group.

'He's right you know' said Erik Fernan the lead doctor who had travelled in Karel's car. 'The Watch may be very well trained where their specific job is concerned, but don't forget the poor lad learnt all this from a book ... and from Karel and Sandy of course.'

The two to whom he referred raised their glasses in acknowledgement before returning to the animated discussion on communications they were holding with the specialists. Jean Klock as usual alternating between waving his hands to emphasize some point and trying to tuck his shirt back into his trousers. Since their initial success with the Sentry satellite they had managed to contact another high-orbit satellite that Sandy hoped was simply dormant, waiting for a wake up command, but so far all that they had been able to obtain was a periodic identification signal emitted every twelve hours. The truth was that most of the several hundred commercial satellites had not been designed for a lifetime of more than a couple of decades. It was only the military application ones like the Sentries, with multiple redundancies and backups as well as

EMP shielding, that had managed to survive over fifty years or more. The Sentry had served them well, with its footprint covering an area of almost eighty degrees of latitude, starting in what had been southern Argentina and stretching up as far north as the Great Lakes. They had used the signal to navigate by since confirming its reliability and accuracy by means of some old-fashioned map reading. Accurate to within ten metres or so, even at coarse acquisition, the signal had been patched directly to the Gevcars' own navigation computers, taking much of the strain and responsibility off the hands of the pilot, particularly on the longer stretches over water. Best of all, of course, was that they could now speak to the Hold over the comm link, which allowed them private and untraceable conversations, a great step forward from the old short wave alternative.

They had left the coast of South America at a point a couple of hours northwards of Buenaventura, just a day after departing the village where they had freed the slaves. With a nominal cruise speed of eighty to ninety knots, the two cars had crossed the five hundred plus klicks in just over three hours, the highest average speed they had ever achieved, hardly surprising of course as the trip was over water without any obstacles. They had made their landfall at Coiba Island in mid-afternoon and without much trouble found a place to spend the night, over on Damas Bay on the eastern coast. The next day they had continued northwards keeping a couple of klicks off the coast until noon when the increasing swells forced Karel to decide to come ashore again rather than face a seasick crew. They had made their landfall at the southern end of a long curving coast, a place called Coronado Bay in southern Costa Rica, according to the Hold maps. They had driven inland a couple of dozen klicks following overgrown tracks upwards away from the sea before picking up the remains of the old Pan American highway which paralleled the coast running south-east to north-west. No longer were they insulated from the past as they rode through villages and towns, deserted, wrecked, dead, but still towns, full of the remains of the life that had once sustained them, now mouldy heaps of bones, metal and bricks, mostly scavenged by those who had lived a bit longer. Nature too had taken giant strides to recover what was rightfully hers, for where explosives and pickaxes had been unable to complete their demolition work, the rains and the resulting streams and rivers, the occasional seismic action, aided by wind and the burgeoning new vegetation, as well as by termites and fungi, all worked hard together to complete the task of erasing all signs of man's passage.

San Isidro, Villa Mills, Cartago, San Jose, Heredia, Ajuelo, Naranjo, San Ramon, on and on, an endless litany, akin to reading from the Book of Names. At Lake Nicaragua they took again to the water, 150 klicks of renewed speed, a relief after the forty or fifty klicks per hour on the road. In the remains of Managua they saw sign of recent habitation but found nothing save for a pack of wild dogs that stood off rapidly when the Gevcars drew to a halt. The long and winding road took them up through the hills, and down again to the fertile plains where bananas, coffee, sugar cane and other crops to feed the industrialized North American Federation once grew.

At latitude twelve degrees north after leaving Guatemala City behind, still following the Pan American highway up through the mountains, their plans of continuing up the western side of the isthmus went awry. At first they didn't pay much attention to the occasional patches of grey vegetation, but soon it became obvious that the patches were some sort of fungus growing on almost any type of plant or tree. Patches that became larger and more numerous as they drove along the winding road taking them further north. Inside the grey patches, which seemed to consist of some form of stringy glistening growth that covered everything, there was no movement of any sort to be seen, no animals, no birds, simply sheets of the growth hanging waving in the wind. Karel ordered both cars to full bio alert, and, after half an hour's discussion, reluctantly stopped to allow Lee Sun Yan and Miguel Pardo to take samples for analysis. The two scientists worked for less than fifteen minutes, the worry on their faces becoming increasingly obvious, before reporting back to Karel. On hearing their comments he took the decision to turn back immediately and look for an alternative route, which in the end meant that they were forced to go back to Guatemala City, a distance of some seventy or eighty klicks. At Miguel Pardo's insistence the car's external disinfectant spray systems were activated before leaving the area, so as to be sure that they didn't accidentally carry any spores to areas as yet unaffected. The two scientists, working only with the limited instruments carried in the Gevcars, had not been able to determine the exact structure or the origin of the blight, but it was clearly a man-made phenomenon, a symbiotic growth of vegetable origin which could and did easily adapt to living off animal flesh as easily as it did off trees and other vegetation.

Their new route took them north-eastwards, climbing up into the mountains again, before reaching the Sierra de Las Minas and turning to follow the Montagua River down to the east coast. From there they had followed the coastline for two days, sometimes by sea and sometimes by land, until arriving at Tulum, the ancient Mayan city, situated on the coast of the Yucatan Peninsula just under a hundred klicks south of where the holiday resort of Cancun had stood before being swept into the sea by the earthquake-generated mud slides of 2008 which had killed over a million people in the first twenty-four hours.

The meal was uncharacteristically silent as they sat around the fire eating the delicious barbecued pork. Lee as usual put to rest the theory that small people need a smaller food intake as their energy requirements are lower. She came back four times for a fresh piece and only after that was picked clean did she sit back eyes closed, a blissful expression on her face. Herb Kramer who had finished his own dinner two servings earlier and who had been watching her with mounting awe, burst out laughing, and in a minute at least half the team who had also been watching her delicately putting away all that food, had joined him. At this outburst, Lee cranked open her eyes unable to understand why so many people were staring at her and laughing, and it was only when Matt offered her another piece that the reason for the hilarity dawned on her. Putting on her best inscrutable oriental face she looked around, eyes innocent of any guile.

'I was hungry,' she said, before starting to laugh as well.

After breakfast the next morning, which in contrast to the previous night had dawned foggy and damp, with visibility limited to a scant hundred metres, Karel and Jock gathered the crews together outside one of the cars to discuss the route planning for the next part of the trip.

'I imagine that most of you will be anxious about where we go from here,' said Karel, 'Jock and I, along with Threejays, as well as with some help from Sandy and Jean, have worked out a tentative route that we intend to follow from here. As you know we were forced over to the east coast by the presence of the fungus, so it doesn't seem to make much sense to attempt to cross over again further north, specially as we eventually have to be on the eastern flank of the mountains anyhow. So, we have attempted to work out a route that will take us northwards with a minimum degree of risk, in other words keeping as far away as possible from the old population centres, from military installations, and so on. This isn't only to avoid any current residents who might be feeling possessive, but to keep clear of any latent radioactivity or toxic wastes, chemical dumps or whatever. I needn't remind you that we all saw the effect of that sort of thing only a few days ago.'

'What about taking the ocean routes? We made great time on those, and there's unlikely to be anyone to bother us. Don't you think we could ride all the way up the Pacific coast?' asked Alice Folsom, Herb Kramer's backup pilot from Jock's Gevcar.

'We did consider the option, and in fact we will be doing a fair bit of over water stretches. But bear in mind that in any really long stretches away from land we would be at the mercy of storms, high winds and so on. The Gevcars are a fantastic piece of engineering design, but they're not true ocean-going vessels. Eventually if the North American option turns out to be hopeless, we may have to attempt such a run, for the moment we should I think limit such trips to four or five hours at the most' replied Jock, 'look, let's run through the plan, and then we'll answer questions, and we can discuss any further alternatives or suggestions you may have, OK? Threejays, would you do the honours?'

Threejays stood up and walked to the Gevcar where she taped on a map across which a pencilled red line had been marked. She stood for a moment checking to see that her handiwork wasn't about to come unstuck and end up on the ground, and then swung round to face the crowd, pale eyes like searchlights shining from her dark skin. Using a laser pointing device she began to explain.

'Starting from where we are now, the first leg will be over water to the island of Cuba, where we'll be making a landfall here at Punta Gorda. From there we'll head eastwards using the old highway wherever possible, eastwards past Pinar del Rio, skirting round Havana and eventually hit the coast again near Matanzas. Then we'll do our next water leg up to the Keys. Key West used to be around 140 klicks from the island, but for obvious reasons won't be seeing much of it, so our first landfall will probably be Big Pine Key, which as far as I know should still be there, and then ...'

'Whoa there, hold it, what have I missed?' Asked Erik's assistant Sanjay, raising his hand, I can't remember hearing anything about Key West.'

'Oh, Oh, Oh!' moaned Matt Wilton, holding his head in mock

pain and rocking back and forth. 'Doctor, such crass ignorance is giving me a pain!' He continued to act for a few more seconds as laughter broke out.

'Sanjay, where were you when you were supposed to be in your history class? Key West was an island, a very low-lying island, get the point? It's all in the Hold tapes you know.'

'Damn, yes, I vaguely remember now. Not much feeling for dead names I'm afraid. I was born long after the waters rose you know.' Sanjay grinned apologetically. 'I imagine Big Pine stood higher out of the water, hmm?'

Threejays smiled patiently. 'Right people, let me continue. We'll then continue north-eastwards, if the weather turns bad we'll come ashore and sit it out. After reaching Marathon we'll turn due north and continue straight up through the Everglades where we'll be unlikely to meet anyone. We should be able to make good speed for the next five or six hundred klicks as we'll be travelling over swampland for the most part. We intend to travel paralleling the old route that runs between five and ten klicks inland from the Gulf Coast. Once we get to the latitude where Tallahassee is ... sorry, was ... well, we're not sure, we'll turn westwards and head in a generally westwards direction until we hit the Mississippi valley.' Threejays stopped and looked around. 'Any questions so far?'

'Yes, how much information do we have on surviving population centres? I imagine some must have survived in some way,' said Erik Fernan looking over at the map.

'Let me take that one,' said Karel. 'Although I spent a long time travelling around I never got out of South America. However, over the years I picked up a lot of news, sometimes first hand over the radio, sometimes second hand, and sometimes as obviously distorted stories, passed on from mouth to mouth. When we were preparing this I had the Records people in the Hold track down every reference they had regarding groups of people, towns, cities and so on, starting from when the Hold was built. What we've ended up with is a fragmented history of the last fifty odd years.' He stopped, gathering up his thoughts and then continued talking. 'Mostly the big cities collapsed under their own weight, more often than not the big cities consisted of a business centre, enclaves of upper-class homes surrounded by barbed wire fences and guards, and enormous areas of poorer neighbourhoods, all too often little better than slums. When the trade and business infrastructure began to collapse, first at international level, then at national level and finally at local level, everything went haywire. Without food, power or water the poor had nothing further to lose, so they came out and attacked the rich areas. They attacked with everything they had. And the rich enclaves responded in kind, not with more cruelty, that would hardly have been possible, simply with more efficiency. In the battle of the cities they used guns, toxins, genetically enhanced viruses, air sprayed Nogrow, poisons, hell, you name it, a full-scale orgy of destruction. So, I don't think we'll find much left besides ruins in the big cities. ... In the smaller towns, who knows? I believe that it's likely that we will run across surviving societies, but there's no guarantee they'll be friendly.'

'Tumbes was friendly enough' said Maria Sanches.

'True, but they had been really isolated and didn't feel too threatened, I think it just depends on what the local history has been. Threejays, why don't you go on, we can continue on this topic afterwards.'

'When we reach the Mississippi valley we'll travel upriver, we don't know for sure how much of the original river still remains. No doubt many of the old levees were destroyed, but we figure that if we can travel over water or swampland, we'll make better speed. We'll have to keep away from all the old high-population areas, and what Karel has just explained should be reason enough. Our objective is to hit the south-east coast of Lake Michigan. Then we'll continue up the lake, keeping a few klicks offshore, cross over into Lake Superior which means around seventy-five klicks over land, head westwards as far as possible, coming ashore near Thunder Bay, and then head north-west towards Winnipeg, then on to Regina, Calgary and up the Banff valley where the other Survival Centre is supposed to have been. Once we get up there we'll have to do a lot of searching. The Hold records have given us a lot of data, but we'll still have an awful lot of surface to cover, and we should also be prepared to be disappointed.'

'What are the chances really Threejays?' asked Brendt, 'and what if we don't succeed?'

'The chances are reasonable, even better than reasonable' interrupted Karel. 'I found the Hold, although it took me a long time,' he smiled gently, almost sadly, 'and at the end if Bob hadn't got to me I could even have missed it altogether. I knew to within ten, perhaps fifteen or so klicks where you were. Close enough you might think, but a massive job for one man on his own. But now things are different, we went through the Hold design specs from start to finish, we followed up every obscure reference the Records' computers held, and now at last we have an ace in the hole.' This time the smile was wider, and happier. He looked at Sandy who stood and moved forward, pushing back the lock of hair that always seemed to slip out from any sort of restraint.

'The people who designed the Hold were probably among the best and brightest humanity has ever produced, the best it will produce for a long time to come. They thought in terms of decades, of generations, not like the politicians of the day who only craved votes for the next election. They tried to cover every eventuality, backups within backups, contingency plans within contingency plans, and one of them even thought that we, or at least someone like us, might have to search for one of the other Holds from outside.' She stopped, thinking perhaps for a moment of the builders of the Hold who still reached out to help the future they would never see. Around her the crews sat, as would children listening to a particularly clever or entrancing fairy tail.

'So they gave us a sort of key. A sequence of notes transmitted on a particular wavelength, in a particular sequence at a particular time, and if things are still working, we should get a homing signal from one or perhaps two transmitters.'

'And all this was cleverly hidden from us?' said Brendt, a trace of resentment shading his face. 'I mean, I know that you already explained at the first meeting that the two Council members who were supposed to hand down the knowledge failed to do so, but I can't see why things weren't registered properly in Records.'

'Well, perhaps it was, but don't forget that even with expert system computers such as yours you have to know what to ask for otherwise the thing is still just a high-speed idiot. Look, perhaps the reason you people in the Hold knew nothing about the other Holds for a long time was that the knowledge was deliberately concealed because the founders felt it was better that way. I can imagine that the psychologists and human resources people who set up the organization were the best and most dedicated available, so they must have had good reasons for ensuring that each Hold developed independently. One can only be amazed at how far the long arm of coincidence reached out.' She smiled, 'serendipity really I guess, two unlikely and unconnected events started the wheel turning, and the

115

result is that here we are today, half way round the world from the Hold. Firstly, Herb and David found the Gevcars and the tapes on the other Hold, and then Karel arrived bringing with him confirming evidence that yours wasn't the only Hold. After that we went down to Records and started digging ... easy really.'

The rest of the day they spent wandering around the ruins, some of the Watch out on a longer walk finding a cavern entrance which led to an underground lake. In an abandoned building, apparently part of what had once been a holiday cottage complex, they found maps showing a vast network of flooded caves which had attracted divers from all over the world. The faded brochures expounded on the wonders of the rock formations hidden from the light, stalactites and stalagmites, formed before the flooding, now submerged, pillars in a great cathedral of eternal dark, lit only by the artificial light of divers' torches. The group immediately wanted to fetch the diving gear, of which there were three or four sets, and go off exploring, but Bob drew a line at that sort of adventure. The mist lifted shortly after midday leaving them a view of the sea, dull and greyish without the sun which chose to remain hidden behind some high cloud cover. The whole area was reverting to its original state, before the coming of man. The vegetation around them grew lushly, many of the old buildings, once carefully uncovered and cleaned by keen archaeologists, were well on the way to being covered from view again as vines and creepers wound their way in from the encroaching jungle. There were encouraging signs that the wild animals and birds, once almost vanished, were also making a recovery, for there were a fair number of species to be found, darting through the trees and the bush. Inevitably, the dark side of the coin was also present, for they also came across one or two mutations which were obviously the result of toxins or radioactivity, apparently healthy animals with shrunken extra limbs hanging from their bodies. Erik, at the request of several members of the crew, repeated his check of the remains of the wild pig they had eaten the previous night, and was once again able to give their previous night's supper a clean bill of health much to everyone's relief, although none of them had shown any immediate symptoms of anything.

'It's difficult to imagine the life of the tribes that lived here,' Janine said, knees drawn up to her chest as she sat with Bob on one of the old stone walls overlooking the ocean. 'We know so little about them, there's no personal stories, no anecdotes, they're not real.'

'Oh, I don't know, look at all the legends. I can imagine them being based on some real event, I mean, don't forget, most of their history was oral, so things got distorted in the telling. Only once the story became a legend and the way of telling it, even to the exact words became set, did the alterations stop, and by then of course the bridge from reality to fantasy had been crossed.'

'Mmm, Bob, what will our legends be? Will we have them do you think? Sometimes when I'm alone I forget I'm a highly trained professional, and I wonder what it's all for. How can so few of us do anything?'

'Jan love, that sort of thinking never got anyone across the next hill. Each one of us is worth something. We all have a small part to play, and whether we succeed may be decided to some degree by the fates. But, there's one thing I'm convinced of, and that is that the right action at the right time can make an awful lot of difference.'

'I envy you your certainty.' She leaned back, turning to look at him, and then rested her head on his shoulder.

'I'm certain of other things too,' Bob continued, as he slid his arm round her shoulders drawing her in, stroking her hair with the tips of his fingers. 'In the Hold I'd never met you directly, though I suppose we might have crossed at some point in time. Now I want to be with you, I can't visualize being without you.' Pausing, 'when we get back ...'

'Yes, oh, yes, when we get back' she sighed, smiling as she turned to him, lips reaching for his.

The weather remained poor for the next two days, with gusty winds pushing the sea into a confused and choppy pattern. Although they could easily have made the trip with the aid of the GPS and the on-board computers, Karel chose to let them all relax and take it easy. And so, it was not until the morning of the fifth day since their arrival when the cloud cover lifted and a watery sun began to shine again, that they set out towards Cuba, some two hundred klicks over the horizon. The cars travelled on parallel tracks about three klicks apart, their ninety-knot speed raising two glistening feathery tails. In the second car, Herb Kramer cracked open one of the upper hatches and they roared along accompanied by the blast of the wind blowing in through the opening.

The island came into sight shortly before midday, but rather than come ashore immediately they altered course to the north and began to run up the coast. After a quarter of an hour, and much to their surprise, they spotted a plume of smoke rising from a village on a hillside above a small crescent bay which according to their charts bore the name of Guadiana. Slowing down to a sedate fifteen knots, but still keeping well apart, the two Gevcars turned and swung round, heading for the coast. The beach below the village was a narrow strip of yellowish sand on which half a dozen narrow-hulled fishing boats rested, their mooring lines running up to the tree line nearby.

With Karel's car remaining offshore in a lazy circle, the second car came in and up the beach. In the upper turret Matt sat leaning forward, eyes sweeping back and forth in the old familiar movement learnt far away and long ago in the dry valleys near the Hold. As the car settled its weight down some seventy metres from the nearest hut, sinking into the sand, sending out a small storm of particles, the rear hatch opened and Brendt and Peter, leaped out of the car with Brendt in the lead, and raced for the trees, spreading out as they went. From the co-pilot's seat Jock watched them disappearing into the bush, and sat waiting for any reaction from the village, trying to watch everything at the same time as well as to concentrate on whatever sound might come from the surveillance microphone which swung back and forth in its port, pointing in the direction of the huts. The huts were crude yet sturdy constructions, raised on stilts above ground. Under roofs of woven palm leaves set in walls of whitewashed wattle, the huts looked clean and organized, cooking pots either of pottery or cast iron, it was difficult to tell at a distance even with the aid of binoculars, hung on hooks, while from a number of hemispherical mud ovens smoke issued forth, the smoke which had attracted their attention in the first place. From a series of racks some brown leaves hung drying in packs, facing the still watery sun which in these tropical latitudes shone with a lighter more orange colour than it did over the Hold. The ground between the huts was mostly bare earth, but there were stone footpaths leading off in different directions. After two or three minutes the three Watchers stepped out from behind the huts, waving the all clear signal. Sandy called the other Gevcar on the radio and they too drifted in, passing over the breakers and grounding on the beach a few dozen metres away.

They explored the village finding plenty of traces of recent habitation, but no sign of any of the inhabitants. Beyond the huts

SEASONS OF CHANGE

the land crept upwards into low hills, a number of tilled fields separated the village from the natural growth which covered most of the hills. In these fields a variety of crops were to be seen: maize, carrots, potatoes and what appeared to be peanuts. Miguel, whose professional interest was aroused, observed that all the growths were fungus and blight free, and that the locals obviously had some knowledge of land care as a number of fields were lying fallow. The place was spartan by the standards of the Hold, but nevertheless in a benign climate offered no real hardships to the locals who obviously lived off whatever hunting fishing and the nearby fields and trees could provide. In a way people such as these away from the mainstream of society were the ones who least mourned its passing, if anything they might even have felt relief with the lessening of the fallout, chemical clouds and gases, and poisoned seas.

'You are pisco, no?' The question, delivered softly in barely comprehensible Anglic, galvanized the Hold team who jumped practically as one body, searching for the source. Standing beside a bent and old mangrove tree stood a figure no higher than a metre and a half, clothed in a loose woven robe, and set in a smooth brown ageless face were the brightest green eyes anyone had ever seen.

'We don't know what piscos are,' said Maria recovering rapidly from her surprise, 'we come in peace, umm, we would like to talk with you.' She walked closer to the little figure and then squatted down on her haunches, removing the implicit threat of greater height. The others, at Jock's signal, followed suite, sitting or squatting where they were, and as if it had been a signal, a dozen more locals emerged from the undergrowth. Several carried the result of the morning's hunt, a small wild pig, and a brace of partridges, none were much taller than the first one. Their dress code was as variable as their height was uniform: robes, loose trousers and shirts, shorts that were almost loincloths, all obviously home woven cotton with a minimum of patterned designs. The most surprising external factor among the locals was their eyes, which were all the same bright green.

'My grandfather, he tell that one day the pisco with their fine machines come back to visit us,' he spoke slowly, obviously choosing the words carefully. 'I welcome you, we have learnt from our old ones that many times ago you have helped to drive off the others, also gringos, who came to take our land and our fish.'

'Thank you for your welcome, we are just passing through on our

119

way north,' Maria waved vaguely out to sea. 'We have come far and are strangers to these parts. Would the pisco and the gringos you mention be people from the NAF?' Seeing the puzzled look on the little man's face she tried again. 'Americans perhaps?'

'Yes pisco, from America, my grandfather he say, from America.'

'We are not pisco then, but if we can help you in any way we would be happy to do so. Also, we would be happy to hear your stories and legends. We have plenty of food we can share with you if you would permit us to stay here with you until tomorrow.'

The little man said something to the nearest of the locals who nodded and headed for the largest hut at a trot. The words had been incomprehensible and yet familiar, Maria had not understood them, but she had the feeling that they must be a distorted version of Anglic, perhaps mixed with some other language, presumably Spanish. She made a mental note to check and see what information the computer had on that idea. As these thoughts raced across her consciousness their host smiled and nodded.

'We would be honoured to have you stay with us and to share our meal with you.'

Karel, who had been sitting on the steps of one of the huts, suddenly started, looked around and then walked over to the Gevcar, which with the main drive off was now resting on the beach, operating off the solar panels which covered the rear part of the roof.

'Sandy, get me the Hold will you, someone ought to be at the desk already, it'll soon be time for the regular schedule.' Sandy who had been sitting at the comm panel looked quizzically at him.

'I need Records to look up some history on this place, I seem to remember that in the early twenties, before Copernicus, there was some trouble here, and that the NAF came in and cleared it up. One of the last overseas incursions probably. The little fellow mentioned pisco, I'm betting that it's a distortion of Peace Corps, you know, the old aid to poor countries thing, I think they were still around at that time.'

At the village, the crew from the Gevcars, feeling like giants among the diminutive locals, sat around, objects of much curiosity to their hosts whose number seemed to increase all the time as groups kept on coming in. From what Maria had been able to make out there were seven or eight villages much like the one they were in, each with a population of a couple of hundred, each with a specialty: fishing, hunting, fruits and vegetable, root crops, woodwork, ironwork and so on. Lee Sun Yan and the other members of the science team who had been fascinated by the uniform size of the people had been busily scribbling on a scrap of paper. When they finished they were clearly pleased with the result, for when Jock looked over at them they were happy to explain.

'This place is a genetic anomaly, even within a particular race or strain it would be unusual to find such uniformity. We can't say for sure what took place here, but it is likely that some of the original gene pool showed a high resistance to the disease seeding that almost certainly affected the island. The survivors kept certain the genetic traits, among them their small size and light coloured eyes, obviously highly dominant factors, those with different characteristics must also have lacked the disease-resistant genes, so they died, maybe not right away, perhaps they became sterile, but in any event they are no longer. With a breeding pool of fifteen or sixteen hundred they have survived without degenerating, a rather smaller gene pool than we would have expected, but nature has a way of coming out on top in the end.' As Lee finished her explanation, Sandy arrived carrying a short printout.

'You were right Karel, in 2022 the island was attacked by a strong force of Muslim extremists who after a week and a half managed to wipe out most of the local forces, they used CBW agents over much of the island, mostly Sarin derivatives. Many of the participants were disgruntled NAF citizens so naturally they felt involved. The NAF government waited for the UN to take action but as none was forthcoming with the Security Council deadlocked over the matter, the Marines were sent in. After another week or so they had cleared up most of the resistance, as you can imagine the toll on the civilian population was horrendous, a fatality rate estimated at over seventy-eight percent. After this the Peace Corps were sent in to help rebuild, the last records held in Records are dated from early thirty-one and are radio traffic transcripts, mostly about pulling out.'

The visitors, having intended to only stay overnight, spent a full week at the village, more of a study session for the scientists than anything else. As they had first suspected, the locals were truly self-sufficient with the low-level technology they used, and their genetic pattern made them apparently resistant to most if not all of the remaining poisons that might still be around and active. After some persuasion Erik was able to take a few blood samples for analysis when they eventually returned to the sophisticated laboratories in

121

the Hold. The most interesting exchanges took place with the farmers, and while the Gevcar specialists were able to suggest a number of improvements to the way things were being done, they also came away with a plenty of practical and simple ideas which could be applied to any farming society. It was clear to both Karel and Jock that the survival of a small but functional group, without any hi-tech help was in many ways a humbling experience to the crew from the Hold, who all had been born and bred to place their faith in science.

On the morning of the seventh day after their arrival, and after thanking the islanders for their hospitality, as well as promising to return, they set out once more. Leaving the coast to head inland, they followed the old highway past Pinar del Rio, skirting the remains of old Havana which had been largely destroyed during the fighting, maintaining a generally eastwards course until they reached the coast again at Cardenas, where they spent the night in the abandoned port, having covered almost four hundred klicks in just over seven hours including the midday stop. The following morning, with the reddish purple globe of the sun barely over the horizon, lighting up the mares tails of the high cirrus clouds barely discernible through the haze, they turned northwards, accelerating rapidly up to their standard over water speed of just under ninety knots, racing for the Keys which lay unseen over the horizon 190 klicks away.

[Extract – 2025]

(The following reports are excerpts from the minutes of the Site 3 Steering Committee meeting held on 30 April 2025. It is to be noted that all records related to 1 January 2018 to 31 December 2025 have been classified as restricted and can only be accessed with the authorization of the Council of Elders.)

The removal of any documents from the Records Hall or the copying of any information relating to this period is strictly forbidden.

Commissioning and Start-up Phase Construction Contract Report: Detail finishing work is continuing on Levels A to C and with the exception of the roofing panels for Level B, which were lost when the Shinan Maru was torpedoed last month in the Gulf of Mexico, all the non-structural linings along with their insulation panels have been completed.

Auxiliary equipment for the maintenance workshops and stores has been delivered and is now being assembled, completion is now planned for week 24 versus week 18 originally foreseen in the Masterplan. This delay is due to the non-availability of some of the originally specified materials of construction.

A fire in the Level C Zone 4 electrical room has been traced to faulty materials, which have now been fully replaced. It is gratifying to note that the fire detection and alarm system worked flawlessly and that the damage was limited to one secondary switchboard.

All six hydroponics units are now in production. Units 1 and 3 have now completed their fourth crop of assorted fruits and vegetables with higher than expected yields. The remaining units have successfully completed their first cycle and final parameter adjustments are being made prior to returning the units to service.

Attachments:

- Fire Damage Report
- Technical Status Reports on All Systems
- Bio Report: Hydroponics
- Commissioning and Start-up Time Schedule (Adjusted)

Staffing Report: Site 3 staffing is now complete with the final intake having completed their full training schedule. The COPEEV (Continuous Personnel Evaluation) staff have begun work on the basis of the programme agreed upon at the last steering committee meeting. All the specialists involved are agreed that in order for the system to work smoothly all Department Heads must be made aware of the programme. Special induction courses are being prepared and will be tested on selected personnel before the end of the quarter.

Attachments:

- COPEEV Organization Structure Handbook
- Programme Time Schedule

Power Subcommittee Report: The Site 3 TFR workup is on schedule with power output now being at thirty-three percent of nominal. All redundancy safety system checks have continued to prove successful. Power loading has been transferred to Transformer Cells 1 and 2 and the ventilation and life-support systems for Levels C to F will be transferred shortly. CERN has indicated that it is under pressure from environmentalist lobbyists to cease supplying TFR technology outside Europe. So far no problems are expected in the completion of the remaining scope of supply items (mainly spares for auxiliary systems), and CERN has already undertaken a feasibility study of alternate subsuppliers for these outstanding items should any form of embargo be imposed on exports outside Europe.

Attachments:

- Layout Site 3 Power Installations
- TFR Commissioning Time Schedule
- Delivery Schedule for Outstanding Items

News Item Summaries: The Japanese parliament has issued a statement announcing its dissolution after a marathon negotiation session which has lasted practically non-stop since the beginning of the year. Power has now been returned to the supposed heirs of the original warlords who ran the country as a group of separate city states prior to the start of the Meiji Dynasty and the introduction of Western ideas. Shinto has been re-established as the official religion, and members of other faiths refusing to accept 'the errors of their ways' are being executed in public ceremonies. Many aspects of Western technology have been outlawed, including the ownership of private vehicles, television and radio stations as well as other mass communications media, industries connected with electronics goods, and all shipbuilding except that of fishing vessels.

The states of Texas, Arizona and New Mexico, hard hit by the TZ6 bubonic virus, have seceded from the Union and closed their borders to all comers. The North American Premier speaking from Billings, Montana, called for them to withdraw the statement and threatened to send in National Guard units to back up his demands. Independent observers have discounted this possibility given the lack of power of the Premier since the vote of no confidence last March when Alaska voted to increase royalties on its oil production by a factor of five.

A study recently released by the EU shows that the incidence of leukaemia and other cancers in children born in Finland, Sweden, Norway and Poland since the Russian Federation war of 2024 have increased sevenfold to a level of 150 per thousand live births. The study also reveals that only thirty-two percent of pregnancies lead to live births. Analysts expect that these rates will decrease slowly over the next decade as the half-lives of the isotopes resulting from the war decay.

Chapter IX

The complexity of the pattern on the screen was spellbinding, never still for a moment, the vibrant hues and colours succeeded one another with a smoothness that belied the sophistication of the algorithms that had created them. Spirals and cartwheels, ever turning, ever faster, metamorphosing into tubular worm shapes, which, as though seeking to return to the unknown place from whence they had come, turned inwards on themselves appearing to the observer to blur and be sucked into nothingness as fast as they were created, to be immediately followed by new patterns, rebirth without end. The accompanying music that had begun softly and slowly had speeded up to accompany the visual display, the notes becoming more galvanic with each passing movement, each chord building on the previous one, a complex sonic structure, up to the final almost electrifying climax which seemed to transcend the boundaries of the cabin, reaching out into the heads of the listeners, before winding down to a soft finale, accompanied by the glowing patterns shifting down through to the ultraviolet end of the spectrum before fading into blackness.

After a moment during which the audience remained silent, still entranced by the piece they had been offered, the round of applause which broke out was both loud and spontaneous, accompanied by shouts of congratulation. Janine stood up from the console seat where she had played and bowed low, accepting the praise due to a fine performance.

'Oh, Jan!, that was truly beautiful,' cried Sandy, tears running down her cheeks. 'Oh my word, it's a long time since I cried at the beauty of a concert.' Karel, sitting at her side, reached over and hugged her. Jock, nodding his head up and down, his eyes sparkling, seemed unable to speak, nor was he alone as many of the crew who had gathered in the central cabin could only smile and make approving noises. This was the first Sonolite concert they had heard since leaving the Hold, and in fact most of them had not known that Janine among her many accomplishments was also a skilled concertist.

'Much of civilization may have gone down, but not all that was beautiful is lost. That was the best concert I've heard in, oh, too many cycles to count, long before you were born anyway.' Karel spoke softly, 'Sonolite was I think one of the few great achievements of the twenty-first century, the melding of human skill, feeling and creativity with the high-speed supercooled processors able to handle vast amounts of information. If the Hold can bring Sonolite back into the world, then the adventure will have been worth it.'

'Come my dear friend, a bit too melodramatic I think,' Jock smiled. 'It's very beautiful, but perhaps we should think about rebuilding other things first before we get round to concert halls?'

'Oh ye of little faith, Jock you're missing the point, of course there are more immediate concerns, but look at it this way, if we can rebuild one, just one concert hall, then we will have succeeded, for the other things will already have been done. Food for the spirit my friend, food for the spirit, just as necessary as food for the stomach.'

'Well said Karel, I'll drink to that.' Threejays raised her glass in salute and took a drink, an action followed by most of those present including Jock.

The mood in the car was optimistic, they had covered the distance from Cuba to the Keys, and then on up through the Everglades without any mishaps or delays. The Everglades, which according to the Hold information had once been an enormous expanse of freshwater swampland with a wide variety of wildlife, had fared poorly in the intervening years since the descriptions had been entered into the records system. The higher than average sea level, even though it was only of the order of half a metre, had wiped out much of the old vegetation converting much of the fresh water into a brackish undrinkable mix, the result of occasional spring tides and storm waves which had swept inland powered by the seasonal hurricane cells. There was still plenty of life to be seen, kelp like plants flourished in the place of the high swamp grasses, and the manatee, freed from the passage of man's fishing boats, had obviously recovered, but gone was much of the bird life for which the area had been famous. Their track had taken them northwards past Naples whose towers still stood, apparently undamaged, but without any sign of life, up as far as what an old and very weathered signpost claimed was the Myakka River State Park.

They had parked the two Gevcars a few dozen metres apart as usual, hidden from view among the overgrown bushes and trees of an old and abandoned campsite. On the banks of the river, the remains of two or three log cabins still stood, roofs caved in but with parts of the walls still intact, including oddly enough several windows with glass and the ragged tatters of what had once been curtains. Around them the warm night was filled with sound, the croaking of frogs, the chirping of insects and the occasional squeaking sound which they took to be bats. They had arrived a couple of hours before sundown having taken only seven hours to cover the six hundred klicks from the Cuban coast. Having found a reasonably elevated and therefore dry piece of land to stay, they had watched the invariably beautiful sight of the sun sliding down out of the sky slowly turning from orange to red to purple, colouring everything its rays touched, until at last the afterglow which had starkly silhouetted the horizon, faded into the blackness of the coming night. The impromptu after-dinner concert had been an unexpected bonus to the evening, and had taken place as a result of Janine and Brendt arguing the merits of Sonolite versus classical Strauss waltzes, with the former claiming that Sonolite could provoke a far greater emotional response, and then setting out to prove it.

The first stage of the day's journey up to the Keys had been entirely uneventful, as had the short run up to the mainland, both made under a hazy but almost cloudless sky. The waters over which they sped had varied in colour between turquoise and deep blue depending on the depth and the type of bottom. There had seemed to be far more fish life than what they had seen over on the Pacific coast, and they even saw schools of dolphins which tried but failed to keep up with the speeding Gevcars. It had taken them well over half an hour of cruising along the coast to find a suitable place to come ashore which had been near the town of Flamingo. After that they had paralleled the old road leading northwards, keeping away from any of the larger towns. The Gevcars had been able to make good speed over the swampland, although once or twice they had to detour to avoid heavily forested areas. There was no sign of recent human activity, nor any apparent reason for its absence save for the scarcity of truly dry land. The travellers were also relieved to note that all their instrumentation indicated that the level of residuals was extremely low, a fact which the science team put down to the cleansing effect of the hurricanes which swept the area every season and would be starting again fairly shortly.

'Lo Karel, any problem? Want to talk about something?' Jock eased himself down into the empty chair next to where Karel was sitting at one of the fold-down tables in the meeting cabin gazing into space.

'Jock. It seems that sometimes I am easy to read.' He paused, looking over at the smaller bald man. 'To tell you the truth I'm trying to work out the risks of crossing over to the Atlantic coast, and I haven't yet come up with any satisfactory answer.'

'The risks shouldn't be very different from going up the Gulf Coast, we'd be just as likely to run into trouble there as here. But I don't see the point, after all we're going to swing west when we get off the peninsula.' Jock stopped talking suddenly, took a breath and said 'Canaveral, the space centre! That's what you're thinking about.'

'Yes, I am. I did a launch from there before the Copernicus mission, made plenty of friends. I can't help wondering if anything is left. You know, much of the space centre was on the islands and could only be reached over causeways, if someone had chosen to defend the place and had blown the crossings, only a full-scale military assault would have succeeded. Local guerrillas would have been repulsed. Oh, of course they could have taken the place using plagues and radioactives, or even with heavy artillery, but what's the point of destroying what you want?'

'Well I understand what you're feeling. I have no objections as such if you want to take a look, but we'd have to do some planning just in case the space centre is occupied and they turn out to be unfriendly.'

'We had some contact as late as mid-twenty-four, they did what they could to give us a hand when Guyana was destroyed. We didn't get much in the way of local news of course, but enough to know that they were holding their own against take-over attempts. I don't know, I really don't know.' Karel looked up suddenly seeming older and more worn out.

Jock didn't hesitate any longer. 'Karel, let's go for it. At the Hold we had no contact with them, but that doesn't mean to say they aren't there, after all we ourselves kept a low profile. Minimum transmissions, passive reception, scrambled signals, you name it, we didn't want to be found.' He grinned. 'Perhaps these people were the same.'

'Thanks Jock, I'll speak to Threejays in the morning when we've looked at the charts.'

Despite it being early in the season, the sun's heat an hour before noon was already oppressive. Karel and the others lay flat on the roof, cloaks spread over them, looking out towards the buildings of the old space complex eight klicks away across the water. Sweat trickled down from his hairline, and ran round the glare specs frame, finally to drop off down to the warm concrete. The buildings seemed to shimmer in the rising heat, as though sliding in and out of focus. Nearer to them were some other structures, apparently abandoned launch pads, most of which showed obvious signs of decay if not destruction. They had been watching for over half an hour, during which they had detected no sign of any movement, but as their viewing angle only allowed them to see objects seven or eight metres above the ground the lack of movement was at best inconclusive evidence of lack of occupation. Across the Banana River on Merritt Island, hidden in the haze, the vegetation gave the appearance of being man-made with defined areas of different colours, though being even further away than the buildings it was difficult to judge if this was so. Later on, Karel decided they would have to cross over to check.

The Gevcars had approached the old space complex from the south, having cut across almost due east from their campsite finally to hit the coast three hours later just outside a deserted and wrecked town which they took to be Fort Pierce. The two cars, keeping their usual safe distance apart, had sped up the intracoastal waterway with David and Herb at the controls, both Techs enjoying the sensation of speed down the narrow straits. They had got as far north as the old Cape Canaveral town from where they now lay watching, having decided earlier that a discrete approach was called for. The comm unit on Karel's belt beeped softly, and without the spread cloak which covered him appearing to move, he reached down and slid the unit up to his ear clicking the microphone twice to indicate that he was listening.

'Jean here, Karel, we've suddenly started picking up some low-power VHF transmissions. The stuff is in clear, and it's definitely local, the signal strength is too low to travel farther than fifteen or twenty klicks.'

'What are they saying man?' Karel grimaced. 'Are you trying to keep it a secret?'

'Sorry, sorry, most of it seems to be in speech code. Look, why don't you come back to the car? We could break into the band if you want to.'

'You're probably right, we'll be right down. I hope they'll still be on the air when we get there.' He clipped the comm back onto his belt, and rose into a half crouch. 'We'll head back, Jean has picked up some radio traffic. Remember to keep down behind the wall, I don't suppose anyone is watching, but you never know.'

Back at the cars, which they had parked inside an old warehouse, empty now except for bits and pieces of debris and a thick covering of dust, which had lifted like a magic cloud when the cars arrived, they listened to the voices coming over the speaker.

'Thirty-seven to thirty-nine, what's the reading now? Over.'

'I make that thirty-two percent,' came the reply, a female voice. 'That is three two. Time to tell assembly to ...,' the voice faded out in a hiss and then returned, 'six on the pumps. Over.'

'Nineteen here.' A third voice joined the conversation. 'We were over there and ... at thirteen or fourteen ...' Again the speaker was drowned out by the carrier wave hiss.

'... assembly here, we have people from industrial here as well, they reckon ... so it's about fifteen minutes more ...'

'Assembly from thirty-seven, we copy, good to hear ...'

Jean reached over and turned down the speaker volume, and then turned to Jock and Karel who had been listening with him to the voices.

'It's all like that, between the low-powered signal and the fade outs it's bad enough, but the speech code is meaningless without the key.' A smile twitched at Karel's lips, a smile which brought questioning looks from the other two.

'It's not a speech code, though I can't fault you for thinking that it might be, they're referring to the launch pad numbers. I imagine every pad bunker has some people living in it, and what's more important they've managed to keep up some technology. How can we break in to their conversation, Jean?'

'I've already set the frequency, all you need to do is talk into the mike.' Karel thought for a moment and then leaned forward.'

'Kennedy Complex, Kennedy Complex, this is Captain Karel Houseman, ESC, come in please, come in please. Over.' He sat back, waiting, watching the microphone, willing the speaker to answer, but hearing only the subdued hiss of the wave.

'Kennedy Complex, I say again, this is Captain Karel Houseman, ESC, Copernicus mission, 2023–24. I knew Jack Knowles at Flight, also Pete Harden. I also flew from the Cape in twenty-two with Spider Magee on the Aegis Seven mission. Come in please. Over.'

'Ah. ... This is Pad 37 for Captain Houseman. Please identify your location. Over.'

'Houseman for thirty-seven. I'm just south of you. We picked up your transmissions by chance. Over.' Karel replied, not wishing to give an exact location or to reveal that they had in fact come searching. The speaker remained silent for several minutes other than for its characteristic hiss, during which those in the Gevcar chatted quietly, no sign of their inner tension detectable in their voices. Five minutes became ten, and then fifteen, until finally the speaker buzzed into life again.

'Houseman from Pad 37, come in please. Over.'

'This is Houseman. I'd like to meet with you if possible. Over.' After a moments pause, a new voice came over the speaker, a voice that seemed somehow thinner, older than the previous one.

'Hello Karel, long time no see. Did you ever get over the dizzy spells while you were up on Copernicus? I always did say that you guys in the ESC were a bunch of pansies. Over.' Karel sat stunned for a moment, then his face split into an enormous smile as he grabbed for the microphone.

'Spider? Spider! I don't believe it! Christ man, I thought you'd be flying a harp by now you old goat. Unbelievable, Spider, how did you manage to survive the collapse? Over.'

'Same as you obviously. By thinking ahead. We heard something about Copernicus from Vandenberg when you went down, but that was, oh, I don't know, fifty or more years ago. My God, man. Where are you? Come on in and we can chew the fat, for we surely must have some tall tales to tell each other. Over.'

'Yeah, you bet, we're in Cape Canaveral town, I've got two vehicles and a bunch of friends, we can be up by thirty-seven in a few minutes, but I imagine you've some defences around, so we'll need some guidance. Over.'

'Yeah, right. Get over to Gate One, then stop. Someone will be there within fifteen minutes to bring you through. Looking forward to seeing you, yer damn pansy.'

Spider Magee was as good as his word. It took the Gevcars five minutes to pull out of the town and reach the entrance to the old Air Force Station, on the way they passed several very old and rusted wrecks which they took to be the remains of earlier attempts to get into the base. After a few more minutes they saw a small car speeding down the road, and as it came nearer they were able to see that it was in fact a large electrotrike of the type that had been popular with local patrol organizations before things came apart, the civilized version of the cross-country trikes they had ridden out of Mendoza on. The machine pulled up, and one of the two men riding on it got off and walked towards the cars. A middle-aged man, skin burnt by the sun, with a thin thatch of greying hair coming down out of the cap he wore, he stopped, obviously impressed with what he was seeing. Reaching the nearest car, he looked around at the group of people waiting, and making the obvious choice, addressed himself to Karel.

'Captain Houseman? My name is Ken Magee, I'll guide you through.' He stopped and then spoke more informally. 'My uncle sends you his greetings, he's looking forward to seeing you.'

The two cars travelled up the road under the direction of their host, soon leaving the man on the electrotrike behind. Every so often they left the road and followed a circuitous path, avoiding so their guide explained, the numerous minefields that had been laid down decades before during the troubles, but which were still active and dangerous, even to large armoured vehicles as the Gevcars. In a number of places the sea had obviously broken through the defence walls for whole areas had become salty swamps, destroying the older launch pads that had once been there. Some of the old reinforced structures were still standing, tower support foundations, blast diverters, stained and mildewed, broken in parts, mute witnesses to remind man of unattained dreams and broken promises, to Karel a message filled with ineffable sadness, they had come so close, so close, only to fall back again. Now the stars had become unattainable specks of light in the night skies. North of complex fourteen they saw massive dikes and land filling, millions of cubic metres of rock and earth which had managed to do the job of keeping out the rising waters, for there was little sign of damage, and the rows of fruit trees grew protected by low walls. They finally stopped in a parking area halfway between pads thirty-four and thirty-seven, parking the Gevcars in the leeway of some abandoned buildings. Karel descended first, followed by the rest of the crew, all using glare specs and hoods, looking somewhat like a congregation of monks on the way to church. Across the Banana River, half hidden in the haze, the enormous bulk of the Vehicle Assembly building loomed, still apparently intact though at a distance of five or six klicks it was impossible to see if it was undamaged.

'Still standing, but the north face is full of holes.' Ken Magee, as though sensing Karel's unspoken question offered the answer. 'Shall we go? The others will be waiting inside.' And so saying he turned, leading them towards the low grey concrete building that stood two hundred metres away, surrounded by low trees and bushes.

As they reached the building, their guide indicated a ramp leading down to a roller curtain in which a personnel door had been set. As they got near the door opened, and several people stepped out, followed by a large wheelchair pushed by a young man. In the wheelchair sat a legless man, a small man with an almost boyish face, eyes shaded by the wide-brimmed bush hat perched on his head. Karel broke his stride for an instant and then without seeming to hurry, moved on ahead, leaving the others a couple of paces behind. Arriving at the chair he bent over to embrace the smaller man, receiving in turn a hug from the thin wiry arms.

'God, Spider, I can't believe it.' Both of them talking at the same time, all other thought and activity swept away into irrelevance for them, crossing a gap of fifty years. 'Karel man, it's good to see you!' Patting each other on the back, 'what the hell did you do with the pins? I always did say you were too lazy to walk if you could ride.' 'Lost them way back, you on the other hand still have that big hooter, and a nice decoration to set it off.' Karel reached up, unconsciously touching the long thin scar running down his cheek. Still talking, the two men were herded inside, while Jock having first introduced himself was now presenting the rest of the team, except for the on duty Watchers who had stayed with each car.

Inside the building, they were led down a bare concrete passageway, passing a number of rooms, until they arrived at what was obviously the canteen where they were all invited to sit. The Hold people felt immediately at home, for much of the layout was not unlike what they were used to in the Hold, albeit of a much simpler and more basic nature, with a few improvements which had been added over the years. Originally designed as a command centre for the launch pad, with a number of auxiliary and storage rooms attached, the place had been extended and made habitable. Spider, as he was known to one and all, his original name having long since been lost, explained that only six of the old launch pads were occupied with a total population of between 250 and 300 people, as there were a number of regulars who came and went according to the season.

'We started out with ninety-two people, mostly Space Agency employees of course, trying to survive the mobs that took over practically everything in the area. We grouped together and fought off the attacks, luckily for us there were at least half a dozen separate bands so we managed to keep them fighting among themselves. Eventually the attacks petered out, some groups were wiped out, others just disbanded and wandered off, I don't know, anyway eventually we were able to begin putting things together.' Spider ran his hand across his forehead as his mind ran over the events of so many years ago. 'I guess the worst period was between twenty-seven and twenty-nine, we lost almost a third of the original group, after that more people kept arriving, word of mouth I guess. We peaked at 362 somewhere in the mid-thirties. Most of us are rather on the old side, and the troubles took care of our fertility. We keep our numbers up with new arrivals more than with births, the miscarriage rate here is far too high, still too many toxic residues, though with no capacity for serious investigation we can only guess at that.' He stopped, a small, tired, little man in his wheelchair. 'Still, having heard your story about the Hold, I feel hopeful for the first time in years, not for me perhaps, but at least for the younger ones. We've kept a very low profile here for all these years, trying to avoid calling the attention of unwelcome guests, hence the VHF radios, but of course that also cancelled out our chances of getting in touch with you earlier.'

Jock, who had listened quietly to the story, nodded his head and spoke up, his deep rumble clear over the general background noise.

'Spider, as you know, our Hold is a very long way from here, so in practical terms immediate help is out of the question. Nevertheless we'll set up a communication link with a relay over Sentry. Sandy tells me that should be easy now that they've cracked most of the access codes, at least you won't be alone any longer. In time we will come for you, the Techs back in the Hold are working on our first homebuilt Gevcar.' He smiled. 'It won't be anything like the ones you saw, but it will be enough, and now that we know where you are we'll be able to improve on the route. In a cycle or two we'll be here, I'll take a wager on that.'

'Thanks, and that's from all of us,' replied Spider. 'You'll be on your way up north before too long, and I sure hope you find the other Hold, Australia's an awful long way from there if you don't. We can supply you with a fair bit of information on what it's like going north, at least as far as the Lake Michigan. We have people who were up that way, mmm, let me think, not longer than five years ago anyway.' He thought for a minute, and then continued. 'You know, I'm sure we can refine your route quite a bit, one way or another we know pretty well which areas have to be avoided, at least within a thousand klick radius of here, yes, we can definitely help you there.'

After a light meal served early in the evening, the visitors sat around with the Cape locals, spread out through various rooms as people from the other launch pads had drifted in to greet the visitors. Many questions about the Hold were asked and answered, and here even more than in Tumbes there was a feeling of comradeship generated by the similarities of the two societies. Jock, Karel, Spider and a few of the others had retired to Spider's quarters in one of the wings of the complex where they sat sharing a glass of brandy, a product not even the Hold, for all its technology, could match.

'Tell us more about how you managed to get by all these years,' said Karel. 'Then, in exchange, I'll tell you my tall tales, though sometimes even I think it was a sort of dream now that I've found the Hold.'

'Well, as I said, after the worst period we began to rebuild what we could, no industrial base of course, just scavenging off the past. The military always was generous with its stores of equipment, food, medical supplies and spares for almost everything you can think of, so one of the first things we did was to secure the old Air Force base. At first we could only be out for short periods of time, so we more or less lived in the launch bunkers, but eventually the rad levels dropped off and we were able to start growing things to supplement the C-rations.' He made a face of disgust. 'You can live off them, but after a while you begin to doubt the wisdom of doing so. Even today we're still not quite self-sufficient with what we grow on the islands, so we still have to send out hunting parties. We get up as far as southern Georgia and as far west as the Mississippi valley, normally that's enough. Much of the old wildlife has started to come back, and of course the cattle and pigs which managed to survive are now wild as well. At first we were wary of eating the meat, but now if the animal appears to be normal and healthy that's enough for us.' He paused. 'Not very scientific, but we're short of natural science people aside from a couple of semi-trained doctors, the rest of us, the older ones I mean, are mostly technical.'

'At the Hold of course we avoided that problem.' Jock took up the conversation with his usual quiet rumble. 'In comparison with you lot, we had it easy, you've done wonders here.'

'Too little, too late, but even then better than nothing.' There was no bitterness, only a deep sadness in Spider's words.

'Well, I don't know, you've kept going here against enormous odds, you never had the chance to be isolated and self-sufficient like we did. You may be, as you say, scavengers of the past, but you've kept a small technological society running. Our job is to start to rebuild a better world, so what you've done here is already a nucleus for a fresh start. If it didn't exist, then we would have to start from scratch. Spider, believe me, you've done a great job. How many other societies have your people come across which were like your own?'

'Mmm, I suppose we could say one or two, different of course, but still with a lot of basic technical know-how intact. One is up near Dayton in an old Air Force base, the other, we haven't heard from them for quite a while, is, or perhaps was, just south of Denver. For the rest, plenty of small tribes, some savage, some simply agricultural, it's difficult to know why some were successful and some weren't.'

'Not really,' replied Jock. 'As Karel can confirm from his own travels, those that survived successfully had strong-minded technical leadership. Men and women with guts, determined to ensure that at least something survived. Whenever you had people filled with nothing but the old I'm better than you syndrome, or my belief is right and yours is wrong, things fell apart, with the survivors fighting and killing each other over petty differences. No society led from the rear survives for long when the chips are down. Leadership is an odd thing you know, some people have it, whether they like it or not, but if you don't have it, you won't learn it, however hard you try. This is one of the reasons why Karel is our leader although he was not of our Hold, but a newcomer. Getting things back together again won't be easy, with the birth rate where it is, we'll need every civilized human being we can find, otherwise it won't work.' He stopped, shook his head and offered a shrug. 'My apologies, I've got onto my hobby horse again.'

'Yes, well I do the same myself sometimes,' Spider replied. 'I imagine you people will want to turn in, it's been a long day for everyone. You know where your quarters are.' Taking the hint that Spider himself was tiring, the group dispersed to their own sleeping places leaving only dim night lights to illuminate the barren corridors.

Ten days later, with the last of the loading completed, the moment for goodbyes had at last arrived. Spider sat upright in his wheelchair, eyes gleaming with excitement, while Karel squatted at his side talking quietly. The rest of the team went round saying their farewells to the forty or fifty Cape people who had come out into the cool damp morning air to see them off. Threejays wore a worried frown, for on her shoulders had fallen the responsibility of ensuring that the new members of the crew knew what to do. The three Hold members who had chosen to stay on at the Cape, scientist Samantha Alessi, Sanjay's young medical assistant Tammy, and Watch member Peter Whade, all looking rather forlorn, but still resolute in their decision.

The general concept of switching people had come into being without anyone really being aware of why, how or even when. Karel, Jock and the others had had several long discussions with Spider and his lieutenants about the possibility of exchanging people. The idea had first taken root when Samantha had proposed staying on to Jock, mainly because she was interested in the animal husbandry work being done on the nearby Cape farms. The concept seemed to Jock to contain some merit, so after a preliminary talk with Spider and Karel, the leaders had sat down to review the relative needs and experiences, both from the side of the Cape as well as that from the travellers. The end result was that after a call for volunteers on both sides, the Cape was receiving a scientist, a doctor and a Watcher, while the Gevcars in turn obtained Ken Magee, Linda Olsson, a fuel cell specialist, and a deceptively old looking man who went by the name of Jojo, whose reputed competency with weapons, both on land and at sea, made him an interesting addition to the Gevcar teams. All this left Jock's car one man short, with only one scientist as Linda had gone to Karel's car as a replacement for Patric, not to mention leaving Sanjay alone to run medical services.

An unexpected bonus for the Gevcars was that the hydrogen tanks were once again brim full. Even with the capacity to run for over a cycle without refuelling, it was good to know that the tanks were full, and to the Cape it was no loss as their recovery plant was capable of producing far more hydrogen than they could possibly use. Much of the same technology used for the Gevcar fuel cells had also been applied in space vehicles, and in fact the Cape had several prototypes still running to supplement their other energy sources.

One by one the crew climbed aboard the cars, until finally only Karel was left outside. 'Well, Spider, old friend, time to fly again. There's so much that I could say, but you know it all anyway. Perhaps we'll meet again, who knows? The fates brought us together for this little bit of here and now. Good luck, keep in touch.' Karel bent over and hugged his old friend, and then turned and walked off towards the waiting Gevcar, back straight, head as high as ever.

'Bon voyage, you old pansy, and don't forget to send a postcard.' Spider's jaunty attitude and brave words covering the sadness he felt as his old friend left on a journey from which he was excluded.

At Karel's order the power units whined into life once more, a tremble running through the Gevcar hulls, and then as the power came up, the cars rose off the ground as though tied together into a single unit, throwing out particles and dust, forcing those on the apron to cover their eyes and hold onto their headgear. The cars spun round and slowly headed off to the east, following the safe route off the Cape indicated by Ken Magee who rode in Jock's car, up beside Herb Kramer in the co-pilots seat.

Their passage across to the opposite coast of the Florida peninsula was rapid and untroubled, as if their short stay at the old spaceport had brought them luck. Three hours later found them moving at a steady forty-five knots up the old highway towards Tallahassee still over 250 klicks away to the north, back once more on the route they had planned a two and a half weeks before during their stop at Tulum.

Shortly after midday, under a low leaden sky which seemed to herald the coming of bad weather although there was hardly a breath of wind, they passed the town of Perry, now long abandoned, but instead of continuing northwards as they had originally planned, they turned off to the west towards the coast and then out into the gulf, a refinement to their route which had been suggested by Spider's people, rather than travelling overland. Once away from the coast the Gevcars rode the swells easily and it wasn't long before they crossed the bay and came ashore again. Much of the low-lying land bordering the Gulf of Mexico had returned to swampland with the disappearance of the old levees and dykes, whether by the hand of man or simply by the passage of time, but they managed to find a place to stop, again in an old national park. The following day they awoke to a steady drizzle which fell depressingly from a uniformly grey sky in which not even the least colour or shade variation could be seen. After the usual after breakfast planning session they set out again, following the old highway westwards for over two hundred klicks, with visibility limited to a small circle barely a few hundred metres in diameter. They cruised along at the best possible speed, avoiding the remains of old wrecks and craters which decorated the highway, mute testimonies to the savagery of the civil wars that had racked the world, passing a series of small abandoned towns whose now meaningless names figured only on the old maps. The land around them seemed undamaged, but most of the cultivated fields had been overrun and absorbed by the regrowth of the natural vegetation, leaving little trace of the hard years of labour that had gone into clearing and planting the fields.

Chapter X

The great sleek snout hung at its lowest position, blackened and streaked, gaping holes where the windows had once been. The passage of time had pitted and corroded much of the stainless steel skin, but even with rotted tires and a buckled landing strut where someone had attempted to set a fire, the hundred-year-old aircraft retained an aura of greatness.

'Originally conceived as a strategic bomber capable of undertaking the entire mission at a speed of Mach 3.0,' read Petra from the computer print she was holding. 'The XB-70 Valkyrie served as an aerodynamic research vehicle. Only two were ever built, and one was lost in a crash. Much of the airframe is fabricated from stainless steel honeycomb-core sandwich, and the wingtips fold downwards in cruising flight to increase stability and reduce trim drag. It was designed to make use of a phenomenon called 'compression lift,' achieved when the shock wave generated by the aeroplane flying at supersonic speeds supports part of the aeroplane's weight.'

She stopped reading while the exploration team from Karel's Gevcar, led by Brendt who had now changed over as a result of the shuffle made at the Cape, walked slowly along the sixty-metre length of the sleek aircraft. Yet another fragment of the world that had forever vanished, a dream of flight that would not be repeated for a long time to come, if ever. Even though the delta-shaped machine that sat on the cracked concrete had been relegated to the museum long before the Fall, its performance superseded by later generations of aircraft, its appearance still drew the eye, a mantis waiting to strike, waiting and waiting.

'We'd better be heading back soon,' Brendt said, pocketing his watch, 'Spider's contacts must have been wrong, there's nothing for us here.' The small group turned, retracing their steps towards the burnt out hangars at the eastern end of the old base. They had come to what had once been the Wright Patterson Air Force Base trying to make contact with the group that Spider Magee had mentioned, but had found no signs of any recent habitation. Since leaving the Cape a week earlier they had seen occasional smoke but had not come across any other humans. Their route up the Mississippi had been a sound strategic choice, for with much of the nearby land flooded or at least swampy they had been able to cover several hundred klicks every day, skimming over the waterlogged land without much effort. The slowest days were when they were forced to deviate from the river to avoid the old cities, many of which were still standing. They had seen Memphis in the distance through the binoculars, and that had been close enough. Seen through the haze and distorted by the rising heat waves, the fallen houses and wrecked buildings told the same old story. Office tower blocks, all the shiny gold plated glass all gone, blackened empty shells of their former selves standing silent guard, surrounding a flattened criss-crossed patterned and glassy plane six or seven hundred metres in diameter where the busy hub had once been. Nothing living, nothing moving, no more would the bustle of business return here, and the rad count still higher than any doctor would have recommended to any patient who wanted to have a long and healthy life. Further up the river at St Louis the great metal arch had still stood, outlined against the red of the evening sky as black streaky clouds slid in from the side finally to obscure the view. The gardens and park were gone, replaced by rough soil and rubble, and the buildings from what they could see through the binoculars were half fallen and empty. No one had slept much that night. They had miscalculated the distances, and the gathering darkness had caught them nearer than they liked to the city. The next morning they had got under way earlier than usual, leaving the sleek arching monument behind them.

From there they had left the Mississippi valley cut overland to the north-east to Dayton where they now were. Off the river their advance had been slower as they kept to secondary roads as most of the highways seemed to be blocked with the rusting remains of vehicles, a sort of graveyard where the foremost sign of North American opulence had come to die. They had arrived early in the morning and the four scout teams had spent the day searching the base and the surrounding area to no avail, leading them to the conclusion that Spider's information was long out of date. Arriving back at the Gevcars they made their reports to Karel and Jock, and after a brief meal the cars were on their way again, heading northwards again, leaving the Valkyrie to its lonely vigil over the remains of the old museum.

*　　*　　*

142

The grey-blue surface of the lake, rippling and scintillating under the yellowish orange light, seemed almost friendly. Capable of producing wind-driven storm waves and surges up to two metres high, seiches as they were known, which had battered the shoreline over untold years, the waters now seemed almost inviting, while overhead skimpy greyish white clouds drifted around, reforming into ever new patterns, occasionally dimming the sun's yellow orange globe. Twenty klicks away, the towers of Chicago could still be seen, seemingly intact, reaching up into the sky, beckoning to the visitors. Through the binoculars it was even possible to see the trapezoidal shape of the Hancock building, and behind it the mass of the Sears' Tower, once and for a short time the tallest building in the world. But the old Chicago had perished, so the records from the Hold said, for the city had been dusted before the end of 2030, wiping out the remaining hundred thousand or so inhabitants who had managed to survive in the ruins where anarchy had prevailed for the better part of the previous decade. As was often the case half a dozen splinter groups from across the political spectrum had claimed responsibility and the NAF president, speaking from an unknown location, announced that the culprits would be caught and punished. Unfortunately by that time the good citizens of the windy city were no longer interested in empty promises. To the crews of the Gevcars the city seemed remote, a place they knew about from history tapes, but having been born and bred into a different world somehow softened any feelings of pain provoked by the fall of such a bastion of civilization. Filled with the hope of rebuilding, they felt some curiosity about the past, and wonder at the complexity of life in the great cities, but only passing regret.

Keeping a safe distance from the coast of Lake Michigan the two cars accelerated up to their cruising speed of ninety knots and rapidly ate up the distance to the northern end of the lake. Behind them the wakes sprayed up and out, spreading in a long thin triangular shape, adding to the impression of power and grace as they swept over the placid surface of the lake. Miguel Pardo insisted on stopping for a few minutes to take water samples from the lake in order to compare results with those given by the Records system, and after half an hour's work was pleased to find that the eutrophication, produced by the dumping of half treated sewage and agrochemical runoff during the better part of the previous century, had diminished. Three hours after leaving the southern shore they swept into Green Bay, all systems on alert and all eyes sweeping the shore for any sign of activity. Little trace remained of the lakeside villages where busy city folk had once vacationed, being mostly built out of wood, the passing years had taken care of the once neat little houses which succumbed to the harsh winters and high winds. Now in the middle of summer, their timber frames bent and broken, half covered by weeds and young trees which had sprouted again after the toxic chemicals in the soil had decayed, these old buildings watched soundlessly as the two Gevcars sped by. Nature, observed Miguel, had a way of winning in the end, years of acid rain and wind-borne fallout from fossil fuel plants, and incineration plant waste had contributed volatile organic compounds, PCBs, and heavy metals, which had all but destroyed the natural vegetation of the area in the first quarter of the twenty-first century. Now, half a century after the passing of industry, nature was again making a comeback. Slowing their pace, the two cars followed the old road up past Kipling village, climbing slowly upwards through what had once been the Hiawatha National Forest, until the point where both lakes were visible, and then began the descent to Lake Superior. They stopped for a brief lunch on the shore of the lake, just east of Marquette, keeping to the routine which somehow represented an anchor in the ever changing scenery through which they travelled.

Contact with the Hold had become increasingly difficult as they approached the northern end of the Sentry footprint, and all Sandy's expertise in enhancing the signal with the aid of the on-board computers could not entirely eliminate the temporary fading which led to repeats and misunderstandings in the daily communication routine. Since the first simple use of the Sentry as a navigational aid, they had accessed the wide range of communication programmes which still kept them in touch with Tumbes and with the Cape, but the distances involved were such that the atmospheric disturbances were having an increasingly negative effect. The midday sessions were also a chance for Maria to observe and record the team's behaviour and performance. Prior to their departure from the Hold, she and Erik had briefed Karel and Jock on the problems likely to appear within small isolated groups of people under great strain, and had agreed to report regularly to them on the matter. So far, there had been no serious trouble, thanks in no small measure to Karel and Jock's careful selection, a process they had based both on the Hold psychological profiles as well as on their own intuition. The four new additions from the Cape had fitted into the team almost seamlessly, although as Maria herself said, it was only reasonable to expect people from a vaguely similar background to adapt well. Even with known psychological profiles there were surprises: Janine's ability on the Sonolite was one of them; Petra had turned out to be an expert carver, able to produce exquisite representations of animals and plants from gnarled and twisted bits of wood; and Jock, without compromising his qualities as their leader, could spin a story guaranteed to keep their attention riveted for as long as he felt like talking.

In the afternoon they made a short run of just over 130 klicks up to the north shore of the Keenaw Peninsula. They had hoped to be able to continue until later in the day, but in the face of a stiffening breeze which first covered the watery sun with high clouds, soon followed by heavy grey thunderheads, building up increasingly choppy waves, Karel decided to call a halt. They came ashore and took shelter between two low hills from where they overlooked the angry waters to the north. The storm, when it finally broke at around five in the evening, was something to behold. Great bolts of lightning streaking across the sky from cloud to cloud, as though gathering up their strength, and then pulsing down to the land in five or eight second bursts, leaving forked and twisted images engraved on the retinas of those who watched. Some strikes were even close enough to produce a breathless tingling feeling as the air around them became charged with millions of volts, the hair on their heads standing up, sending goose pimples running up and down as the hissing sound permeated through the Gevcar's open hatch. The cars themselves were, at least according to the design specs, more or less immune to such strikes, but even so Jean, seeing the advancing front, took the precaution of rigging up a lightning arrester a hundred metres away, using a length of pipe and some spare copper cable filched from the stores. As they watched, the horizon vanished under an advancing grey curtain, seemingly almost solid water, the wind gusted around them, whipping trees and bushes into a frenzied dance under the premature nightfall produced by the enormous black thunderheads which covered the sky. The first drops fell, large and solid enough to be painful, forcing them to seal the Gevcars' hatches, and then the tempo increased until the downpour enveloped them, cutting them off from the outside world, with visibility two or three metres at the most. Even inside the shelter of the thick armoured hull it was possible to hear the moaning of the wind and the roar of the falling water. After the first moments, the downpour eased up, allowing them to see down to the shore. The gale force winds pushed the waves up into breakers which rushed in to pound the land, releasing bursts of spray which reached up to meet the falling rain. The pitch of the incoming waves was so short that no sooner had the first broken than its successor was rushing in, each wave taking with it some part of the waterfront as it receded. To the Watchers inside the cars, warm and dry, the violence of the storm was still shocking, as someone was heard to remark, although later no one was sure who it had been. 'If we have to go outside, I volunteer to stay here. After all, there's no point in all of us getting wet,' which seemed to sum up the general idea quite clearly.

The next morning, the storm had vanished as if it had never been. The sun rose up over the horizon far clearer and more brightly orange than anyone had seen for a very long time. On the land around them, however, the effects of the storm were clearly reflected by the slashes produced by newly cut stream paths, fallen trees and stripped bushes, and in some cases areas of fresh mud slides, even though the slopes had not been particularly steep. After breakfast, they resumed the trip westwards across the lake where the confused wave patterns could still be felt in the pitch and yaw of the heavy vehicles which advanced more slowly than usual in order to limit the shocks as they rode over the waves. They came ashore near Thunder Bay, another deserted town seen in the distance and headed off along the old Winnipeg highway, which like most old roads was empty except near towns or wherever fighting had taken place. In these more inhospitable latitudes, where short, hot summers broke into the endless pattern of long, cold snow-filled winters, the land lay empty. They met no others, either individuals or groups, and the great plains once covered by waving fields of golden wheat had now returned to their original state of rough grassland, empty except for the passing of the Gevcars, heralding the return of man after half a century of absence.

For the next five days they travelled on westwards under a hazy but almost cloudless sky, the great rolling plains turning slowly to low hills, becoming more arid, and then creeping up until they became foothills to the Rockies. They lost a considerable amount of time in avoiding the larger cities and towns on the route, particularly the area around Calgary. Only once or twice did they see signs of smoke in the distance which could have been the result of naturally produced fires, but which Karel chose to ignore, despite some protests from the doctors and from Threejays. Animal life on the plains was scarce, occasional herds of deer, once a brood of horses led by a magnificent golden brown stallion who led his charges off on a divergent course when he spotted the Gevcars racing towards him. The single most amazing sight was one they were privileged to see just after dawn on the fourth day when, coming over a low ridge they almost drove into a small herd of American bison. As the two Gevcars came to a halt in a cloud of small stones and dust, the males, perhaps twenty or twenty-five in number, turned as one to face the cars, offering their thick bony skulls as if they were shields, while the females and calves retreated to the rear.

Finally they reached the general area in which the second Hold was believed to be, and after half a day of random searching during which they found absolutely nothing, settled down to a painstakingly meticulous grid search, hill by hill, valley by valley.

'I don't know why we can't get an answer, but I'm beginning to fear the worst,' said Sandy to Jock as they worked through the daily transmission routine, her voice toned with the frustration she was feeling.

'I know, but the Hold can't just have vanished, there were too many safeguards for that.' Jock ran his hand over his head, pushing back the hood of the cloak. 'Perhaps Karel has some ideas, I'm afraid mine have all been used up.'

'If only we had more time, the window is pretty tight at only fifteen minutes a day, it only allows twelve signal repetitions which means two days at each site in order to complete a reasonable directional scan. If only the wavelength wasn't so directional.' She looked up as Karel and a couple of others came over from the table which had been set up in the shadow of the cave entrance. As always the glare specs gave them all a sort of vaguely sinister appearance, specially as they had got used to only having to use them for a couple of hours at noon. Now that they had entered the higher latitudes, however, they had been forced to extend the period to five hours a day due to the higher uvee. It was easier to adapt to pleasanter conditions than harsher ones, as Jock was happy to remind anyone who complained about having to continue using the protection gear.

'You know,' Jock said, 'I never really appreciated until now what

Karel faced when he set out to find us, an accuracy of ten or twenty klicks doesn't seem very much on a map, but here in this sort of terrain it's an awful lot. We're just going to have to go about it methodically like Karel did. Work our way up and down every valley, one by one, and hope we get lucky.'

From the mouth of the cave where they were sitting, Sandy looked out down a wide U-shaped valley, the floor of which was almost obscured by trees save in the middle where a stream meandered down, with the slopes sweeping up to peaks well over 2,500 metres above the floor. But for Sandy the awe-inspiring view barely existed, her world focused down to the signal which flowed outwards, begging for a reply.

'Hi love, no luck eh?' Karel looked thoughtful for a moment before continuing. 'You know, I've had a funny idea, it came to me last night ...'

'While you were snoring you mean?' asked Sandy, making an effort to snap out of her mood, a smile twitching her lips to show she was only pulling his leg.

'No, seriously, Sandy. Hear me out, it may seem to be a bit too far out, but. ... Well. ... Do you remember how the Sovs used a double relay to get a signal to that lost shuttle? We were taught it as a case history at the Academy, it must have happened in fifteen or sixteen, somewhere around there anyway.'

'I can't really remember any details, but I do remember the case study. How's it going to help us?'

'The gist of the matter was that they were stuck in an orbit without enough fuel to relocate. Their ground control systems were all fouled up as a result of sabotage, or perhaps some accident, I can't remember, so anyway, what they did was to link up over a surveillance satellite to their unmanned station, and then order the supply shuttle which was coupled there, to undock and boost to their orbit.'

'So how does that help us?'

'As you know, I spoke with the Records people this morning, the link was extremely poor, but I think they understood me. They're checking the orbital records for this part of the sky. If they could just find something, and that's a big if, then we could try to use the Sentry to redirect a signal to it. If it works, if we find a bird with a directional array, we could attempt to get it to transmit the signal down on the whole area, or at least on sectors of it. Then all we need

148

to do is reprogramme it to listen for the homing signal, and we can cover a much larger area than sending the signal ourselves where we practically have to check out each valley individually.' Sandy sat still, open mouthed.

'Karel, that's the craziest idea I've heard for a long time. Look how long it took to crack the Sentry code, now you want us to do it again on another satellite? Look I'm not saying it can't be done, but it won't be easy.'

'Karel could be right you know,' said Jean Klock who had joined the group in time to hear Karel's idea. 'We no longer need to do all the work ourselves. Look,' talking faster now as his enthusiasm grew. 'If there is a satellite overhead, and if it will answer a probe from the Sentry, then the Hold computers should be able to crack any code. Now, we aren't near enough to get a clear signal through to the Sentry, but the Hold can talk to the Cape, pass on the message and the Cape can relay to the satellite via the Sentry, certainly better than we can, up here we're lucky if ten percent of the signal gets through.'

'Maybe you're right, but we'll still keep on going at it with the local search, we've only been here eight days, we've searched maybe one-third of the likely area, so we have to keep going. There are plenty more valleys that we haven't scanned yet.'

'I agree with you Sandy,' Jock smiled, his smooth skinned face creasing, 'we'll work on both fronts, I'll get hold of the other Elders at the next contact and push them a bit. I know our computer resources, if there is in fact a satellite in a suitable orbit, then Records should have some info on it, it shouldn't take more than a couple of days to crack a code.'

It took them longer than a couple of days, a lot longer. It was two days before Records produced data on three possible satellites, two military and one civilian, none of which had been active in the last four decades. It took three days until one of the military satellites finally acknowledged receipt of a signal sent from the Sentry, and after that it took a another four days to decode and process an acceptable instruction set and to reprogramme with the new transmission instructions. All of the transmissions being done via relay over the Cape. That in itself had been a hard nut to crack, for Spider had been wary of announcing his presence with a high-powered transmission, even though it was highly directional and up into the sky, but finally he had acquiesced. Because the military satellite was in a lower orbit, it was only in position every so often, and not always within the time window set by the Hold designers for the location. Meanwhile the Gevcars continued their search, leapfrogging from valley to valley, sending out their signal and waiting patiently for the reply. They met no others, although on two occasions they came across villages which had obviously been occupied not more than a few months previously. As they had walked through the deserted streets and houses, Brendt and Janine both claimed to have the feeling of being watched, but although they left written messages in prominent places no one attempted to make contact with them. The mood in the group was still hopeful, but conversations were beginning to carry overtones of false jollity to hide the general disappointment at the lack of any concrete results. Only Karel, having spent so many years of his life searching, seemed to be immune from the depression that slowly permeated the group.

It was only in the late afternoon of the fourteenth day since their arrival in the Banff area to the west of Calgary that they were rewarded by a weak but still distinct high-pitched sing-song of a homing signal, triggered by the old satellite broadcasting from almost nine hundred klicks over their heads. The duty crews had been setting up camp for the evening when Jean's shout brought them all running. Suddenly it was as if a party was in progress with everyone hugging and pounding each other on the back. Threejays sat in the doorway of one of the cars, tears streaming down her face, Bob and Janine swayed back and forth locked together in a tight embrace, Jock wandered around in a daze, patting anyone who stopped long enough to allow him, Herb and David kept telling each other that they had known all along that the other Hold would be found in the end. When the initial burst of excitement died down, several people proposed initiating an immediate search for the entrance to the Hold, but both Karel and Jock vetoed this, agreeing that the best plan was to make a fresh start in the morning. As Karel pointed out with a quiet smile, it had taken them almost four and a half moons to get this far, so if the Hold was in fact there, it would surely still be around the next day. It would also, he pointed out, give Sandy and Jean time to triangulate on the signal source to see if they could cut down the final search area.

[Extract – 2020]

(The following reports are excerpts from the minutes of the Site 3 Steering Committee meeting held on 4 August 2020. It is to be noted that all records related to 1 January 2018 to 31 December 2025 have been classified as restricted and can only be accessed with the authorization of the Council of Elders.)

The removal of any documents from the Records Hall or the copying of any information relating to this period is strictly forbidden.

Phase II Construction Contract Report: Heavy movement on site is proceeding on schedule, approximately sixty percent of the blasting has been completed. All galleries for Levels D to F have been cleared of debris and work on the linking tunnels is expected to start in mid-September.

The first four tenders for basic building work have been issued, and bids will be in by the end of the month. The remaining three tenders are in preparation and should be ready before the end of the year. Contract placement is expected to take place before the end of next March, two months ahead of schedule. Negotiations to guarantee the secrecy of the project are proceeding well and no problems are to be foreseen with any of the possible contractors.

Design work on the accessory systems has been delayed in order to incorporate a number of significant modifications, therefore the specifications will not be ready until the beginning of November. This delay comes as a result of the additional safety audit on life-support systems requested in the previous Steering Committee meeting.

Attachments:

- Safety Report: Redundancy Philosophy
- Accessory System Status Listing
- Phase II Layouts
- Phase II Time Schedule (Adjusted)
- Cost Control

Power Subcommittee Report: Detailed schematics for the TFR have been completed and piping work for main and primary redundancy systems is well under way. The first batch of materials specifications and listings has been completed, covering about seventy-five percent of the total. Simulation (dry) tests on the expert system have been completed with a reliability rate of eighty-three percent. The corrections in the programming logic are expected to be ready by mid-October when a second test will be executed.

Core fabrication at CERN has been initiated and is proceeding on schedule. All statements and reports issued to the public continue to make reference to the EC grid reactors only, so far there is no indication that this subterfuge has been detected.

Attachments:

- Materials Listings: Cover Sheets
- Simulation Test Scenario Listings
- TFR Construction Schedule (Adjusted)
- Reactor Layout: Update

Hydrogeological Report: Both boreholes have successfully competed their pumping tests operating at thirty cubic metres per hour. The aquifer dynamic response has been better than originally forecast with a depression of only 1.80 metres and a recovery time of thirty-five minutes, independently of the operating time. Total dissolved solids have increased by 11.5 percent since the first analysis, but have shown no further variation during the last three months. This situation is expected to remain unchanged.

A placement for a third well within the N1 layer has been selected, however this well will not be sunk unless the existing wells show any sign of decay.

Attachments:

- Well Construction Drawings
- Water Analysis

News Item Summaries: A major power blackout has all but cut off Scandinavia from the rest of Europe. Reports say that the simultaneous outfall of seven power stations caused the collapse of the interconnected grid system, leaving almost all the Scandinavian Peninsula without light, heating, power and communications. All airports have been closed indefinitely as a safety measure, although most are equipped with standby generators, fuel is scarce and the decision was taken to save this for emergencies. Because of the time of the year the death toll is expected to be low, except in the far north.

The Presidents of Monaco and Liechtenstein have agreed to sign a mutual defence pact, by which an act of war on one of them will be taken to be an act of war on both nations. Both countries, for many years tax havens and resorts for the very rich, have only very limited armed forces. A joint announcement, however, revealed that these defence forces are equipped with tactical nuclear devices with a short-range missile delivery system of Chinese origin. How the weapons were obtained is not yet clear, but it is believed that they were purchased from Angola after the surrender to the Namibian army.

In its first action this year, Israel attacked the cities of Aden and Abu Dhabi using Galahad missiles equipped with conventional warheads. Both missiles were targeted on the centres of government and according to Israeli sources were accurate to within ten metres. Israel has warned that unless terrorist training camps are removed within seventy-two hours a second strike with nuclear warheads will be made. The UN has moved UNDEF forces into the area and has warned that such action will be met with utmost severity.

A UN Health Commission has warned that unless action is taken rapidly, the Ebola C virus which has reached the pandemic stage in central Africa could spread to South Africa and to the Middle East despite the rigid quarantine regulations that have been in force since the beginning of the year. The statement claims that if enough healthy carriers can sneak through the border controls on foot there is a danger that the spread of the virus could go out of control.

Chapter XI

The pages were slightly yellowed and crinkled, even to the point of seeming to be brittle. The top few sheets were mouldy at the edges despite the care with which they had been packed into the sealed pouch, which in its turn had been inside a plastic container. In the glowing light of the lantern that sat on the desk in what had once been the general services area on the second level, they resembled sheets of parchment, scrolls containing some ancient wisdom, instead of a story about death. Matt and Erik sat together, heads bowed, totally absorbed in what they were reading. Occasionally some sound could be heard, filtered and distorted through the long, dank passages, as the other search groups worked their way through the Hold, but the two men read on, oblivious to the outside world. The walls in the room had once been a cheerful yellow golden colour, like sunlight on ripe wheat, now the paint had pealed in parts, and streaks of dampness decorated the corners. In the far corner filing cabinets had been left open, as if someone in a hurry had removed a file and not bothered to replace the rest of the papers which lay in a damp mass, now quite unreadable.

The writing was small and untidy, uneven, as though the writer had been unaccustomed to writing longhand, in places the pages had become stuck together with dampness and the writing blurred. As they separated the pages, occasional words were lost, but the general context was enough so that the gist of the message was unchanged. The first twenty or so pages listed people's names and skills, followed by equipment lists of various sorts, and after that by names of places and distances as though the unknown writer had been planning a trip. Beyond that the writing became a journal of sorts.

> This is our story, the story of Survival Centre North, the Citadel as we had begun to call it. I don't know if anyone will ever read this, but even so I feel it is the least I can do to pass on the story of our failure in this place. We came close to fulfilling our founder's dream of surviving the Fall with our knowledge and abilities intact, ready to start again. But it was not to be.

In the end the old ways are sometimes the best, with all the power off except for some emergency lighting, all the computers are down, so here I am. Pen in hand, back to longhand writing, my wrist is already sore from the unaccustomed exercise, I hope the result is readable. I believe that when the weather improves we will have to leave, but it seemed wrong to do so without leaving some sort of record of the events of the past three months.

For the record, my name is Peter Sonderjheld, and I am, was is perhaps a better word, a member of the Council of what was supposed to be a survival habitat. I am a psychologist, and my specialty is administration, so unfortunately I cannot give you many details about the building and structure of Survival Centre North as it was designated. The centre was built from 2017 to 2025, the result of a private investment plan by a group of industrialists, and became fully operational in February 2025 with the arrival of the first groups of residents, all carefully chosen, screened and exhaustively trained. We were supposed to hold a maximum of around 10,000 survivors, but of course we never came anywhere near that number.

In a way I suppose the death knell was the bombing of Calgary, early in October 2024. At that time there were only a few of us already installed, most of the construction crews had already left and the reactor was already on stream. At the time we were busy working out the logistics in preparation for the arrival of the staff, we heard about the bombing, but it was somehow a remote problem. I think we felt in a way that it was the justification for the enterprise of which we were part. In any event at something like 200 kilometres from ground zero, we felt quite safe, for inside our artificial womb we were cut off from the troubles, after all, it was our job to survive. Later of course we would go out and offer assistance, pick up the pieces as it were, and make a fresh start.

After the Centre staff arrived we were extraordinarily busy, indoctrination lectures, specialist courses, task forces for this and that. The days slipped away, turning first into weeks and then into months, news from the outside was sporadic, and grim. A number of contingents failed to turn up, disturbing, but only slightly so, certainly not a major worry as we had more than enough staff to run the Centre. We celebrated our first six months, our first births, and settled down into the routine of living in a giant prison, a prison of our own choice, but a prison nevertheless.

Even after six months the Library and Records staff were fully occupied cataloguing all the stacks of high-density discs that had arrived at the last moment. I imagine much of it was meant to have been sent earlier, but the situation in the last few months had deteriorated alarmingly. Not only the Calgary bombing, but also all over things seemed to be unravelling at an unprecedented rate, what little news we got from the outside by tuning in to audio and video bordered on the apocalyptic, entire towns wiped out in orgies of mindless destruction, farmland laid waste by poisons spread at random. Back in the Middle Ages, Ned Ludd may have hated technology, but what has been happening outside for the last five or six years can only be described as suicidal, some sort of collective malady.

In October 2025 the first group of survivors from the outside arrived in the valley, numbering around two hundred, and set up camp on the river. They were spotted by some of our people who were out on a survey mission, and we then watched them from a distance for a week or so, until eventually the decision was taken to let them know who we were and to invite them to join us. Not an easy decision certainly, for knowing how much effort had gone into the selection of the Centre personnel, I for one was reluctant to just go down and invite them to join us. In the end the vote in the Council was passed more on humanitarian grounds than on anything else. So be it.

18 March. I see that so far I haven't put any dates on this journal. For the record then, today is, I think, 18 March 2026. I wrote the above introduction in two sittings around a week ago, say the 10th and 11th. I can't remember setting the date index on my watch so my reckoning may well be a couple of days off. One way or another it doesn't matter. Here in our insulated little world, all the days are the same, except that everyone has certain days off from their 'jobs.'

To continue with the story. Needless to say the group of survivors from the outside were delighted to join up with us. Our medical staff gave them a rigorous check-up before pronouncing them fit, hungry, thin, in some cases with injuries, but not carriers of sickness. Throughout the next two months we continued take in people, probably something like 350 in all, but never again as big a group as the first one. In mid-December, the 15th in fact, a date that those of us who lived through all this will forever remember, a small group of men, seven of them, all in good health well equipped and claiming to be the remains of a military unit, turned up at the entrance to the Centre. They had, again so they said, followed the tracks they had found, hoping to join up with a larger group for protection. We checked them out, they turned in their weapons, all perfectly normal. Two or perhaps three days later it started, several people, including four of the newcomers went down with fever.

The next day the number was over fifty, all with high fevers, ugly reddish swellings in the neck, under the arms and in the groin. We sealed off the Centre by sectors, with the medical staff working round the clock checking people. The last batch of newcomers, both the sick ones and the remaining three healthy ones were screened again, this time a far more exhaustive study than we had been using. The head of the medical department reported to the Council in the early hours of the morning of 20 December with the news that we were facing a variant of the bubonic plague, probably a genetically enhanced version, and that the survival rate was likely to be below ten percent. At that time the death toll was already over 360, with almost as many more on the critical list. The problem of what to do with the bodies was a pressing one, we had of course planned to deal with some fatalities, but our facilities were completely ...

They reached a point where several consecutive pages were so stuck together that their content had become lost, Erik glanced at his watch and was amazed to see that only half an hour had passed since they had found the room. He shook his head, trying to get rid of the feeling of having lived through the time about which they were reading. Separating the damaged pages for later examination, they continued reading.

if that was all, but of course as a solution it was quite useless. The Council, myself included, voted to complete the inoculation, even knowing that the effect would be minimal, because we felt that some sort of positive sign was needed.

27 March. We finally found out what had happened. One of the supposed soldiers, on his deathbed had confessed to being a member of the New Luddite Rising, he claimed that the six had been given vaccines and then inoculated with the plague so that they could act as healthy carriers. It was only when he realized that the vaccine had failed that he chose to unburden his soul, and unfortunately he knew nothing of the disease itself. The only coherent piece of information was that the NLR had found out about the Centre somehow and had sworn to destroy it.

28 March. I took a rough head count today, there are only 407 of us left without any symptoms of the sickness, and another twenty-eight down with fever, the worst of it is there's nothing we can do except inject tranquillizing drugs, nothing seems to work any longer, but at least the infection rate seems to have dropped off practically to zero. The damnable thing is that we'd come so close to having it under control.

In January, having lost over half our population, something like 2,400 people, the research people developed a vaccine which not only prevented fresh cases, but also even pulled back some of those who had lain at death's door. We set about trying to pick up the pieces, burying the victims in a mass grave just down the valley from the main airlock, those who dug the pit came back weeping, we have lost so much, too much. The vaccine worked, and there was once more hope in our hearts, but it wasn't for long, for after a two-week respite the disease struck again, with slightly modified symptoms. The designers of these tailor-made self-mutating diseases ought to be burned alive for what they have done, anything else would be a kindness. By the end of the month we had lost so many people that it was becoming difficult to keep all the essential systems going.

Some groups, about five or six hundred in all, I don't know exactly how many, left the Centre under their own steam, hoping to find better conditions elsewhere, they took most of the vehicles we had, but even so many went on foot. I tried to talk their leaders out of what I saw to be a folly, mid-winter is no time to set out on such a desperate journey, even if they planned to head south to the warmer weather. They left the Centre on 28 and 29 January, none of them have returned to us yet so I don't know what happened to them.

The remaining technical staff tried to prepare new people to help them keep things running, but little by little we began to abandon whole sectors of the Centre, turning off water, heating, ventilation and power, attempting to leave things in working order for anyone who might come after us.

29 March. Going back over what I have written I realize it seems a bit disjointed, but that's the way it was in reality. The last week in February was our most critical time. The reactor was turned down to standby condition. In this state I am told it generates enough energy to keep its own control system running and to supply heat and light to a very limited area. All the door and airlock systems were turned off leaving only the possibility of manual operation by turning a handwheel. Of the twenty-eight sickness cases, only seventeen are still alive, but at least there have been no new cases these last two days. The medics say that the variant was a short-lived variety, designed to be used prior to an invasion, and that its cycle time is only a few weeks, they believe that there is no further danger of infection now, even to people not so far exposed. We are living on the lower levels now, bleeding what little power is available from the reactor to keep warm and to cook with. Outside winter is upon us with a vengeance, with a major blizzard piling snow against our main door, we couldn't go out even if we wanted to.

3 April. Time passes, I had intended to write a few lines every night, but some days I'm so tired that I just drop onto my bed at the end of the day and am out like a light before I know it. The designers of this

great Centre never visualized having to keep it running with so few specialized people, normally we could run the whole place on automatic with a shift of not more than 30 or 40, but with so many inexperienced hands around, things have a habit of going wrong, sometimes irretrievably. Yesterday, or perhaps it was the day before, the control system on the lower level hydroponics tanks issued a pH alarm (I know enough to know that this is related to the acidity of the water). The duty watch took note of the alarm, accessed the control system and set up what they thought was the correction routine, unfortunately it was a sterilization routine and the result is that we have lost over sixty percent of the hydroponics vats due to a warm caustic soda rinse. As soon as he realized what had happened, the technician aborted the cycle, dumping I don't know how many thousands of litres of alkaline liquid into the water recycling system which dropped out of service as a result of the overload. The technician, a medical technician in fact, can hardly be held responsible for his lack of training, but that's the way it is, there are so few of us that everyone is doing all sorts of half understood jobs, and accidents do happen. I am reminded of my history lecturer at college, a perfectly rational human being in all aspects save one. He was absolutely convinced of the presence of a metaphysical being he referred to as Murphy, who, so he claimed, was responsible for ensuring that things go wrong. The basic precept of this belief was the statement that if anything can go wrong, then it will. Ridiculous of course, we by our actions, by our care by our attention to detail determine whether or not things will work. Certainly not some fellow called Murphy.

4 April. I see reading over what I wrote yesterday that I failed to mention our situation with regards to the plague. As it stands now, of the seventeen cases we had last week, only eight are still alive and looking as if they might pull through. The best news is that we have had no new cases in over a week now. Perhaps we have a chance after all.

9 April. Outside the weather has improved a bit. Yesterday we got the airlock open for the first time since the snows came. There are only 402 of us left alive now. The remaining plague victims died, and worst of all, five healthy people more took their own lives. I have been talking to people as much as possible, I am fearful suicide will be the choice of many. Arnold Hogsdon, the Logistics Department head, now that his superiors have gone, tells me that our dried food supplies will see us through a year or two, always supposing we can count on a minimum of power from the reactor. The hydroponics of course are out for the moment but he believes that things can be put right eventually.

Clearly our mission is now over, it will be hard enough to survive ourselves without thinking about going out to help others. Already there are signs that our organization is falling apart, petty squabbles about who occupied which rooms, or how the food is divided up. I am the last remaining member of the old Council, I hear occasional grumbles about why should I be obeyed or looked up to. The odd thing is I cannot answer the question, but the fact remains that people constantly seek me out to demand that I make decisions, arbitrate in their discussions, listen to their woes. All I can do I am doing, but why me, why me?

13 April. It is after midnight now, we held a meeting today and the decision was taken to abandon this site and head south. I was one of the main proponents of the idea, for with so few of us left there is no point in living on in the Centre. Here in the Centre we are only scavenging off the past, we have to get out and fight to survive, and if the price is a more primitive life, then so be it. We will begin preparations in the morning, with the objective of getting away by the end of the month.

There has been a lot of discussion as to where we should head for, my own feelings are that we should try to reach somewhere like southern Kentucky. We have to find somewhere with good farmland, not too far from the coast, but not on it, hilly rather than flat land, with warm summers and not too cold in winter. Not an easy task, but not impossible either. In my function as quasi-leader, today I performed a wedding, a meaningless ceremony from the legal point of view, but none the less important for that.

18 April. I often wonder if I am right in leaving this journal. Perhaps it would be better if we just vanished quietly into the darkness. Before this disaster we had much to hope for, to be proud of, now having been destroyed by our fellow men's short-sighted bigotry, my main feeling is one of embarrassment. Are there no limits to our stupidity? Couldn't we have foreseen that this might happen? Perhaps it might be better to destroy the whole complex, wipe the slate clean, I just don't know what to do.

At least it is good to see that our people seem to be motivated by the coming move, teamwork does wonders for the spirit. Our preparations are well under way, most of us of course will move on foot, divided into four groups of around a hundred people as this will make the organization easier than keeping in one large group. Our heavy supplies will be placed in the electric carts, what isn't certain is that there will be adequate roads or at least tracks to see the cars through. Time will tell.

The destination we have chosen is on the eastern slopes of the Appalachians, a town by the name of Ararat in the old state of Virginia (ref. 36° 36' 1" N and 80° 30' 38" W) where two of our surviving members come from. They have assured us that we will be well received and that the area around the town is easily defendable. The name at any rate seems appropriate although I don't know if anyone other than myself has noticed. We are taking most of the portable comm units so as to be able to locate other groups, who knows, it's about time we got lucky.

28 April. Tomorrow at dawn we will be leaving this sad place. We have left as many instructions as possible for any that may stumble across it, though hidden away as it is this seems unlikely. The reactor has been put on safe shutdown with all the interlocks in place, we discussed the possibility of leaving it running, but in the end it seemed safer to pull the plug. Almost all the auxiliary systems have been left in working order, pipe lines have been drained, machinery wherever possible oiled and protected. Arnold has worked round the clock preparing additional instruction sheets which are being posted up, perhaps they will serve some purpose if anyone comes here after we have left.

God bless.

There were no further entries, just a scrawled signature. The two men sat quietly for a while until finally Erik rose, picking up the pages and began laying them back in the container in which they had been found.

'A brave man. ... Come on Matt, I think Karel and Jock will want to see these, it's almost time anyway, we'll only be a few minutes early anyway.'

They returned back the way they had come, hurrying, despite, or perhaps because of the bad news they carried with them. As they walked along the dank corridors, the empty and dark doorways stared at them, their world became the sphere of light thrown by the lanterns they carried, and the walk of little more than five or six hundred metres seemed to stretch away in front of them.

On this, the second day in the survival habitat, they were still being cautious about where they went, and still worked in pairs, each team staying out for a period of not more than two hours before reporting back to the entrance bay. So far they had only penetrated the first two levels, finding most of the personnel airlocks closed but still operable by hand. They arrived back at the entrance bay just as Jock himself came in through the auxiliary airlock to the outside. Erik called out to him at once.

'Jock! Over here, you'll need to see this.'

'Lo Erik, what's up? I've been talking to Sanjay over in the infirmary, down that passage by the way, about two hundred metres. He says that there's evidence that some sort of ...'

'Bubonic, modified. It's all here Jock.'

'Where did you find the info? Is that a Records' document? Never mind, tell me later. Are we in trouble? Is there anything on the propagation characteristics? Even if it's airborne it should be harmless by now, this place has been sitting like this for a long time and from what I know most tailor-made stuff was short lived.'

'Yes, that's what it says here,' said Erik handing the pack to his brother. 'But we'll get onto it right a way, I'll need a day to be sure though.'

'Get to it.' Jock turned. 'Matt, get Karel at once, bring him here, I'll be waiting outside. Then get down to the reactor room and give Herb a hand, he says he could go a lot faster with some more help.' He spun on his heel heading back out towards the lock. In the yellow light of the lantern, which had been placed on a pile of crates, his shadow preceded him, flowing out like a wave over the doorframe, into the outside twilight.

Four days later the entire crew except for the Techs and Matt stood gathered in the entrance bay while Jock and Karel discussed the past days' tasks with everyone. The two Gevcars sat side by side a few metres away, noses pointing towards the open lock through which the setting sun's deep red light streamed in, tinting everything it touched with blood. Several of the crew glanced in the direction of the cars, and then at their blistered hands, for some of them had spent over two hours the previous day cranking away at the manual gear system, watching the huge doors slide open for the first time in over fifty cycles.

They had been working almost without a stop since they had finally found the entrance to the centre the day after receiving the homing signal. The entrance locks, blasted into the rock beneath a low overhang, had been carefully disguised to resemble the rock face, and if they hadn't known exactly what to look for they would have passed on by. It had been a day of seesawing emotions, the hope of finding the second Hold after receiving the signal, soon dashed by the obvious fact that the locks had not been operated for a very long time. There had been no problem in cracking open the smaller personnel lock, for the previous residents had left clear instructions engraved on a thin sheet of plasteel which had been bonded onto the door. Even though spring was well on the way to becoming summer, the wave of cold air that swept out as the door swung opened had seemed to bring ill tidings. Karel had divided them into five teams which he sent in with strict instructions to touch nothing, to stay on the entrance level, and to return in not more than thirty minutes. The teams wore their cloaks, as much for warmth as for anything else, as well as breathing masks, although there didn't seem to be much chance of anything virulent still being around. At the end of the first thirty minutes they met again at the entrance lock. The reports were uniformly negative, nothing living had been found, and there was no indication as to what had happened although it was obvious that the departure had been more or less planned. A number of things had obviously been stripped and removed, but on the whole things had been left moderately clean and tidy. The strange and perhaps frightening thing was that almost all the personal belongings such as might be found on a non-residential level had been left untouched, as if the owners had departed to somewhere where they would have no need of them, a fact which once it had been pointed out by Maria Sanches led to some unpleasant speculation. Now the situation had become clear, mainly thanks to the journal left by the unknown Peter Sonderjheld, validated also by all the evidence they had found throughout the Centre.

To have come so far, to have found the second habitat against all odds, but to have found it cold and dead, had been a bitter blow, particularly for Karel who had in more ways than one, dedicated his life to the search. They had all held high hopes of finding new colleagues with whom to work in the battle to rebuild something of what had been destroyed.

'I wonder how much longer?' said Karel. 'Herb said he thought he might be on stream by eight thirty and it's past that now.'

'Give the man a chance Karel, he's worked miracles with what he had available.' Threejays countered, coming to the defence of the absent Tech. Karel nodded to her, accepting the implied rebuke gracefully.

'I know, we're all impatient. You more than most, carrying us all like you do.' She smiled at him, almost sadly. No sooner had the words left her mouth than the emergency lighting fixtures set along the walls at regular intervals began to come on by sections, the light seeming to race down the passage towards them, and past them on down the opposite passage. There were varied expressions of delight from the little group, as they headed off down the passage towards the power sector. As they reached the doorway, expecting to have to crank it open, they heard the servo whine, and then with a clunk, the door shifted and slid aside, revealing a delighted Herb inside.

'Told you, told you. I was sure we could do it.' He beamed at them, accepting the congratulations as his due.

'Once we got the computer up with help from the auxiliary unit in the Gevcar it was easy, just had to watch really, it's all preprogrammed. Most of the work was checking that all the moving parts still worked, and that the communication links were still in place and undamaged, and that the basic signal i/o's, input/output signals, were still valid. After that the computer ran all the checks for the remaining i/o's.'

'So what does that give us?'

'Well, Jock, we're on standby plus five percent. That's as high as I care to go for the moment, and it allows us to scram in not more than a minute and a half if we're pushed. So far all the parameters are within limits though there are two temperature readings which are oscillating more than I would have liked. In practical terms, this means that we can give you limited lighting throughout the whole place, power the main bay lock, give you heating and ventilation on Level A, where we are now by the way. We've confirmed that the levels here are named the same as at our own Hold, though the layout is different in parts.'

'What about Communications and Records? I'd like a look there,' Sandy asked. 'It would be interesting to see if we can rig a patch using short wave bursts to transmit compressed data off to the Hold, they'll have the staff there to do a far better analysis than anything Jean and I can do here.'

'Well, let me check the files in the power sector to see how much we would have to divert for that.' Seeing Sandy's face drop, he added, 'I imagine it should be possible Sandy. We could leave some areas in the dark, and much of the auxiliary services equipment only needs to run for a few hours a day with so few of us here. Give us a couple of hours and we'll be able to give you a definite answer.' Herb turned to leave, and then turned, remembering his last piece of information. 'By the way folks, this place is designated as Site 2, Karel's info was absolutely correct.'

The Tech team did even better than Herb's promise, for two and a half hours later David came back into the office on Level B which the group had adopted as their meeting place since getting the power back on, and announced that the Records' computer had power again. Sandy, Jean Klock and Janine who was temporarily assisting them disappeared at once in the direction of the computer room, such was their hurry that they left their teas sitting in the mugs, slowly getting cold.

The Watch people, led by Brendt and Bob, now that the initial survey had been completed, were at something of a loose end while the specialists all seemed to have found something to occupy their time. At Threejays' suggestion, they organized themselves into two groups which went off to do a thorough check of the personal quarters up on Levels D–F. As they set about rummaging through cupboards and drawers, they were gripped with a feeling of prying into someone's private life, letters, books, children's toys, family photographs, clothes of all sorts, outerwear, intimate items, electronic devices of all sorts, all available for scrutiny by total strangers. In general the décor of the place was similar to that of their own Hold, though the cold and damp had taken its toll. In the kitchenettes of the married quarters, items of desiccated food still sat, best before dates long gone. Some rooms were neat and tidy, some were in a mess with signs of the arrival of the sickness, or showing signs of hasty departures. Occasionally they found a room that had been stripped for some reason or other. After the first hour the work had become repetitive and automatic such that only things out of the usual or that might mean something were noted. In others the quality of the search might have fallen off, blunted by boredom, but the Watchers, trained to observe, to notice details and differences, used the same skills and patience that made them superb guards and scouts, to analyse and separate what might be relevant. There was no apparent slackening of effort or precision despite the monotony of the job. All the cameras they found they set aside for later processing, in the hope that the resulting pictures might reveal some relevant item.

After the third hour Brendt's team working through the northern end of Level E, received a nasty surprise in the form of a corpse still lying under the sheets on a bed, at first sight simply asleep, a closer look revealed the mummified skin, drawn onto the bones like a dark brown parchment, tufts of curly black hair still clinging to the skull.

Brendt called Erik on the comm unit he was carrying as soon as he had ushered the others out of the room. Erik arrived a few minute later, panting from his run to get down from the medical labs which, like in their own far off Hold, were up on Level F.

'It's OK Brendt,' he said between deep breaths. 'My word, I'm really out of shape, whew, too much riding around, back at the Hold I used to go to the gym at least once a sevenday.' He paused for breath again and then continued. 'Whatever killed this guy is quite harmless now, but a tissue sample will be great help in confirming what he was hit with. You fellows just keep going.' He looked grim. 'Call me if you find any more surprises.'

'Sure thing doc.' Brendt smiled, but the humour failed to reach his deep blue eyes. 'You're welcome to them.'

On balance, and at the end of a gruelling six days, Brendt was forced to admit that the idea of exploring the place had been worthwhile, for they had built up a clear picture of how the Citadel had been betrayed and had fallen from the fragments of information they had gathered. Most of the older-style film had decayed to a point where it was useless, a number of the magnetic media recordings were however still intact, and they were able to see parts of the daily lives of those who were no more. Clearly it was all very interesting, the only problem of course was that it had no bearing on the here and now, it was simply fifty-year-old news.

Karel was over the worst of his disappointment. His own decades' long search had been full of ups and downs, and he knew that to succumb to pessimism was a bad option. They would continue to search this place, obtaining as much useful information as possible, hopefully more clues as to the final site, and then the chase would be on again, this time for Site 1, hidden somewhere in the Australian Outback, just an ocean away.

Chapter XII

At noon on the thirteenth day since their entry into the Citadel as they had taken to calling it, for to them the word Hold was the name for home and this dead place was as far from home as they could imagine, Karel called a meeting in one of the conference rooms on Level E. The décor in the room was quite different from that of the room in which the first meeting back in the Hold had been held. The general impression was one of stark utilitarian efficiency, for the room was a study in black and white without a drop of colour save for a painting depicting a green-white mountain lake set in a steep-sided tree-covered valley. The black wall-to-wall carpet, contrasting with the pure white walls and the white synthetic surface of the table, held no thought of relaxation or of pleasure, it was a room that demanded only work and dedication to a cause. Only the end wall broke the monotony, set as it was with a variety of technological devices including wall screen, vid-player, music station, electronic clock and comm console, all currently out of use. The group sat loosely around the table, with Karel and Jock at the far end facing the wall screen. Overhead in their recessed ceiling bays the white hot glow of the lighting spots served only to highlight the austerity of the room.

'Well people, we've finally reached the moment I have been hoping to avoid ever since leaving the Hold.' Karel's tone was sombre. 'There is nothing here for us at the moment. Someday perhaps this place will be a starting point for a more ambitious expedition than ours. Herb tells me that with a staff of twenty-five or thirty Techs and scientists this Centre could be fully operational in a couple of moons. We have neither the people nor the time.' He looked around making eye contact with most of them. 'Sandy and Jean have downloaded copies of much that was in the databases here, unfortunately we haven't been able to set up a reliable link to the Hold in order to pass that data on. As far as we can tell the satellite we used to retransmit our signals via the Cape has gone down, and we're too far away from the Sentry footprint to do a direct patch, so I'm afraid we'll have to wait until we're further south.' He paused for breath. 'Meanwhile, I have therefore decided to push on to the third site.' He held up his hand to forestall the murmurs that swept through the others. 'It's now almost five moons to the day since we set out. I had hoped that by this time our mission would have met with success. Finding this place was in itself a sort of success. But at best a bittersweet victory because the inhabitants of this Centre, the Citadel, cannot be here to share it with us. We have also lost a member of our team getting here, a friend, that isn't an easy price to pay. We have made new friends on the way, but this is not where it ends, it isn't enough for us to go back to the Hold with this knowledge, we must take this as a new beginning and push on.'

'But we planned for six moons, seven at the most,' said Alice Folsom, the co-pilot from Jock's car, 'some of us have families to get back to.'

'Yeah, it's all very well for you, I'm for going back as well.' Jules Borman said, 'we've found this place, someone else can take over now.'

'Jules!' Bob's voice, pitched only slightly above normal, cut across the noise of several conversations like a knife. 'The Watch does not abandon a mission. Never, ever. If you think otherwise then the interviewers made a serious mistake.'

Miguel Pardo looked around. 'Karel my friend. You too Jock, I too am becoming tired of this wandering, my talents would be better used back in my labs. We set out with high hopes, unfortunately too high, perhaps it's time to accept that, and to decide accordingly.'

'I didn't join up with you to give up, I joined to go on and on, for as long as necessary' said Ken Magee, looking round as if daring anyone to defy him.

'We should vote on this, that's the Hold way of doing things' Alice Folsom coming in again, looking around as though gathering support.

Jules, still not deterred by his chief's rebuke, took up the discussion again. 'At least you should consider the opinions of those who think we should turn back,' he went on. 'This isn't a dictatorship you know, we all ...'

'Enough!' 'Stop!' Jock and Karel's almost simultaneous orders brought silence to the meeting room. For a long moment the only sound was the distant hum of the air-conditioning unit, and then Karel rose to his feet.

'Back at the Hold, when your Council asked me to lead this

expedition, I laid down a number of conditions, conditions which your Council deemed acceptable. Among these conditions I stated that I would be willing to listen to everyone's opinion along the way, but that the lead decisions would be mine and mine alone, unless I chose to share them. I have in fact talked this over with Elder Fernan and we have agreed on the course of action. I want to make it absolutely clear that this isn't a matter of my personal wishes, the decision is based on what I am firmly convinced is the best decision for the survival of the whole. To go back is to accept defeat, the Hold on its own can survive, perhaps for several generations more, but in the end it will fall.' He stopped, letting the silence lengthen. 'You were picked as being the best team the Hold had to carry out this search, your personalities include an above average willingness to face the unknown. If you give up, then the Hold will remain turned inwards.'

'Karel is right, I know you all fairly well, and I know a fair cross-section of the people back in the Hold,' said Maria from where she was sitting at one end of the long table. 'If the Hold is to fulfil the mission which our founders set for us, then there is no other choice. We must find the third site.'

'But what if it too is dead and deserted?' asked Miguel.

'That is a bridge we'll cross when we get to it, you as a scientist should know that.' Karel replied, ice blue eyes looking straight at Miguel who began to feel uncomfortable under the intense scrutiny. Icy blue eyes seeming even colder than the mountain lake shown in the picture behind him. 'We'll be leaving here as soon as Herb and his boys can put things through a safe shutdown.' He looked over at Herb who held up two fingers. 'That will be at dawn two and a half days from now.'

'And how the devil are you intending to get across to Australia, it must be at least seven or even eight thousand klicks over water?' Still Alice was not willing to give up, 'and to think of going round the Aleutians is even crazier ...' Karel let her wind down to a halt and was about to reply when Jock held up his hand and turned to her.

'Alice, perhaps you missed the point. This is a command decision. Even if I disagreed, which I do not, I would be bound obey it. There is only one leader, and that is Karel. No one ever said our search would be easy or without any danger. You knew that when you agreed to join this expedition. We will be leaving two and a half days from now. All of us, and that is final.'

The dissenters looked around at each other, faces strained and unhappy, but none of them chose to take the issue any further. Finally Miguel went as far as to give Jock and Karel an assenting nod. Sandy, who had been wondering if Karel would have to call a vote, visibly relaxed, and taking Jean by the arm took him off, talking about some communication problem or other. Jock nodded almost imperceptibly to Karel, the corners of his mouth lifting in a slight smile, signalling his approval at the way the situation had been defused, then turned back to the table.

'Right. There is much to be done before we leave, and not too much time. We'll be leaving this place, but our people will be back sooner or later, so we don't want them to think we're a bunch of slobs. That means leaving it in an even better state than we found it, so let's get on with the work.'

They rose from their places, taking with them folders, papers and maps. Threejays tidied up the last things, replacing them as they had been, taking a last look around before turning out the light and closing the door. The stark utilitarian look of the conference room was once again plunged into darkness, silent, to wait dormant for the next awakening, whenever that might be.

From where they were high up on the cliff it was possible to see the great ocean swells rolling in, coming out of the fog-covered horizon in seemingly endless progression, each one almost identical with the one before. Occasionally the orange-yellow outline of the sun could be seen behind the cloud blanket, but it was still too early in the day for it to burn off the low-lying ground fog. It had stopped raining early in the morning, but the air was still redolent with the smell of damp earth and vegetation. This was the first time since the grey blight in Central America had forced them to turn eastwards that they had seen the Pacific. The bluff on which they stood overlooked the southern end of the Grays Harbor bay, some 120 klicks as the crow flies from Tacoma, which, as was their practice with the larger cities, they had made a point of avoiding. On the shore below them the waves crashed and thundered, throwing up clouds of spray which hid much of the narrow beach. On both sides of the bay's narrow entrance the remains of fishing or perhaps holiday villages, for the most only the skeletal remains of the higher buildings, could be seen, the rest having been long ago dragged down into the sea by endless succession of winter storms.

Their route down from the Citadel to the coast had not been an easy one. Not wanting to go too near Calgary with its high background radiation count, they had followed the Bow River for a few klicks south-eastwards, and then turned south following the remains of an old road which wound its way through the Spray Mountains leaving Mount Allan and Fisher Peak to the east, passing to the west of the snow-capped peak of Mount Sir Douglas and then later turning westwards along an old secondary and often washed-out road that led towards Cranbrook. In many places they had found the road blocked by old rock falls and had been forced to detour round, a time-consuming exercise to say the least. On two occasions even this proved to be impossible, and so rather than turn back they had blasted a way clear using charges extracted from one of the missiles placed inside a piece of steel tubing fired by remote control. At some moments and in other circumstances the trip would have been a delightful trek through beautiful scenery, for despite mankind's best efforts much of the vegetation and wildlife had managed to survive and thrive. Any visitors from the past would of course have noted the oddly coloured sun, distorted by the atmospheric haze which turned what had once been blue into grey, but the changes were relatively few. The visitors would surely have marvelled at the multi-hued sunrises and sunsets so much richer than in previous centuries. Maybe they would have wondered at the number of dead trees, and surmised that perhaps a great fire had come that way, killing off trees and driving out the wild animals. All in all, it was remarkable that many things remained the same, a tribute to Nature's versatility and stubbornness. As the crow flies the distance from the Citadel to the town of Creston on the southern end of the Kootenay was about 240 klicks, the two cars covered just over two and a half times that distance and it took them three days, three days of frustration after frustration as there was no earthly way of increasing the pace. Even Jock, usually the epitome of patience and understanding, was heard to remark that if they wanted to go any faster they had better leave the car behind. Once south of Creston they had been able to pick up the pace southwards following the old roads, passing abandoned towns and villages, some burnt out, others intact, but all empty of any life other than the occasional wild dog. Reaching the old interstate road, they turned westwards to the coast, detouring round the Spokane area although there was no reason to suppose it would be inhabited. With the hills around them it had not been possible to see much of the town, but what little they did see from the roadway they were following, looked long abandoned.

The trip down through the last ranges towards the coast should have been awe inspiring, for here stood some of the greatest peaks of the continent. The weather however had other ideas, leaving Janine and Alice who had been studying all the photographs included in the data from the Gevcar computers sorely disappointed. Practically from the moment they left Spokane the clouds closed in round them as a series of squalls which blotted out anything further away than a klick or two swept in. Every time the weather appeared to be clearing giving them some hope of seeing something, a new patch of wet would appear from the west, and once again their world would turn to grey. The Gevcars, able to go where no ground car could ever have gone, were immune to the weather conditions, swamplands, lakes, torrential streams. All of these were there simply to be crossed under the able hands of the pilots whose skills had grown immensely since leaving the Hold.

Up on the headland, the whine of the Gevcars power units seemed to be diluted by the wind, separated by a distance of some hundred metres two sets of eyes scanned the bay area, checking for movement, heat sources, fuel emissions or any other sign of human activity. Even with their technology, they were hampered by the weather conditions that limited their scan area to a radius of three or four klicks, enough to guarantee immediate safety but not much more. After ten minutes or so, and after cross-checking with Bob on the intercom, Brendt announced that the area was in principle safe, and suggested that they head down to the coast of the bay, seeking a place out of the wind to stop for a rest. By the time they reached a likely clearing still a dozen or so metres above sea level, the sun had begun to come through the mist, bringing some feeling of warmth to the day, a most welcome change after the last three days of almost uninterrupted rain and drizzle. Coming at last to a halt, the two cars settled onto the damp ground, side by side, positioned nose to tail so as to allow all round surveillance. The sound of the power units dying down to a subsonic moan as the doors hissed open allowing in the scent of wet earth and vegetation, and allowing the weary crews to step out and enjoy the sounds of the woods around them.

Sandy and Jean as ever began setting up the directional dish and began trying to contact the Sentry which they both insisted should be just within range now that they were a few hundred klicks further south from the Citadel. Jean as ever spent about one-third of the time trying to tuck his shirt back into his pants, accepting with good grace the usual round of disparaging comments from anyone who happened to be around. Threejays retired to her desk to catch up on her journal, and most of the other members of the crew found things to do. It was as if after departing from the Citadel the old routine had suddenly been switched back on again, throwing them once more back into the pattern which had held them together throughout the trip up from the Hold. The tension which had built up over Karel's decision to carry on to Australia had receded, and the group was once more operating as a highly trained team, differences shelved, at least for the time being.

Bob and his Watch crew set off down to the shore, heading eastwards, away from the mouth of the bay along the stony beach, in the direction of where the villages of Ocosta and Markham had once stood. Mostly the shoreline was quite open allowing them to walk without hindrance along the stony beach, and whenever they met a larger boulder than usual or came across a fallen tree, they simply skirted round the back before coming down to the shore again. The trees, mostly different varieties of fir and pine grew bordering the shoreline, reaching back up into the hills, their tops lost in the fog that swirled around, giving them a sort of spectral look. It took them until lunchtime to reach a point from where it was possible to see the towns of Hoquiam and Aberdeen which still stood tucked into the hills on the northern side of the bay. Bob set up his scope and began to scan the area slowly, his head swinging slowly back and forth following the old Watch pattern. Not wanting to miss anything, he took his time, for at this distance there was still enough haze around to make really clear viewing impossible. The others were looking around quietly, poking through the remains of a fishing cabin which had once stood up on a ledge above the high water mark and now rested right on the waters' edge, with the surges running up lapping at the old beams. Matt and Jojo, the latter the new member of the team who had joined them at the Cape, were attempting to pull down a metal plate bolted to the structure when Bob's shout brought them running.

'Look, over there, do you see that fallen tower to the left of the reddish patch? Go left about ten degrees. ... Do you see them?'

'I can't see anything unusual,' replied Matt who had reached the scope and was bending over it. 'What did you see?'

'Canoe, maybe more than one.'

'Got him, yes. ... Them! There's two of them, one with, I don't know, maybe three people in it, have you got a comm unit with you? We should call back to the cars.

'No, mine was down, I left it with Linda to see if she could fix it, we'll have to head back.'

It took them two hours to reach the clearing where the Gevcars were parked, and all of them, despite being young and fairly fit, were sweating profusely by the time they arrived. Karel and Brendt questioned then closely about what they had seen, and after some discussion it was decided that one of the cars would cross over to the other shore immediately as there were still at least four hours of daylight left. Ten minutes later the Gevcar slid down across the beach rattling the smaller pebbles and stones, throwing out twigs and dust particles. Once out into the bay, the motion of the gently moving waves, miniature versions of the great ocean swells which pounded the Pacific coast, was hardly noticeable. Even keeping to a moderate speed it took them no more than fifteen minutes to reach the point near where the canoes had been seen. The Gevcar siren wailed once, twice, an eerie almost mournful sound, reminiscent of the lighthouses of days gone by. They drove up the beach and powered down, settling down onto the stones with a soft scrunching sound. With the cabin access hatch open, and the weapons platform on alert, for the friendliness of the locals was by no means guaranteed, they sat down to wait and see if anyone would put in an appearance.

'I don't think we're going to have any luck,' said Matt after the first ten minutes had passed.

'Let's wait a few more minutes' replied Maria who had accompanied the group. 'Perhaps they're waiting to see what we do.'

'Well, after some of the things we've seen, I don't know that I'd be all that eager to go rushing out to welcome some weird machine that came and sat on my beach' mused Petra who was at the controls. 'In fact, I'd probably be downright wary. But I agree, let's give them a few more minutes.' In the end, they grew impatient with sitting doing nothing and powered up again and moved out. For the next two hours they cruised up and down the coastline, scanning the shore for any sign of activity. Sometimes they stopped and drifted along, a few centimetres above the surface of the water, with the power turned down to minimum so that the spray cloud from under the skirt was hardly wider or higher than a handspan. Above them the day lightened for a while as the sun broke through the clouds, and then darkened again as evening swept in from the east, the sky sinking into orange and then down to red. With the sun already hidden behind the hills which sealed off most of the western end of the bay, and the purple-black shadow line creeping inexorably towards them across the bay, Petra finally called off the search and swung the car back towards their campsite.

By the time they got back, only the last tinges of purple still showed over the hills, but darkness had fallen, and if there was any moon it remained hidden behind the clouds cover which had closed in again. Their disappointment at not finding the canoe people was tempered by the news that Sandy and Jean had once again established contact with the Sentry satellite and through it with the Hold and with the Cape. At the Hold, the Council after receiving a briefing from Jock, had echoed their disappointment at finding the second Hold abandoned, but were delighted that the site was intact and had already set in motion plans for a future expedition. They had also, after going off the air for over an hour, approved the plan to continue the journey to the third site, a fact that when announced served to still much of the worry over the trip, although in practical terms there was little the Council could have done should Karel and Jock have chosen to go against its wishes. After a quiet dinner the crew retired to their sleeping quarters, even the hardest Watchers having given up the idea of sleeping out as the ground was still soaking wet after the rains.

'Seriously Bob, what do you think the chances are of getting to the third site?' Janine lay on her side facing her partner, her loose hair cascading over her shoulders, the golden lights reflected in the light from the reading light above the bunk, to which they had retired after the evening meal.

'Well, my money is on Karel. Look what he's done with his life, he doesn't know how to give up. We know enough about the Site location to make the risks of the trip worthwhile.'

'So which way would you go, round the coastline up by the Aleutians?'

'Me? No, I'd go the quick route, wait for a spell of good weather and set out at high speed. If we can count on a few days without storms ... I mean we could cover as much as four thousand klicks in a day without pushing the Gevcars too hard.'

175

'But there will be some arguments won't there? Alice won't sit quiet, probably not Jules either.'

'Jules will obey his superiors, he has no choice, he's Watch.' Bob's voice and expression were bleak. 'As for Alice, I think you'll find that Karel and Sandy will bring her round.'

'I'm sorry lover, I didn't mean to bring the conversation round to this,' Janine leaned in close, brushing her lips down his cheek, 'I'm just being a worrier, being able to ignore problems that have no immediate solution isn't one of my strong points.'

'Well, I'll forgive you that,' said Bob with a lazy grin. 'After all you do have a couple of other good points.' He continued, letting his eyes run over her full rounded breasts which lay half hidden in the shadows.'

'Pig,' she replied, pushing him playfully, and then pulling him down to her as he turned off the light.

The briefing began after breakfast. As on previous occasions Threejays pinned up the maps and after a few introductory remarks began to talk about their planned route.

'We've had a lot of discussions with Karel and Jock, as well as with the pilots on the best routing. The route we've finally planned is that we will head south to a point slightly north of east of the Hawaiian archipelago, and then head out towards the islands. That means a sea trip of between 3,200 and 3,500 klicks without stopping.' Threejays stopped talking and raised her hand for silence as a wave of murmurs and comments starting to come from her audience. 'Hear me out please, please, let me finish and then we'll open for discussion. Let's call this part of the trip the first phase. The initial decision we have to make is how to go south from here. There are several land routes, and of course we can head out offshore a couple of klicks and then come back in the evening. Our jumping off point has not yet been finalized, but we are in principle thinking in terms of the Eureka area, somewhere between latitude forty and forty-one North. A number of bays and protected areas are available, and we are already close to the minimum distance for the first leg. Any questions so far?' Looking around, seeing a number of raised hands. 'Yes, Alice.'

'You already know what I think about this trip. But, as I have no real choice, I will go along with you and give my best effort despite remaining firm in the belief that the risks are high.' Alice looked around and then, nodding briefly to Threejays, sat down.

'Jules?'

'I am of the Watch, a fact which Bob and Brendt had to remind me of, and I apologize for my outburst the other day. I'm with you all the way, I'll do my part.'

'Thank you Jules, I know you will.' Threejays looked around again. 'Maria?'

Maria looked thoughtful for a moment. 'I think we're all feeling better about this than when we were at the Citadel.' The psychologist smiled slightly. 'We came a long way to find the second site, and when things didn't turn out quite the way we wanted, some of us felt that it was just too much, that everything was falling apart. That isn't the case, we are a team, and a good one, our Gevcars and all our equipment is in great shape if David and Herb are to be believed.' She turned to where the two Techs sat and waggled a finger. 'Although sometimes our Techs forget that machines need people to run them.' Herb smiled, but David was unable to resist a quip.

'Ah, doctor, if only you could psychoanalyse a machine. ... Seriously people, given a reasonable break in the weather we could cruise at a speed as high as 150 knots if we really wished to. At that rate we wouldn't need all that much time.'

The briefing continued for a further hour and a half, and included discussions as to the pros and cons of the alternatives, where they finally decided that the best route was to follow the coast road for a day while the weather calmed down, and then to complete the journey by sea. Sandy passed on the decision to the Hold over the satellite link, where they received almost immediate approval from the Council, though Jock thought to himself, not for the first time, there wasn't much the Council could do if they decided they didn't like the decision. Karel announced that they would leave after breakfast the following day, so that they might have another go at finding the canoe people, although the general opinion was that if they didn't want to be found, there was little hope of success.

[Extract – 2022]

(The following reports are excerpts from the minutes of the Site 3 Steering Committee meeting held on 28 September 2022. It is to be noted that all records related to 1 January 2018 to 31 December 2025 have been classified as restricted and can only be accessed with the authorization of the Council of Elders.)

The removal of any documents from the Records Hall or the copying of any information relating to this period is strictly forbidden.

Phase III Construction Contract Report: Work for Phase III is within the Masterplan Time Schedule. The removal of the heavy digging equipment which should have been completed last month has been held up due to subcontractor labour unrest as a result of the modifications introduced into the pension plans by the government. Both Betchel Brown Corporation and Techint Worldwide are currently negotiating at senior ministry level to try and break the deadlock. Building work on Level A is delayed by at least seventy-five days, however on Levels B and C is ahead of schedule. If the equipment removal problem is solved within the next month, then Betchel Brown is of the opinion that by redeploying more resources to Level A, much of the lost time can be made up.

This problem has not halted the start of accessory system installation on Levels D–F which is advancing satisfactorily. Over seventy percent of the accessory system tenders have already been issued, and the engineering specs for the remaining items are expected to be completed by the end of the year, two months ahead of schedule.

Specifications for detail finishing of Site 3 installations have been completed and tendering is under way. So far the first three tenders have proceeded to the pre-award discussions and there is every indication that the resulting contracts will be between five and eight percent under budget.

Attachments:

- Security Report on Labour Situation
- Accessory System Status Listing

- Phase III Layouts
- Phase III Time Schedule (Adjusted)

Power Subcommittee Report: Reactor construction is now fully under-way with primary components distributed in seven manufacturers. Resistance to the CERN TFR construction plan, which was initially high, has slacked off as a result of the low profile maintained regarding component construction locations. There is a slight delay versus the original schedule which is the result of high temperature metallurgical problems in the core support elements, where some of the test parts showed higher than expected creep rates.

Simulation studies using the central control expert system will be finalized next month. So far the preliminary results have been well within standards, and it may be feasible to increase the reactor power rating by up to 3.5 percent.

Attachments:

- TFR Simulation Schematics
- Construction Schedule – CERN/TFR/S3

Hydrogeological Report: As required in the technical specifications, the thirty-month borehole performance tests have been carried out on both N1 and N2 wells. The results of these tests fully validate on site routine analysis and show practically no variance in component characteristics. Dynamic levels are within five percent of the original pumping tests indicating that the aquifer permeability has not been affected by the current rates of extraction. These are the final set of semestral tests and unless variations appear there would appear to be no need for an extension of the test contract. Final payment has now been made to the perforation company.

Attachments:

- Water Analysis

Staffing Report: The primary personnel selection procedures prepared by KPMG Andersen have been submitted for approval. The review phase will be completed at the end of October after which the Steering Committee will have a further month for Final Approval.

The problems involved in recruiting selected people for a project whose existence is still secret and where no details of any sort can be revealed until the applicant has accepted all terms and conditions are not easily overcome. With the state of the world as it is there is bound to be some suspicion directed at the selection staff, at least until the project objective can be revealed.

It has been strongly emphasized that while from the side of Site 3 there are no limitations of any sort regarding race, creed, or politics, the recruiting of people showing strong prejudices in any of the three mentioned areas is to be discouraged.

Attachments:

- Site 3 Personnel Selection Concept Outline
- Skills Listing
- Masterplan Time Schedule (Staffing)

News Item Summaries: After a six-month international effort to improve the situation, all UN Defence Forces were withdrawn from Sri Lanka as of 00:00 GMT on 25 September. This decision has been taken as a direct result of the bombing last week of the UNDEF Headquarters by supporters of the Tamil Resurgence Party. This attack using a one kiloton tactical nuclear device wiped out approximately six square kilometres causing a death toll which will run to over seventy thousand people, not including those who die from fallout effects over the next few years. The weapon is believed to have been obtained from one of the Islamic Republics. The EU government has once again condemned the use of nuclear weapons and called for an agreement to ban their use and to set up a timetable for their deactivation and destruction.

NASA has issued an official statement declaring that the Heisenberg mission to Mars has been lost due to unknown causes. Messages were received normally up until July last when a power failure in the main module caused two of the on-board computers to crash. Communication was re-established within a few hours and the astronauts reported that although their life-support system had temporarily shut down, there was no immediate problem and that they expected to have a patch solution in place within a few days. Further garbled transmissions were received until mid-August when they ceased altogether. Today would have been mission commander Tom Herdeck's thirty-fifth birthday.

India and Pakistan today traded accusations about border incursions by each others' troops although no fighting has been reported. The situation remains tense since the war two years ago when the two nations clashed for the eighth time since 1947. So far neither nation has resorted to nuclear weapons since the so-called Short War of 2005 which left twenty-four million dead. It is believed that between them these countries still have at least forty to forty-five warheads totalling over eight hundred kilotons.

NAF forces on the island of Cuba today declared that the Muslim World Army which invaded Cuba eight weeks ago had been effectively wiped out although a few resistance cells were believed to be operating in the mountains. The death toll among the civilian population is reported to be extremely high although no accurate count has been made available to the news services. The MWA has been accused of using chemical and biological agents outlawed by the UN since the Fair War conference in Madrid last year.

Scientists for Life, a non-profit group working out of the Ross Station in Antarctica, has presented a report indicating that the melt-off rate of the ice cap is occurring at least six to seven weeks earlier than in the previous year. They emphasize that it is not yet possible to make an accurate forecast on the total retreat of the ice cap in comparison with 2021; however, should the temperatures follow the same pattern, then the result will certainly be a larger ice melt.

Chapter XIII

It was raining again. Not the torrential downpour they had experienced on Lake Superior, but a fine drizzle that fell at fifteen or twenty degrees from the vertical, bent by the wind which blew steadily out of the west. To step outside from the Gevcar was like stepping into a fine spray from a fire nozzle. The infinitely small droplets collected, condensed and flowed down forming rivulets that fell to the ground. The drizzle, seemingly innocuous, soon soaked everything it touched, after five days even the Hold cloaks were beginning to feel damp, although in fact only the outer surface a few molecules thick could have absorbed any water. It was more a feeling of dampness than a reality, but to the people of the Hold it was an intrusion, an anathema. The Hold crowd were, Karel mused to himself as the Gevcar drifted slowly along the narrow winding road, too used to the controlled temperatures and humidity supplied by the ventilation system, and even those who went Outside usually found any storms to be of short duration, for in general the climate tended to be dry. Even Ken Magee and the others from the Cape were rapidly getting fed up. Down at Canaveral there were storms, even hurricanes during the season, but they were soon over and done with, this unending drizzle was another story altogether. Only Sandy other than himself was unaffected by the weather, years of living rough soon taught one to take the good with the bad, and if in this case the bad was sitting in a comfortable seat gazing through the windscreen as they moved slowly along the remains of a country road, then so be it. Without much effort, he could stretch his mind back across the years to other rain storms. Once just south of Vitoria, up on the Atlantic coast, he and Jose had been caught out in a downpour while they were trying to salvage equipment from an abandoned iron ore pelletizing plant. They had been soaked to the skin in an instant, almost flattened by the strength of the falling rain which beat painfully on their backs as they raced for cover. Yes, a gentle drizzle from the comfort of the Gevcar was definitely a superior option.

The weather had in fact closed in the day they left Grays Harbor bay. The front had come in across the headland, inbound from the ocean, as if a great grey and impenetrable curtain were being drawn across everything, cutting off the view and dulling all sounds. They had set off fairly early in the day, following the coast road southwards, crossing Willapa Bay at the top end, then on down across the Columbia River bridge which much to their surprise was still standing, though much of the town of Astoria on the southern shore had vanished. Following the old winding coast road limited their speed to an average of around forty or forty-five klicks per hour, and at times the drizzle thickened to such a degree that they had to stop and wait for the squall to pass. Occasionally, as the road came near the shore and if the drizzle let up a bit they would see the waves crashing into the beach below, a sort of entropic performance, as the land was dragged, particle by particle, grain by grain into the sea, a remorseless process already aeons old. By the fourth day, with the weather showing some sign of beginning to let up, they came to the outskirts of a town called, according to their maps, North Bend. The first Gevcar, Jock's as it happened, had just passed a branch in the highway where a dual lane highway led off westwards towards the sea and into the town, when Herb suddenly registered that from the corner of his eye he had seen signs of human habitation down the road. The Gevcar slowed to a halt, spinning round in its own length and returned slowly to the branch in the road. Looking down the highway, it was obvious that someone at some point in time had gone to a considerable amount of effort to ensure that the road into town could not be taken at speed. Across the road not far ahead and clearly visible despite the rain was a large well constructed roadblock, covering about two-thirds of the total width, and at intervals beyond that further constructions, each preceded by a series of signposts, blocked the way making it necessary for any approaching vehicle to slow down and take a zigzag path through the obstacles. Some of the signposts showed the ravages of the passing years, but as far as they could see through the drizzle most were still quite legible.

'Stop. Wait. Do not advance,' read Herb peering through the windscreen with the binoculars at the signs as he brought the car to a halt, suspended inches above the pitted tar surface. 'Friendly lot aren't they?' Jojo, who had been riding in the co-pilot's seat, grunted a reply as he too watched for any signs of movement, while Sandy having seen the situation, talked rapidly to Jean in the other Gevcar half a klick down the road behind them.

'Look at the next one. Watch out! We love visitors. But the last one who didn't follow the rules met a mine. Great sense of humour too. ... Do not make any sudden moves, we get nervous easily. I like that one too,' Jojo's eyes continued to scan the road. 'Brendt, Matt, why not power up the cannon, I don't see anything alarming, but better safe than sorry.'

'We're already doing that man, keep a watch,' Matt's voice floated down from the turret. As they continued to wait for any sign, Jock climbed up into the cockpit, easing himself into the chair beside Herb.

'I don't somehow think we're going to be attacked, if they wanted to they would have tried already. I'm afraid that it's up to us to prove we mean no harm.' Jojo looked at him, his face wrinkling in a humourless smile, his slate grey eyes unable to hide the adrenaline rush he was feeling. Jock turned slowly to look at him, making eye contact, and then nodded, almost imperceptibly.

'I imagine you'd like me to walk down that road and maybe get my head blown off? Ah well, Ken always did say I was too foolish to refuse a dare.' His lips twitched, and then he slid out of the chair and headed back towards his bunk, still talking over his shoulder. 'Give me a minute to get my gear together will you?' In less than a minute he was back, agreeing on last-minute details with Brendt. 'Crack open the rear hatch for ten seconds, then close it again, I'll head off down the road. If I stop and raise my hands well above my head it'll be because I'm following instructions but that I believe that our hosts are friendly. If I put my hands behind my head, it's because I've seen something I don't like. I'll try to keep out of your line of fire by keeping to the right-hand side, near the ditch. If you're in trouble fire anyhow, I'll take my chances.' He shook hands with Brendt and disappeared off towards the back of the Gevcar.

As Jojo walked along the side of the road he whistled tunelessly to himself, a sound that could hardly be heard more than a couple of metres away. As he got nearer the first roadblock, he was able to appreciate that the whole affair was a highly professional job, in fact, he probably couldn't have done it any better himself. 'What in the name of seven devils,' he wondered, 'am I doing here? I always manage to open my big mouth, Spider keeps telling me never to volunteer, so what do I do? I stand up to be counted.' Shaking his head to himself without once stopping his careful scan of the road he continued his lonely walk. Off on both sides of the road there were raised areas, which, if the job had been done properly, would hide gun emplacements of some kind, probably light anti-tank rockets. In order to get through the block, any vehicle would have to slow down to negotiate the concrete pods which dotted the whole width of the road. 'Yes,' he mused to himself, 'a very nice job indeed.' At first sight and from some distance, they appeared to have been placed at random, a sort of surrealistic garden filled with oddly shaped geometric concrete blocks. Close up however, it was clear that there were paths through, only of course if one cut ones' speed to practically nothing. The roadblock itself was a massively solid affair reaching to the height of a man's chest, a mix of poured concrete and metal plates, carefully planned and constructed, a job designed to last out the years, nothing hurriedly thrown up to stop an advancing enemy.

Back in the Gevcar, now motionless except for the whine of the power unit which kept the massive bulk of the machine hovering motionless just above the surface, Sandy listened on the directional mike to Jojo's steps and to his whistling, almost lost in the mulch of general background noise which resulted when the gain was turned up high. A hundred and fifty metres back up the road the second Gevcar had now come to a halt. Jock could see a head sticking out through the upper hatch, obviously engaged in scanning the nearby fields with binoculars, while Sandy abstractly registered the occasional comments coming in over the comm unit as she concentrated on the feed from the directional microphone.

Jojo came up to the first block and passed through, heading diagonally across the road towards the next one. 'So far so good, so far so good?' The refrain passing through his head as he walked on, still whistling. The second block passed uneventfully, accompanied by another warning sign. Back in the car, his figure, growing smaller in the distance seemed to pass in and out of focus as the drizzle lifted and returned, as though unwilling to depart the area.

'Stop!' The high-pitched command, shouted from somewhere near the third roadblock came as Jojo reached the next sign post, which carried an unequivocally clear message: 'You should obey instructions, otherwise you will soon be dead.' 'Right son' he muttered to himself, 'here's where you earn your keep.'

'Keep your hands in view at all times. Walk to the left hand side of the road, then advance slowly.' The voice continued, all echoes lost in the soft dampness of the air. A young boy's voice? A woman even? Jojo obeyed, slowly raising his hands straight above his head, strolling along as if that was exactly what he had intended all along, trying hard to see where the person giving the orders was hidden, though with the roadblock still at least a hundred paces away that was a difficult task.

'Tricky devil' he muttered, barely moving his lips, hoping that the mike he knew was pointing at him from the Gevcar, now well behind him, would pick him up. 'Dirty trick really, keeping me away from the safety of the ditch, can't say I blame them. I'd have done exactly the same.'

'What did he say?' Jock was leaning forward, trying to catch the sounds from the speaker.

'I think he was complementing them on being tricky,' replied Sandy as she inched the squelch dial round, trying to cancel out more of the background noise. 'After all, he put his hands straight up to indicate that he was obeying instructions but that he thought things were OK.' She reached for the intercom button and spoke softly to Matthew up in the turret. 'See anything Matt?'

'Nothing, I thought I could see movement a minute ago on the right-hand edge of the block, but to be honest I'm not sure. With this drizzle it's difficult to tell.'

Jojo continued to advance until he was within some three dozen metres of the block, nothing, the thought crossed his mind, a well thrown grenade couldn't cover. The same idea probably crossed someone else's mind, for he was ordered to halt, and then to sit down, keeping his hands above his head. From what he judged to be the right-hand side of the road a few metres in front of him a voice called out to him using clear unaccented Anglic.

'If you are carrying any concealed weapons you should say so now, later will be too late.' Definitely a woman's voice. Curiouser and curiouser thought Jojo, echoing the words of a long-forgotten fictional character.

'Only a knife on my left hip, the other stuff on my belt is harmless, water canteen, C-rations, and so on,' replied Jojo, still keeping his hands straight above his head, though he was beginning to feel the strain. 'Listen, I'm going to remove my knife and then leave my hands where you can see them, but I'm getting tired of waving them in the air,' and so saying he did exactly that, with a feeling that it was important that he keep the upper hand.

'Right, stand up again and face away from the wall, you will now be searched. Please remember that you will be covered at all times.'

As the speaker finished, a heavily garbed figure slid out from behind a bush just out of Jojo's field of vision off to the left and trotted over, slightly crouched, as though trying to present a smaller target. Jojo stood still while he was frisked, a good job, but he knew he could have slipped a small weapon through undetected.

'Follow me.' said the figure in a low almost inaudible murmur, and then it stepped back and trotted off to the right, jumping lightly over the ditch and stepping up to a half buried rock which emerged from the front of the roadblock. Much to Jojo's surprise, the rock swung aside, apparently without effort to reveal a cleverly concealed entrance, visible from where he now stood but not from farther back up the road.

'What a nice little cave' muttered Jojo, half turning his face towards the barely visible Gevcar, hoping that the directional mike would pick up enough to warn the others about the hidden entrance, as he ducked down into the doorway. As the rock slid into place behind him, he was filled with a momentary sensation of absolute stark terror as the walls soundlessly reached down to crush him, squeezing the breath from his labouring lungs. After a second or two during which he couldn't even move, save to reach out to steady himself, reason returned as the higher functions of his brain took over, pushing the primitive panic instinct into the background. He took a deep breath, and time resumed its normal pace once more. He stepped forwards following the retreating figure, now pulling away from him. The passage, which as far as he could judge led off at an angle away from the roadblock, was not entirely dark, for at intervals of fifty metres or so some sort of dim light fixture hung from the curved ceiling. After the third light, or perhaps it was the fourth, the passage curved round to the left, leading to a door behind which a set of stairs led upwards.

He emerged into another passage, this one obviously above ground. He followed the figure in front of him until they reached a wide arched doorway. The door swung open silently as they reached it, leading to a room with a large window looking onto a field dotted with the broken remains of some old constructions, now mostly overgrown. Outside the drizzle still fell, hiding the distance.

'You may sit.' The speaker was an old, wrinkled woman, sitting in a high-backed but comfortably cushioned chair covered by an embroidered shawl. A very old woman, Jojo thought, correcting his first impression.

'One hundred and seven, to be exact,' she said as though reading his thoughts. 'Over there,' pointing to a chair set at a small table off to one side of the window. Jojo walked slowly to the indicated place and sat, mentally estimating the distance to the old crone, though he didn't feel particularly threatened, and had no intention of trying to jump her before one of the others in the room could stop him.

'You'd never make it.' The voice became toneless, flat. She waved her hand vaguely indicating off to the opposite side of the room, now behind Jojo's back. He turned slowly in his seat, seeing for the first time the two very efficient looking crossbows that pointed in his direction, feeling the chill run up his spine. 'Damn but that old dame is sharp. You're slipping, me old son, slipping,' he thought to himself, and then abandoned such useless self recrimination as he examined the weapons with interest. Hand-powered they might be, but these were hi-tech versions of the old medieval invention. The difference was that with the strength of the high-tensile bow and the woven monofibre string, the hardened quarrel would go clean through a man's head, and then some.

'Not slipping, just tired perhaps,' the woman's voice sent a shock coursing through Jojo's veins, a shock he tried not to let her see in his eyes. A mindreader? Telepathic? He'd heard of such things, in fact Karel had been talking about that a few nights ago back at the Citadel. Abruptly he stopped and began to think nonsense thoughts.

'You're quite right Joseph, I can read superficial thoughts.' The old woman paused, obviously amused at Jojo's jaw, which had dropped when he heard his name mentioned. 'I don't make a habit of it, it's rather tiring.' She waved to the two assistants who held the crossbows. 'All right, you can go now, he means no harm.' The crossbows were lowered, but the two women remained where they were, still alert, ready to defend the old woman if necessary. She smiled, a trace of amusement drifting momentarily across her wrinkled face. 'Go. I'll be perfectly safe.' Turning to Jojo she said 'I may be their leader, but sometimes they treat me like a valuable piece of property with no mind of its own.' Jojo sat quietly for a moment watching her, now not so sure of what he was seeing, old? Yes, from all outward aspects, yet suddenly her bearing and movements were those of a much younger woman.

'I'm, ah, I don't know,' Jojo stuttered, trying to get his racing thoughts back into some semblance of order, 'I'm with friends, we're passing through. We mean you no harm, and if there's anything we can help you with we will.' He stopped suddenly unable to suppress the unbidden answer to something that had been bothering his subconscious since his arrival in the room. There were no men. No men at all. Was this old crone the leader? Whoops, he'd better be careful what he said, it was never a good idea to be offensive, even without meaning to, to those in positions of power. 'Excuse me, ah, umm, what do I call you?' He stopped, feeling almost embarrassed, imagining that his thoughts had been captured, rather like a small boy caught doing something he shouldn't.

'You may call me Tante, everyone else here does, even those I'm not biologically related to. I think before we continue talking it might be a good idea to go up to the road and call your friends in, they're probably getting worried by now. After that I'm sure we'll be able to satisfy your curiosity,' she observed, just a trace of humour touching her eyes.

Jojo thought for a moment assessing the possibility that the whole thing was a carefully set trap, but discarded the idea almost at once. His sixth sense indicated that that all the moves so far had been born of caution but were not hostile. He looked back at the woman again, made and held eye contact for a long second, and then nodded his head in agreement.

'Selena will take you back to the road again. We'll meet again in a while. Farewell.' The old woman, Tante? Didn't that mean something? The memory tickled somewhere in the back of Jojo's mind. Tante rose slowly from her chair, pushing it back and left the room, followed by one of the other five women who had remained after the guards left. Jojo looked around, scanning the four faces before him, waiting, the next move was now theirs. The youngest, a tall woman with hair the colour of ripe corn, taller than Jojo himself probably, nodded to him and indicated that he should follow, and then exited through the same door through which they had come in.

When they reached the exit to the road, she tugged at a lever set into the wall of the passageway well out of the normal field of vision, and the doorway slid open again. As they stepped out into the gentle drizzle, Selena turned to him and handed him back his knife.

'Tante says you're alright, so you can have this back.' She watched him for a second, her grey eyes giving nothing away, except perhaps, could it be, a trace of amusement? 'Come on Joseph, I'll walk with you.'

'Ah, look, call me Jojo will you, I've been called that for so long now that Joseph sounds wrong, OK?' She nodded, and together they set off down the road to where the Gevcar waited, barely visible through the thin curtain of the rain.

Jock leaned back in his chair, lowering the fine bone china cup to the saucer, a piece of china so thin that the shadow of the scented herbal tea remaining could clearly be seen even though the light in the room was not particularly bright.

'So, finding the Citadel deserted we decided, after, I might add, some discussion, to push on to the third Site. That, in a nutshell, more or less covers our story I think.' Karel, sitting beside him, holding another cup between his massive hands, enjoying the aroma drifting up, nodded his head, agreeing with Jock's story. The old woman, Tante as they begun to think of her, nodded her head slowly.

'I feel sure that there is still much to tell regarding your Hold, but that can wait. I imagine you are wondering who we are and why we are here.' She looked around, as though enjoying the attentive silence. 'Have any of you ever heard of the Übermorgen Foundation?' Without really waiting for an answer she continued talking, her eyes taking on a far away look as in her mind's eye she gazed back over the years. 'I don't suppose any of you were even born when the Foundation started up. Yet another of those California crank ideas,' she smiled softly. 'Only this one worked. After a fashion anyway. The Foundation was set up early in the eighties with the stated objective of improving resistance to disease through applied genetic engineering using donated human material. All quite true of course, but not the whole truth, not by a long stroke. The real work was to develop viable genetic clones with the objective of improving the race, the next step along the evolutionary ladder.'

'I read something a long time ago about that sort of thing,' observed Sandy. 'But I understood that that sort of work had been banned because of its racist aspects.'

'Oh yes, much of what we did was proscribed. The eternal human approach, ban what you fear, pretend it never existed. But we were never racist, we took samples, genetic material from anyone who possessed one of the characteristics we considered worth breeding for. Male, female, white, black, yellow, it made no difference to us. Our funding came from individuals who saw in our research a means to produce clones of themselves with the hope of transferring their mind, essence, call it what you will. Of such things are stories woven.

The idea of having a dormant clone on standby as it were had been around for a number of years, even at the end of the twentieth century. I'm afraid that it was never quite that simple. It took forty years to get somewhere close, but producing fully grown clones as replacement bodies, ready to be quickened when needed, remains fully in the realm of fiction. I joined the Foundation in the mid-nineties, ninety-four I think, soon after I graduated in micro-molecular genetics, a nice way of saying that I knew a pitifully small amount of theory and was totally lacking in practical experience. But, we worked at it, with the world crumbling around us, we worked on it. We moved up here after the West Coast riots of twenty-one, we felt we had become too visible as the cutting edge of nanogenetic technology. In this place, hidden away from the eyes and therefore the minds of the anti-science sects, we continued to work.' She laughed mirthlessly. 'The Luddites never did find us, they firebombed our old labs about three months after we left. There was great rejoicing that the great geneticist hell-hole had at last been wiped from the face of the earth. In fact all they destroyed was a carefully set up front of old and useless equipment we had purchased on the quiet and staffed with agency hirees. We started out redoing the original tissue work done by the old Roslin Institute in Edinburgh. We moved on to embryonic stem cells and by the mid-twenties we were growing organs from original genetic material and using them as transplants on anyone who needed them.' She stopped talking, reaching out for the glass that sat on the arm of the chair. She took a number of small sips, her hands quite steady, and continued her story.

'Five years after that we produced our first clone, the product of genetic material taken from twelve carefully screened donors. A healthy female baby, normal in every aspect, we named her Una. She walked at four months, spoke her first words at the end of her tenth month. At age three her IQ was 125, soon after that it was high enough to be meaningless. We cared for her, cherished her and she grew up with us. In all aspects a great success. Physically she was also outstanding, she was never ill, her reaction times were quite extraordinary. In her the Foundation achieved its goal.'

'What became of her?' Threejays asked from across the room. 'I sense that you are talking of her in the past.'

'Oh, no, not at all. Una, and her sisters for that matter, are fine. I am an old lady now, and most things are in the past to me, though I fully expect to be able to continue for several more decades.' She glanced at her guests. 'I can see you looking sceptical, don't be deceived by my apparent cosmetic age, I like it this way, though it wouldn't be too complicated to make me look much younger if I so wished it. Some of us do, and some of us don't.'

'You can adjust your cosmetic age?' Sandy leaned forward. 'At first thought that's rather a shock, but I suppose not altogether surprising. I read something about that in the Records back at the Hold while searching for something else.' Sandy stopped, still watching their host. 'But I still have another question. Why are you all female? Is that adjustable as well?'

Tante smiled, a trace of bitterness evident in the gesture. 'I imagined that someone would eventually ask that. Several of you, starting with Jos ... Jojo have wondered about that. We do in fact have some males here in the Foundation though you may not have crossed paths with any yet.'

When I said our techniques worked after a fashion, I meant exactly that. You see, in theory we can produce male or female clones at will. In practice no viable male clone has survived much beyond a couple of months, after that they all suffer from an extremely rapid ageing process which destroys them in a few weeks. Even with all our skills we haven't been able to solve the problem yet. We believe it to be related to the fact that certain DNA strands are more susceptible than others to various toxins, toxins now found everywhere, including the tissues of the cell donors.' She took a deep breath, tightened her lips for a second before continuing. 'We are scientists here, not monsters, after the sixth failure we took the decision not to go beyond cellular experimentation before solving the problem. We are still working on a number of promising options, at least we now have the problem isolated down to two gene sets.' She rubbed her forehead, as though searching for a lost idea. 'Our puzzle now is why in natural births there is still a fair proportion of males, quite a bit lower than fifty percent certainly, but still appreciable, while we are unable to clone any successfully.' The Hold people who had been sitting around the large comfortable room listening to the old woman's story seemed suddenly to realize the implication of what they had just heard about the clones. They looked around at the two dozen or so women who had joined them, none of whom appeared to them to be much over twenty-five or thirty. The old lady in turn watched them for a moment.

'Yes, you're right. Some of them are. All different, conceived *in vitro*, and grown in the amino tanks until physically viable.' She gazed around, sensing the uneasiness in the visitors and then continued talking. 'The process of growth is entirely natural, only the gene selection is artificial. In an earlier age they would have been reviled as constructs, abominations, but to me they are our sisters. They offer us some small hope of continuity. Mankind has done a fine job of destroying itself in the last century. Here at the Foundation we hold out the hope of immortality, not for ourselves of course, but at least for our genetic material. Of those who were originally here on the staff of the Foundation, only twenty-five remain, including myself. We have another 672 people here, some are our children and grandchildren, others came to us over the years, but many of them have been cloned. They are fully human and in every sense they too are our children. Out of the total, only a 145 are male, and many of those are people who drifted in over the years.'

Jock Fernan who had been sitting near the back of the room next to a window looking out down to a small semicircular cove, watching the play of the waves as they came and went on the beach, now stood up and spoke quietly. As ever, despite being a relatively short man, his deep gravely voice gave him a natural authority which commanded immediate respect.

'I am sure that I speak for all of us when I say that as far as we are concerned what you have done is admirable. Please believe me when I say that we are not shocked by what you have done, though perhaps at first thought we are slightly uncomfortable with the idea of beating nature at her own game, but that is all. We have our own achievements, we have met others along the way who have also held out against the Fall. We too have used technology to survive, I cannot fault you for what you have done, quite the contrary. I hope that eventually you will be able to meet up with our own biotechnicians, we have worked more in the area of food growth genetics than with human cloning, but I'm sure there will be common ground.' He smiled. 'Enough said on that topic for the moment I think, one thing I really would like to hear more about is how you managed to survive all these years here without being attacked.'

'When the Foundation first came here, we put it out that we were part of a religious order building a retreat. At that time the town was already half deserted so we had no trouble from the locals. We were

193

able to grow some food during the summer months up in the valley, and the rest came from our laboratories. About ten or perhaps eleven years after we arrived a large slice of what had become the Californian Republic coastal area was wiped out when the Oakland fault cut loose. After that there were fewer and fewer visitors from the south, and we became more and more self reliant. We set up defences, you saw some of them on the way in, but basically we just kept a very low profile.

'You say much of the coastline was wiped out by a big quake?' Karel sat forward. 'I never knew that. 'It must have been after we landed.'

'Landed? We?' It was Tante's turn to look puzzled.

'Captain Karel Houseman, late of the European Space Corps at your service,' Karel bowed slightly, obviously enjoying himself. His bright blue eyes, highlighted more than ever by the tanned skin and by the scar on his face, seemed to sparkle with some inner amusement. 'And let me introduce you to Sandy Cook, communications and telemetry specialist, Copernicus mission, 2024.'

'Copernicus ... I remember, you had some trouble with the groundstation and had to delay your return to Earth. Some anti-technology group attacked something or other, I never heard anything more after that.'

'Yes well, that would fill a book all by itself, but I interrupted your story, please go on.'

'Where was I? The Oakland fault. ... It really was the big one, a few years late according to the doomsday millennium fanatics, but it eventually arrived. Nobody really knows how many people were lost during the quake and its aftermath, but I would guess not less than forty million.' She stopped, looking somehow weighed down. 'The numbers are meaningless, but of course you know that already. We lost much of the most productive area of the west coast. A number of other faults cut loose in sympathy, and at the end of the day a strip of coastline some forty miles wide and four hundred long had changed shape forever. Some of it disappeared into the sea, including much of the Bay area, new land emerged forming islands, slopes were levelled, and flat land looked as if a giant had crumpled it in a fit of anger. So, here far away from the worst of it we set up defences as well as we could. We took some light damage, but nothing that couldn't be repaired, and basically battened down the hatches as it were. We were incredibly lucky that none of the major northern faults went. With the Cascades just a few klicks away to the north, there was every chance of that happening, but even the volcanoes remained quiet. We heard that Mount Hood had blown its top off, but as the wind was blowing inland we got none of the ash fall so we never knew about it until years later. Over the years a number of small roving and disorganized bands attacked us, on several occasions we lost some people, but we were able to beat them off, not an easy task for a bunch of research scientists, I might add. If they had got together it might have gone differently, as it was we were able to defeat them thanks to being well armed and prepared. We have made the surrounding area look as uninviting as possible, and as you can imagine there are few enough visitors nowadays. We do still take in stray people who wander in by accident, but you are the first real visitors we've received in a long time, three or even four years probably. Yes, we have survived, our logistics haven't always been easy, protein mash from the food vats may be healthy enough, but it's not very appetizing, and there's always the problem of trace minerals. We used to have supplement pills, but they ran out a long time ago, nowadays we use a mix of natural salts.'

'What about vitamins?' asked Janine, 'have you managed to solve that problem?'

'Oh yes, we can synthesize practically all the necessary vitamins, and those that are missing are supplied by the fruits and vegetables we grow up the valley. Was that a problem for you in your Hold?'

'As far as I know it never was, we still have plenty of mineral tablets, but we grow much of what we eat in hydroponic gardens where we fertilize appropriately, and we also have a vitamin synthesis plant.'

Tante talked on as the evening fell, telling of the years of hardship the Foundation had gone through, of the successes and the failures. Much of what she told was a repeat of what Karel and Sandy had seen for themselves in other places during their wanderings after leaving Mendoza. For the Hold people it was in a sense new, although the communications monitoring systems had told them much of what had happened over the years, the story was different when told by someone who had lived through the collapse.

One of the current worries in the Foundation was the lack of balance in the sexes, for with only female clones being viable, the only source of new male blood other than by traditional births was the Outside, at least until the genetic problems were solved. The current balance was around five to one, as a result of which many of the old social conventions regarding formal couples had eroded away, giving rise to a more flexible concept of partners and extended families. In fact, the matter was further complicated, or eased, according to how one looked at it, by the cloned children who grew up in the knowledge that they had ten or twelve parents who they could rely on. With such a small gene pool to draw from, the geneticists were particularly careful in allowing natural births, for the threat of a negative reinforcement was always present in the background.

In the morning, after a breakfast of fresh fruits, Erik, Sanjay and some of the others including Karel and Sandy visited the laboratories. The Hold medical staff had made a number of medical advances over the years, particularly in the field of tissue replacement where they had managed to produce a universally acceptable skin graft for use in dealing with accident or burn victims. Here in the Foundation the field of nanogenetics had been taken orders of magnitude further down the line. Finally, and after visiting several labs filled with flasks filed with incomprehensible sensors, the visitors stood in awed silence in front of a glass-sided tank resting on a massive black marble table. Inside the tank, eyes closed, a perfectly formed human baby floated suspended in a pale green fluid. As if sensing their presence the embryo moved slightly, shifting its position, the head turning towards them, a tiny hand unclenching and reaching out towards them. Tante stepped up to the tank, reaching out her own hand, and as the hands touched, separated by the layer of glass, the baby's eyes snapped open, unfocussed for a moment and then changing to stare at Tante and the Hold visitors. The tiny mouth moved, forming a smile of welcome as a feeling of warmth and contentment washed over them all and then vanished, abruptly as it had come, leaving them wondering whether it had ever been.

Chapter XIV

The breeze blew gently offshore as they walked along the steep beach a few metres above the high water mark. Overhead a small flock of seagulls swooped, flitting over the waves, rising and falling in unison with the grey frothing surface of the water over which they flew. Karel shaded his eyes as he turned to watch the gulls, his eyes squinting behind the glare specs at the unaccustomed brightness of the yellowish sun which gazed down from an almost cloudless sky. As if to flaunt his grey mane, bound with a stained band at the nape of his neck, the hood of his cloak was pushed back. Tante walking beside him wore a wide-brimmed hat, tied down with a strap which ran down under her chin, keeping it safely in place despite the best efforts of the wind.

'The procedure is quite painless, we use a local spray anaesthetic to numb the area before carrying out the procedure. You won't even notice the implant after a couple of hours. Believe me, this is our stock in trade, and we're very good at it.'

'Of that I have little doubt,' retorted Karel. 'It just seems extraordinary that you can take a man's cells, modify them genetically, and then replace them and in effect add two score more years to his span. Somehow it seems like cheating the clock.'

'Cheating? No of course not, we're not taking anything away from anyone, it's your own genetic material which we grow as stem cells and then replace in whatever part needs them, having first removed the ageing proteins of course.'

'But as I understand it, these new cells won't grow forever, I mean the effect will be temporary.'

'As I said earlier, this isn't the door to immortality, not by a long stroke. We can slow down and even reverse the process for specific organs, but after a time nature takes over again. All we are doing is buying time. Of course, in theory we can repeat the process time after time, but don't forget each set of cells is for a particular organ, or a piece of tissue or bone. This isn't a whole body treatment, you're only getting an implant with twelve specific cell types, heart, lungs, liver, kidneys, and so on. Eventually things will decay to such a point where we can't keep up any longer. Look at me, I've got at least five decades to go, but eventually all the ...,' she paused, 'repairable ... parts will have been treated, but the rate of decay will be such that further treatment will be useless. Unless of course we make some startling breakthrough, but I don't think that that is a realistic expectation. We've some fine equipment, we've made some improvements, but unless we get some industrial backing things will eventually fall apart.'

They continued walking in silence, Karel's mind still full of the offer Tante had made him. To be young again, well, to have a rejuvenated heart at any rate, an improved immune system, to be able to hear the high notes again, it seemed like something out of a fantasy novel. And yet, here beside him walked a woman who was 107 years old, and within the old shell which she kept from choice, her body would be good for another fifty or more years. It was an incredible thought.

'You know of course that in the Hold almost all the old technology is available? They can design and build literally anything, at least within certain size and weight limits, Jock can arrange for all this to be available to the Foundation. We spoke yesterday with the Council using the Sentry link we told you about, and they are delighted with this new contact. After fifty years of looking inwards, the Hold is now awake and active. Even if the search for the third Survival Centre fails, the Hold will go on, now with a heightened sense of purpose. The Gevcar technology will ensure that they keep on searching, and they already know where you and the Cape crowd are. I think at last we have reached the point of inflection and that the Fall is over.'

'I hope you're right Karel. I too feel optimistic about this new stage, we have much in common, but even more to offer each other. Yes, maybe you're right.'

Again they walked in silence, stopping occasionally to look at some object that the tide had left deposited on the rough, sandy beach, a curiously shaped log, a brightly coloured seashell, pieces of kelp, darkened and squishy, but none of the innumerable man-made objects they both remembered from childhood holidays at the beach. After a while Karel stopped, gazing out to sea. Finally he turned to Tante and began to speak slowly, as though feeling his way through unknown territory.

'Jojo spoke with Jock and myself about his first meeting with you.

At first we found it hard to give credence to his story, but after some thought on the matter I now believe him to have been telling the absolute truth, although part of the story was pretty unlikely,' Karel paused for breath, but was interrupted before he could go on.

'I wondered when you were going to bring the matter up.' She paused, 'Jojo did of course tell you the truth, after all, why would he hide the matter? Science and inheritance can do strange things when they work together. Let me sum up matters for you, then if there are any questions, I'll be happy to answer them. We have no secrets we need to hide, least of all from you people.' Seeing Karel's assenting nod, she went on. 'Some time ago during one of the early implant sessions when we were working with memory retention cells, we noticed that after each session we began to have very limited telepathic abilities. Nothing spectacular, but the three of us who had the transplants found we were often able to guess what someone was going to say, that sort of thing. We ran all sorts of tests with mixed results, some days we were scoring well above average, others just normal. We isolated the gene group that seemed to be responsible and did another implant, and then another, and it worked, though not for everyone. I have certain abilities that seem to be permanent now, with training I have improved them. I believe these were latent abilities which most of us have to some degree, the treatment merely heightens the faculty, brings it to the surface as it were.'

'You can read minds then? Quite an achievement. What about other psychic abilities, telekinesis, teleportation, and so on?'

Tante laughed. 'You must have read too many sci-fi books as a child. I can read superficial thoughts, but only if the person is unaware of my doing so, as soon as they realize what's going on the jumble of emotions effectively blocks any further contact. To some degree I can sense moods, call it a sense of heightened empathy. With some of the others we can even exchange information over a distance, a relatively slow process and with considerable mental effort, a phone call would be easier, assuming we had phones to start with.' She laughed. 'That's where the training comes in. As for the rest, no. None of us can move objects through space, nor transport ourselves, or anything like that.'

'That's not all you've done though.' It was a statement, not a question. Karel stood watching her eyes unblinking. 'The other day in the lab, the clone ... the child ...' He left the sentence hanging, begging a reply. Tante allowed a small gesture to escape her, a sort of apologetic, maybe even regretful shrug.

'We have tried to make our new sisters better than ourselves or the ones before. We look for intelligence, for physical health, resistance to diseases, for beauty, for strength and agility, for longevity, and of course for telepathic abilities. Leana, the baby you saw in the tank, has already demonstrated some amazing talents. Her education has already begun. I talk to her almost daily, so do some of the other telepaths we have. We teach her about the world, nature, science, about our society and about people, her capacity is amazing, she keeps asking for more, and because we don't want to overload her we limit the amount of information we give her at a go.'

'Is she the first?'

'No, but certainly she's the most powerful. You felt her reach out to greet you all, her empathy with others is almost overwhelming.' Tante looked quizzically at Karel. 'She said that she would like to meet with you when she leaves the tank, she wanted you to share your experiences in space with her.'

'She wanted to what?' Karel's voice carried a high note of shock. 'How can she possibly know about that?'

'I think that probably she represents the next step for humanity. No doubt it will be a long time before the whole race carries her genes, but the time will come. You will speak with her?' A tone almost pleading.

'I can hardly refuse, you have made your knowledge available to help me, but in all honesty, even if that were not the case, I would still do so, if nothing else because of my insatiable curiosity.' Karel laughed, a laugh echoed by Tante.

'You'll have to be careful about that, a long time ago, at least a century before I was born, there was a story about insatiable curiosity, something about how the elephant got his trunk.'

They walked back towards the Foundation buildings, talking amiably about a variety of subjects, but mostly about Karel and Sandy's adventures during their search for the Hold, a topic which fascinated Tante, who for all her own adventures had spent a very static life in comparison. The sun now almost overhead, for it was coming up to noon, still shone from a cloud-free sky, and the gulls, which had soared and swooped with such abandon, had now vanished, driven to their places of shelter by the high uvee levels. A prime example of a species adapting to changes in the environment in order to survive. The two humans also took care, Karel with the hood of his cloak now drawn over his face, and Tante with the brim of the hat curled down to give as much shade as possible. When they reached the maintenance building, they found Herb and David sitting amid what appeared to be pieces of a machine that had exploded, both wearing magnifying lenses strapped on their heads, happily chatting away in an improbable mix of Anglic and technobabble to several of the Foundation staff, including some of the men. Seeing Karel approaching, Herb got to his feet and came over, face alight with the satisfaction of doing a technical job again.

'My word, Karel, you can't imagine the ideas I've got for improving the handling of the sterile incubation tank waldo. I can modify the logic circuits to the servos, and remove a whole section of the extension without sacrificing any performance. The thing is miles behind what we have back in the Hold ...'

'Come on Herb, stop wandering off, I've not got all day holding this terminal board you know' called David, enjoying the possibility of nagging his senior, and getting a laugh from the rest of the group.

'Ah, well, I can see we're not really wanted here' grinned Karel as he and Tante continued on their way towards the main complex.

The bright beam of the theatre lights clicked off, and the two surgeons turned away, beginning to strip off their gloves. Karel lay quietly for a moment, not dizzy or anything, but mildly sedated from the local anaesthetic he had received while the implant was placed in his chest. He decided after a moment that he felt no different, no younger. And why should he, after all, it was only slightly modified pieces of himself that had been implanted. The whole procedure had taken sixteen days, starting with a blood sample as well as some skin scrapings which had been processed by the gene-splicing technicians, and the resulting hybrid cells force grown in a nutrient vat. In theory, so he had been told, it would be possible to grow a clone to full maturity, but of course it wouldn't be him, just a genetic twin who would, if quickened, acquire its own distinct personality. Karel could see the dangers involved in thinking that it would be possible to grow an unquickened clone to maturity and keep it as a spare parts bank. Or worse, as a vacant seat in which to transfer the mind and personality, although the Foundationers assured him that such a concept was still so far out of reach that it wasn't even worth wasting time discussing the ethics of the matter. Still, the idea was rather frightening. He shook his head clearing away such thoughts, returning to the present.

Within a couple of days it would be Sandy's turn for an implant. They had talked it over for a couple of days before making up their minds, but if they were honest, neither of them had felt any serious doubts. As was natural, their ... what could one call it? ... sense of wonder, joy of living, whatever it might be, which had accompanied them throughout their travels triumphed over the idea that they should simply live out the years they were given. Sure, one had to play the deck of cards as they were dealt, but if you could sometimes get hold of the Joker and change the rules, well, why not?

Life was made up of millions of small coincidences, this place, this time around, it all seemed to fit together. After the first few hours, Karel had been only mildly surprised at how well the Hold visitors had fitted in at the Foundation. Gears meshing. Despite totally different backgrounds and social contexts, they found a surprising degree of coincidence in the way they looked at the world, and in the deeply rooted belief of service to the larger community of humanity. The intervening years after the Fall had taken them down different paths. In the Hold along the way of the hard sciences, from machinery, engineering and on to advanced physics, in the Foundation on the other hand, the concept of moulding body and mind into a single superior entity through advanced medical and genetic techniques had prevailed. Both these societies had turned inwards, protecting their knowledge and themselves. Now, after almost two generations once more they were looking to the world, inspired more than anything else by the thought of what Karel and Sandy had been through to reach this point in time.

Yesterday, on the roof of one of the storage buildings, he had seen Jean Klock, helped by the Techs as well as by the Foundation maintenance crew, setting up a satellite dish they had found down in the town and with much trouble disassembled and transported up to where it was being rebuilt. Both of the communications specialists were certain that they could set up enough equipment to enable full and permanent communications with the Hold over the Sentry link. Both Sandy and Jean had never quite ceased to worry that the Sentry satellite might fail, leaving them without any means of direct communication, but they accepted that there was not much that they could do about the problem. Before leaving the Hold they had traced out the orbital paths of the Sentry satellites which had once comprised and important part of the NAF defence system. Sixteen high-orbit satellites, eight for each hemisphere, each with a footprint covering from a latitude of fifty-five degrees to over thirty-five degrees into the opposite hemisphere, a footprint a couple of thousand klicks wide. To date and in addition to the original Sentry, they had only managed to obtain a short-lived contact with one of them out over the Pacific, which left them no nearer having some sort of backup link with the Hold. Some day in the future, probably via the Cape, they would regain the capacity for launching new and even better satellites, for the moment however they would have to continue to steal help from the past. Of course they could still set up a very poor and scratchy short wave link, which unfortunately had the handicap of being available to anyone who happened to be listening in on the same wavelength. Meanwhile, they had slipped back into the old routine of a daily noon contact with the Hold during which news and more often than not gossip were exchanged. The conversations had become three and sometimes four way affairs, for now not only was the Cape taking part, but also Tumbes had come on the air with the aid of the Hold Techs who had arrived there after an almost trouble-free trip using the newly built Gevcar. That event had occurred while they had been out of touch beyond the footprint searching the remains of the Citadel. What a milestone, yes, what a milestone, a new city joining up represented a turning point in the affairs of men, for again it was time to build. Communications of course would be the key to the new beginning. If only they had been able to avail themselves of the facilities the Sentry's offered while searching for the Hold. They had had to rely on short-range hand-held comm units, and all too often the damn things went on the blink, always at the worst possible moment.

He could picture in his mind's eye as clearly as if it were yesterday. After five days searching, there they were at last, Jose and Susanne waving their jackets and jumping up and down. Jose had been holding the comm in his hand and kept pointing at it, as though wanting Karel or Sandy two hundred metres away across the river to talk to them. They had driven the electrotrike back to the half-broken bridge half a klick away and, with considerable difficulty, driven over it to meet up with the others. Jose had arrived, panting, dragging an exhausted Susanne behind him, leapt onto the trike and yelled to Karel to get out of the area. They had made it out, but only just. Jose had found the locals to be extremely unfriendly and had been hiding out waiting for Karel to show, unable to call him on the broken comm unit. Yes, if only they'd had the Sentry as backup, it could have saved them an awful lot of risks. Sandy and Jean had high hopes for the Sentry over the Pacific, certainly its footprint should cover at least the eastern half of Australia giving them a direct link to the Hold. Of course the two comm specialists were more ambitious than that, they wanted to get the orbiting cameras working again, that would give them weather coverage over half the world, what a dream. Well, whatever happened, they would go on. To give up now was unthinkable, more so after the failure of the Centre, the last Survival Centre of the trio just had to be intact and working, yes, it had to be. The Hold scientists too had become immersed in the ongoing projects within a couple of days of arriving, most specially Lee Sun Yan whose field of expertize tallied closely with the genetic work going on here, though as she admitted, it was like a primary school student trying to understand university level science.

Karel's eyelids fluttered, blinking repeatedly as he started to sit up. The med-bed behind him folding up to accompany the movement, then stopped as he lay back, realizing that he wasn't over the effect of whatever it was they'd given him. The bed sensing his change of mind slid back, leaving him in a comfortable half-elevated position. He blinked again, aware now that his mind had been wandering a bit. He looked over at Sandy, sitting quietly across the room watching him, the ever-present stray lock of grey hair curling down over her forehead. She absently pushed it back, a movement so familiar and yet so personal that it triggered in Karel a sense of immense yearning, bringing a lump to his throat. As though sensing this, his partner came over to the bed and gripped his hand, a sharing that the years together had brought them, a giving and a taking of strength. He relaxed again, smiling.

'Roll on the next seventy-six,' the white bushy eyebrows twitched. 'We've piles of time now.'

'Oh, yes my love, all the time in the world now, thanks to the Foundation. I'm looking forward to mine. Mmm, you know, it's almost seventy-seven, isn't it?'

'Aye, I suppose so ... I seem to have been away a bit, sorry. A funny feeling, things seemed terribly confusing for a while, time out of joint, but now they're clear again.'

'Yes, the medics said the anaesthetic might have a mildly narcotic effect on you. Apparently some of the components in it were originally synthesized from mushrooms. You were mumbling away about Jose and Susanne, I think it was about the time we got cut off near ...' Sandy paused, annoyed at herself for not being able to remember the place. 'Blast, I must be needing the implant ... Natal, that's it! We only just got away that time. The medics said you can eat something light if you want. Anything you fancy?'

'Only you my love, only you.' He lay back, relaxing, and the bed, obedient as ever to his needs, slid down. 'But later, now I think I'll just sleep a bit.' Sandy sat quietly beside him, feeling the hand twitch for a while and then relax as Karel slipped into a deep sleep. Was it her imagination, or did the long thin scar seem to be fading, impossible of course, nothing could work that fast. He had got that while defending her from a rather angry cannibal somewhere on the outskirts of the ruins of Sao Paulo, and it would stay with him forever. After a while she got up quietly, and after adjusting the light blanket over his chest, left the room.

They sat in a loose semicircle round the briefing board, Threejays as usual had been assigned to present the planning. Several of the Foundationers had joined them, curious to hear what was being planned. Jojo, feeling rather self-conscious sat with Selena beside him, a condition which had become increasingly frequent over the previous week or ten days. They made an unusual combination, he half a head shorter and broad to match, still looking a lot older than he really was, even after the rejuve implant, while she looked childlike and vulnerable. That impression was definitely misleading, for Jojo had seen her practising with the crossbow and her aim and speed were remarkable. A few days after their arrival at the Foundation, Jojo had chanced across Selena and had got talking to her, shyly at first for he was a man of few words. Somewhere a chord was struck, and the friendship blossomed. She was fascinated with his practical no nonsense approach to life, a technique acquired long before he wandered into the Cape at the age of seventeen, already a battle-hardened veteran. He in turn was charmed by her youth and vitality, which coupled with her extraordinary intelligence and naïveté, made her a continuously interesting person to be with.

The developing relationship had not escaped notice, to the point that Karel and Jock who had spent some time talking about possible changes in the composition of the group which would go on to Australia, included her in their short list of possible acquisitions.

They had also at long last found with Tante's help a suitable replacement for Patric in the form of Alexandra Lowe, a middle-aged woman who in fact was at least two decades older than she looked. Both Karel and Jock had been greatly relieved when the Foundation had agreed to help them find a suitable science specialist, for much of what they saw on the journey, and in particular the mutational capacity of the uvee and other radiation on plant life, needed a specialists interpretation which none of the original crew could supply.

'With the fresh information we have, it now seems that this is as good a starting point as we'll find. We had originally planned to continue down the coast until somewhere near the point where the over water trip to the Hawaiian islands is as short as possible. Unfortunately the post-earthquake coastline further south from here bears little resemblance to our maps.'

'How much does it really matter?' asked Petra, 'I mean, we've often gone through uncharted territory. And probably will again.'

'True, but given that we have absolutely no charts at all, I think that the benefits of leaving from Coos Bay outweigh the extra klicks over water.'

'What is the exact distance?'

'As best as we can calculate, the shortest distance run is 3,860 klicks. At ninety knots we can cover that distance in under twenty-four hours. ... Quite a thought isn't it?' There was a silence, a silence which stretched as people thought about the distance and the risks. Threejays continued talking.

'Of course we have no way of knowing if the weather will allow us to travel all that way at that speed. Quite likely it won't, and the trip may take two or three times as long. But there is no doubt, no doubt at all that the Gevcars can make this trip. The Gevcars are better than any boat or ship ever built. Even without power they'd be able to float safely, and that is an unlikely event. No storm however big could sink them, however uncomfortable we might feel inside, we can seal up and the life-support system is good for at least a week.'

'You know my feelings about going on,' Alice Folsom spoke up from where she sat, looking upset but defiant. She glanced across at Jules, as though seeking support. 'I can't go on. I want to go back to the Hold, this is all too much for me. I've spoken to Tante, she says I can stay here for now. Eventually someone from the Hold will get here.' She broke down, head held in her hands sobbing quietly. Jules

Borman who had expressed such strong feelings about not going on earlier looked over at Brendt and then stood up.

'I know that a few days ago I spoke out against going on. I don't know what happened to me, I can't explain it, but I've spoken to Brendt and Bob and I surely want to be part of the team which goes on.' He walked across to Alice and touched her shoulder. 'Alice love, I'm sorry I can't stay with you, but I've got to go on ...' He patted her shoulder and walked back to where he had been sitting. Jock rose to his feet and walked up to stand beside Threejays.

'Look people, if there is anyone else who has serious doubts about coming with us, now is the moment to decide. You can stay here in the Foundation until such time as a Hold crew gets here. I estimate that will be in a cycle at the earliest, but not later than sixteen moons according to the way the new Gevcar development is going. Let me know before the end of the day please. Carry on Threejays.'

'Several of you have been asking about the situation in the Hawaiian islands. Unfortunately we have very little information. The old reports we have from the Records say that Hawaii itself was evacuated in twenty-seven after a major earthquake and eruption which ripped the top of Mauna Loa, that's the major peak, and dropped much of the western side of the island into the sea. Oahu was hit by the Chinese back in twenty-one, and between the typhus A pandemic and the heavy fighting most of Honolulu and Pearl Harbour were destroyed. What happened after that is anyone's guess as there were no further data items other than some annotations which said that it was believed that several low-yield tactical neutron bombs were dropped once the NAFDEF forces had been evacuated. Whatever the case may be, we'll stay clear of that area. Maui or Molokai seem to be the best spots to aim for, at least we have no negative reports about them, the population was lower to start with ...'

'Why bother to go there at all?' Sara Mesada asked, looking mildly surprised at herself, her golden hair glinting redly in the light of the sun which shone through the plate window. 'After all, both Herb and David have said that there's enough fuel for a couple of years, so what's the problem of going on for a week or two without stopping?'

'Let me answer some of that please, Threejays,' said Maria, interrupting Threejays who had begun to open her mouth to reply. 'Of course it may be possible to do as you propose, but you have to remember that the pilots need to rest, even working in shifts the watches have to be kept, and there's no real need to push everyone to the limit. The islands are pretty much on the route, so even if we lose a few days looking around there's no big problem. The main point here is that we'll all get a chance to get out and stretch our legs, instead of being cramped up in the cars. OK?'

The briefing continued for another two hours with the planned route across the Pacific being mapped out and discussed. They worked as a team, Janine handled the logistical problems, Sandy and Jean setting up the communications schedules, Herb, David and Petra worked out the duty watches. Alice now fully committed to staying on still sat with them but took little part in the discussions. The co-pilot's seat would they had decided be taken by Matt, while Selena, the girl who had originally led Jojo into the Foundation, would be joining them for the rest of the trip and would be paired with Erik as a member of the medical team, while Maria Sanches switched to Jock's car. The last remaining item on the agenda was to set a departure date, a date by which all of the crew who wished to would have had their implant. Thus, after further discussion, a conditional departure date of 8 July was set, almost exactly seven moons since they left the Hold, weather and other conditions permitting of course.

Evenings were the best time. With the deep purple of the sun's swollen belly beginning to kiss the haze blurred horizon, the need for glare specs and hoods lessened. In the long summer twilight, the day's dying light shifted down through shades of red and purple leaving a wine red afterglow with the thin wispy clouds high in the sky reflecting some light down to the earth. It was a time for swimming in the sea, even a time for surfing on the breakers when the waves weren't too fierce. It was a time for taking up the long lost art of beach combing, and a time for lying on the still warm sand, relaxing after the day's work was done, enjoying the fulfilment of doing nothing.

Bob slowed his trot to a walk, breath coming in gasps. After the three-klick run, Janine was now fifty paces ahead of him and drawing effortlessly away, a reddened image on the paler coloured sand of the beach. He had always considered himself to be fairly fit, it had been part of his Watch training, but Janine was something else, a natural athlete, every part of her perfectly conditioned. Matt too was ahead of him, just a dozen paces behind the girl, but still unable to catch up with her despite his youth. Realizing without having looked back that he had given up, she turned and trotted back moving gracefully like a huntress, nothing to show of the hard muscle rippling under the silky skin, the subtle movement of her shirt holding the promise of wonders within. Jojo, Selena and half a dozen others came down from the dunes where they had been sitting, backs to the Foundation buildings, to join the runners.

'Lazy devil, I could do better than that on one leg' called Erik, laughing as he arrived at the bottom of the hill. Even in the poor light it was possible to see that there was noticeably less grey hair in his goatee than two weeks earlier, one of the early visible effects of the implant.

'Yeah, sure,' retorted Bob, 'specially if I was crawling.'

'Children, children,' interrupted Jock, joining the fun, 'some of us were born to run faster than others, those of us with shorter legs will just have to make do by thinking harder.' He grinned in response to the laugh, running his hand over his scalp, feeling the unaccustomed presence of the soft yet bristly growth for the first time in several decades. No one else he was sure had noticed the reddish fuzz so far, but he had decided to speak with the geneticists to see if it could be inhibited, the truth was he was quite happy to be totally bald, and didn't see any need for a growth of hair, although he quite enjoyed its effect on other people.

All of the Hold crew had opted for the implants. They were after all a pragmatic people, not given to profound philosophical analyses, a people who accepted that science could be used for both good and evil. But, went the basic reasoning, in a world which suffered from severe underpopulation, and which desperately needed help to get going again, by no stretch of the imagination could there be any damage to others by extending one's own life span. On the contrary it would allow those in a position to help others to do so over a more extended period of time. The Elders in the Hold, when told of the developments over the Sentry link-up, had been cautiously pleased by the news that man was no longer limited to a useful life of nine or ten decades. They saw clearly the dangers of nanogenetics, and also the potential advantages, and of course the implicit power in handling the technology. Tante herself had approached Jock and Karel with her worries on the subject.

'We have developed a technique which is available to anyone here without exception,' she had said, 'we have offered it to you, we shall continue to offer it to anyone, regardless of who they are, barring only obvious misfits, criminals and deviants. Sooner or later there will be those who have received implants and those who haven't, and this will unfortunately be inevitable because we don't possess enough capacity for treating large numbers of people. I want to make it absolutely clear to you, however, that this development must not be used as a weapon, or as a means of suppressing a group, or tribe or sect. Mankind has shown enough barbarity this century without adding more to it. We must do everything in our power to build, not to destroy.'

Jock and Karel without needing any time for further thought, had fully concurred with her opinion, and Jock had explained in even more detail the objectives laid down by the Founders of the Hold. Additionally, he had repeated Karel's earlier offer, placing the vast resources available in the Hold at the behest of the Foundation to extend and if possible improve on the techniques and technology they had developed, should they wish to do so. It was abundantly clear that while the Foundation was streets ahead in the field of genetics and in particular in cloning techniques, the Hold however had retained a far wider range of technologies, many of which would be essential if the discoveries were not to be lost, either by accident or by some external event.

As darkness closed over them, and the last of the day's light was swallowed by the ever-moving ocean, they lit a bonfire and sat around it watching the sparks fly upwards on a journey leading only to their dissolution. The swimmers, back from the sea, crouched near, turning round and round in front of the fire, driving out the cold. Karel and Sandy came down after a while and sat with the group, enjoying the warm sense of camaraderie, a rare privilege in a world turned upside down. Even Lee Sun Yan had joined them, an unusual occurrence since she had vanished to spend most of her time working in the genetics labs, attempting to think of ways in which the new techniques developed by the Foundation could be applied to her own work on genetics which she had been working on in the Hold. Finally, when the chill of the evening reminded them that it was late, the group gathered up their belongings and made their way back over the dunes to the buildings, dim shapes moving through the darkness.

Yes, thought Karel as they walked up over the dunes, evenings were definitely the best time, when for a brief moment they were able to forget the harsh world around them, something that had not been possible since leaving the Hold.

[Extract – 2024]

(The following reports are excerpts from the minutes of the Site 3 Steering Committee meeting held on 2 July 2024. It is to be noted that all records related to 1 January 2018 to 31 December 2025 have been classified as restricted and can only be accessed with the authorization of the Council of Elders.)

The removal of any documents from the Records Hall or the copying of any information relating to this period is strictly forbidden.

Phase IV Construction Contract Report: Work for Phase IV is proceeding within the Masterplan Time Schedule, albeit with some minor delays due to missing materials related to ancillary systems for Levels A and B. This delay is due to problems encountered with suppliers as a result of violent strike actions which have resulted in the destruction of a number of fabrication installations. It should be noted that these actions were not directed at the Site 3 construction programme but formed part of a well-orchestrated plan to disrupt industrial supplies in north-eastern Europe. We expect to be able to acquire all necessary replacement items within the next two months. The Masterplan Schedule has been amended to take this into account. Budget overruns resulting from increased overtime due to shortened delivery times is expected to be less than 0.8 percent, mainly due to low occupation levels in many workshops as a result of the EU-NAF recessionary situation.

It has been noted that an additional risk factor has been added to the project as a result of having to concentrate fabrication in fewer suppliers. Special efforts will be made regarding misinformation strategies to be applied to mislead anti-technology groups.

It is pleasing to report that accessory finishing on Levels D–F has been completed on schedule with a less than 0.0003 percent failure rate. This does credit to the inspection services contracted to follow up the jobs. Detail finishing work on Levels D–F is proceeding as planned and is expected to be completed on schedule. Some areas are in fact already occupied and in service as requested in the previous Steering Committee meeting. Minor design changes resulting from availability and sourcing changes will not significantly affect the handing over process.

Attachments:

- Adjusted Cost Control
- Accessory System Status Listing
- Phase IV Layouts
- Phase IV Time Schedule (Adjusted)

Power Subcommittee Report: Reactor installation is now fully underway with all primary components set in place and all secondary components, with the exception of the third-level emergency cooling pumps, having been delivered ex-works.

Control system components are currently undergoing dry tests, both at Site 3 and in suppliers' factories. A number of parameter modifications have been requested by CERN due to plasma temperature variations encountered in other installations. Site supervisory staff have also been taking part in these tests and this has resulted in a highly positive feedback which will significantly simplify the TFR commissioning phase.

Attachments:

- Dry Tests Time Schedule
- Change Order Listings

Staffing Report: The initial four-group induction programmes have been completed with a two-week delay. The dropout rate was below five percent, which is only two-thirds of the expected level. In general it can be said that not only have the technical competencies found in these groups exceeded our expectations, but also that the psycho profiling system has proved to be well worth the higher initial costs. The second four groups have already initiated training activities, however no report is available at this time.

Further personnel searches for non-technical staff are continuing, and it is expected to complete the first intake before the end of September.

Attachments:

- Site 3 Induction Programme Report
- Tentative Staffing Assignments List
- Masterplan Time Schedule (Staffing)

News Item Summaries: The European Parliament has by a majority of eighty-seven percent voted to apply entry restrictions to all citizens of the Arabian Independent States as a result of the recent wave of attacks on several refugee communities. This has led to a formal protest from the AIS in the form of cutting crude oil supplies to the EU. Meanwhile the NAF has guaranteed to supply crude from the surplus stock if needed. Further terrorist attacks are expected and security measures across both the EU and the NAF have been stepped up.

The Korean War, which began on 27 June, is believed to have ended after an exchange of thermonuclear weapons. The death toll is unknown but is assumed to be well over thirty million as at least two explosions were observed in highly populated areas. Neither side has made any claims since the start of the war and it is assumed that both leadership cadres have been wiped out. As far as is known no CBW agents were released, but the radioactivity levels in some parts of the peninsula are so high that access will be impossible for several decades. The prevailing winds have carried much of the fallout northwards into the Chinese Republic.

In the Silicon Valley area, a battle for control of the area between rival anti-technology groups has been raging for over a week. Many of the industrial plants have already been destroyed in what analysts say may be the death blow to the NAF circuit industry which since 2010 has been slowly relocating to the EU where better security conditions are to be found. The identity of the groups involved in the fighting has not yet been established.

Medical staff of the Mount Sinai Hospital have announced a new breakthrough in the effort to combat the effects of Nogrow. At this stage preliminary studies have revealed that the conception rate in females treated with a new hormone cocktail is seventeen percent higher than in a control group which did not receive the treatment. The head of the research programme announced that further clinical trials are necessary prior to any sort of release. Scientists hope that in the end they will be able to reverse the population decline in areas seeded with Nogrow, but cautioned that this will not occur for several years. Despite this, the UN Plenary Council is studying a petition presented by a number of member states including the Chinese Republic, requesting that copies of all data be made available immediately.

Chapter XV

Sitting in the comfortable old leather-backed chair, Karel Houseman, late of the European Space Corps, was feeling like a little boy, or perhaps like a freshman cadet on his first day at the Academy. It was a feeling at once of uncertainty, of nervous anticipation, and at the same time of satisfaction of knowing that all he was feeling were images and feelings related to events long since put behind him. He was himself, and at the same time a dispassionate observer looking down through the distorting telescope of the years. And above all he was enveloped in a sense of well-being, of friendship, and of love.

Tante had taken him to visit Leana early in the morning after they had enjoyed a light breakfast together. Karel had been amazed at the change that had taken place in the time since their previous visit, not more than three weeks ago. The baby who had floated serenely in the tank now sat upright, supported by the med-bed, but obviously in full control of her movements, head unsupported. Again he had felt the warmth of her greeting wash over him, followed by a sense of waiting. His intuition told him that the child was asking him for permission to enter his mind. After a moment of hesitation and although he had no way of transmitting his thoughts directly to her, he ordered his body to relax, using long-ingrained, almost forgotten mantras to bring his mind down to its alpha state while remaining fully conscious and awake, thinking thoughts of welcome.

And then without conscious volition, he was young again, a child racing along the dunes north of Zeebrugge, the cold wind from the North Sea helping to push him along. Behind him he could hear the shouts of his friends, Paul and Jacko, as they tried in vain to keep up with his long legs. Out over the sea, masses of dark grey clouds rolled, threatening to let loose their thunder at any moment. He ran faster, knowing that his uncle's beach house was only a few hundred metres away, and that if he was lucky he could beat the rain. He focused again, and was a teenager at the ESC Academy going through his basic training, a whole new world of uncertainties opening before him. At the Academy they trained the cadets hard, fleecing out the

214

weak and the undecided before the real training began. The induction year was followed by three years of intense physical and mental effort. Some subjects seemed irrelevant to the young Karel, after all why was it necessary to review the campaigns of Alexander the Great in order to be a spaceman? Physics, maths, astronomy, and then on to orbital mechanics, telemetry, and other more obscure subjects. And of course there was Sandy, and the joy of new discoveries, of things shared, of loving. Now at last came the day of the ultimate reward, the day they had been waiting for, the day when they flew as supernumerary cargo aboard a shuttle. He could feel again the immense enveloping g-forces pushing him down into his acceleration couch where he lay strapped, harder and harder, accompanied by the drumming roar of the torch as they rode up the parabolic path into low earth orbit. For the first time he felt the surge of release as the power cut, leaving them floating weightless, restrained only by the straps. He twisted his head round, looking out from the viewport where it was possible to see the vast curve of the earth as they raced towards the terminator line, and the world beneath them turned from black to blue, half covered by the intricate lacy patterns of the clouds. As clearly as if it were real, Karel saw the space station swing into view, high above them, spinning majestically against the black backdrop of stars. Somewhere behind him he felt the whine of the manoeuvring jets as the shuttle matched velocities, and his inner ear protested at the gravitational changes as the floor became the wall and then the ceiling the floor. Seen through the port, the station ceased to rotate, and in its place the rest of the universe beyond the window spun round and round and round, the colours changing from blinding sunlight to the blue and green of the earth and then to the blackness of infinite space, speckled with uncounted stars. Some day he knew he would go that way, outwards into the cold depths of space.

Like a film running too fast, his ESC missions succeeded each other. The two-week stay at the UNDEF polar orbit station, the auroras below them covering the arctic in glorious scintillating patterns, complexities beyond anything an artist could hope to capture on canvas. The supply run to Luna as co-pilot, where the rest of the crew went down to the surface leaving him alone. Now he sat alone again in the right-hand seat of the deserted module while the ferry descended to the lunar surface, taking much needed supplies to the scientific station beneath the domes, now in its tenth year, with the fifth dome almost finished. Alone, he sailed along in the eternal silence, ninety-two klicks above the surface of the moon, passing over the giant mountain ranges which seemed to stretch upwards until one felt it was possible to touch the sun silvered peaks. Again he raced along above the dark side of Luna, cut off, separated from his kind by the body of the moon, loving every precious minute of it. The payload lifts for the Heisenberg mission to Mars working in conjunction with the NAF teams, ferrying up the parts that went into building the Mars ship. They joked about it even then, the Marie Celeste of the spaceways they called it. A spidery structural mass of beams, piping, girders and tanks, radio and radar antennas, clipped or bolted on wherever there was room. The envy surged again in him as the fusion engines were lit and the Heisenberg mission edged out of orbit and boosted outwards. He relived too, the overwhelming sadness at the news that the mission had failed to maintain its contact schedule and was presumed lost, a Marie Celeste for the space ways, fiction to reality, and who was to say which was stranger. Cry not for lost colleagues and friends, for they journey ever onwards into the void, Tommy, you may not have reached Mars, but your mortal remains will be the first to leave the Solar System.

Finally the Copernicus mission, one of the few pure science flights, a mission which despite the claims of the Luddites was without any hidden agenda. The heavy work schedule had meant long hours of hard labour for all the crew. As if reliving his time again, Karel gazed through the gold plated glass of his helmet at the surface of the Earth rolling by six hundred klicks below him. It was a view that would never tire him, would never pale into a routine matter. Among his companions his ability to talk his way into participating in every spacewalk going was something of a joke. Even after months in space, each EVA brought something new to look at, and to wonder what was coming next. Although there were significant areas of the planet covered with the cancerous growths of smoke and fire, spreading misery over the globe, the enduring blues and greens with their infinitely varying cloudscapes were always a source of fascination. He felt again the stomach-sickening lurch of fear at losing touch with ground control when the terrorists attacked, followed by the long, sometimes seemingly endless, wait for things to be fixed up again earthside. Finally the despair of knowing they were at last truly on their own, destined to ride the final crazy helter-skelter path to the unexpected landing in Mendoza. If you can walk

216

away from it, it's a landing, you'd better believe it, for he could still feel the bruises the safety harness left across his chest.

The scenes flickered now, as if the arc was burning down, though Karel knew, felt really, that each of those scenes had been carefully recorded by the mind of the child that sat in front of him. A mind so far ahead of his own that he could only wonder at the strangeness of it. With such a one to help us, the rebuilding might not be so difficult after all. And then the contact was broken, and for an instant again he felt the warmth wash over him before it vanished leaving him on his own again, neither lonely nor sad, but on the contrary with a sense of quiet joy at the time he had shared. In the bed in front of him the child watched him, wise beyond her years. Tante sat in the easy chair, eyes closed, apparently asleep, but Karel had the certainty that she too had shared the journey through his memory. Leana's tiny hands waved in the air, not, he somehow knew in an aimless pattern, but wishing him well for the long journey that lay ahead.

During their extended stay as guests at the Foundation they had taken advantage of the time available to make a number of short exploratory sorties with the objective of discovering any neighbours who could perhaps, and this was the optimistic viewpoint, be integrated into the Foundation. The pessimists of course held that at least half the groups they came across were likely to be hostile, and that any contact would only serve to advise them that there was activity in the area. As things turned out, these fears were groundless, and the expeditions did in fact serve a very useful purpose, that of updating the local maps for future reference by the Foundation. The Gevcars found nothing of immediate use on these trips, mostly it was the same sad depressing old story of abandoned towns and villages, buildings and structures slowly falling back into nothingness, covered more often than not by vegetation. The four horsemen of the apocalypse, aided by random sprayings of Nogrow, had come and gone, leaving only emptiness. Occasionally they found places that looked as if they might have been occupied more recently, possibly within the previous half cycle, but never were there signs of activity. All in all the Gevcars made six short trips and covered an area round North Bend some forty or fifty klicks in radius, no mean feat considering the decayed conditions of many of the old country roads.

On 2 July a special ceremony took place, a ceremony that had been planned in secrecy, secrecy that is from the one person it was designed to honour. Karel had arrived back at the living quarters building after spending the day with Herb and David reviewing the navigation computer manuals which both pilots had been studying and modifying so as to allow better handling of the GPS signals they would be receiving. After his shower he had wandered over to the canteen, rather surprised but certainly not worried that no one was about. He had pushed open the swing door only to encounter total darkness, a fact which his brain told him could not be right, for the room had several windows and it was not yet dark outside. As his survival reactions took over, he spun aside, leaping sideways away from where he had been silhouetted against the open doorway, rolling over and up again into a crouching position, reaching for the weapon that was, oh damnation, no longer buckled to his left hip. Before he was able to do anything else, the room lights came on, and he was greeted by a multiple shout of 'Happy Birthday!' In front of him sat or stood all the Gevcar crews, plus a large number of Foundationers, all holding their glasses ready to toast his good health. Sandy came over and hugged him, and then everyone else was there as well, all wanting to congratulate him. The party ran on into the early hours of the morning, and if it was more genteel than some of the times he remembered from the ESC Academy days, it was still quite an event. So much so in fact, that the next day was not exactly noted for its level of productive activity.

With only two days to go before their scheduled departure date, and after several days of almost non-stop programming, Sandy was beginning to worry about the lack of progress. Her fingers rippled over the keyboard hardly seeming to touch the keys, but the CPU up on the Sentry seemed to be impervious to her commands:

New message buffer stores (240, 60, 710 KKL)
Restore shift. Mem display terminal 2B
Orbital parameters: illegal subtype in Block 3510

Sometimes she almost felt that there was a gleeful little elf somewhere in the system who was having a great time thwarting her efforts. Scratch it kid, she told herself, anthomorphism went out a long time ago. All she had to do was put herself in the mind of the long gone NAFDEF programmer who had written the lockout routines:

Relay data incomplete: fatal error
Exit filepack subroutine
Store auxiliary standby cache to OFF

Damnation. It should be easy, easy, a piece of cake. And that's a long unused expression if ever there was one. Hadn't she been the best hacker in the ESC communications squad? One of the best anyway.

After lunch, Karel came across and stood behind where she and Jean worked in one of the outbuildings. She didn't look up nor interrupt her work, but she knew he was there, just as he knew she had sensed his presence. He ran his hands over her head, where the darker brown roots could be seen pushing aside the grey streaks of the years as though by magic. It was late in the evening when the Sentry finally gave up its ultimate secret, the power to open a link channel to any other operational Sentry satellite. The power to link up and reprogramme practically anything. This was what they had been working for, and now finally they would be able to obtain access to the second Sentry satellite. Sandy had talked with Karel about her intention of reprogramming it to shift its orbit to a new position five degrees south of the Equator and then to shift the scan axis twenty degrees further west than the original path, thus covering a better footprint for the whole Pacific crossing. Over the previous months and during the journey they had also increased the available options from the original Sentry's memory banks and command codes until at last the final barriers had fallen. Sandy sat back hands clasped behind her head, stretching luxuriously. Exultation flowed through her like a potent drug. With new information retrieved from the databanks she would not only shift the orbit to guarantee improved communications with the Hold, but also she was almost certain that they would be able to retrieve some photographic images. The enhancement of these images could, at least in theory, be done in the Hold until they were of practical use. That was another challenge altogether, when the Hold received the information, the software specialists there would be free to nibble away at the algorithms necessary for the task. Communications with the Hold, the Cape and with Tumbes had now become routine matters thanks to the satellite links, and it seemed difficult to recall that only five moons earlier such things were unthought of. Yes, things were definitely looking up. She leaned forward to complete the file download procedure, and then turned off the terminal. Patting Jean on the shoulder she left the room, her step jaunty, head held high, feeling better than she had for many years.

At dinner, over in one of the common rooms the usual atmosphere of relaxed calm had changed for one of subdued excitement, not only because of their forthcoming departure, but also because of the news that Sandy and Jean had cracked open the Sentry's code.

'Ah, but I'll be glad to be on the move again,' David said as he sipped his citrus juice, 'we've done about as much as we can on our own here, eh, Herb? In time the Hold people will be here with greater resources, but for us it's time to move on.'

'I tend to agree with you, my brash young friend' replied his companion, peering over the manual he was reading, his newly dark brown close-cropped hair giving him an almost youthful look. 'This life on the move has gotten to me. I confess to having been a stick in the mud conservative. Until we found the Gevcar, now, the more we see of the world, the more I want to see. I'm convinced that the only course open to us is to search for the other Holds.'

'Even though our efforts were useless because the Calgary Centre had fallen apart?'

'All the more so!' Herb's reaction came almost without pausing for thought. 'Now more than ever we must push on. Look, imagine a worst-case scenario and say that we find nothing, no trace of the third Hold. I can't believe that ours were the only three long-term efforts ever made, anyway, we've found the Cape and the Foundation. That's more than enough to ensure that we go on looking, instead of waiting safely in our cave.'

'You bet, those are my feelings as well.' Brendt had wandered over and joined the two Techs. 'I was one of the so-called hot heads who believed that the Hold was eventually doomed to die out if we stayed where we were. To my mind stagnation and decay were the only possible end result.'

'A bit too negative, don't you think?' David leaned back in his chair, 'after all, things in the Hold were working fine, there were plenty of research activities, new developments in AI, the crop genetics work, cryogenics ...'

'I've had this argument before with plenty of people. I don't deny that some areas were advancing, but fundamentally we were a closed society growing inwards. Ask Jock what his opinion is. Why do you think he pushed the Council so hard on the subject of going out? Even without the Gevcars and the records you found, Jock knew we had to do something to fulfil our mission and that the waiting period was over. Even without the Gevcars and without Karel's arrival he would eventually have won some limited concession to mount a short-term expedition. With the Gevcars and with Karel the Council had no other choice but to review their policy regarding outside activity.'

'Well, perhaps you're right. Anyway, it's a moot point now,' David replied.

After a while the group split up, moved around and then re-formed, a sort of social Brownian motion. Jojo sat close to Selena, looking as relaxed as anyone had ever seen him. The years of hard living from the time before he arrived at the Cape had marked his face with innumerable worry lines, but the genetic implant and the easy life at the Foundation had begun to ease away the furrows. Selena at his side looked a mere child, her fair hair tied back into a pigtail which hung over one shoulder, but inside her hair a mind like a steel trap was ever at work. Brendt and Bob had been running through some Watch training schedules when she had happened by and asked to try some of the weapons. Both men had been at first surprised and then astounded by her rapid grasp of every new concept, not to mention her ability in handling unfamiliar weapons. With reaction times as short as any they had seen in the Hold, Selena also possessed that most valuable of qualities, the ability to make rapid and precise decisions with very little hard data to go on. Brendt was even heard to say that it was a shame she had to be on the medical team, a true compliment coming from the senior Watch member of the expedition. Her relationship with Jojo was an odd one, between the toughened veteran and the young woman there seemed at first sight to be little in common, even if one could think in terms of the attraction of opposite. After a while however it became obvious that the natural empathy between them made them a formidable team.

As the day of departure approached, they had all worked hard to get things ready and stowed away, until finally, with the Gevcars loaded and ready by mid-afternoon there was suddenly an absence of things to do. Overhead a thin haze covered the orange ball of the sun, and a pleasantly cool breeze blew in off the ocean. Inside the Foundation, Karel, Jock and Threejays sat at a large round table in one of the old conference rooms, running through their final checklists, while elsewhere most of the remaining crew sat around or found themselves odd jobs to fill the hours until supper. Only Janine, who as usual had done all the logistics planning, still sat near the threesome, ready to take action on any additional suggestions that might arise. Not that she had any worries that they would find anything wrong, she had checked and rechecked her work more than once and was fully satisfied with the results. After Sandy's breakthrough the previous day, the communications team had continued to work, and the results, considering the short time available, were really outstanding. Already they had some photographs transmitted down from the Sentry, to be sure, rather blurred as they had still to be enhanced by the Hold, but in any event clear enough for them to see the general cloud pattern and to know that they could expect a clear run out to the Hawaiian islands.

The Foundation medical staff had spent much time the previous week checking the results of the implants on the Hold people and had pronounced themselves satisfied with the results. Not that all the results had been even by any means, in some cases the reaction times had been very short and in others rather longer, with all three Cape people, Linda Olsson, Ken Magee and Jojo, being in the latter group. The specialists had hesitantly tried to correlate this to higher radiation doses the Cape was thought to have received from the environment over the years, but had been unable to explain why Sandy's progress was almost a perfect match on the average line, and Karel's was one of the fastest they had ever seen. All in all, the recipients of the transplants were without exception delighted with the results, and even Jock had finally accepted that the thickening brush of red hair he was growing in no way diminished his natural authority. A particularly interesting, not to say startling, case had been Lee Sun Yan's reaction to the rejuve implant, very little changed in her outward appearance, but the tests showed that she had begun to regrow a damaged kidney which had been removed several cycles previously by the Hold surgeons.

For Karel the time spent at the Foundation would forever revolve around Leana, whom he had visited several times since the initial session. Without quite understanding why, he realized that he had somehow grown close to this precocious young mind, so young and yet so eager to understand. And so incredibly powerful. Each time he left her he felt immensely relaxed and clear of mind, as if the sharing of a lifetime of experiences were lightening his load, though that was not something that had particularly bothered him. He knew that all through his life he had tried to do what was right, and if at times this had meant dealing out violence, then that had been the only available option at the time. On the second visit Sandy had come with him, and she too had emerged fascinated by the experience. They had both felt, so briefly that had they not compared notes afterwards the event would have faded away as a fanciful notion, a brief moment of absolute and total oneness. Karel was left with the feeling that somewhere inside him the ability to do this at will rested quietly, waiting only for the right key to open the door. That, he thought, would be quite something, it surely would, and then he committed the thought to the back of his mind, for there were more pressing matters to be dealt with.

Early the next morning, soon after the day began to lighten, they prepared to set out once more on their journey, with the sun still hidden behind the purple-shadowed mountains to the east. Out to sea, the horizon was shrouded and distorted in the morning mists, and the beach seemed to vanish into nothingness half a klick or so away on each side. The two Gevcars eased over the dunes like giant beetles, slid down to the beach, and came to rest just above the reach of the waves. There, wrapped in warm clothing to fight off the early morning chill, almost all the Foundation, headed by Tante who sat in a comfortable chair, waited to see them off. With the engines thrumming softly at minimum power, the two Gevcars sat scrunched down into the hard and still damp sand, brooding powerhouses, lit intermittently by the flashing position lights on the hull. The night had been quiet, almost windless, and the swells rolling in to the coast failed to raise much of a spray. Overhead a few early gulls circled and screeched, as though indignant that their territory should be encroached upon by the metal and carbon fibre monsters below them. The crews gathered slowly, splitting off from those who were staying, saying quiet goodbyes to special friends, then heading for the open Gevcar doors.

For the first time since Patric's death, both cars were at full strength, with Jojo switched over to Karel's command, Selena as Erik's assistant and Maria now in the other car. The farewells on the beach were awkward, as such things tend to be, a mix of personal sadness and formal statements, well meant, but not always possible to fulfil. In the end it was Jojo who summed it up the best.

223

'We haven't been here all that long, and yet this place is like home to many of us. You accepted us and made us welcome and we grew together. Thirty odd days is not much, but it is a start. We'll be back to break bread with you again, you can bet on it.' And then it was time to go, the crews climbed aboard their cars. Karel and Jock stopped for a moment beside Tante to say their goodbyes, and then followed the others towards the Gevcars. Karel walked easily down the beach his powerful stride leaving a clear line of prints in the sand, his mind still turning over the old woman's final cryptic remark.

'She placed the gift within you, use it well.'

With the cockpit windows and the top hatch still open, the whine of the engines built up until the great bulks lifted, light as feathers, and blowing a small gale of sand drifted down to the waters' edge. With increased lift, the two cars swung away and punched out through the breakers with only a light rocking motion, while from the open windows hands waved. Even over the sound of the sea it was possible to hear the immense power of the engines as the two cars, now past the breaker line, built up speed and headed out to the south-west, leaving the bay and diminishing rapidly in size, until after a few minutes all that was left was the vague impression of movement in the mist, with the wake pattern soon absorbed back into the movement of the ocean.

'Coming up to ninety knots now,' Petra at the controls, leaned forward as she shifted the joystick slightly, while her other hand played over the touch pad in front of her.

'Course two two zero,' David, reaching over to throw a switch set in the lower left quadrant of the instrument panel. 'Right, autopilot on, did you reset the proximity alarms?'

'Yes, recalibrated for thirty klicks. OK with you? Gives us plenty of leeway.'

'Yo, should be OK. Go down if you like, I'm fine for now. Don't forget to send one of the others up.' David leaned back, adjusting the headrest. His eyes swept automatically over the instrument panel screens glowing gently in the dim light of the cockpit, course, speed, height, power level, tube temperatures, outside to sweep the still blurred horizon, and back to the instruments. He stretched comfortably as his mind wandered, fully relaxed except for the tiny part which continued to watch, even though the computers would detect anything wrong much earlier than he could. The truth was that the habit was now so ingrained that he couldn't have stopped even if he wanted to, and although David didn't know it, it was the same vigilance that pilots throughout the ages, both at sea and in the air, had always maintained, conscious of the responsibility handed to them.

'Hi, not bothering you am I?' Erik Fernan eased himself into the seat recently vacated by Petra. 'I enjoy coming up here occasionally, there's not much to do aft at the moment.'

'Sure,' David replied. 'I was just going to call back and see if there were any volunteers, you know what a stickler Karel is that at least two of us should be in the cockpit.'

'Do I hear a note of complaint?' Karel peered in from where he stood behind them on the access ladder, a slight grin on his face, a face that had already lost much of the harshness as his skin regained its youthful elasticity, the scar now a thin barely visible line.

'Uh, no sir, definitely not sir.' David smiled back, knowing full well that Karel didn't mind the occasional ribbing, knowing also how important the order was.

As the morning wore on and the klicks flowed by, the sun rose behind them, emerging from the mountains, a fiery flattened wine red ball. Ahead of them the mists dissipated, leaving only the endless swell over which the two Gevcars rode easily, their parallel courses separated by a couple of hundred metres. With the controls set on a slightly higher than usual lift, the rise and fall of the cars was less noticeable, though if one concentrated on the horizon for too long the feeling of the constant up and down became uncomfortable. Invisible in the sky and off to the south, the Sentry received and retransmitted their position signals with unvarying regularity, giving back in return GPS confirmation reports. Soon after leaving the Foundation, Jock had spoken briefly to the Council Committee in the Hold, but for the moment there was not much news to give, other than to say they were on the move again. From the Hold side the news had been good, for the new Gevcar had returned safely from Tumbes, having found a better and more southern crossing route to the Pacific, instead of following their own overland route and only reaching the ocean near Arica. They had brought back with them a group from Tumbes, leaving behind some of their own specialists to work at improving things for the Captain, who had specifically sent Karel and Jock his best wishes. Unlike their own trip, the new car had run in to several heavy rain storms while travelling up the bulge of the Pacific coast, storms which had produced a number of impressive flash floods, forcing them to turn aside or wait out the storm on a number of occasions.

By midday they had covered the first nine hundred klicks, moving through an apparently deserted world of their own, as their electronic eyes and ears reached out and found nothing. Only twice had they spotted shoals of what they took to be dolphins, but these were off their course and Karel chose not to go nearer and investigate, much to the disappointment and pleas of the science teams in both Gevcars. They ate a prepacked lunch, missing the freedom of the Foundation, or even of the earlier part of the trip when they had stopped to allow people to go for a walk and stretch their legs. Here the best they had been able to do was slow down to a crawl and open the top hatch, allowing the entry of the fresh tang of the sea. Despite the urgings of the younger members of the crew, Erik refused point blank to allow anyone out onto the top of the cars, for the uvee count was well above the acceptable limits even for short exposure times. After this break, Petra, now again at the controls of the first car, brought the speed up to their standard cruise speed once more. As though joined by an invisible string, the two cars sped on across the empty ocean, the distance between them constant to within a couple of metres. In Jock's Gevcar, with Matt at the helm, the job of following the other car was handled with unfailing electronic precision by the autopilot, but he still maintained a close watch on their progress. As the hours passed, the lack of outside stimulus became quite noticeable with most of the crew retiring to their own business. The only exception was the resumption of a community card game over the comm between the two Gevcars, which held the almost undivided attention of the Watch members, the game being a derivative of an obscure game called Contract, in which old-fashioned physical printed cards were used. The day wore on, and the orange ball of the sun crept across the sky, slowly overtaking the speeding Gevcars before beginning its fall from grace into the western ocean ahead and off to the right. The great Pacific swells continued to live up to their name, with only small ripples decorating the surface of the water, throwing sparkling patterns in all directions, while in the billowing tail wakes behind them, rainbow patterns writhed and mutated endlessly.

Just before twenty hundred hours, Matt Wilton, who under Herb's direction was acting as group navigator announced that they had covered half the distance to their destination. With the state of boredom in the cars, the announcement was greeted by a muted round of applause, as well as by a few ribald comments from those who threw doubts on the accuracy of the calculation, claiming that members of the Watch had never been very good at mathematics. While most of the crews tuned in to their bunks after the evening meal, the two cars bore onward through the night, manned only by the duty pilot and one other member of the team, with shift changes every two hours. Erik had protested that this was rather hard on the pilots, although the matter had been settled when planning the trip, but in fact, none of the four supposed victims of this arrangement were much bothered. Occasionally the cars rocked as they rode over a larger than usual swell, generated who knows by what happening thousands of klicks away, earth tremor, minor seaquake, there was no way of knowing. The forward-ranging electronic scanners, distant descendants of the weather radars developed in the last decades of the twentieth century, gave the pilots plenty of warning of such events, allowing for any minor course adjustments that might prove necessary. Both cars kept their running lights on, not only to allow visual contact to be maintained, but also hopefully to show any third party who might be around that no secret night attack was intended. The on-board computers had been programmed to detect and analyse any indications that were fed to them by the sensor arrays, but, as Karel never got tired of repeating, it always paid to be careful.

Chapter XVI

At first Herb thought it might be some figment of his imagination when the faint image persisted through several scans, he wondered about the possibility of minor screen glitch. The image blipped again, definitely something large off to the south, but at least sixty klicks away. The monitoring system chimed softly, calling his attention to the signal. Glancing at the digital clock in front of him and noting that the time was four twenty in the morning, he regretfully depressed the alert stations buzzer, knowing that he would receive little thanks if the thing turned out to be a false alarm. As with all professional highly trained crews there were no questions asked as everyone slid out of their sleeping quarters and moved quickly to their stations.

'Weapons, standby. Power on, coming up to standard.' Sara from the upper turret, curt, bitten off words, uncombed hair hanging over her eyes.

'No target, no range.' Ken Magee on the ranging computer, barefoot, but otherwise dressed.

'I've advised the others, they're going to alert stations as well.' Sandy, at the comm station, cool calm and collected as ever.

'Tell Petra and David to switch the Doppler rate on their scanner and see if they get a clearer signal.' Matt watched the ghostly image intently as he reset his own screen. Behind him Jock watched the image for a moment, and then picked up the comm microphone which linked them to the other Gevcar, but before he could say anything the speaker came to life with Karel's voice.

'Jock, you there?' The voice continued without really waiting for a reply. 'I don't want to go in at night. At this range we should be nearly invisible if the Gevcar specs are to be believed, but I'd still rather wait for first light. We'll go to a holding pattern at a speed of twenty knots, square box, with a ninety degree turn say every fifteen minutes, that'll give us a five klick side. We'll keep two klicks apart, I'll lead. Come round to one eighty and pull in behind us.' The voice stopped although they could still hear some background conversation coming from the other car. 'Let use know when you're in position and on the same course, and then we'll execute on my mark.'

'OK will do Karel, that sounds reasonable. What's your plan? After this I mean?'

'We'll wait in this holding pattern until it begins to get light, keeping a close watch on the signal. Petra tells me it appears that it might be moving very slowly, though at this range it's difficult to be sure. Then when it's light we'll separate by twenty klicks or so and go in. I think the best plan is that I start ahead of you and go in at a fairly low speed, then, when I'm near, you can run a high-speed diversion for us without coming within range of any short-range stuff they might have.'

'Right, OK with me,' replied Jock.

'Right, I suggest we try to get a bit more rest, for the moment we can stand down from alert stations.'

By six thirty in the morning with the first light trying to break through the purple haze on the eastern horizon everyone was up, dressed and a concentrated ration breakfast had been served. The screen images of the object they had detected remained vague. Sandy, in Jock's car, had attempted to obtain a scan report from the Sentry, but the IR camera was either deficient or unable to pick up an image, for the decoded signals, even if still unenhanced, showed nothing. After a brief exchange, and with the comm unit turned to a short-range combat frequency, Karel's Gevcar left the circular pattern they had been holding and set off in the direction of the object. At a distance of twenty klicks out, the image had solidified to the point where Petra was certain it was from a large ship, and that if so the ship was almost stationary. Karel ordered the speed to be brought down from sixty to thirty knots, and edged their course over slightly so as to pass the object. At a distance of fifteen klicks out, with the haze still making any visual sighting impossible, the second Gevcar started to come in, moving at ninety knots on a course that would take it past the ship on the opposite side at a distance of around five klicks. As they continued to approach, with all their electronic warning systems at full power, the tension grew, for there was no way of knowing if they would be met by some sort of attack, however unlikely it might seem.

'I can't imagine why anyone would wait on the high seas on the off chance that someone might come by,' Karel had said. 'But for all that I'm not willing to risk them being unfriendly. Anyone who has survived on the open ocean for all these years is quite likely to have an itchy trigger finger, and I'd hate for us to find out the hard way.'

As they came closer the haze appeared to thicken at one point, leaving a dark area, as though a hole were sucking away at what limited light there was, and then the amorphous mass suddenly resolved itself into a giant aircraft carrier, rust streaked and listing slightly to port side, motionless in the water. It took all David's willpower to drag his eyes away from the giant ship, back to the cockpit panels. Without needing any instruction he swung the Gevcar round in a slow arc, keeping a constant distance between them and the carrier.

'Frequencies clear, no transmissions on any of the usual bands.' From Jean sitting at the communications panel, headphones perched on his head, listening intently as he worked the comm computer.

'Cannon locked on target. Ready to fire.' Brendt said quietly, almost aloofly at ease, ocean grey eyes watching intently. Curled up like a steel spring, ready for instant reaction, thought Karel as he glanced across.

'Nothing, clear on the IR,' Petra called out. 'The signature isn't quite even, but it's not that unusual. I'd like to see the deck, that would tell us more.' A forlorn hope at the moment for the deck was a good twenty metres above their present height. Jean spoke quietly into the microphone, telling Sandy over in the other Gevcar what the mysterious signal had turned out to be, while the Gevcar came round the bows, which even at five hundred or so metres distance appeared to be coming down on them.

Karel ordered the speed to be lowered to a mere five knots. Off to their right, bursting out of the haze, clearly visible now that the sun had begun to creep upwards through the early morning clouds, Jock's car made a splendid sight. Now moving in excess of 140 knots, well above the surface of the water, its passing generated an enormous wake which boiled up three or four times the height of the speeding car before beginning to fall back, dissolving into an untidy pattern of spray which sparkled with the colours of the morning sunlight against the stone grey horizon. Erik, without any duties for the moment had the presence of mind to take some photographs of the scene. The Gevcar passed out of sight behind the carrier. They scanned the sides of the great ship, taking time to check each entrance and opening in the hull as carefully as possible. After ten minutes during which they circled the derelict, with the second car well off to the west, still moving back and forth, though only at sixty knots now, Karel ordered David to take the Gevcar in closer.

The rusting sides of the massive vessel loomed high above as Petra brought the Gevcar in as close as she dared. The great ship seemed to remain motionless on the ocean, unlike the car which rode up and down on the slow swells. They had swung in close under the high flattened stern trying to decipher the corroded name, but it had proved to be impossible for much of the area had apparently been ground off at some point in time.

'So, what do we do about it?' Karel sat back in his seat staring out through the viewport. 'I personally doubt that there is much on board to justify the effort, and perhaps the risk of getting on board.'

'My first opinion was the same as yours, but now I'm not so sure' replied Janine, 'I've been doing some quick checks on the currents in the area, and by rights that carrier ought not to be there.'

'How so?'

'Well, there are two major currents which shift north or south according to the season, but is seems to me that any object caught in the drift should sooner or later end up on the north American coast, either north near Alaska, or south, down past Baja.'

'It wouldn't be the first time that currents have changed,' said Brendt from where he sat at the galley table, 'we know nothing about the long-term oceanographic changes, but it doesn't seem unlikely that all the nukes forty or fifty years ago could have wrought changes in old established patterns. After all, they certainly changed the sunlight distribution on the planet.' Threejays remained unconvinced.

'Of course you're quite right about the climatic changes resulting from the dust clouds thrown up into the stratosphere. But still, that ship is an anomaly. My feeling is it must have been under power not so long ago, days, weeks, months, I don't know, but I'm sure its not years.' The Gevcar continued its careful run down the side of the ship, coming round the bow where one of the anchor chains hung downward, vanishing into the darkness of the ocean. The Gevcar slid round, emerging into the orange glow of the morning sunlight again. High under the peak, it was suddenly possible to see the once proud ship's name, highlighted by the angle of the sun.

'There, look!' Brendt's shout made them all jump. '*Abraham Lincoln*, she's the *Abraham Lincoln*.' Janine peered through the small side window near her desk, and then began to tap at the keyboard in front of her. The Hold Records database did credit to its long defunct creators.

'*Abraham Lincoln*, ninety-two thousand tonnes. Length 352 metres. NAF nuclear powered carrier, built 2007, saw service in the Persian Gulf 2008–12 and in the Far East conflict of 2015. Carried a maximum of eighty-five combat aircraft, plus several helicopters, and six hundred marines. Armed with four Cougar SS one kiloton missile launchers, as well as a number of conventional guns and six batteries of Vulcan 20-mm cannons. Unrefuelled range in excess of one million nautical miles at twenty knots. Maximum speed in excess of thirty-eight knots. That's all we have here, there'll probably be more in the full Records base.' The Gevcar continued round, heading back towards the stern again. Brendt continued to examine the carrier carefully, head tilted back to gaze up at the overhanging bridge structure far above them, his deep blue grey eyes moving to and fro as he scanned the ship, noting the long flaking rust patches, places where some superficial damage had dented the toughened steel hull, scars of unknown battles fought long ago. Then suddenly he sat up, watching intently, and then called out, tension noticeable in his voice.

'I saw something moving up on the bridge. Petra, pull away. Now! Stop us at half a klick or so.' The Gevcar slid sideways, rotating, throwing spray up onto the rusted plates, and then surged forward and away, the wake building up into a white tail behind it as the pilot poured on the power, yelling at everyone to strap in.

From five hundred metres away, twelve pairs of eyes stared intently at the carrier, Karel spoke briefly with Jock, and the second Gevcar took up station lined up directly astern of the carrier, Bob Cantor's careful hands rested on the sighting controls in the electric cannon, ready to fire at the first sign of anything untoward. Knowing too that he dared not make a mistake, for one of those terrible shells would rip the carrier apart in a split second, the heat from the incoming projectile vaporizing everything in its path as it travelled on its way into the bowels of the ship. After spending a further fifteen minutes studying the carrier, trying without any success to detect further movement, the Gevcar moved in close once more, coming up under a sealed hatchway some fifty metres along from the bows on the port side, while the other car remained astern and on the same side, making sure that their field of fire was still clear.

Close up, from where Brendt, Jules and Jojo stood on the roof of the Gevcar, it was possible to see the marks of years of hard service, unpainted dents and scrapes. At the waterline, the hull was covered by thick growths of vegetation that hung down into the blue grey depths of the ocean. The bottom of the hatch was almost level with the roof of the car, and oscillated back and forth as the Gevcar rose and fell with the wave motion. For all David and Petra's skill, the gap between the two vessels remained unstable, narrowing until it nearly closed, and then widened again to over a metre, showing the deep blue water writhing and flowing four and a half metres below. Judging the distance as the two vessels came together, Jojo leaped across the gap, to hang precariously on the ladder built into the hull, while his feet scrabbled for a foothold. Hooking himself onto a ring set beside the hatch, he reached over and began to try the long swing handle. A couple of pulls were enough to convince him that a different approach was needed, and unhooking the hammer which had hung from his belt, he began to batter away at the handle. Over on the roof of the Gevcar, Brendt looped his own safety cord to a cleat, holding on to Jojo's line with both hands, ready to pull in rapidly should he slip from his precarious perch on the side of the carrier. After half a dozen blows, the handle showed its disdain for Jojo's efforts by breaking off suddenly, too near the shaft for it to be of any further use. Jojo's comments on the matter resulted in Jock having to apply his Elder's authorization password to overwrite that part of the journey records from the computer. Up on the roof, Jojo once again chose his moment before leaping back to the Gevcar landing in a catlike spread, from where with Brendt's assistance he scrambled away from the edge.

'David, this is Brendt, we'll have to try to find another hatch, this one's out of the question.' Brendt spoke to the cockpit using the throat phone pinned to his collar. 'Work your way back round by the bow again, warn Jock, I don't fancy being vaporized just because Bob gets an itchy finger.'

The Gevcar moved out and away from the steel wall that towered over it and cruised back round the bow while the Watch team on the roof searched intently for any other possible opening. As luck would have it, there was a twin hatch on the starboard side, so once again the Gevcar edged in close, allowing Jojo to leap across again, though with the slight list to port, it meant that he had to jump upwards almost a metre. This time the task of entering the ship proved to be easier, with the second hammer blow the handle spun round to the

233

open position, releasing the perimetral cleats. Jojo slowly leaned his weight, and the hatchway swung open a few centimetres, protesting the unusual movement with a long drawn out screech.

Stepping into the hatchway, Jojo leaned his weight on the door again, and with a further screech it swung back until with a resounding clang it engaged the holding clamps on the bulkhead. He gazed into the passageway which stood revealed, the light of the day illuminating only the first eight or ten metres after which it faded into blackness. Unfortunately, this second hatch was on the shady side of the carrier, and although the sun was now fifteen degrees over the horizon, its orange ball was useless as far as this particular lighting job was concerned. After consulting with Karel, who in turn spoke with Jock, it was decided to allow the Watch team to proceed into the carrier, with the proviso that they keep together and keep in touch on a continuous basis, taking with them some relay units so as to avoid the steel walls of the vessel cutting off their communications. Karel's instructions, dredged up from the memories he had of visiting a UNDEF carrier while still a cadet, were precise and to the point.

'You will find the nearest stairwell which should be immediately off the passageway, and proceed upwards to the flight deck. Check each door on the way up so as to ensure that the clips are dogged home, they can be opened, but the noise will buy you some time. Head upwards to the flight deck, from there see if it's possible to climb up to the bridge. Any logbook, journal, or chart you can lay your hands on would be of interest. Above all, be exceedingly watchful, the ship may not be deserted. Take a needle gun each, but nothing heavier. Check the rad count frequently, I think we can forget about biohazards out here, but even so don't touch anything that's sealed. '

'Aren't you being rather pessimistic about all this?' asked Brendt as he stood in the hatchway looking down at the Gevcar's open cockpit window a metre or so below his perch, from where Karel was watching the exploration team.

'Probably. But I'd hate to say that it was all clear and then be proved wrong.'

'Right, we'll be on our way then.'

'Roger that. I can see some sort of bay above you, probably two decks up, you should be able to get to it fairly easily. Tie one of the ropes there, then in an emergency you can rappel down to us, or even into the water if necessary.'

They set off down the passage, checking each doorway they came to, the first two of which turned out to be empty storerooms. As they went, their radiation counters clicked reassuringly slowly, indicating that there was no excess radiation to deal with. The third door led to a stairwell leading both upwards and downwards into pitch darkness. While Sara and Jojo waited on the landing, Brendt ran lightly down to the deck below them, lighting his way with the lantern clipped on his shoulder. Nothing he found there indicated recent occupation, but remembering Karel's instructions, he made sure the clips were set, before returning to the others. They made their way upwards, stopping to check only that the clips on each door they passed were set, before continuing on their way. The air around them was cool and damp, but not to the point of being unduly musty, so obviously there was some natural circulation through the decks, even with closed doors and hatches. The access to the open bay proved to be much as Karel had forecast, and leaning over the rusty railing they tossed out a rope which landed on the roof of the Gevcar where Selena, who had come out onto the roof, grabbed it and tied it down with a sliding noose to the Gevcar. Two decks higher, they reached a larger door on which the word 'Hangar' was still clearly legible. The three exchanged a look, and then with Sara and Jojo standing well back against the bulkhead, Brendt turned the lever which yielded easily though noisily, and then pushed the doorway open and slid over the sill, crouching low.

The inside of the cavernous hangar was almost dark, lit at intervals by the entry of daylight through some open hatchway or scuttle. The doorway through which they had entered was at the forward end, and off towards the stern they could see the dim outlines of a number of aircraft, as well as untidy piles of equipment. There were no signs of movement nor of lights, and yet the three of them were brushed by the feeling that the place was not deserted.

'I'm covered in goose pimples, and it's not because of the cold.' whispered Sara as she followed Brendt into the hangar and advanced a few metres away from the door. She switched on the powerful sweep lantern she carried and its intense white beam cut through the twilight illuminating two sets of eyes low down and some sixty metres away which sparkled for a moment, shifting to the left and then vanishing abruptly, as though turned off.

'What the ...? Did you see? Not human, possibly a cat ...' Jojo whispered excitedly.

'Better check in Brendt, let's see what Karel suggests,' said Sara as she continued to sweep the lantern back and forth trying to see where the eyes had gone. Brendt nodded his agreement and spoke into the comm unit.

'We're into a hangar deck,' reported Brent, 'we saw something moving, Jojo thinks it could be cats, I don't think we'll catch them, but their presence could mean that there are people around as well. What do you think, should we head aft through here or continue upwards to the main deck?'

'I think it would be better if you go back and continue up the stairwell. Close the door behind you. I've seen plenty of cats who lived and survived quite happily without us to help, and if they're really wild, then you might do well to leave them alone, at least for the moment. All cats really need to survive and prosper is a food source, and on a ship that would be rats, so be very careful where you go, a pack of rats could be absolutely lethal in an enclosed space, specially in the dark.'

'Will do, we're on the way.' Leaving the hangar they retreated to the stairwell and continued upwards for a further two flights of stairs, emerging at last into the daylight through a steep stairway that led up to the flight deck. The sheer size of the deck was overwhelming, after the reduced size of the Gevcars, and their position seemed awfully exposed. Up at this height the wind seemed to be stronger than down on the Gevcars, though Brendt knew that this could be simply because they were out in the open, but it was still vaguely unsettling to feel the little gusts tugging at their cloaks like phantom fingers. Putting their glare specs on, although the sun was not yet high in the sky, they set off in single file towards the control tower island which emerged from the deck something like a hundred metres away, being careful to keep several metres between them. Off in the distance they could see Jock's car, keeping position half a klick away, and had they chosen to do so they could have walked to the edge of the deck to see their own Gevcar far below.

On reaching the island, Brendt, who was in the lead, avoided the nearest doorway and walked on until he reached the second entrance. Unfortunately this proved to be either locked or jammed, for their combined efforts were unable to shift it even a millimetre. The next hatch they came to led only downwards, but after some discussion between themselves and over the radio with Karel, they headed downwards into the darkness once more. No sooner had they reached the deck below, they came to a sudden halt when Sara hissed a warning.

'I smell something, sweaty people, dirty clothes, I don't know, but it's there.'

'Are you sure? I can't smell a thing.' Jojo peered at her as they stood on opposite sides of a dimly lit passageway, lit by what little light filtered in from the stairs down which they had just come. 'But the back of my neck tells me you're right, there's definitely someone or something here.'

'Keep it quiet, we don't want to miss anything,' whispered Brendt. 'I'm going to try the hatch here at the end.' And so saying advanced up to the door and, pulled at the handle, trying to make sure that if it moved it would do so slowly. With a soft scraping sound the door swung back to reveal a room fitted with tables. Unlike most of the other compartments they had seen, this one was lit by the daylight that streamed in through the open scuttles. The place was empty, empty that is except for the smell of fairly recent cooking, probably not as recent as the morning, but also not more than a couple of days old.

Brendt reported their find to the Gevcar, and was told to stand by. As the minutes trickled by, the three Watch members explored the eating area nervously, looking into cupboards and containers. There was no fresh food anywhere, but several cases contained vacuum-packed dehydrated foodstuffs, the shelf life of which had long since been exceeded, though Jojo's own experience was that if the sealing had not been broached, then there was a good chance that the contents would still be edible. The comm unit Brendt carried beeped softly, announcing a call, he acknowledged the call, and was rewarded by Karel's voice.

'I've decided to change tactics. You've been aboard for an hour and a half, and on a ship that size if anyone is hiding and doesn't want to be found, then we have no chance. Get yourselves back onto the flight deck, stay within easy reach of the stairwell you first came up. We're going to try talking to them, if they're there to start with that is. Let me know when you get there.'

The siren on the Gevcar whooped repetitively, the sound beating against the carrier again and again, and then as the echoes died away, Karel's amplified voice boomed out across the water. 'Hello on the carrier *Abraham Lincoln*. We are an exploration team from a Survival Centre in South America. We mean you no harm and wish to speak with you. We found the carrier by chance. I repeat, we were not searching for you, we found you by chance. If you need any help we will try to be of assistance. Please show yourselves to our people on the flight deck. We will wait a further half hour and will then leave.'

As five minutes turned into ten, and then into fifteen without any sign of anyone, it began to look as if either there was no one aboard, or perhaps that they were so wary that they were not going to show themselves. The three explorers sat around the top of the stairwell, with one of them taking a quick walk down to the open bay every few minutes. With their hoods pulled up and the glare specs on, a person from an earlier age would have been forgiven for imagining that they were watching druid monks holding some sort of meeting. It was Sara who saw them first. The first door they had tried on the control tower island swung open, and a figure stepped hesitantly over the threshold, shading its eyes against the brightness of the sunlight. Behind this first figure came five more, two of whom were obviously children, hands held by the adults. As they had previously agreed, Brendt and Sara rose and went to meet them, crossing the wind-swept expanse of open deck, while Jojo remained at the top of the stairway, reporting back to the Gevcar. While he talked his eyes swung to and fro, watchful for any trick, and his hands were never far from the concealed needle gun strapped into his sleeve. As the distance closed, the group resolved itself into three men, a woman and two male children. Finally they halted, facing each other at a distance of some three metres.

After a brief pause, Brendt spoke. 'I'm Brendt, this is Sara. We mean you no harm. We found you by chance on our radar, and came on board because we were puzzled as to how the ship could be adrift out here.'

The older of the men, a grey bearded man of medium height with a heavily discoloured and wrinkled skin out of which peered his black slightly slanted eyes, straightened his back and spoke. 'My name is Flowers, Jack Flowers. I represent the tribe. We haven't been adrift for long, we were anchored on a reef off Kauai but a storm three and a half weeks ago dragged us out to sea.'

'Kauai? That's part of the Hawaiian Islands isn't it? That's where we're heading. But how have you survived? From the food and water position I mean.'

'We, the tribe that is, have lived on the island for years and years, most of us were from the islands originally, but others have drifted in as well. The carrier grounded on the reef some time ago and we were exploring it. There was a storm and our anchor dragged, by the time we realized, it was too late, we were out at sea. That was, oh, twenty-seven or twenty-eight days ago, fortunately we'd stocked up some food, dried stuff mostly, and there are still fish around. Before the storm took us, we had even restored some power with an old engine, gave us light, some power tools. A number of people had even moved aboard when that happened. We had also stripped a number of useful items and taken them ashore, that's why we're on board now instead of safe back home.' He smiled bitterly. 'Living off the past may not always be the best solution, but sometimes it's the easy option.'

'How many of you are there on board then?' Sara asked, still squatting down from smiling at the two children who had responded with shy smiles. 'You certainly kept very quiet when we turned up. We weren't sure until you actually appeared, that there was anyone aboard.'

'Well, we've had unwelcome visitors to the island in the past, and there was no way of knowing.' He shrugged apologetically. 'We've fought several battles with gangs of pirates a couple of years ago. We beat them off, but the tribe lost some good people, we're over twenty thousand in all, but we can't afford to lose doctors or engineers, there's no way of producing new ones. Luckily for us there were only thirty-six of us on board here at the time of the storm. We're thirsty rather than hungry although we do have some water. Look, come on up, most of us are up in the tower under the bridge. Will your third man join us?' Brendt thought for a brief moment and then waved Jojo over, knowing that if he was wrong, then all three of them could end up as prisoners, or worse.

As they made their way up to the higher decks, they continued to question their new acquaintances. 'Your tribe seems to have kept in touch with technology, we've seen others that have become purely agrarian, and others that have fallen back into savagery.'

'I can imagine that you have. I can still remember times when every house had electricity, there were cars and planes, television, and so on. I was a child of course, but the memories remain. Our people farm and fish, but we also maintain a self-defence force, medical staff, we rescued the dentist's equipment from this ship by the way, we even have a loose central administration. We have some machinery, a couple of generator sets are still running, tractors, and so on. The problem is of course that we can't build anything new, and at some point in time we're going to run out of fuel which will affect some of our infrastructure. In the long run it's better not to rely on what we can scavenge.'

Arriving at the fourth deck, they were ushered into a large compartment where they met the other members of Flowers's group, a group with a mix of men and women with ages varying from ten to over sixty. Most looked reasonably healthy, although even those who had started out on the plump side were now rather thin as they had been on short rations since their unplanned journey had begun. There was a mixture of races, with a clear predominance of original Hawaiian stock, with a few Negroid and Caucasian faces thrown in for good measure. After chatting for some minutes with them, explaining again who they were, it became clear to the Hold people that they would not be able to leave these thirty-six people adrift. Finally, Flowers asked the question that was on everyone's mind, which was what could the Gevcars do to rescue them from their predicament, to which Brendt replied that he would have to consult the expedition leaders in the Gevcars.

Opening the comm line to the car, Brendt passed on the problem. 'Karel, us three babies are doing just fine,' using the speech code to indicate that everything was in order. 'Pass the message to Bob that he can relax now. We have a bit of a problem to deal with, there are thirty-six people here on the carrier, including a number of women and children. As I see it there are two options open to us, either we attempt to take the carrier in tow and trail it all the way to the islands, or we take the people off.'

'Let me talk to the Techs about it a second, though to be honest I can't see us towing that monster across hundreds of klicks of open ocean.' Karel went off the air for a full ten minutes before returning with the verdict that they couldn't risk the tow, although from a purely technical point of view it might be possible. He therefore proposed transferring the refugees across using nets so as to avoid losing any into the ocean. As they heard the decision, a wave of relief swept through the small crowd, smiles breaking out on worried faces.

In practice the whole affair of transferring the Hawaiians to the Gevcars turned out to be far more complex than expected, and it wasn't until after three in the afternoon that the transfer of eighteen passengers to each car had been accomplished, and all the participants including the Gevcar crews were thoroughly exhausted.

Several times they had come close to dropping people in the ocean, and it was only thanks to the Gevcar crew's fast reactions that the incidents only resulted in a good scare. As it was, Brendt ended up with a bruised shoulder and some rope burns across his back as a result of leaping out to catch a woman who lost her grip and was sliding down the side of the hull into the sea. Had the weather turned on them, the results, Jock knew, would have been quite different, in fact they would have been lucky to manage the transfer at all without loss of life.

'I want to say thank you for your help.' Flowers sat opposite Jock sipping a cup of coffee, crowded into the canteen which like most areas of the Gevcar overflowed with people. 'Many would have left us adrift, some might even have sunk us or killed us. When we reach Kauai our tribe can offer you little in return for this service other than our hospitality, and of course our commitment to participate in your efforts in any way we can be of use.'

Jock smiled. 'I really do appreciate your offer, I've given you a summary of the Hold's mission, but the truth is we can't hope to build the world again on our own. We'll be needing all the help we can get, and it won't be only today or next week, our job will go on for cycles and cycles. When we set out almost seven moons ago I didn't really know what to expect, or even if we had any chance of success. Today I know we have a future, also that the job ahead of us will be hard and long. I would even dare to say that I hope and expect that our children will continue after us when we are gone. The job of rebuilding even a small part of what we have lost will need all the help we can get, so I thank you for your offer. Be assured we will be accepting your commitment.'

Leaving the carrier adrift, they resumed their journey, with a slight change of course now that they were heading for Kauai. Sara had wanted to attempt to rescue some of the cats which they had seen on hangar deck, but the islanders had assured them that the cats were quite feral and had in any event been on board the ship before she ran aground on Kauai. Karel had considered sinking the great ship in order that it not represent a navigation hazard, but the truth was there were unlikely to be many ships around, so in the end they watched it dwindle to a speck on the hazy horizon before disappearing altogether. Once the novelty of the high speed as the cars skimmed over the waves wore off, the guests settled down as well as they could in the limited space available lying in passageways and under tables, trying to keep out of the way of those members of the crew who were on duty. As the purple sun sunk into the sea ahead and off to the right of them, the speed was reduced slightly to eighty knots, which according to Petra's calculations would bring them up to their destination at around nine in the morning when the sun had already burnt off the early morning mist. Once again, with only the duty crew fully awake and David and Herb at the controls, the two machines bored on through the black night under a thin high haze which hid all but the brightest stars from their view.

[Extract – 2021]

(The following is a summary from a special report prepared for the Site 3 Steering Committee meeting held on 2 September 2021. It is to be noted that all records related to 1 January 2018 to 31 December 2025 have been classified as restricted and can only be accessed with the authorization of the Council of Elders.)

The removal of any documents from the Records Hall or the copying of any information relating to this period is strictly forbidden.

INTRODUCTION

Over the past two years a private research group has carried out extensive studies regarding the world situation and its likely development over the next decade.

The compilation of valid data has been complex, and is a mix of on-site reports, Sigint, Elint, and reliable second-hand information. Forecasts have also been based on the extrapolation of statistical data as well as on psychological profile studies. As such there will be inaccuracies in the study and the conclusions may not turn out to be one hundred percent correct. Nevertheless, it is the joint opinion of the group that any deviations from the proposed scenario will not be significant.

The basic conclusion of this report fully validate the original decision related to the construction of a Survival Centre.

DISCUSSION

The full report presented to the principals has been summarized in order to present a quick overview of the situation. The topics below have been selected as the most relevant.

A. Conflict Scenarios

Contrary to previous forecasts, none of the so-called local scenarios have led to wider reaching conflicts. To date these conflicts have taken the form of proxy wars where the larger powers (NAF, EU, SOVREP, PRC, etc.) supply weapons, financing, technology and training to third parties while themselves remaining aloof from these conflicts and on occasions even acting or at least giving the appearance of acting as peace brokers. It is to be expected that as local situations become more critical due to failing infrastructures and to lack of food, further localized conflicts will break out. The dangers of these smaller conflicts is that the level of fanaticism involved becomes greater and this leads to even more determined efforts to destroy the perceived enemies.

B. Population

As stated in the previous report two years ago, world population peaked at almost 5.8 billion in 2018–19. Since then the rate of decline has increased by at least thirty-eight percent though exact figures have become difficult to obtain. It would be reasonable to suppose that the current level is of the order of 4 billion ± ten percent. The reasons for this are twofold. Firstly, food production, particularly in Africa and parts of Asia, which has been largely destroyed by pests and wars, has been unable to keep up with the demand, even taking into account population declines. Until recently this situation was alleviated by assistance from the NAF and the EU; however, with the curtailment of these aid programmes a number of large diebacks have taken place. This situation is likely to worsen in the future. Secondly, the development by Roche Labs of Nogrow, the airborne contraceptive virus, originally presented as a great step forward in the field of birth control and put on sale in domestic use aerosols, has also placed in the hands of those who have it, a most potent weapon. This virus has been on the market since the beginning of 2017, but as of mid-2020 a number of illegal large-scale population eradication programmes have been detected. It is known that at least sixty-eight areas have been sprayed in the last year alone using low-flying aircraft for dispersion, with success rates of close on one hundred percent. This study foresees further increasingly rapid population decline, particularly in the poorer areas of the world, as well as in the poorer sectors of the advanced nations. It is also feasible that if terrorist groups obtain large enough amounts of Nogrow, the more advanced nations will also be at risk. If these trends continue, and this seems fairly likely, the total world population may drop as low as two billion ± fifteen percent by the end of the decade.

C. Social Disruption

The level of social unrest has increased steadily and will continue to do so for the foreseeable future. Many cities and towns have in effect become fortified enclaves, where those inside live in fear of attacks from the vast numbers of poorer citizens living outside. This has meant that many medium-sized towns have been all but abandoned, with the consequent disruption of the general productive and economic cycles.

This is further exacerbated by the continued attacks of anti-technology groups who have been successful in destroying much of the underlying infrastructure necessary to guarantee the continuity of the industrial society as we know it. Many advanced programmes have already been terminated, with space technology, biotechnology, communications and energy generation being particular targets for terrorist actions.

D. Nuclear Weapons

The use of nuclear weapons in 2019–21 has increased in comparison with the previous period (forty-seven air or surface explosions versus eighteen); however, the last year has seen a sharp downturn in their use, mainly as a result of pressure by the major powers. It is to be foreseen however that the so-called surgical strikes will continue for an indefinite period. Several cities in the NAF and the EU have been targets for nuclear strikes using land-delivery vehicles. It should be noted there are still over 150 nuclear devices unaccounted for, and while some of these may have been destroyed, there is a more than likely chance that some have fallen into the hands of extremist religious and ethnic fanatic groups.

The weather pattern disturbances resulting from the fallout and atmospheric dust produced by these explosions will not be known for a number of years. It is however already clear that the lack of sunlight on large areas has seriously affected the crop production capacity.

Conversely the use of radioactive dust seeding has the potential for being far more destructive, with large tracts of land in Eastern Europe, North Africa and Asia having already been rendered uninhabitable. Unlike the technological capacity for the production of bombs, the production of radioactive dust produced from spent nuclear fuels has proved difficult to control. It is our opinion that further large-scale seeding is to be expected, and that this will not only result in a large number of deaths, but also will convert large tracts into wastelands.

E. Chemical and Biological Weapons

The use of CBW agents has increased and it is fair to state that the situation is no longer manageable by the major powers because there are at least forty independent nations producing and selling CBW agents. Most of the agents currently in use are genetically modified viruses with increased virulence as well as reduced active lifetimes. This allows infected territories to be invaded and recovered fairly rapidly. The success of recent attacks carried out in the Middle East against the Kurdish territories has done much to encourage the further uses of CBW agents.

F. Global Warming

This is one of the few areas where previous predictions have been pessimistic. The latest studies show that the rate of increase has slowed down to less than half the previously estimated values. This is in part due to the restrictions placed on the use of the so-called greenhouse gases after the Amsterdam Conference of 2009, and also as a result of high-level dust clouds resulting from nuclear explosions (see point D above). The average sea level rise is now expected to be less than 0.5 metres. This will still mean the permanent flooding of low-lying areas near the coast, but a number of cities and towns hitherto under threat of evacuation will now be able to survive provided the necessary flood defences can be completed in time.

G. Economy

The financial structures of the capitalist nations are already under severe strain, and the burden of keeping a large percentage of non-productive people will steadily increase. Although the NAF and the EU blocks still exist as trade groups, there is a high probability that in the short-term trade and tariff barriers will come into being to protect local economies. Many of the large multinational corporations have already been forced to sell off and/or divide back to regional or even to national companies. This is leading to rising costs and reduced productivity, which in turn results in loss of earnings to shareholders who in the end will withdraw their funds from the productive cycle.

CONCLUSIONS

Within the next decade the collapse of the global economy is inevitable. Local economies may survive by using lower levels of technology, but it is clear that the world is facing an increasingly grim scenario. The remaining financial markets will continue to oscillate wildly as new rumours arise, and sooner or later trading will cease as investors pull out of the market.

Terrorist and/or local armed group actions will increase in frequency and violence as factions fight for the control of an ever diminishing bag of resources.

Healthwise the world is facing diebacks from plague and radiation on a scale not seen since the Middle Ages. The city enclaves present particularly tempting targets and it is to be foreseen that only a very few of them will survive more than ten or twenty years. Many small isolated villages will survive this disruption basically intact, but will in the long run be reduced to a primitive technology agrarian society.

NOTE APPENDED BY THE STEERING COMMITTEE:
In view of the above, every effort to speed up the construction of Site 3 will be made, regardless of the cost involved. In particular the TFR construction plants will be given additional protection against the possibility of terrorist attacks. Staffing studies will be brought forward in order to be able to initiate personnel searches at an early date.

Chapter XVII

The arrival of morning brought with it the knowledge that the sky was overcast, wiping the colours from the sea and sky, depressing everything into shades of grey. Petra had chosen a course that allowed them to approach from the north, thus avoiding coming near any of the other islands. Both Jock and Karel had questioned the islanders at length on the state of their home, and in particular about the after-effects of the Chinese attack on Oahu as well as from the Hawaii earthquake.

'I can still remember the reports on the Chinese invasion, our people were monitoring the radio day and night for over a week,' one of the elderly women from the carrier had told them. 'We took in several boatloads of escapees, they really were the lucky ones, most people were sick from the epidemics and couldn't even make the attempt to get off the island. I don't know why the Chinese never attempted to land on Kauai, we'd have been a pushover compared with Pearl.'

'Lucky for us they didn't' chipped in another of the rescuees. 'We wouldn't have been here today to tell the tale, that's for sure.' He stopped suddenly, rubbing his forehead tiredly. 'I can still picture in my mind's eye the day the nukes went off. We could see the mushroom clouds quite clearly ... three of them, misshapen, bent over by the winds but so big, miles into the sky, I don't know ... don't know.' He stopped unable to go on, while one of the other islanders took up the story.

'We were more than lucky that day, because the wind was blowing south at thirty, maybe thirty-five knots, unusual for that time of the year, but it saved us. We got no fallout at all, and the medics said the direct blast exposure was insignificant at that distance. After that there were no more boats, we heard later that the bombs had been neutron bombs, people killers, some even said the NAF had dropped them as a last resort to stop the invasion. I don't know, there probably weren't that many of our own people left alive by then anyway, between the epidemics and the Chinese on Oahu, things weren't that good.'

Six years after that, the islanders went on to tell, Mauna Loa on Hawaii had blown itself out of existence, but once again Kauai had ridden out the crisis, although the resulting tsunami caused considerable damage to the coastal towns and left a large number of casualties. Across over two hundred klicks of ocean they had been subjected to ash falls over a period of weeks whenever the winds blew their way, but eventually that too had diminished. In the intervening years since then, the islanders had basically kept themselves to themselves, not seeking trouble, but keeping a watch out to defend themselves against it. They had tried to keep contact with other survivor groups distributed on the islands, but over the years the contacts had diminished, mainly as a result of the smaller groups being absorbed into others. The island had been attacked by marauders on several occasions two years previously, attacks which they had beaten off. From what they had been able to ascertain from the prisoners they took, the attackers had been based on Lanai where they were living a very primitive existence. Driven more by hunger than anything else, the pirates had set out to conquer their neighbours, an effort which had resulted in their destruction by the better-equipped Tribe on Kauai. Since that time there had been no further incidents, although occasionally they had seen sails on the horizon off to the south.

And so it was that shortly after nine o'clock on a grey morning, the island of Kauai loomed suddenly out of the mist as the Gevcars roared over the breakers and swept into Nawiliwili Bay on the south-eastern end of the island. They came ashore, and at Jack Flowers's indications came to a halt on what had once been the Lihue golf course, now an area of crops and grass fields. Above them and in the distance, the tree-covered land rose up towards the Waialeale ridges, still hidden in the low clouds, adding a sense of mystery and uncertainty to their surroundings. Around them, after the first moments of surprise, the town came to life, as people came out to see what the strange fast-moving vehicles had brought them. As soon as they came to a halt, Jack opened the roof hatch and sat shouting and waving like a madman at his Tribe, cutting short he told Karel later, the defence squad activities which had been set in motion as soon as the Gevcars had been spotted coming across the water. In less than ten minutes the two Gevcars were surrounded by masses of people, curious on the one hand about the strange newcomers and, on the other hand, rejoicing and cheering at the safe return of one of their leaders as well as the other islanders, back as it were from the dead.

Once the visitors had disembarked, they had been escorted to meet the other leaders of the group, a process which took until well after midday as the roads leading away from the place where they had parked the Gevcars had become more and more crowded as word of their arrival spread. The leader of the Tribe was an imposing figure, well over two metres tall with a girth to match, with close-cropped curly brown hair and a dark face at odds with his pale green eyes. He was dressed as were most of the locals in trousers and shirt with sandals, but his sense of presence was such that no one could have mistaken him for anything but the leader. And yet, as he greeted Karel who was a full head shorter, it was clear to one and all that he was greeting an equal who was in every way as powerful as himself, for such is the aura of true leaders that no fancy trappings are needed to enhance their position.

The locals seemed anxious to show off their achievements, and the meeting turned into an impromptu tour of the main town. Much of the original infrastructure on the island was, they were able to see, still standing, and even down on the shoreline, higher now than it had been decades earlier, many things had been rebuilt after the tsunamis from the eruption had battered the coast. Over at the south-western end of the town however things were a different story, for many of the buildings had been wiped out by a vast mudslide seven cycles earlier which had swept down without warning from the upper slopes after several days of intense downpours. It was rather humbling to see roads that vanished into the hillside leading to homes which no longer existed and to see buildings whose top floors emerged from the now overgrown hillside. The tribe had lost over a thousand people in a matter of hours, a major tragedy in such a small community. The current population, the census taker proudly told them, stood at 21,262 as of that morning, spread out all over the island, with the greatest urban concentration still being the north-western end of the old town of Lihue. Given that the original residents had not been selected with survival skills in mind, the Tribe, which was the name they had given themselves, had been fortunate in having a large number of fairly young professionals who were not only able to keep things running, but also had done much to pass on the knowledge to the next generation. Over the years, many of the machines had failed, and even with the extensive skills on hand, it had been possible to repair only the more basic mechanical and electrical items, while microprocessor-based elements had all but vanished. To Karel and Sandy who were the only visitors really old enough to remember society prior to the collapse, much of what they saw was like something out of a historical film depicting mid-twentieth-century technology, though with more sophisticated know how, obtained from the books and records available. They were taken to the hospital, which turned out to be an odd combination of modern knowledge but without the machines and equipment normally seen in such surroundings. Gone were the ECG and EEG units, as well as the highly sophisticated computer-assisted tomographs. What remained was the more basic equipment, manually controlled dialysis units, X-ray machines, basic operating theatre equipment. Erik, Selena, Sanjay and Maria wandered through the building, marvelling at how the place had been kept running throughout the years. Unlike the Foundation where medical science had been the prime mover and where stocks of spares and replacements were still available, here the islanders had had to make do with what they had on hand. Many items of the old technology had been lost, with manufacturing facilities having to be abandoned when the spare parts stock became exhausted. Nevertheless, there was still a small textile plant in operation, two generating stations, several well-equipped machine shops and a number of lesser industries. On the city services side, a waste water treatment plant was still operational, street lighting still existed, though on a reduced scale, and most households had electricity although a couple of power cuts per week had become the accepted norm as the technical staff struggled to keep the old equipment running. This by any criteria had to be rated as a success, and both Karel and Jock had agreed that if Tumbes and Kauai could produce functioning societies under such adverse conditions, then surely there was hope for the future of mankind.

The first social event to celebrate the arrival of the visitors was held that very night, much to their surprise, for most of them would have been happy to retire early. Luckily for them, the whole affair turned into a pleasant and amusing gathering, with both sides exchanging their stories.

The Chief, for so everyone referred to him, threw back his head and laughed. 'Why the tribe? I'll tell you why young ladies.' He said, answering Janine and Alexandra Lowe's question. 'At the beginning, long before I was Chief, and there weren't more than a couple of thousand of us, we had set up our base in the area up above the Wailua reservoir, that's north from here, by the way. So, along comes a delegation from the folk who had elected to stay down in the town. Finding us there, living off the land, they looked down their noses at us and said that we looked like a tribe of savages, that we were a disgrace to the people of the island, and so on. So it became a joke, we were the tribe, and our leaders became the chiefs, and of course in time it stuck with us. We weren't really savages of course, we lived in normal houses, there were villages, we had phones, farm machinery, the electricity generating station, it was just that we had decided to try and be self-sufficient. You have to realize that this was after the Oahu invasion, and it was painfully obvious that the NAF would not be coming back to take care of its citizens stuck out here in the boondocks as it were. We extended the existing farms, we planted new crops. Did you know this island was once called the garden island? Yes it was, and things grew, and we survived, bartering with the townsfolk for what we needed. We grew as well, as more and more people moved into the area and set up their own farms. We never had too many rules, looking back I think that was the secret, you could do what you wanted as long as you didn't damage anything or anyone else. But if you did, the tribe dealt with you swiftly and harshly, there was no room for anyone who didn't pull their own weight.'

'But what happened to the people who stayed on in the town?'

'Ah, well they weren't so lucky were they? They were the posh ones, but without the know how necessary to keep things running. For a while things worked, some died from injuries, accidents, some from disease, some eventually left the town and came up and joined us.' He shrugged, running his hands over the thick white beard which hid much of his face. 'In the end the Hawaii quake finished off what few were left of them, wiped out most of what was down near the coast. The truth is, we've suffered far more from natural disasters than from any man-made problems. Lately things have been a bit more stable, but around ten years ago, after a period of relative drought, we began to get intense and frequent storms, winds in excess of one hundred knots, short lived but very heavy downpours. Lately things seem to have calmed down again, but I imagine the world-wide weather pattern is still in a turmoil.'

Brendt looked thoughtful. 'Yeah, the weather has certainly done some crazy things. But tell me, how did the leaders manage to get things organized enough to survive as a social group, that surely can't have been easy?'

'Well, I was a young man back then, little more than a kid really, but I guess the main thing was that everyone who was there had come up of their own free will. They weren't obliged to leave the town, and if they did they weren't obliged to join the tribe, plenty didn't at first, but they knew that if they did, then they had to go by the rules. My father brought his family up here, he was a founder member, at that time the group was really small, I think the first lot were only fifty or sixty people, but they got organized in the summer homes up there, they voted on who the leader was to be, and then they backed him up, all the way down the line. Within three or four months our numbers had gone over five hundred, and in two years we were two thousand or so. This would have been in, let me see, probably twenty-four, all a long time ago now anyway. As I said, the secret was in having very few hard and fast rules, and in making sure they were obeyed without exceptions. It kept us going, it still keeps us going.'

'That, and education.' Maria sitting three or four seats down from the Chief looked at him.

'Yes, you're right, we were blessed by an inordinately high number of teachers in the early group, some retired, some still in activity. They insisted most strongly to the early leaders that unless some sort of teaching system was set up we really would be savages by the end of the second generation. I wasn't too happy about it at the time but they were surely right, and compulsory education up to the age of eighteen has become part of our system.' He sighed. 'Of course, we have lost some of the high-end knowledge, but our people believe that we have more or less stabilized the situation in the last few years. Teachers are an honoured profession among us, and so it will remain.'

As the evening meal went on, the Gevcar crews and the islanders, the Tribe, as they called themselves, exchanged histories, telling tales which had already begun to grow into legends as the participants died and all that was left was what they had told their children. Only a couple of hundred of the tribe members, plus Karel and Sandy could really remember events from the time of chaos. As always, Karel and Sandy's travels and adventures proved to be a great attraction, all the more so because of the unassuming way in which they were told, playing down moments of great danger or excitement. The tables at which they sat had been placed in a large hall in what had once been a large department store, but was now used as a gathering place for special events, and the arrival of the Gevcars with the survivors off the *Abraham Lincoln* was certainly that. There were at least three hundred people sharing the dinner, all anxious to see and talk to the newcomers, for although from time to time people arrived on the island, nothing like the Gevcars had ever been seen. Had the travellers come upon such a society shortly after leaving the Hold, they might have been amazed. Yet, in the seven moons since they had left the Hold, they had in a way grown blasé, accepting each new stop with equanimity, thinking of Kauai more as a simple stopover on the road to the final site which they all hoped would be there. A number of the older members of the tribe noticed and complemented Karel and Sandy on their youthful appearance when learning their ages, not realizing that in the three weeks since the implant had been made, the genetically altered stem cells had worked wonders. The Hold crew, after a recommendation from Maria, did not make any mention of the treatment they had received, for longevity and good health were more than ever prized possessions in a world where the four grim horsemen still rode abreast, harvesting at random.

The fact that Karel had been an astronaut soon became known, making him a figure of wonder, almost mystical, as if a God from the distant past of mankind walked among them. As Sandy said with a tolerant smile, with his flowing hair now turning a mixture of blonde and white tied back in a ponytail, and the Hold cloak flowing back as he went from place to place, he certainly looked the part. To the few hundred islanders who were old enough to remember the last days of space exploration, Karel's presence was a message from the past that not all was lost, that still the best of the previous world lived on.

Having decided not to stay overly long on Kauai, yet reluctant to leave their hosts without offering some concrete signs of help, Karel and Jock decided to extend their stay for more than the couple of days they had first envisioned. The visitors followed much the same pattern they had done back at Tumbes, soon finding places where their expertise could be put to good use. The medical team ended up in the local hospital, the scientists began giving lectures on genetic manipulation of plants and animals, the Watch joined up with the local militia, and the Techs along with Sandy and Jean began dismantling some of the old communication and transmission equipment they found dotted around the island to see if it was possible to set up a new link through to the Sentry satellites.

By the end of their second week on Kauai, most of the jobs they had set in motion were reaching a point where the locals would be able to continue. In particular and thanks to the comm teams' ability, the communication set-up had become a successful reality, with an old dish aerial and a patchwork of old equipment now linked with the small but spreading Hold contacts. From the Cape to Tumbes, and from the Foundation to the Hold itself, the network spread, uniting them more than anyone would have believed possible. From Spider Magee over in the Cape, came the welcome news that an expedition sent up to Virginia had returned intact despite having been ambushed several times. The news they had brought with them was encouraging, for they had made contact with the remnants of the Citadel Survival Centre including the children of Peter Sonderjheld who had left the journal the travellers had found. Even Karel, normally pragmatic in his assessments, had been prompted to make a philosophical comment about meaningful coincidences. From the Hold itself came the welcome news that the computers had at last broken the encryption algorithms on the Sentry imaging system, and with it the latest download of incredibly clear weather system photos covering the majority of the Pacific basin. Sandy had handed the prints to Threejays who almost crowed with delight before vanishing to study them.

In spite of the intensive work programme, several of them including Karel, Bob and Janine had also found time to hike to the top of Wainiha ridge using an old trail which wound its way up from the now long deserted town of Waimea on the south-eastern coast. Climbing up through the lower levels, pushing their way through the heavy undergrowth, they came at last into the mid-level grasslands peppered with stunted bushes. Passing from a world of deep verdant green vegetation, burdened with humidity which dripped continuously, running off the surface of their cloaks, it was almost a shock suddenly to emerge into a land of sun-parched brownish green, which as they continued to climb soon became a series of sharply pointed rocky outcrops leading to the higher ridges. The going was rough as they approached the highest parts of the ridge, encumbered as they were with the Hold cloaks and glare specs, but in the end their efforts had been rewarded by an unparalleled view over most of the island, the deep verdant greens stretching down to the blue Pacific which rolled in as it had done for uncounted centuries. Across the ocean off to the south-west they thought they could just make out the low shape of Nihau, almost lost in the haze. Despite their elevation over sea level all else was hidden, Oahu, the next nearest island, remained hidden from view in the haze, while the orangey yellow sun burned down stifling under their cloaks and glare specs.

The next morning, still feeling rather stiff after the long hike, even after a good night's sleep, Karel lay quietly, listening to the early morning chirping of the tropical birds that nested in the tree outside their window. Through the open curtain he could see the dim outline of the row of palm trees, silhouetted by the light of one of the occasional streetlights which swung to and fro in the gentle breeze. Beside him Sandy lay, still asleep, her breathing deep and slow. More by habit than necessity he leaned over, and with gentle fingertips brushed back the stray lock of hair that hung down over her forehead, a lock now returning to its original golden colour, though there was still plenty of grey hair in evidence. Her eyes flickered, and she rolled over, snuggling into him, sighing in comfort. He reached over, his fingers brushing feather lightly back and forth across her bare shoulder, an action at once possessive and unconscious, his hand simply doing what it had done uncountable times over five decades. After a while, as the first flush of dawn began to light up their room, he felt within him a sudden pulse of desire, a fire that had lain dormant for the past few years, now awakened he realized intuitively, by the stem cell implant growing in him. As though aware of the change, Sandy opened her eyes, her arms stretching up round his neck as she drew him down to her waiting lips, and then for a while there was only the two of them, moving as one.

Afterwards, all energy spent, as they lay side by side, just touching, still one, eyes closed, sweat drying slowly in the cool dawn air, Sandy stroked his arm. 'Oh my love, it's been a while ... I didn't realize how much we had been missing, it's hard to realize we had almost forgotten the beauty of loving.' She smiled, almost shyly. 'I can't tell you how glad I am that we found the Foundation. I wouldn't have missed this for all the world.'

'Me neither lover.' A lazy smile curved Karel's lips.' It's every bit as good as it ever was, isn't it? I feel so alive these days, I never said much to you, but the truth is I was beginning to feel weary of the never-ending search, but now I feel we could go on for ever.'

As the days passed, their thoughts turned more and more to the journey that lay ahead. As was usual after dinner, they gathered in the lounge of what had once been the Sheraton Hotel and golf resort, at least so the weathered brass sign on the door still said. Threejays lounged back in the easy chair, hands clasped behind her head as she listened to Jock and Karel arguing about the best route. A small smile twitched her lips when they eventually turned to her to ask her opinion.

'I'm way ahead of you people, while you've been busy on other matters I've been working through the various options available, with help from Janine and the pilots.' She grinned her small characteristic grin. 'You've just finished discussing some possible options which consider going on via the Marshall Islands, and from there on to New Guinea and then southwards to the mainland, or perhaps to the Solomon Islands and from there on to Queensland on the mainland. Once one gets to the Marshalls there are plenty of other island-hopping options open. Now, I've also thought of those, but there's a third option which would mean a slightly longer run, and that's to go south to the Western Samoa group, and from there westwards to Fiji, Vanuatu and on to Australia.' She stopped, obviously waiting for some sort of comment, which wasn't long in coming.

'Alright Threejays, I'll buy it, you can stop looking so smug, what's the advantage?' asked Jock, adding with mock resignation to Karel. 'The problem with Threejays is that one always has to leave something for her to pounce on and gloat.'

'You mind your Irish tongue my friend,' came the retort. 'Has it ever occurred to you, oh esteemed leader, that we're coming up to the typhoon season, or at least what used to be the typhoon season?' Jock looked at Karel and shrugged as Threejays continued in her best lecturer's voice. 'Typhoons are tropical cyclones, most of them are born and run just north of the Equator, anywhere from say 160 degrees east to 130 degrees west. The records show that sometimes they stray south of the Equator, but that hasn't been a frequent occurrence. They normally start to appear around mid-July and can run as late as October. Now, I've been studying the data in the computer, plus some additional feed I asked the Hold to send me, plus the latest set photos we have.' She paused, gathering her thoughts. 'I can't pretend to be a weather expert, even less so with the scant data available, but if the current conditions hold, then we can expect a big storm within the next few days, and it will be cutting across from the Marshalls, heading eastwards.'

Karel looked thoughtful. 'I saw the photos of course, and there is a cloud mass north of New Guinea, but the centre doesn't seem to have moved much over the last couple of days, and it's still well to the east of the Marshalls.'

'I know that, and there's no guarantee what will happen, but correlating the data we have gives a more than even chance that the depression will coalesce into a mayor storm which, at least so the statistics say, will run towards the Marshalls at anything up to seventy knots. So, I feel we should either stay put here, Kauai isn't under threat, or head south where we'll be better off. The extra klicks we'd pay for that aren't even worth considering.'

Karel smiled. 'Caught out again,' he grimaced. 'I'll admit we hadn't taken the point into such deep consideration.'

'Look Karel, I admit that typhoons are notoriously difficult to predict, and even then, are liable to change course on very short notice. So, if we head towards the Marshalls we could run into some heavy weather, and even if we have some sort of advance warning, it could cut across our course within a very short time. The alternative is of course to wait for what appears to be an extended clear period, but I think everyone is anxious to get under way again as soon as possible, I know I am.'

'Welcome to the club, so are we.' He stopped, looking at the others, his bright blue eyes seemingly lost in thought. 'You know, it's a pity we didn't plan more over water legs right from the start, 'I know that it's easy to be clever after the event, but we would have saved an awful lot of time if we had only dared to do so.'

Jock nodded his head. 'True of course, but let's not forget that on our first real over water trip up past Panama we had to come ashore because of the short swells which affected several of us. I know I was feeling queasy at the time anyway.'

'Hmm, and don't forget Karel, that if we had done everything over water we wouldn't have made contact with Tumbes, or the Cape, or even with the Foundation,' Threejays pointed out. 'And I for one enjoy feeling younger and more alive than before.'

Karel nodded in agreement. 'Yes, of course I agree with you, and I wouldn't have it any other way. So, on to the next point. When should we set our departure date for? We've been here, what, two weeks?'

'Two days into the third sevendays,' replied Threejays. 'From what Janine tells me we could leave as early as the day after tomorrow if we wanted to.'

Jock shook his head. 'I think we should allow our hosts a little bit more time, how about completing the sevenday?' he asked looking around, and receiving affirmative nods from his two companions. Threejays looked doubtful for a moment before replying.

'OK, I'll keep an eye on the storm front as long as the Sentry holds up, as long as we head south we should be able to cut across the storm long before it gets serious. Now that the Hold boys have finished the enhancement algorithms, we can get high-definition pictures as often as we want, but ...'

'More information would be even better.' Jock finished the sentence for her. 'We'll tell our hosts that we'll be leaving in five days time at dawn. We'll have to get Miguel and Sun Yan down from that place they've been working way up the valley. As usual, I don't suppose they'll be happy about that, scientists never are when someone interrupts their research work.'

Turning away from the window through which he had been waving at the well-wishers on the beach, now growing smaller and smaller as the Gevcars picked up speed and the curtain of spray covered their view, Jock stretched and looked across at Matt who sat relaxed at the controls, jiggling the joystick lightly to adjust their course through the reef.

'Well Matthew, off again into the great unknown.'

'Yep,' came the reply. 'I was getting bored already without any fixed duties. It's all very well for the Techs, the science specialists and the Medics, but for Petra and myself. ... Well, there's not been that much to do.'

'Not much to do?' David peered into the cockpit from the stairway down to the main cabin where he had been standing. 'Not much to do?' he repeated. 'I saw you doing not much with that girl the other evening at the farewell party!'

Matt opened his mouth to reply, then closed it again, turning a bright red which came close to matching the colour of his hair.'

'Relax, carrot top, just joking, just joking' continued David, delighted with the reaction he had obtained, as he retired down the steps, leaving Matt without any possibility of answering.

'Blast,' Matt grinned, 'I'm just never fast enough with the witty answers, he beats me every time.'

Jock smiled. 'I wouldn't worry too much, David's more than a match for most of us, as far as I know only Threejays can manage to get the better of him on a regular basis ... mmm, probably Selena could as well if she really wanted to, but she's probably too kind hearted.' He watched the last of the offshore rocks slip by, started to yawn, and caught himself. 'Don't know why I'm sleepy already, it's early in the morning. Well, I'm going to do some work on my report, nudge me if you need anything.' Matt nodded absently, deeply involved in the as yet untarnished pleasure of handling the massive Gevcar as they accelerated up to their cruising speed.

Behind them and off to the left the second car followed their curving course as they cleared the reef and turned south towards their destination which lay far to the south, a small spot in the immensity of the Pacific, an island not quite eighty klicks long by twenty wide, with, according to their carts, the unlikely name of Urolu. Ahead of them the ocean and the sky met indistinguishably in a steel grey wall, while behind them the peak of Waialeale fell away into the ever-present haze. From off to the south-east, still only thirty degrees or so above the invisible horizon, a watery pale red sun made the occasional unsuccessful effort to break through the high wispy overcast, as though peering out to see where the speeding Gevcars were, before hiding once more.

By noon the crews had once again got used to the slight corkscrewing motion as the cars slipped over the great swells at over ninety knots, albeit with some help from Erik's medicine cabinet. Even with the lift set at one metre above the surface and with the autopilot tuned to compensate for wave motion, the ride was not entirely smooth. Herb and David had, it was clear, added enormously to their piloting abilities since the first over water run four and a half moons earlier, reducing the discomfort to only a small part of that experienced in their earlier runs. The day continued overcast, and with the absence of the sun, and the great wakes left by their passing seemed somehow cold and distant, pallid manifestations of great energy, soon re-absorbed again into the ever-shifting bosom of the great ocean. The distance to their first destination, the islands of

Western Samoa, chosen on the basis of information available to them in the Records' computer, lay just over 4,200 klicks away from Kauai, in theory a mere twenty-four hours at their full cruising speed and even less at maximum speed, although the pilots had allowed twice that in their planning so as to take into account unexpected detours or other delays.

As evening drew to a close, with the dull coloured sea and sky slipping down the grey scale towards the blackness of night without even a glimpse of the setting sun to colour it, Karel sat at his desk behind the cockpit as was often his wont. Lately he had taken up the habit of going over all the information available on the third site, correlating again and again the scant data, looking for some additional clue to narrow down the search area. After their experiences with the Citadel he knew that the search would not be easy, although from what he had been able to find out about the surrounding territory, they could at least expect somewhat better signal emission and reception conditions than they had encountered in the mountains, a fact which would hopefully shorten the time until the site sent out its automatic recognition pattern. Always supposing the thing worked that is. After hours of research and cross-checking he had the name of the area where the last site was to be found, Uluru, even the name seemed to be mysterious, a message from the distant past. The white men who had arrived in Australia long after the place had been given its name, had only reached that part of the continent in the second half of the nineteenth century. They had called the massive rock outcropping by a new name, Ayers Rock, but in the end the older aborigine name prevailed. Uluru, the biggest monolithic surface rock ever found, and somewhere within a circle which was probably some twenty klicks in diameter lay the third Survival Centre, Site 1 according to the old records. Three hundred million square metres to search, shouldn't be too bad, not too bad at all. Karel smiled to himself, he had faced tougher challenges before. After dinner, a meal which produced more than a fair share of grumbles as they re-adapted to their travel rations instead of the fresh island produce, they spoke briefly with the Hold, reporting to the Council the days progress, and receiving in turn the latest Sentry weather photos.

Later, Karel had returned to his desk, and after a while, lulled by the distant thrum of the power unit and the almost hypnotic motion of the Gevcar as it sped over the dark ocean, his breathing slowed and his lean frame slowly relaxed into sleep. And as his mind slid down through its alpha rhythm, he knew with absolute certainly but without understanding how, that Leana watched over him.

Chapter XVIII

The man stood up slowly, stretching his back which ached from crouching in the scant shade of the spinnifex bush, he turned carefully before sliding out into the open, so as to avoid being scratched by any of the inch-long thorns which decorated every gnarled branch. Under the wide brim of his stained old bush hat his jet black eyes swept the horizon once more, the glare specs looking rather incongruous under such an ancient piece of headgear. He scratched his scalp through the thick brown curly hair which covered his head like an unruly mat, as though something inside his skull bothered him. The brownish desert stretched away from him on all sides, dotted occasionally by sparse clumps of vegetation, stunted eucalyptus, spinnifex bushes, and other grasses, all covered in the pervasive dust which at the slightest breath of wind would leap up forming dozens of dancing dust devils, hazing the view even more than usual. Out of his sight behind the large boulder off to his left would be the distant shape of the domes of Kata Tjuta, the Place of Many Heads, a group of twenty-eight reddish conglomerate sandstone rocks, towering out of the surrounding desert. A place of legend covering thousands of years of Aboriginal history, inextricably linked to Uluru where the old cave paintings still guarded the tunnels into the rock. He looked around again, seeing no unusual movement, and with a slight shrug bent down and picked up his small pack which he threw carelessly across his shoulder. With a final look around, he set out towards the entrance to his post some hundred metres distant, moving easily across the dry land as only one born to it can, leaving no visible track whatsoever.

They were coming, the strangers, quite soon too, he sensed, stretching his mind to its limit, yes, soon, they were coming, and some among them had the gift. In the evening he would speak to the Council, and if the strangers proved worthy, they would make them welcome.

'Land Ho!' The cry rung through the Gevcar, bringing everyone to the windows, looking to glimpse the land that meant the end of the long ocean crossing. Jean passed the news back to Sandy in the second car a klick and a half behind them, and then the orders to reduce to forty knots as David cut the throttles and the car seemed to sag as their headlong rush slowed.

Petra studied the GPS printout carefully checking their position against the computer printout, and then peered through the high-powered binoculars. 'You're right on the nail, David, that should be Magnetic Island just off to the right, and that will be Bowling Green Bay to the left. Didn't they just give these places some weird names?'

Karel who was sitting in the third seat in the cockpit looked over at the young co-pilot and smiled. 'Read your history child, there's a reason for every name, you know.'

'Right, give me a course when we come round that headland,' replied David, indicating the point ahead which was rapidly growing in size as the cars raced across the water.

The trip from Kauai had to all intents been an anticlimax despite all Threejays' worries. They had met no typhoons, no tropical storms, no giant waves, only the unending swells of the great ocean. The threatening mass of cloud off towards New Guinea which had made Threejays propose the southern route had quietly dissolved away, leaving days of high overcast and occasional spotty sun. They had found no recent traces of anyone at their first landfall in Western Samoa, just the abandoned remains of towns and villages, some intact, and some destroyed. They had moved on, and 2,500 klicks later had come across some frightened and shy natives in what had once been the spreading city of Noumea in New Caledonia, natives who fled as soon as they realized they had been spotted. They had wasted a few hours trying to convince the tribesmen to come out, but in the end had pushed on towards the mainland, pausing only to stop to admire the beauties of the Great Barrier Reef, where fish played as though man had never been. Skimming slowly over the crystal clear almost perfectly transparent water, they could see the coral growths which made up part of the vast coral reef which, after dozens of generations of human interference, still stood defending the eastern coast of Australia. Under the effect of sunlight the colours varied from green through to dark blue, with flashes of yellows and oranges. Colours that they had thought lost forever under the orange sun, but here out in the Pacific rim, the haze seemed to have lifted, reminding them that the Earth could live again if it was allowed to.

They had watched a school of dolphins playing nearby, effortlessly keeping pace with the two Gevcars' reduced speed. In the evening Karel had brought them to a halt on a low semi-circular coral island which emerged barely a couple of metres above the sea, where a few thin palms clung tenaciously to life. They had swum out from the beach under the purple light of the setting sun, and the memories of the dolphins which had played with them and allowed themselves to be touched would be with them forever. Selena above them all seemed to possess some special talent, for without any apparent hesitation the dolphins had allowed her to hang on to their fins and enjoy a high-speed ride round the lagoon.

Now, nine days after departing Lihue, they had reached the Australian coast. The two cars cruised slowly in towards the shore, their hulls glistening from the spray, coated all over except for the windscreens with a thin white film of salt, the product of their days at sea. Off to the north it was possible to see the dim hazy outlines of a number of buildings which according to their charts should be the city of Townsville. They came ashore moving shudderingly through the breakers, separating to a distance of some four hundred metres as indicated in the procedures set up by Karel so as to ensure that no single event could harm both cars. In Jock's car Jean sat at his console, head bowed as he scanned the airwaves for any sign of activity. Band by band went by, and all that came to him was the quiet hiss of the headphones and the occasional muted whistle and klick of some distant interference. Up in the electrogun turret, Sara sat quietly, the cannon fully powered and waiting, while just below her Bob stared at the blank ranging screens. The two cars moved up through the dunes, occasionally losing sight of each other for a few minutes until they reached the remains of an old road.

'Which way boss?' Herb, looking over towards Jock as he jiggled the joystick keeping the massive Gevcar practically motionless as it hovered just above the weathered and pitted tarmac surface.

'Turn right, we'll move slowly towards Townsville. Move out until we're about a hundred metres seawards from the road, Karel will do the same on the other side.'

'Will do. David, do you read? We'll parallel the road off to the right.'

'Yeah, we'll be on the left and a bit behind you, watch out when the road turns to the left and joins the main road, according to Janine's map reading there used to be a village of some sort at the crossroads,' replied David from the other car as they ploughed their way through the bushes which bordered the road.

As the cars advanced, leaving behind them the coastal dunes and pushing their way through areas where tropical vegetation still grew on the low rolling hills which bordered the coastline, they passed a number of what had once been posh summer homes, now lying toppled and burnt. More than once they saw small shrivelled piles which were obviously the remains of corpses, long eaten and rotted by the passing years, but of recent occupation there was no sign. The land around them had obviously remained fertile, and if at times there had been droughts, there was not much sign of such occurrences at the moment. At the crossroads they were confronted by a large roadblock formed by a column of ten or twelve burnt out military vehicles, including a number of light tanks, now lying hatches open, streaked with the rust of many seasons, some of them half buried in the ditches and covered with vegetation. On either side of the road, the land fell off into swampland, which presumably explained how the armoured column had been ambushed there long ago. Passing a tilted sign on which it was still possible to discern some writing, the Gevcars swung out over the swamp, throwing up a thin spray of muddy water, continuing their slow purposeful ride towards the town.

'... no closer. You have been ... Townsville Defence ... 043' read Jules from his vantage point up in the turret as they passed by. 'Karel, shouldn't we avoid this altogether? The locals don't sound very welcoming.'

'Ordinarily yes, but we need to have some idea of local conditions before we push on into the interior. Townsville was only a small place, otherwise I wouldn't be taking us in. If it had been a large city it would have been different, but I think it's worth the risk.' Behind him Jojo sat quietly, his assault rifle cradled loosely in his hands, his mind disconnected while he waited for the call to action that might or might not come. Beside him, Brendt sat also fully geared up, having left the ranging equipment on standby, but ready take over again if Jules needed his assistance.

The nearer they came to the town, the more obvious it became that a large attacking force had been through, systematically destroying everything in its path, for hardly a building stood intact. Every few minutes the Gevcars stopped, carefully scanning the land ahead for any signs of activity, in addition to continuing with the

266

radio watch, neither search giving any indication of the presence of man. Finally, with the sun beginning to tilt downwards to the west, and knowing they had only a few hours of daylight left, they entered into the main town itself. The scenes of destruction that met their eyes were frankly terrifying, and more than one crew member had difficulty in restraining the gag reflex that was the instinctive reaction to what they were seeing. This had been no ordinary attack, for even after many years the savagery of the fighting was evident in the rows of bleached heads which decorated the railings of many buildings, eye sockets staring blindly at the passing visitors. Along the remains of the waterfront boulevard stood several sets of crudely built gallows, and although the ropes had long since rotted away to nothing, the piles of bones alongside gave grim witness to their enthusiastic use. Calling a halt, Karel positioned the Gevcars in open courtyards a couple of hundred metres apart, but where they could still provide covering fire for each other should it be required. The two watch teams plus Matt, with Karel himself in the lead, set out to investigate the immediate area, advancing carefully through the rubble which covered much of the street, always careful to not have more than three people in the open at any one moment. Grimly conscious that the small team of eight would prove no match for any large group that lay in waiting, however disorganized they might be, Karel talked almost constantly to the cars using the throat mike taped under his cloak. Many of the buildings had gaping holes in them where explosions and artillery shells had ripped out entire walls, some had been burnt out, but curiously, the windows of the upper floors of some office blocks eight or ten stories high still had glass in them, and neither the force of the explosions nor the obviously intensive fighting that had taken place had damaged them. In one dead-ended alley there were skeletons stacked dozens deep and the marks of bullets and flame-throwers could still be seen on the walls. They continued the advance through the deserted city under the orange glare of the sun which burned down on them through the thin haze, throwing shadows into stark contrast with the rest of the scenery. They moved slowly, under their hooded cloaks and behind the glare specs they moved as grey ghosts might, except for the sound of their boots on the broken surface and the occasional dry cough of a cleared throat. By fifteen thirty they had quartered an area some ten blocks square, finding nothing living except several packs of grey brown rats which had all but ignored their coming. Wherever possible they tried to glean information on what might have happened and who the attacking party or parties had been, but there was painfully little evidence to support any theory except for faded graffiti on the walls, obviously left by the victors. Finally, sick at heart, the exploration team returned to the Gevcars, several of them weak kneed from vomiting at some of the sights they had seen, sights which even the all enveloping blanket of time had not softened nor faded.

'I feel that we should move on as rapidly as possible, striking inland away from the coast,' Karel leaned over the table where he had been looking at the map. 'We don't know enough about what happened in Townsville to draw any reasonable conclusions. From the evidence we have gathered, the fighting took place only some eight years ago, and I use the word only on purpose.' He paused, checking to make sure that everyone was getting the point. 'If all this had happened thirty, forty or more years ago, there would be little danger in running into the perpetrators. But, eight years ago is not very long, and any large band that existed then could conceivably still be operating in the area, even if we haven't come across them yet.'

'But it's still a gamble, even if we set off towards Charters Towers as planned, we could still run into them,' pointed out Threejays, looking worried.

'Yes.'

Brendt cleared his throat. 'There's not that many options open. If we had found people here it would have been helpful, as it is ...' His voice trailed off.

'That's about it, we'll head out a few klicks, the maps shows a place called Brookhill, perhaps there'll be something there.' Karel picked up the map and began folding it, signalling that the meeting was over.

'Just one thing, more of a suggestion really.' Ken Magee, not usually very vocal at the best of times made Karel pause and look at him inquiringly. 'There's supposedly an airport three or four klicks to the west, at least it's shown on the maps. I'd like to take a look at it, there might still be a flyable machine in which we could go up and take a look around. After all, this wasn't a Luddite attack, I mean these people used technology to fight. If we could get up to say three or four thousand feet it might be possible to see smoke or other signs of habitation.'

'I'm not sure I could still fly an unknown aircraft, I haven't sat in a cockpit for over thirty years now.' Karel looked regretful.

'No, but I have. We had a couple of ultralights at the Cape which we kept in working order, I last flew one six or seven moons ago. The idea came to me because I saw the remains of a poster stuck up on a wall while we were exploring.'

Karel looked at him, and then shook his head. 'I didn't know that, tricky devil that Spider, he never said anything. No Ken, I hate to disappoint you, but I don't think it's worth the risk. Look, those things make quite a noise, and they can be seen from way off, so we could attract some unfriendly attention. No, I prefer to keep the group together.'

'Yeah, I guess you're right, but it would have been nice to get up in the air again' Ken grinned, not the least put out by Karel's rejection of his idea.

The fall of evening found the two cars moving slowly southwards, leaving the destroyed town centre behind them. Passing through what had once been a charming suburban area they could see that the destruction had been less intense, and that while most houses had obviously been ransacked, not all that much damage had been done. Much of what damage there was had in fact long since been covered by the spread of vegetation from the untended and overgrown gardens. In some way the lush tropical flowering plants provided a grim carnavalesque picture, while the waist-high grasses made it seem as if the building floated on a sea of yellowish green waves. There were no signs of any recent habitation, though on a number of occasions they saw movements in the bushes, or once or twice even in the houses, but these turned out to be animals of various descriptions, from feral cats to packs of wild dogs, obviously the distant descendants of abandoned family pets. With the distant and distorted purple globe of the sun starting to sink into the horizon, hidden behind the now more spread out buildings and trees, they came at last to a halt in a grove of eucalyptus trees.

With the guard shifts set up among the Watch team, and the perimeter alarms set, a practice which they had not had to do since before reaching the Foundation, a frugal meal was served inside the Gevcars. With a strict no lights policy, there was not much further activity and even less conversation, aside from Jock and Karel contacting the Hold with the usual end of the day report. After a while, other than for the changing of the watch, the Gevcars soon lapsed into silence as the night rolled over them.

The two cars were under way again as soon as it was light, following the old road, first almost directly south, and then swinging westwards towards Charters Towers. Moving at speeds not much in excess of thirty knots, keeping their usual distance apart, they took over two hours to reach the town, which much to everyone's relief turned out to be basically undamaged aside from the destruction wrought by the passing years of sun and storms. Several times they saw indications of more recent activity, articles of old clothing which couldn't have been out in the open for more than a few weeks, the remains of dead dogs, killed within a period of a couple of moons. On full alert now, they edged towards the centre of the small town, hardly more than a large village really. As Karel's car reached the central square, now an area totally overrun with long grasses and bushes, they saw a small figure dart out and run across the road ahead of them. Stopping the Gevcar, Karel gave orders to Brendt, Jules and Jojo to attempt to follow the runner and see what information they could obtain. As the three Watch members set off at a trot down the narrow lane down which the figure had disappeared, being careful to keep several metres apart, David slid up into the gun turret, leaving Petra at the controls.

As they reached the first corner some fifty metres long, Jojo caught sight of the figure vanishing around the next corner.

'Hey, stop, we only want to talk' he shouted, trying to catch his breath at the same time, while Jules who had been close behind ran up and passed him.

'I'll follow him this way, go round the block, perhaps he'll run that way.'

Jojo nodded, and set off at a trot, followed closely by Brendt who had been bringing up the rear, moving slowly and carefully, constantly scanning the buildings, watching for any sign of activity, his trained eyesight noting which things belonged, and those that were not right, and cataloguing their degree of risk. Jojo reached the next corner and turned left, hoping to be able to see their quarry as he crossed ahead of them, even though the street was half blocked with abandoned vehicles. Still fifty metres ahead of him, the small figure darted out from a pathway that ran between two houses, started to cross the road, but catching sight of Jojo, spun round and cut off down yet another path. Jules and Jojo reached the point

270

where the figure had vanished at more or less the same time. As they debated what to do next, a second figure, larger than the first stepped into the road some twenty metres away.

'Look out, to your right,' yelled Brendt, as he ran to the left trying to get to a place where he would have a clear field of fire should that prove necessary. 'We're not here to harm you, we just need information.' He shouted, still on the move, watching horrified as the figure raised the weapon he had been carrying pointing it towards the other Watch members. Jojo, with a reaction time that would have done credit to a man many years younger, spun and leaped towards the shelter offered by the curb, while Jules, a fraction slower threw himself towards the entrance down which their original quarry had run. The figure seemed to hesitate for an instant, and then continued to swing the weapon up, bringing it to bear on Jules. With a twanging sound, a set of three short stubby crossbow bolts leapt out, and as though it were an echo came the dull sound of Brendt's needle gun, followed a split second later by the duplicate noise as Jojo fired as well. Two of the bolts missed completely ricocheting off the wall, but the third caught Jules high in the shoulder, and with a yelp of surprise and pain he slid down the wall. The attacker, caught simultaneously by the two needle bursts, appeared to leap backwards, his chest and head turned almost instantly into a mass of splintered flesh, dead long before he reached the ground.

'Jojo, see to Jules. I'll guard.' Called Brendt as he raced for the shelter offered by the other side of the road, scanning constantly for any movement, finding none. Jojo stooped by his fallen companion, using his scarf to bind the wound which he realized was painful rather than fatal, and then between them they half carried, half dragged Jules back the way they had come while Brendt called for the car on the portable comm.

Back in the Gevcar, Karel immediately ordered them to move ahead, wanting to get them away from the town as rapidly as possible. Dropping his kitbelt, Brendt climbed straight up to the turret, relieving David who scrambled down and headed back for the cockpit.

'Shit, we made a mistake there,' Jojo sat on the bench and looked ashamed, 'we should never have split up like that in enemy territory. Sorry, I should have stopped Jules.' He looked across at Karel.

'No Jojo, if anyone made a mistake it was I. Trying to catch that runner wasn't the best idea, but I felt that we really need to know if there's any serious opposition in the area.'

Erik ducked into the compartment. 'Well, he'll be OK, stiff at the shoulder for a long time, but luckily nothing vital got hit.' His announcement brought an immediate lightening of the tension. 'But,' continued the doctor, 'I've given the bolt to Linda and Sun Yan, they'll try to check for toxics, although we're not really set up for that.' Karel looked sharply at him, and he went on. 'Relax, just a precaution, I don't actually expect any problems.'

'Karel, you're wanted on the comm' Janine called, peering in. Karel left the room, followed by Jojo still looking rather glum.

At the communications desk, Jean Klock handed Karel the microphone, indicating that the other Gevcar was calling.

'Jock? ... Yes, I'm afraid so, ... no, not a set-up, we just got unlucky, We'll get out of the place and then stop, according to the map there's a low hill a klick or so further on. Keep the distance and we'll rendezvous there. ... Right, yes. ... Out.'

Half an hour later, with the red sun still trying to break through the morning haze, the two Gevcars sat concealed by a straggly bunch of palm trees. Below them, in the shallow valley through which they had come, the town of Charters Towers sat, not a movement to be seen, not a wisp of smoke stirring the air, not even the flicker of a light to indicate that there were any inhabitants. The first thing Karel had done when they stopped was to take Jojo and Brendt outside and after debriefing them had spoken quietly to them for a few minutes.

'We as a group are here to help people. You may be thinking that what you did down there was wrong. It wasn't. We make choices all the time, I have made that same choice before, more than once, the taking of life is never easy, but to allow yourselves or a companion to be killed is worse. You had a tough decision to make, and very little time in which to do so. You are both highly trained, today that training paid off because you definitely took the right decision, and the fact that Jules is with us and will recover is more than sufficient proof of that. Let there be no doubt at all of that. I commend you, you took the right decision.'

The group spent over an hour discussing the next move, but in the end the decision was to keep on along the original route, following the road westwards across Queensland, and on into the Northern Territory, and then turn southwards towards Alice Springs. Sara, Brendt, Jojo, Matt and Bob had all proposed leaving the road and heading out across the Outback in a straight line to Alice, a typically bold Watch idea thought Threejays to herself, but once again the necessity of getting some idea of the local situation prevailed. With the decision taken, and Jules propped up as comfortably as possible in his bunk, the Gevcars once again powered up and headed back down to the road, trailing their usual cloud of dust and sand flung out from under the skirts. Before leaving, they did some crew shifting, with Selena and Sanjay exchanging places, a suggestion made by Erik as he wanted Selena to keep an eye on Ken Magee who had complained that the area round his implant had become very sensitive and itched periodically. The only member of the group who looked rather glum was naturally enough Jojo, but he accepted the matter with as much good grace as possible. As they progressed on their way, following the broken remains of the highway which climbed upwards away from the coastal plains, the land became drier and drier. The colours began changing from the multiple shades of green that marked the fertile zone where tropical and subtropical plants grew and prospered, to the dull reds, ochres and greys of the desert. Scrubby trees and bushes replaced exuberant palms and ferns, with only the occasional half-dried group of eucalyptus trees signalling the presence of a spring or a small trickle of water. If ever there had been fences, they had long since gone, torn down, if not by man, then by time, and only in the small towns which had lived off the road was there a reminder that man had once come close to dominating this great land. Soon the road all but vanished, and they were forced to cover longer and longer sections relying only on the GPS signal beamed down to them from the Sentry, a signal which as they moved westwards would become weaker.

Two days later, with the still warm wind sighing through the promise of the cooler evening, the small group stood in silence, a silence broken only by the occasional scuffing of their boots on the stony ground. What had to be said had been said, now there was only the silence of individual mourning. Karel and Jock had spoken briefly of those they had lost, followed by a few words from most of the rest of the crews, fragments of the memories that bound them together. The air around them was still thick with dust and smoke, and the sweetish smell of death brushed their nostrils. Behind them, barely fifty metres away, the two Gevcars stood silent, hatches open, as if they too were watching the scene. The nearest one, even in the dim red light showing the effects of the battle, scars and dents gouged into the plasteel armour surface, with almost half the rear of the left side blackened by the bursts of the incendiary shells. At the centre of the loose circle in which they stood, three markers, hastily manufactured out of plasteel strips welded together, two planted on rough somehow obscenely small mounds, the third just hammered into the hard soil which in the dull red light of the dying day, seemed to be covered in blood. Karel's eyes gazed over the scene, as though replaying a film slowly, perhaps in the hope of finding out what else they could have done, trying to see what other decisions had been available to him, perhaps just remembering.

Across the shallow depression which marked the path of some long dried up river and beyond the grove of young eucalyptus trees which clung to the hillside somehow drawing up the water which gave them life, the pall of dust and smoke still towered up into the sky. No longer was it the thick threatening mass with a fiery base that it had been three and a half hours earlier when the bolts from the electrogun had wiped out much of the town, and with it half the hillside. Now, dissipating thinly, a mere shadow if its former self, the cloud was just a reminder of the events which had cost Sanjay, Jules, and Petra their lives, as well as wounding Janine. Karel brushed back a sliver of blonde hair that had slipped out from the band which held his ponytail. How easily they had been trapped, despite all their training, how damn easily. They had accepted the situation at face value, and after all, why not? How could they have known it was a damnably clever trap?

After leaving Charters Towers they had moved on westwards at a good forty knots, until at a point still some twenty klicks distant from the spot on the map called Hughenden, they came across the small band of travellers. They had approached carefully, one car hanging back to offer support if needed. Coming in closer, and seeing that there were women and children among them, Jock, whose car was in the lead at the time had stopped and offered assistance. The story they had been told seemed to fit in with all they had seen so far. The group, a dozen in all, had claimed to be fleeing from a large group of bandits that had abducted them a week earlier from their homes in Hughenden, but due to luck and a general lack of care by their captors, they had made good their escape the previous night and were now trying to get home. The information they had on the bandits was limited, only that they appeared to be nomadic and had been heading northwards with the intention of reaching Cairns where they apparently had some sort of base. Most of the refugees were healthy looking enough, though rather on the thin side which seemed to be the general condition of much of humanity. Having talked the matter over with Karel on the radio, they had picked up the travellers and continued on their way towards the town, while behind them their long dusty trail marked their passing as they raced over the dry stony desert.

Arriving in the town, it was easy to see that the place was obviously inhabited, for there were several semi-cultivated fields, irrigated, so they were told, by water from an artesian well. Although many of the houses lay deserted and ruined, the inner part of the town had been made into a rough fort by building walls and blocking roads. Inside these walls lived, so the refugees told them, almost two thousand people, surviving as best they could. Moving into the town, the Gevcar had pulled up at one of the makeshift gates and come to a halt, opening the hatch so as to allow their passengers to disembark. After a couple of minutes, the old rusted brown bus which formed part of the roadblock began to be moved to the side, and the group headed towards the opening gap.

In a way it was luck that saved them from all being captured or killed, luck that put the right man in the right position at the right moment. It was luck that it was Brendt who saw it first, Brendt, whose watchkeeping talents went so deep that even while relaxed his eyes continued scanning everything, registering what he saw, sometimes noting things for future analysis, mostly discarding the data as irrelevant. As he watched from his vantage point up in the turret, a splash of light had touched his peripheral vision, a splash he saw as he turned his head, which originated from a long metal tube projecting from the upper floor of a building off to their right, a tube now swinging round to point at them. He had stabbed at the alarm button, yelling at the same time into the intercom, warning David who was at the controls of the car, while at the same time he fumbled for the activation switches for the missile launcher. Down in the main cabin, the last three remaining passengers, realizing that their game was up, drew weapons which they had kept concealed in their clothes. Sanjay, who had been changing the dressing on Jules' shoulder walked into the compartment unaware that anything was amiss and took a knife thrust straight in the chest, and fell back

275

clutching himself as the front of his shirt turned crimson. Jules, hearing the commotion, levered himself up from where he had been lying, reaching for his needle gun which he kept in the drawer above his bunk. He staggered out of his compartment, taking in the situation at a single glance, bringing up his gun and shooting Sanjay's murderer neatly in the head, the spread of the needles being hardly noticeable at such short range. He spun round and froze, gasping with the sudden pain that shot through his damaged shoulder, blurring his vision with whiteness. The hesitation, though only momentary, gave the next man his opening and Jules took a bolt in the neck from the compressed air gun fired by the bandit who was standing nearest the hatchway which at that time still stood wide open. The bandits had then given up any idea they might have had of reaching the cockpit and had made a dive for the door, knocking down Janine who had been outside saying goodbye to the rest of the group, shooting at her as she rolled on the floor, but missing by a hair's breadth. At this time the tube Brendt had noticed had shown itself to be a grenade launcher, for with a screeching roar, a rocket-propelled grenade had swept down, hitting the Gevcar well aft of the doorway, instantly killing at least three of the supposed refugees as well as Petra who had also been outside helping them. The Gevcar surged sideways, but the worst of the blast was channelled upwards and away by the slope of the plasteel armour which had been designed all those years ago for precisely that function. The two bandits who had just stepped down from the car were also blown away, flung into the side of the car like rag dolls, but Janine who was still down on the ground was protected from the worst of the explosion by their bodies and despite the shock didn't quite lose consciousness and was able to pick herself up and stagger towards the Gevcar despite the pain in her side. Jojo who had flung himself down from the cockpit where he had been sharing a coffee with the pilots, had reached the door and just managed to drag Janine into the safety of the Gevcar as David slid the power up to maximum. The car had lifted half a metre almost vertically while at the same time swinging round in the place where it stood, the hardened plasteel nose destroying part of the front of a building beside the road with a shuddering crash during the turn.

In the second car a few metres behind them, Herb had desperately changed course, ploughed his way straight through a shoulder-high brick wall, throwing debris in all directions while up in the cockpit

Bob and Sara raced through the electric cannon power-up sequence. Inside the Gevcars a few moments of chaos had prevailed until Jean and Sandy had hooked up the command link which put Karel, Jock, the pilots and the gun crews on a priority channel. As the car had retreated back down the road, Brendt managed to put a missile straight into the window where the enemy launcher had been, removing most of the top floor in the resulting explosion. At this time the cars began taking hits from other hidden weapons, hits which were deafening rather than damaging, for being of relatively small calibre they had bounced harmlessly off the toughened hulls. Reaching a distance of around five hundred metres from where they had first stopped, Bob, who had been repeatedly reporting a weapons' ready condition, finally received permission to fire the electric cannon. The effect on the buildings where he aimed the bolt had been immediate and devastating. There had been an incredible bright flash and then an orange-yellow fireball reaching greedily outwards, blasting away everything in its path up to a radius of well over one hundred metres and scorching things twice as far away. The two cars, with the controls set at maximum lift, had been thrown aside by the expanding shockwave, but by good fortune no one was injured. The Gevcars had bulldozed their way up the valley, continuing to fire the electroguns whenever a confirmed hostile target had appeared, until after the seventh shot there was very little left of the centre of the town and a huge firestorm was streaking upwards into the sky, sucking in oxygen from the outside to feed its hunger. Inside Karel's car, Erik worked desperately to try to save Sanjay, whose life bubbled slowly out onto the dark green floor of the car, staunching the flow of blood from the great wound he had received from the long saw toothed knife. At the same time Janine and Linda had done what they could for Jules, but with his spinal chord almost severed by the bolt, they had no chance of saving him and it was only moments before he slipped across the border which divides coma from the long night of death. Shortly afterwards Sanjay gave a last shudder and flopped back, leaving Erik banging his fist on the floor in frustration although even with the resources of a fully equipped med-centre the chances of pulling Sanjay through would have been remote.

They had given up any effort to mop up any surviving bandits after the first half hour during which they had taken eighteen prisoners who now lay face down taped together near the cars. From the prisoners, mostly still in shock, they had learned little, other than the confirmation that they were in fact based in the Cairns area some four hundred plus klicks to the north-east on the other side of the Gregory Range, and that in all there were ten or twelve thousand of them. Alternating threats with subtly skilled questions had in the end revealed that the bandits had survived over the years by raiding across the continent, moving in large groups of at least three hundred members, one of which had been holed up for the past few months in Hughenden. The organization was one of local chiefs reporting on an informal basis to a so-called High Chief in Cairns. The High Chief it became clear was usually the leader with the most bloodthirsty lieutenants to back him up, and was in any event a position that changed hands fairly frequently. In Cairns there was still some basic technology including some short wave transmitters that were operated off hand-cranked generators, the hands being provided needless to say by the unlucky slaves who had been allowed to live. The conclusion was that although it didn't seem very likely, it would undoubtedly be wise to suppose the worst, which was that the bandit leaders had been warned of their presence, and might even be making preparations to come out in search of the Gevcars.

Now, with the coming night nibbling away at the last of the afterglow they stood around the markers, markers which were all that remained to remind them of their friends. As the light turned from purple to black, one by one they said their farewells to their dead companions and made their way back to the Gevcars.

[Extract – 2025]

(The following reports are excerpts from the minutes of the Site 3 Steering Committee meeting held on 15 November 2025. It is to be noted that all records related to 1 January 2018 to 31 December 2025 have been classified as restricted and can only be accessed with the authorization of the Council of Elders.)

The removal of any documents from the Records Hall or the copying of any information relating to this period is strictly forbidden.

Commissioning and Start-up Phase Contract Report: With the exception of the eight areas listed in the attached documentation, mostly related to auxiliary services on Levels B and C. Equipment-commissioning activities on all the other levels have now been successfully completed. Formal handing over is scheduled for 15 December next. Only thirty people still classified as external personnel are now on site, and all areas now fully under control of Technical Services. It is estimated that pending points on the handing over lists will be completed by the end of the year. Site design changes implemented in the period since the last Steering Committee meeting have been limited to the utilities area and have not affected personnel or the operation of Site 3. The hydroponics tanks have been stabilized at the new settings as proposed by EUROPS and the previously detected pH fluctuations have all but vanished.

The six-monthly cost-control forecast for the completed scope of supply now stands at 98.2 + 2.7 percent when adjusted for inflation. The 0.2 percent improvement over the previous semester is due to the final negotiations with Sigma Automation in relation to the CPU modifications in the central control room, as well as to the lower price paid for the final piping delivery.

Attachments:

- Technical Status Reports on all systems
- Bio Report: Hydroponics
- Pending Points Listing Level B
- Pending Points Listing Level C

- Commissioning and Start-up Time Schedule (Adjusted)
- Cost Control Summary Report

Staffing Report: The first COPEEV (Continuous Personnel Evaluation) reports have been received and are currently being analysed. The first conclusions indicate a very high degree of participation and acceptance by personnel at all levels. The first series of training programmes for backup personnel are nearing completion despite some delays in their initial implementation. Some improvements have already been suggested and will be included in the next series. Several requests have been made for the induction of external personnel, particularly in the TFR control room department, these are under review and a decision will be made on the matter next week, taking into account that the Site is still 9.2 percent below optimum staffing.

Attachments:

- Revised Personnel Backup Training Programme
- COPEEV – Preliminary Results
- Staff Listing (Revision G)

Power Subcommittee Report: Power output on the TFR is now at seventy-three percent of nominal with all systems operating within their standard parameters. At this level all Site 3 systems are fully operational within the design specifications. Higher power demands could eventually prove to be necessary only when standby units are run in parallel and in any event will not exceed the maximum allowable levels as established in the operational guidelines agreed upon with CERN. The CERN scope of supply has been finalized with the deliveries of spare parts' inventories as well as all technical documentation as per contract and the corresponding provisional acceptance certificate has been issued. Payment via the usual cut-out banks has been ordered.

Attachments:

- TFR Start-up Compliance Report
- Operational Parameters Summary Listing

Appendix: Site 3 Denomination: Based on a recommendation by the Personnel Psychology Unit, a survey was carried out to obtain suggestions as to the name by which Site 3 should be known in the future. A number of proposals were included in the survey, leaving the way open for new suggestions. The first six preferences expressed in the survey included almost the entire vote: the Hold (forty-one percent), the Keep (twenty-two percent), the Centre (thirteen percent), the Citadel (ten percent), Safe Haven (seven percent) and Survival Centre South (five percent). The results will be announced at the formal handing over ceremony next month.

News Item Summaries: Despite energetic protests at the UN General Assembly, the dumping of spent nuclear fuel from French power reactors in the Pacific has continued unabated. French scientists claim that given the great depth of the Marianas Trench, coupled with the low emission rates, there will be no significant danger to the environment. This has resulted in a new wave of bomb attacks on French installations including an attempt to halt the reconstruction of the Eiffel Tower, originally damaged during the Shiite rising of 2019. Responsibility for the attacks have been claimed by at least seven separate and antagonistic anti-technology groups.

Fighting in Colombia reached a new peak two days ago when a bomber wing flying out of Lubbock, Texas, delivered a total load of two thousand tons of chemical incendiaries in a blanket bombing attack intended to destroy underground drug laboratories belonging to the Patria Nueva group, which claims to be the legitimate government of that nation. Defence forces throughout the Texas Republic have been put on full alert to counter expected reprisals. The North American Premier has issued a statement expressing regret at the attack, which failed to censure the Texas Republic or to be an outright condemnation of the event. This is seen as an attempt at bridge building with the end objective of having Texas rejoin the Federation.

Several EU news agencies have reported the arrival of groups of refugees from the Baltic Republics with stories of the use of chemical and biological agents in recent fighting between rival power factions fighting for the control of the east Chechnya oilfield complex, one of the few fields still operating in the east bock. The UN representative in the area has promised that a full investigation will be made to see if the terms of the Madrid Human Rights Treaty of 2015 have been infringed, and that if this were so, to present a formal protest.

Elements of the NAFDEF Far East fleet mutinied this week while on patrol south of the Java Straits. After two days of fighting the ringleaders surrendered and have been placed under arrest. There was some light damage to the *Weasel*, a 2,500 ton guided-missile corvette, as well as to the *Scorpion*, a fast-attack submarine. A spokesman for the navy announced that no nuclear weapons were involved in the incident which at no time posed a threat to anyone other than to the crews of the vessels involved.

The Commission on Population has reported that the survey carried out in England, Cornwall, Scotland and Wales during 2023–24 has shown that the total population has declined to 19,790,526, the first time in over two centuries that the number has fallen below twenty million. The Commission forecast indicates that although the rate of decrease appears to be dropping, the minimum has not yet been reached. The causes of the spectacular drop since reaching a peak of over seventy-five million in 2012 are given as the intensive use of Nogrow, sickness due to CBW agents and to radiation, and suicides. Coupled with this phenomenon has been the move away from the bigger cities, many of which are almost deserted, towards smaller towns and villages, which are more easily defended against attackers.

Chapter XIX

They stood side by side in the early dawn, the tall fair man slightly in front, gazing out towards the northern horizon though they knew fully well there would be nothing to see yet. His companion pushed back the old hat, worn more out of habit than anything else, for there was no need for any headgear in the chill of the early morning. The silence was companionable, comfortable even, only when there were concrete statements did they speak.

'Yes, I feel them too, you were right, Eddy. A very long way away still of course.' The fair man turned to his companion who gazed back, his jet black eyes unblinking.

'But moving ... fast too. Maybe this time. There have been so many false hopes ...' He scratched his scalp through the thick brown hair. 'We'll have to let them find us of course, Keep policy won't permit anything else.'

'Mmm, agreed.'

'Come on then Richard,' said the shorter man taking off his hat. 'My stomach tells me that supper shouldn't be far away now.'

After a moment or two they turned and together walked back towards the carefully camouflaged doorway which lay just inside a small cave. Above them the immense mass of the arkosic sandstone stretched up, vanishing into the predawn gloom. Out towards the east there was the faintest promise of light, while overhead the haze was thin enough to see half a dozen bright stars, a sight which brought a smile to the lips of the fair man as he gazed upwards, pushing his lank blond hair back from his high forehead. Stepping carefully on the rock so as to avoid leaving any prints, even though they knew the constant winds would soon cover them, they ducked through the doorway beyond which a dimly lit passageway could be made out, stopping to peer at an illuminated display panel set into the rock. From somewhere deep inside the subtle murmur of machinery could be discerned, and occasionally the sound of conversations drifted out. Finishing their task, the two men glanced one final time out of the doorway before they turned and headed off down the oval roofed tunnel. Behind them a proximity sensor beeped gently, and the heavy door whined softly and swung closed, settling on its seals with a faint thump. In the distance a wild dog howled, the wind-borne sound both plaintive and threatening.

Janine shivered, drawing her cloak closer, even now, seven, no, almost eight moons after leaving the Hold, the emptiness of the night still bothered her slightly. So much silence, though if one stood still long enough the small noises of the night could sometimes be heard, the sighing of a gust of wind, the scrabbling of rodent claws in the sand, or the howl of a distant dog. Dingoes, not dogs, she had checked the Records' computer and had found that the wild dogs were in fact a specific breed known as dingoes, tough, untameable, indomitable, a number of adjectives had been stated. Behind her she heard Bob stepping down from the Gevcar and walking towards her. She knew it was him without needing to turn around, other people walked differently, transmitted different vibrations. She hadn't talked to anyone about her heightened sense of awareness, somehow it seemed rather fanciful, and she would hate to have Jock or Karel think she was slipping, and then suggesting that she have a quiet talk with Maria. She turned slightly as Bob came up to her, snuggling into the arm he offered, carefully so as not to put any pressure on her cracked ribs which were still extremely sore despite the medication Erik had issued her with.

Breakfast had been served and consumed by the time Jojo and Brendt returned from their scouting expedition, covered in dust and sweating slightly from their long dog trot through the bush, although the night had not been warm.

'Whew, I hope someone left us some breakfast, I'm famished.' The deep blue eyes swept round. 'I bet our red-headed friend has eaten my share,' said Brendt making a determined effort to puncture the moments of gloom that seemed to settle periodically on the group since the battle of Hughenden.

'Come on Brendt, just because I once made a mistake,' Matt flushed slightly, unable to refuse the challenge though everyone knew that the whole thing was only a joke.

Karel walked across to them. 'Well, anything of interest?'

'We reckon the place is clean,' replied Jojo, pausing while he took a sip from his cup. 'We hung around well over an hour and a half and there was no sign at all of any sort of human presence.'

'The one thing we do think Karel, and I know we've discussed this before, is that ten klicks out is too far, we're wasting far too long getting there and then getting back. Not to say getting bloody tired, implant or no implant.'

Karel was adamant. 'Maybe. I suppose we could bring it down to five klicks, but certainly not less. I made one serious error of judgement at Hughenden and that's something I have to live with, but we can't afford to go into a town without some prior recon. And, I don't want to bypass every town, otherwise we might miss seeing or hearing about something which could later help us with the search.' He had forced through the policy change whereby before going anywhere near any town, a Watch team, composed usually of two members, was sent in for a look before bringing the cars in. So far they had carried out the procedure three times, finding nothing, but Karel obviously had no intention of giving up on the idea.

Before the topic changed, Jock stepped forward. 'Karel, I've said as much before and I'll say it again, this was very much my mistake as well. There is no need for you to shoulder all the burden, we were well and truly taken in by the treachery. We'll here no more talk about blame if you please.' He stood leaning forward slightly, as though giving his words even more emphasis, eyeing Karel unblinkingly, until finally the latter nodded and the meeting continued with other matters.

There were very few towns in the Outback through which they were now travelling. Since leaving Hughenden three days earlier they had passed through Richmond, a deserted shell of what it had once been, Cloncurry, where a community of what could only be described as primitive sheep farming tribes lived, but made it quite clear that strangers were not welcome, even when obviously friendly overtures were made. And now Mount Isa, yet another dead town, serving to remind them of the effectiveness of Nogrow and of the world-wide disease seeding carried out decades earlier. The mood in the Gevcars had picked up a bit in the last couple of days, but the memory of the loss of their companions still hung over them like a dark cloud. It was impossible not to dwell on the shock of losing three members of the tightly knit team, although their daily activities went on, their minds numbed now by the thin shell of acceptance. Before leaving they had released the eighteen terrified prisoners, for it was one thing to kill in the heat of battle and quite another to execute people cold bloodily after the fighting was over. This, even though they knew full well that they would in all probability have been murdered had the shoe been on the other foot. There had been no argument on the matter, none whatsoever, for they all knew that to stoop to such savagery would be the negation of their mission which had taken them halfway across the world to this place and time. Even Karel, who had had no qualms about wiping out the slave traffickers in Ecuador, had no doubts on the matter, for once the fighting was over, it was over.

The Gevcars had suffered no profound damage to their systems though both cars had taken repeated hits from different weapons, a credit to their long dead designers. Even the effect of the missile on Karel's car had been limited to some burnt wiring and cracked components which had soon been replaced by the Techs. After the battle was over, they had contacted the Hold with their sad news, a contact which also left Sandy and Jean worried because of the decreasing signal strength. Somewhere not too far westwards yet another Sentry satellite orbited, or at least was supposed to be orbiting, but so far the comm crew had been unable to raise any reply, though Sandy was broadcasting almost continually on the directional array, aiming for the quadrant where the bird supposedly flew.

After breakfast and the routine planning meeting, they got on the move again, heading westwards, following the remains of the old main road which were for the most part buried under the shifting sands and scrubby vegetation. Passing through Mount Isa and then Camoweal, both long deserted, they entered the old Northern Territories. The day began hazily, but by midday the yellowish globe of the sun had penetrated the ever-present dust and glared down on them, an angry eye in the heavens, waiting to burn their skins and eyes should they go out unprotected by cloaks and glare specs. Behind them the dust clouds blossomed and grew, eventually thinning out to be reabsorbed by the surrounding haze which tinged everything in ochre browns. Advancing at a modest forty to forty-five knots, the drive became an endless challenge to the pilots who struggled to stay alert, for here unlike their trips over water, there was no possibility of using the autopilot due to the roughness of the plain. To go any faster only increased the danger of rolling the Gevcar down some hidden gulch, and to go much slower meant to travel inside their own dust cloud, for at the high lift levels which were necessary due to the condition of the ground, there was that much more dust to contend with. Before arriving at Tennant Creek, which was the next town they aimed to pass through, they reached the crossroads where the road headed south towards Alice Springs, and tired after the long day's journey, decided to call a halt earlier than usual. They parked the Gevcars in the shelter of two large sheds in a long-abandoned industrial complex, carefully concealed from anyone passing on the road, though none among them thought that event very likely.

As Jock and Karel sat in the canteen with the pilots, going over the route planned for the next day, Jean burst in, shirt-tails as ever blowing in the wind.

'We've got it! We've got it!'

Jock leaned over grabbing his arm which was excitedly waving up and down as though sending a message by semaphore to some Watcher on a distant hill. 'I imagine you mean the satellite, just slow down long enough to tell us, will you,' he said good-naturedly.

'Yes, of course, sorry. It's just that we've been trying everything since we reached the coast without any luck, and now we've got it! We found it by looking where it wasn't supposed to be ... it was Selena's idea too, she simply asked why someone couldn't have moved the orbit a bit, the same way as we did with the Sentry over the Pacific.' He paused, more for breath than for effect. 'And there it was, twenty degrees too far west. Sandy reckons that during the troubles they lost one of the European satellites, so they shifted the Atlantic one eastwards and the far eastern one to the west, thereby covering most if not all the gap.'

'And now? Can you tap in, or will there be other codes?'

'Of course.' Jan looked indignant that anyone should see fit to question his and Sandy's abilities.

He was as good as his word, for by the following morning they had once again re-established a clear link to the Hold as well as to all their other outposts, and that wasn't all. Sandy, whose old skills were now more finely tuned than ever, had been able to repeat her earlier trick and shift the orbit back to somewhere close to its point of origin. Initially, both she and Karel who were the only ones with any sort of experience regarding space vehicles, had rather been wary of the reliability of the Sentry satellites. They had felt that after so long in space bombarded by micrometeorites, subjected to the intense heat of the sun and the absolute zero of space, not to mention the possibility of EMP damage from nuclear explosions, the satellites might prove to be faulty. And yet, such was the level of redundancy built in that none of the fifty-year-old satellites showed any sign of problems, though their internal diagnostic routines did indicate some minor malfunctions. Still, they worried, knowing all the time that their worry made no difference whatsoever to the small pack of hardware and software which spun through the vacuum far above them, far too small to be seen through the thick haze which covered most of the earth. The next morning before starting out, the two comm specialists sought out Karel and Jock to discuss a new idea they had come up with, which was the possibility of trying to reprogramme the Sentry into sending out an omnidirectional signal with the hope that the missing Site might respond. In the end however, the idea was vetoed, rather to their disappointment, for they had been looking forward to the technical challenges the job presented. In the end it was nothing but a risk–benefit analysis, and on the grounds that it was always possible there might be others able to listen in on the frequency, it was decided that it was safer to use the Sentry for a more directional signal once they reached the correct location. They had kept up their daily contacts with the Hold, as well as with Tumbes, the Cape, the Foundation, and with Lihue. Contacts now restored to full strength, contacts which provided them with an anchor of stability in the great sea of uncertainty through which they moved. The Hold computers continuously analysed and correlated the incoming Sentry pictures with the information held in the vast data memories, looking for indications that might shorten the search. Karel and Sandy, remembering how long their own search had lasted, were humbly grateful for all this technological assistance.

It took them only three and a half days to reach a point a few klicks north of Alice Springs, three and a half days during which they saw no signs of any recent human habitation or activity, and in fact not much of anything else except for several large packs of dingoes, some of them fifty or sixty strong. The land around them was dry and cracked, and with the rainy season long gone, any grass that might have sprung up from the dried out earth had vanished. They were able to see that there were still patches of vegetation clinging to the rough broken hills, presumably with roots reaching deep into the earth to tap some subterranean stream. Each evening they watched the deep reddish purple sun sinking into the haze, distorted and flattened by the particle laden atmosphere, slowly dimming until it vanished, while overhead wispy clouds drifted, pretty patterns in the sky, offering little promise of any rain. And each day they rode on across the parched desert, their long ochre-coloured tail billowing out behind them.

Alice Springs, situated in a valley surrounded by high bluffs, had once been a thriving business and tourist town with a population of almost one hundred thousand. Now, it was a dead shadow of its former self, with areas several blocks across consisting of nothing but burnt out buildings from which tangled vegetation grew, as if trying to blot out the debris left by man in his retreat. The dull red-brown hills, almost bereft of vegetation, looked down on the city that lay in the valley. The great outcroppings of red rock were in all probability not very different from two centuries earlier. They had not noticed the coming of man and did not mourn his passing. There were more signs of the presence of water, for trees still grew and in some places wild flowers bloomed, and as they drew to a halt in what had once been a prosperous farm, the general aspect somehow seemed almost welcoming to the small scouting team. Arriving a scant hour before nightfall, they had stopped in the shelter of a family of large boulders, and then with the first light of the morning a party of five of them, Maria, Janine, Brendt, Jock and Jojo, had advanced into the town, acting as scouts before bringing in the Gevcars the remaining few klicks. They found real pleasure in the short walk, enjoying the early morning without need of hood or glare specs, not that this lessened their vigilance, for it was always possible that they might come across an unfriendly welcoming committee. They were crossing a wide avenue, when suddenly Janine felt the presence of strangers, not a threatening feeling, but an unsettling one, which raised the vestigial hairs on the back of her neck. Before she could say anything, they found themselves being watched from one end of the square by a the small group of aborigines who, Brendt and Jojo would afterwards swear, had appeared from nowhere, as though sprung from the bowels of the earth itself. The group, some thirty or thirty-five strong dressed in a mix of traditional costumes and modern apparel, eyed the five newcomers warily, but showed no signs of fear. The men, rough faces lost in a sea of heavily wrinkled skin moved frontward, leaving the women and younger members of the group behind them, not threatening the Hold people, but not openly friendly either. Maria moved forwards, hands open and clearly visible, followed closely by Brendt in a similar pose, but whose needle gun lay tucked up the sleeve of his cloak, ready to drop into his hand should it be needed.

Maria stopped about three metres away from the man she took to be the leader. 'We mean you no harm, we're friends …'

'Frindy ouare?' The speech was rapid and slurred in a strange dialect which appeared to be related to Anglic, at least phonetically, but it was clear that what Maria had said had been understood.

'Yes, we've come from a long way away, across the water.' The last as she waved her hand vaguely towards the east. The man looked blank for a moment, then turned to his friends and spoke in a guttural incomprehensible language. His short speech brought about a brief exchange, and then the man turned back to Maria.

'No worra hrr. Longtm belong peebl longtm gonway. … Bakin dreemin tim.' He spat, in the dust, and within seconds the little wet patch had vanished, absorbed almost instantly by the dry soil.

'We're hoping that you may be able to help us,' continued Maria, 'we're looking for some friends, … out in the desert to the south.' She waved her hands again indicating the direction. The conversation continued at its slow pace, needing frequent repetitions in order to ensure that the messages were getting across. Brendt spoke briefly into his comm unit, and then indicated to the locals that the Gevcars would be coming, miming the gesture and making a noise. Presently, they were joined by the rest of the group in the cars which approached at minimum power as Brendt had requested, but still accompanied by the usual dust storm. It surprised them to see that while the aborigines didn't look too happy at the sight of the massive Gevcars coming down the street, they stood their ground without flinching, and this made them wonder if perhaps some technological society was still functioning in the general area. By the end of the first hour with the aborigines, their ears had become tuned to the odd cut up dialect, at least enough to hold an intelligible conversation. It was abundantly clear that despite their rather primitive appearance and attire, the aborigines were in no way mentally inferior to the Hold people, and that their total lack of reliance on technology was not necessarily a disadvantage. They were a tightly knit society, who, when the reign of the white man had ended, had simply taken up their old customs, customs filled with legends that traced their heritage back into the past. Janine went back to the Gevcar and checked the computer database and was amazed to find that tribal histories went back as much as ten thousand years, an unimaginably long stretch of time, down through which the oral tradition had played a vital role. These rough tribesmen, so they were informed, formed a loosely organized group, wandering across the land, as far north and west as Arnhem Land and as far south as they now were. Their numbers were variable, and anything between thirty and three hundred seemed to be usual according to how many subgroups had gone off into the bush, gone 'walkabout' as they themselves referred to this practice of vanishing for months on end.

They tried to question the group regarding the existence of still inhabited towns, but very little information was forthcoming. For the most part the idea of large numbers living together in one place was alien to the aborigines, and in any event they apparently chose more often than not to ignore the old towns unless they were fairly sure that they were uninhabited. Certainly most of the major population centres of the pre-collapse period were now deserted or at best occupied by a few disorganized groups. Maria was able to understand through contact with other nomad groups, that they believed that the city of Perth on the western coast was still operating as a society, though of course without personal experience, such stories might well be suspect. There were also some vague stories regarding Uluru and the spirits that guarded the great rock, stories which offered Karel the tantalizing possibility that the final site might in fact still be operational in the area. As soon as the rays of the rising sun reached out over the eastern hills, the leader of the group indicated that the meeting was over, and with a gesture of farewell to the Hold people, he led his followers off down the road. Karel who had been about to turn away suddenly felt as though someone was speaking to him from the direction in which the aborigines had gone. He stopped, took a step back, and the feeling was gone.

'You too, Karel.' Selena stood quietly beside him, her eyes a deep almost bottomless blue.

'Hmm, what do you think?'

'I don't know for sure, Tante always said that there were naturals around.' She smiled, 'I think we may have met some. If they come back we can try to work with them, otherwise ...'

'Yes, if they don't want to be found, then we won't find them.' Karel nodded. 'Well, meanwhile there's plenty to be done.'

At Janine's suggestion they divided themselves up into separate search teams and spent the rest of the day exploring Alice Springs, concentrating initially on the library and the various civic and government buildings, trying to find references to any construction work that would indicate that they might be on the right track to finding the last survival site.

As evening fell, the various teams gathered back at the Gevcars, each one listing their findings, or in many cases their lack.

'They were an amazingly tidy lot at the municipal civic centre' Threejays said, when her turn came round. 'There are regular city records up to the end of 2048. After that things became a bit more haphazard, the usual story, declining population, plagues and sicknesses even out here, groups emigrating to other towns, and of course some attacks by roving bandits. As far as I could make out, in the end they gathered up most if not all of the available vehicles and set off towards Perth.'

'How many of them were there at the end?'

'From the reports, something in the region of 6,500 when they left. Less than a third of the number they were at the beginning of the decade.' She stopped suddenly, shaking her head. 'What a stupid senseless thing the fall of society was, and so unnecessary. I know that this was just one medium-sized town, but why? Why?'

'Unnecessary, yes.' Karel looked grim. 'But also inevitable. Threejays, you've seen some terrible sights during our trek, but in reality they are nothing compared with what happened to the world. Millions and millions of human beings died, lives cut short, wiped out by plagues, famines, wars, natural disasters, and heaven knows what else. Blame it on the me and mine syndrome, blame it on the belief that one particular god is better than another, blame it on the have nots wanting what the haves tried to keep to themselves, blame it on the belief that one skin colour was better than another, blame it on the desperation of hunger, blame it on ... oh, I don't know ...' He shrugged helplessly. 'I saw much of it, fortunately at long range for the most part. I certainly can't explain it all to you, other than to say that while individuals may be perfectly reasonable, sane and caring human beings, large groups can easily become tainted with the fanaticism of a few malcontents, and then there's no telling where it ends. All you need to do is look again at the charts we prepared for the first briefing.'

She sighed. 'Yes I know Karel, I know, it's just that sometimes ...' her voice trailed off.

'What else have we got?' Jock chipped in still taking a bite from the ration bar he had opened. 'Who's next?'

'That'll be us.' Selena said from where she squatted comfortably, her back leaning on the nearest Gevcar. 'I think we may have found something interesting, but we'll have to go back tomorrow.' Herb nodded his agreement, running his fingers through his short cropped hair, now no longer grey but light brown, and took up the report. 'We started at a construction pound out at the southern end of town. Found nothing of any interest there, except for the address of the vehicle registry office. So we went to the place where all the vehicle registries were kept. The place is an old warehouse building and its pretty much wrecked, but obviously no one was much interested in old paper records, so there was much that was still readable. We also found some computer discs, but either the format is different and unreadable, or the things are blank. Miguel left them with Janine to see what she could do with them.' He looked around, pausing before delivering what he instinctively knew was his punch line. 'The interesting thing is that there are indications of a lot of earth-moving equipment coming through Alice Springs in the period between mid-2019 and the end of 2021. Apparently there was a big mining project somewhere south near the Uluru National Park.'

'Yes!' Karel stood up, eyes alight with excitement. 'Yes, that must be it!' And suddenly there was a general babble as everyone tried to speak at once, their spirits uplifted by the possibility that their search might be heading towards a successful conclusion.

That night, after dinner Janine treated them all to another Sonolite concert. This time a piece that began slowly, growing in complexity and power, like an advancing storm. The patterns on the screen were breathtaking, never still for an instant, jumping to and fro as the accompanying sound notes vibrated through the thin desert air. Circles and ellipses, spinning and turning, now faster, now slower, evolving into other more complex shapes, and then expanding outwards as if to accompany the growth of the universe itself, vanishing into the distance, lost into nothingness, to be immediately followed by new and more splendid patterns, joy and sorrow, in an endless indivisible cycle. The music kept pace with the display, each chord the child of the one before, up to the last note which hung in the air as the glowing patterns shifted up to the high end of spectrum before vanishing, leaving their latent images engraved on the listeners' retinas. It was as if a fresh wind had swept through wiping out their pains, for as they retired to bed after the concert was over, there was an air of contentment and optimism.

The next day they organized themselves into search parties with a far narrower focus, civic records, industrial company records, the tax offices, and of course the local newspaper offices. Once again the day was spent rifling through stacks of old documents, persuading old obsolete computer terminals to give up at least some of their secrets and, most difficult of all, in deciding which piece of information was valuable and which useless. It was of course far too much to expect that thirty years after being abandoned the records would be in good shape, indeed, as with most other towns, as social and civil services had been cut back and then curtailed altogether, the upkeep of the bureaucratic structure had become more haphazard, finally collapsing under its own weight. There were records related to an improbably large number of earth-moving and tunnelling machines passing through, data registered not because it had been useful to anyone at the time, but simply because the local authorities had been able to charge taxes on the use of the highway. The newspaper archives, buried in a deep cellar had survived basically undamaged, and on yellowing and sometimes powdery paper. By the end of the day, however, it was clear that every additional piece of information they had obtained corroborated what they already knew: place, time, scale, it was all there. For all of them, and particularly for Karel, this was enormously satisfying, for their onwards course was now more clearly marked than ever before, and when they found the last site, the sacrifices of their companions would not have been in vain.

Having spent a further day analysing the results, a day which also allowed the two Techs to complete the repairs to the cars, Karel finally pronounced himself ready to move on. They held the usual post-breakfast briefing when Threejays explained their route which led southwards, on down through the southern part of the Macdonnell ranges and on into the James range, before swinging westwards towards the Uluru National Park, a total distance of around three hundred klicks. This was to be sure an insignificant distance when measured against what they had already covered, but as Jojo pointed out, one only needed to make one mistake in the last klick to ruin all that they had already achieved. They had seen the aborigines once more in the distance, but when they reached the spot, the place was empty, clearly indicating that the locals, while not unfriendly, preferred to be left alone. Leaving Alice Springs behind, they followed the remains of the main highway southward to the airport which proved to be totally wrecked, and then followed the old road, track really would have been a more adequate description, as it branched off south-westwards and traced its way through spectacular ridges and valleys, though the crews of the two cars had little time to marvel at the sights. All of them without exception were suddenly on edge, as though waiting for some momentous event to occur as they came round some sharp bend, but of course it didn't. Maria with some assistance from Erik spent the day going from compartment to compartment, soothing frazzled nerves as best she could, and although everyone knew why they were edgy, it became increasingly difficult to break out of the mood.

At last, with evening drawing in and the colours shifting from the usual orange-brown towards deeper reds and purple, colouring the thin wispy clouds hanging overhead while the swollen ball of the sun spread itself into the haze which hid the horizon, they reached, at least according to the GPS, a place once known as Curtin Springs Roadhouse, though there were no signs whatsoever of man ever having been that way.

The next morning they resumed their trek through the rough countryside which seemed to take some sort of perverse delight in producing gullies and cutbacks that forced them to detour almost continuously, until at last with the sun already past its highest peak, they came to the old boundaries of the Uluru National Park. Here of all places, an old worn but still readable sign proclaimed the park, and the rules and regulations applicable to visitors were still listed. Rather than pushing on without a clear plan, Karel called a halt for the day, pointing out as he silenced the complaints, that the communications window was already over, and that in any event they needed time to set up the Sentry. Choosing a slight dip in the ground as the centre of the campsite, the Gevcars were parked about sixty metres apart and the crews unloaded the few things necessary for their overnight stay, and for the first time since Hughenden it was clear that a feeling of optimism and purpose had returned to the group.

Sandy shivered. 'Bad thoughts?' Karel stood nearby, the steam rising from the mug of soup he held clearly visible in the last of the twilight.

'No, I guess not. I don't know, we've come so far, I find it difficult to visualize an end to all this.'

'An end? Well, I'm sure there will be plenty more trips to do, even if ... no, I mean when we find the Survival Centre.'

'I didn't mean only this trip, I meant all of it, since Jose found the first discs in Mendoza.'

'So did I my love, so did I.' He spoke softly now. 'I could never have managed it without you, you know, all this way on faith alone.'

'Jose should have been with us.' A slight sob seemed to catch in her throat. 'He wouldn't have missed this for anything in the world, Suzanne also ...' Her voice trailed off.

'Sandy my love, we are here for this moment. Tomorrow and the days after will determine how it all ends, but believe me that Jose is also with us, because I can remember him, and therefore he still lives.' He turned to her, holding out his hand, and together they walked back towards the light of the fire which burned brightly, fed off long dried bits of brush they had gathered before darkness fell.

The group sat in a loose circle round the fire, some in threes or fours, some just with their partners, others alone. From inside the Gevcars the computers monitored the perimeter motion and heat sensors which reached out into darkness, watching for any activity that might mean hostile action, and though out in the bush this was more than enough protection, Brent had also set up a sentry duty rota for the Watch. The rest of them sat watching the flames, mesmerized by the flickering light, watching the sparks fly upwards into the night, soon to be extinguished as their fuel was consumed. They sat around the fire as groups of humans before them had always sat through uncounted generations, for some a moment of peace, for others a time for relaxation and socializing, for others a moment to unload doubts or troubles. Fragments of different and simultaneous conversations hung in the air, and then were lost.

'... didn't know how to fix it so I modified the spare pressure relief valve by reboring the seat and then using a new spring ...'

'... think it makes that much difference, anyway, I'm sure we'll be faster than at the Citadel, for a start there's nothing to cut out directional signals, and of course we'll have the ...'

'... absolutely delicious, there's nothing to touch the ...'

'... wonder if things could have been different. Unfortunately she thought otherwise so we split up and each went our own way, but still ...'

'... a grid pattern isn't that easy in this broken territory, my belief is that we should concentrate on two areas, Uluru itself, and Kata ...'

'... so what? I mean what else could ...'

'... how happy I am that you really consider a long-term relationship a viable option. I know commitment doesn't come ...'

'... hope that we might run into more groups of aborigines. I can't help thinking that the ones back in Alice knew a lot more than we got out of them. Don't ask me why I feel that, but I can't ignore that sort of gut feeling ...'

'... that luck has a lot to do with it. I'm not disagreeing with what you say, but all the preparation and training and instinct come to nothing if ...'

'... and he said: I don't mind, it's my grandmother's!'

'... for Petra, Jules and Sanjay. And who's to say which price is acceptable, don't forget that any price varies according to the scale, individual, a group, society, and so on ...'

Fragments, soon lost, but still part of the whole.

Chapter XX

It was one of Habitat's better days thought Richard Kreel. Engineering had at last got the bugs ironed out of the new environmental simulation programme. He could hear the sigh of the gentle breeze barely rustling the leaves, and there was the faintest scent of spice in the air, not cinnamon, something else, but he couldn't quite place his finger on it. He continued to listen with half his mind while the other members of the Council argued back and forth, until finally he decided it was time to step in.

'Fellow Councillors, let me remind you that our Prime Directive, while vague in some parts, makes two absolutely unequivocal statements. Firstly, that our purpose is to aid in the eventual reconstruction of civilization, and, secondly, that under no circumstances are we to reveal ourselves until contacted by the members of one of the other two Survival Centres.'

'But who's defining what finding is? These people have beamed a signal which is on the correct frequency, has the correct sequence, and is being sent at the correct time.' Tech Councillor Piet Berg replied. As punctilious as ever thought Edward Zeerk sitting further down the table, though he made no comment.

'That's as maybe my friend, but anyone could have obtained the frequency from somewhere, it doesn't necessarily guarantee that they're from one of the other Centres. There are plenty of not so nice people out there you know,' said Med Councillor Rita Master, whose outlook on life could be relied upon to be conservative.

'Seeing as how we obviously won't agree, I propose a vote.' Kreel smiled, for as Chairperson he was responsible for ensuring that agreement was reached. 'We will vote on the following proposition: 'that we will identify ourselves only when the newcomers reveal who they are and what their purpose is, or alternatively when discovered by them.'

'Seconded!' Edward was quick off the mark, for he knew what his companion was thinking.

'Votes please,' said Kreel, his pale face revealing nothing of what he was thinking. One by one, the other six voted, with only Master and one other voting against the motion, which without needing any further statement was recorded as carried.

Only after the others had left the high-domed room in which the meeting had been held did Edward speak, 'I need your authorization to take a small party out, Richard. Say ten or fifteen, mixed or aboriginal of course.'

The Council leader nodded, giving his assent. 'Choose people with the gift of course.'

'Of course,' replied his companion, running his fingers through his thick dark brown curly hair, black eyes gleaming with excitement. 'Of course.'

'Three days, and nothing, damned nothing!' Bob kicked a small stone, which flew off into a nearby bush. 'I can't believe that the Site doesn't exist any more, not to the point where there's no answer signal, therefore they must be hiding.'

Herb smiled as he squatted in the doubtful shade of the netting, his eyes hidden behind the fully darkened glare specs. 'Relax boy, I thought you Watch types came equipped with infinite patience, we've only searched a small part of the area.'

'Yes,' chipped in Matt with a grin, enjoying ribbing his former colleague. 'I don't know what's got into you Bob.'

Over in the nearby Gevcar, Jean Klock carefully marked off another quadrant on the printed chart pinned to the wall opposite his comm desk, the fourteenth since they had started. Even with the Sentry transmitting the signal down to five or six quadrants simultaneously, a vast improvement on their previous situation, and all within the narrow time slot of only fifteen minutes available to them, the search was a long slow business. They had started out dividing the whole area into forty-five more or less equally sized quadrants, and then selecting those they considered to be the most likely zones for a large, hidden, underground construction. The survey started round Uluru, or Ayers Rock as it had once been known according to some of the maps stored in the Record computer, working round slowly as each successive scan failed to elicit a reply. After that, they had moved the transmission target over to Kata Tjuta, Mount Olga on the older maps, and again met with a lack of success.

'That's thirty-one to thirty-six. And nothing yet. Tomorrow we'll do thirty-seven to forty-two.' She tossed down the pencil and leaned in to Karel who had been standing behind her.

'There's something missing here, I can't quite get to it, but there's something missing, a piece of the jigsaw. Never fear, we'll find them, we'll find them.' He shook his head, and then turned way, hiding his disappointment.

Outside the heat beat down on his raised hood, and he could feel the trickles of sweat running down the back of his neck. He crouched in the shade of a small spindly grey bush that grew out of a crack in the rock. A few metres away he could see Selena and Jojo, sitting together inside the open bay of the Gevcar while they sorted through the supplies. Behind him the mass of Uluru blocked out well over half the horizon, for they were parked only a few car lengths away, while off to the left from where he sat he could just see the top of the netting tent the Techs had set up. The days had taken on a sort of pattern, the mornings dedicated to discussing which quadrants to scan and planning the exploration route to be covered by one of the cars while the other remained at the campsite to handle the midday transmission. After that came the comm linkup to the Hold to report their lack of success. In the evenings they went over the day's results, trying not to get depressed at the situation. The plain fact of the matter was that Karel himself was becoming increasingly aware that there was a very real possibility of not finding the last site, for they had already scanned all of the most likely quadrants with no results so far. Overhead the day moved on, the high haze thickening slowly, while Karel, who had sat in the command seat of a space ship, now squatted quietly in the shade of a small bush in the middle of the Australian Outback, eyes closed, feeling no stranger than he had then, his mind sifting aimlessly through the data it held. Every so often his eyes opened and he took in the strange beauty of the Outback, the washed out reds and greens, the haze which blurred the horizon, the immense sense of emptiness which he so enjoyed. He had long ago become used to the open spaces, and sometimes to being alone, for his travels had so shaped him. Even with the Gevcar and the others a few metres away from where he was, he had no trouble in filtering out their background noises, leaving himself free to enjoy the Outback.

It was already late in the afternoon, shortly before the time Jock's Gevcar was expected back that he became aware that they once again had visitors. As his eyes flickered open, a group of aborigines, seven or perhaps eight of them, appeared from off on the left as one faced Uluru. They walked easily despite the heat which could still be felt, the upper parts of their bodies covered in loose flowing light brown capes. Seeing that Karel had spotted them they changed course towards him, seemingly quite unafraid of him or indeed of the massive Gevcar which sat nearby.

'Evnin teyer.' One of the group spoke while they were still twenty metres or so away, definitely Anglic but compressing words together, in much the same way as what they had heard in Alice Springs. They seemed relaxed, and most of them slid their packs to the ground, obviously enjoying the break in their walk. They were, Karel now saw, a mixed group, with three women and two youngsters who appeared to be not much older than he himself had been when he joined the ESC.

Karel, who by this time had risen to his feet, held out his hand in the universally accepted symbol of greeting. 'Hello, good evening. My name is Karel Houseman.'

'Mm Eddy Kreel, these ma peeble,' nodded the man who had first spoken, his heavy lips pulling back to reveal perfect white teeth when he smiled. He pushed up the protective goggles he wore, revealing jet black eyes. 'Lung time since w'so enbody round disparts, an we go pliny walkabut.' He took Karel's hand and pumped it in a grip that made Karel, long proud of his own firm grip, blink with surprise.

'We've come a long way to get here' replied Karel, conscious of the symbolic meaning the great mass of rock that was Uluru might have for these people. 'I hope we're not bothering you here, we could move if necessary.'

'Na prblim mate.' The man leaned on his staff, a piece of gnarled stick the end of which was a fist sized knob. 'Yer welkim here.' This, thought Karel to himself was just as well, for the stick made a formidable close-quarters weapon, and he himself was unarmed.

'I'd be happy if you could join us for something to eat,' said Karel, not really knowing why he did so, but suddenly aware that it was important to talk to these people, wishing at the same time that one of the others would appear to help him out. As he turned to walk the few metres back to the where the Gevcar stood, Selena shot out of the open doorway as though responding to a shout for help, half skidded to a halt, and then in her usual catlike gait headed towards where Karel and the visitors stood. Stopping in front of them she smiled tentatively at them, head cocked slightly on one side as though listening to unheard voices, and then held out her hand, which Eddy Kreel and then the others shook with an air of almost pompous formality. From the open bay in the Gevcar Jock's head poked out, assessing the situation, his right hand hidden behind the hatch frame, as though holding on for balance. Then, seeing from Selena's infinitesimal nod that things were in order, he relinquished the assault rifle he had been holding and jumped lightly down from the Gevcar, raising a puff of reddish sandy dust as he reached the ground half a metre below.

'So, let the others know we have visitors will you Jojo' nodded Karel, and then turning to Eddy and his people. 'Come on over, the others will all be interested to meet you.' Picking up their kit, the aborigines followed Karel and Selena over to the Gevcar, reaching the doorway, they again dropped their things on the ground, and without any show of hesitation, climbed into the car one by one.

By the end of the evening meal, held in the open space between the Gevcars, under the shadow of a closely woven netting pulled taut between the two Gevcars, a sort of information exchange had been established between the two totally dissimilar groups of people. Maria and Threejays had explained patiently to Eddy, Joey, Pete, Micky, Terry, Maggie, Shana and Lina who they were, and what they were doing there. These explanations had resulted in a few questions, questions which revealed that their message had been fully understood, and at the same time, questions which disconcerted them, for they seemed to reveal that either there was a total lack of curiosity on the side of the aborigines, or, a thought which slipped unbidden into the minds of several of the Gevcar's crew, that the group already knew about them. The conversation over the meal covered a wide variety of topics, from the adventures of their trip, to how the aborigine tribes had survived the rigours of the Outback. After dinner came the time for exchanging information with the Hold, as well as for contacts with the Cape, Tumbes, Lihue and with the Foundation, each of which expressed their hopes that the next day would at last bring their long mission to a successful conclusion. As usual there was also time for personal messages which had the effect of cheering them up, but at the same time having the capacity of leaving them feeling down at heart. At the end of the meal Eddy indicated that his people would sleep out under the cover of the tent, leaving the crews to retire to their compartments, with the notable exception of Karel who continued with his practice of sleeping outside whenever possible. After some discussion, and given the isolation of the encampment, they posted no sentries, though Bob made sure that the perimeter alarms were still carefully set and activated.

The following morning, after breakfast and the daily briefing, the search for the missing Survival Centre resumed, albeit with a difference. Under a cooler and blustier dawn, with heavier clouds than they had seen for several days, Karel had insisted on the necessity of searching the entire perimeter of Uluru more carefully. This, he insisted, meant going round on foot, regardless of the time it might take them. This idea had immediately met with the enthusiastic support of the Watch team who were always glad of the chance to do outside work, the neutrality of most of the rest of the crew, and some degree of scepticism from the two Techs. So much so, that Herb had been heard to remark out of the side of his mouth that he hoped they found the site soon, because he didn't feel up to hiking around the twenty odd domes of Kata Tjuta. Somewhat to their surprise, the aborigines were still with them, and even more surprisingly Eddy asked Karel if he minded if they came with them on the trek round Uluru. 'If yer goeen wokabut, we'll tag 'long ifss 'sorite with yer, sport?' a question to which Karel had been happy to answer affirmatively.

According to the information Janine had downloaded from the Records' computer, the perimeter of Uluru was something in the region of nine kliks, though of course this was very much dependent on how they handled the many small gullies and indents which decorated the whole perimeter. They took with them on the trek a new tool, an enhanced image recognition system input device, in effect a highly sophisticated electronic camera based on a concept of Linda Olsson's and developed into a complex set of algorithms by the Hold computer staff. The basic idea, like many such intuitive leaps, was remarkably simple. Take a photo, keep it, then go back later and take another photograph. Run both images through a high-powered analysis system, factor in changes due to wind and rain, and then isolate change due to other sources by subtracting differences.

'Portable, ha! I'd like to see some of those geniuses at the Hold carrying this thing.' Brendt grumbled as he shifted the thirty-eight kilo pack across his back and nearly tripped over a rock. 'This is about as portable as a Gevcar fuel cell! ... I just hope it works, after all this. Stupid thing will turn out to be like the modified vid-units we used to be saddled with on watch, lucky if they worked ten percent of the time.'

'Come on then Brendt, it can't be as bad as that,' Jojo called back to him, already wise to his grumbling about the technological failure rate.

Walking along some hundred metres away from the rock face, they stopped every few minutes, mounted the image device on its tripod, and took a picture. This picture was stored internally and then transmitted back to the Gevcar, from where Sandy boosted it up to the Sentry, and from there off to the Hold, where the image was collated against all the old photos held in the image bank. So far, after three hours and twenty-two images sent, there had been nothing to report. This electronic search was complemented by careful binocular scans made by Bob, Jojo and Sara, who along with Karel and Selena made up the exploration team. They looked for signs of man-made entrances, tracks made by heavy equipment, signs of old blasting, anything that would indicate that heavy construction work had taken place. Eddy Kreel along with Pete and Maggie, the youngest of the three women in the group, had accompanied the search party, taking an interest in the activities, but not participating actively in the search.

They stopped for a brief lunch, trying to keep out of the wind as much as possible, for otherwise each bite they took became an exercise in spitting out fine grains of sand. Soon, shouldering their packs and equipment once more, they resumed the search. At around three in the afternoon Bob spotted what appeared to be a set of man-made steps high up the rock face and with some difficulty, including a ten metre slide which could have been fatal but wasn't, climbed up for a closer look. The shallow steps he found were undoubtedly artificial in origin, but the old signpost on which the word 'This way to the top' could still be seen made it abundantly clear that this had been one of the old tourist tracks rather than the product of any survival site construction activities. Keeping on going round the great monolith, they took photo after photo which were transmitted off for analysis in the Hold. Each computer study, so they were told, took the Hold supercomputer somewhere around fifteen minutes to process, pretty much half the rate at which new pictures were being sent, thus by the time they had rounded the far side and were headed back towards their campsite, the analysis was running around thirty pictures behind. Karel called a halt, for by this time the day's exertions were beginning to tell, and the stops were becoming more frequent. That their implants had indeed worked wonders they all realized, but the fairly sedentary life of the past few months had left them ill prepared for a long trek such as this, all except Selena that is, who showed no signs whatsoever of fatigue, much to Jojo's chagrin, for he considered himself to be in good shape. In the relative shelter of an outcropping which fell outwards from the main body, they leaned against the rock, enjoying the lack of movement and load.

Karel rested his head on the rock, feeling the muscles in his neck and shoulders relax. With a little effort he brought his relaxation routines into play, feeling the tiredness slip away to be replaced by a sense of wellbeing, of clarity of thought. He felt dissociated from the tiredness, an observer, floating, sensing the others around him. And abruptly came a thought, somehow muffled like a sound heard through thick fog, arriving unbidden in his mind: '… later, he's going to see it, he just needs to glance up and …' and then it was gone. Karel sat up, turning to try and look up the steep slope above his head, and then turning again to see the rest of the party, noting immediately that Selena was doing the same, catching her eye for an instant, and then both of them staring at Eddy, Eddy whose eyes were pools of nothingness, or perhaps not quite.

'You?' Karel's silent unspoken mental question reached out, echoed almost simultaneously by Selena's thought. And suddenly Eddy's eyes seemed to change, and he dipped his head a fraction. 'You!' Karel's voice was soft now, yet it carried enough to call the attention of the others. 'You are the ones we're looking for … you're from Site 1!' The statement hung in the air, and then Eddy smiled, the simple aborigine replaced by someone else, a far more powerful intellect.

'Yes. Yes, indeed we are.' A pause, a heartbeat, and then another. 'Of course, you had to find us. We couldn't tell you.'

'A test of some sort.' Selena leaned forward, smiling now.

'Well, of a sort. More of a condition to be met, really. In many ways we took a different road from you, but we too have a charter to fulfil, and we've been waiting for you for a long time.'

Karel sat back again, shaking his head, overcome with emotion. He felt tears welling up, forming and beginning to flow down his face, and then he was crying, laughing, and the others were joining in, all talking at once, and nobody really listening to any of the answers. As he looked around him, Karel recorded the moment in his mind, Jojo and Selena holding onto each other tight, both talking at the same time, Bob shouting the news into his comm unit, Sara sitting on the rough ground unable to speak, and Eddy and the others shaking his hand, telling him that the search was over at last.

It was late evening as the two Gevcars slid over the ridge almost half a klick away from the mass of rock which blocked out the last purple light of the day. Sitting up in the cockpit beside Herb in the lead car, Eddy directed them down a shallow gully facing in the direction of Uluru, no different from thousands of others. Herb glanced over, worried that something might damage his beloved machine, for even with the lights on it was difficult to see all the variations in the terrain, but Eddy just nodded quietly. Soon, they stopped, just in front of two large boulders set some seven or eight metres apart.

'It's a good thing these Gevcars aren't any larger,' Micky Denson grinned, perched on the edge of the lower step behind the cockpit access hatch. 'Otherwise we'd have trouble getting them down the tunnel.' He thumbed the small transmitter which had been concealed in his pouch, and then the ground in front of them split and began to swing back and upwards, sand pouring off, to reveal a ramp leading down into the earth. Micky tugged at the collar of the rough shirt he was wearing, 'I'll be glad to get out of these clothes, damned things itch all the time.' He waved his hand, indicating that Herb should take the car down the ramp.

The steep concrete ramp led down to a well lit reception area where a number of vehicles, including a small helicopter were parked. The bay was lit by rows of high-intensity lamps giving everything a sickly greenish colour, much the same as in the service passageways back in the Hold. Following Eddy's indications, Herb guided the Gevcar over to where a small group of people were obviously waiting, letting the massive vehicle settle slowly. He initiated the power down procedure, and this time there was somehow a sort of finality to it, even though he knew that the Gevcar would be in use for many years to come. Jock smoothed back his reddish brown hair, already long enough to cover half his ears, flicked the door control button, and as the door swung open, stepped down onto the hard concrete of the vehicle bay. Following behind him, Eddy and the other Site 1 people stepped out. In the second car, with David at the controls, Karel and Sandy, now together in the same Gevcar after so long, sat quietly in the cockpit still overcome with the emotion of finding what they had spent a lifetime searching for. Around them the whine of the power unit ran down, the sound falling in pitch until it became inaudible and vanished. After a few moments Karel joined Jock and together they walked the last few metres to where the welcoming party waited, escorted by their hosts, the aborigine dress somehow incongruous in these new surroundings. Behind them a hooter blew its warning, followed by the whine of hydraulics indicating that the ramp was being raised to its closed position.

A tall, thin, blonde man dressed in a pale green one-piece overall stepped forward and held out his hand. 'Welcome, welcome, I am Councillor Richard Kreel. On behalf of us all, welcome.'

'Thank you. I'm Councillor Jock Fernan.' Jock grasped the outstretched hand and then turned to Karel. 'Let me introduce Captain Karel Houseman of the ESC, our leader, and without whom this expedition would never have happened.'

'The ESC?'

Jock smiled. 'European Space Corps,' he paused enjoying immediate and expected effect of his statement. 'Most of us are in fact from Site 3, the Hold as we call it, set down in Patagonia, but we have two ESC members, two from the Kennedy Space Centre, and two from a scientific foundation in northern California. Quite a mix in fact.'

Kreel introduced them to several more members of the reception committee, and then realizing that things were getting out of hand with more and more people arriving in the bay, hoping to shake hands with the newcomers, invited them to accompany him.

'I'm afraid this has got rather disorganized, and you must be tired. I think it might be better if we adjourn to the Council area up on Level F if you agree.' Seeing Jock's nodded assent, he began organizing their way while the Gevcar crews unloaded what they needed of their personal belongings, leaving everything else in their compartments on board the cars. Bob contrived to bump into Karel while handing him his carryall.

'Lock devices in false bottom' he muttered, before turning to Janine who he proceeded to kiss with enthusiasm, an enthusiasm which was returned in full, attracting several comments from the other members of the crew as well as some laughs from the local people. Karel smiled inwardly, shielding his thoughts as Tante had taught him, while he made his way to the entrance to a tunnel

following the indications given by their hosts. The chances that this meeting was some sort of trap were infinitesimal, but he had trained the Watch team himself in this matter and there was no way he was going to change the procedure, not yet. They had talked the matter over between themselves before setting out for the Site 1 entrance, and had agreed that the SOP would be kept. Better safe than sorry, to coin yet another old but none the less valid term.

Leaving the locked Gevcars behind them, they boarded four or five electric carts which, passing though an airlock of the same design as those in the Hold, whisked them down the tunnel. A tunnel that according to what they were informed, and which tallied with their own sense of direction, sloped slightly down and led towards the great monolith that was Uluru. Arriving at the other end, they passed through another airlock, emerging into a small, pleasantly lit bay, from which they were ushered in to elevators and taken up to Level F, having started from Level A.

As they walked and rode through the survival Centre, they found the place around them to be familiar, and yet strange, for there were subtle differences, in the same way that the Citadel had been different. The clothing of the people they passed in the passageways was different, not so much in colour as in style, and the colours of the walls were different. But around them the hum of the air system, the slight changes in pressure as airlocks opened and closed, the colours of the lighting systems, as well as the visible technical features told the Hold people more surely than anything else that they were home again, a different home perhaps, but home nevertheless.

It took them two more days to get organized for a formal presentation. Two days during which Jock spoke frequently with the Hold, as well as with their other friends in Tumbes, in the Space Centre, in Lihue, and most specially in the Foundation. Congratulations and well wishes poured in, from one and all. Sandy and Jean worked overtime helping the Site 1 communications staff to set up their equipment to use the Sentry links. In small groups they talked with local specialists, exchanging histories and experiences. The two councils also held conference meetings over the link, meetings which also covered their respective histories, and began to touch on their joint future.

Site 1, the Keep as its 7,217 inhabitants called it, had been built at the same time as the other two Survival Centres. Unlike the Hold, however, the knowledge of the other two sites had been kept intact, known to a dozen people. The Keep too had been given its mission, basically the same as that of the Hold, but with an additional condition, that under no circumstances were they to initiate a search for the other sites until a period of sixty cycles had passed. Why this additional condition had been added was something only the Construction Steering Committee could have answered, and they were long gone. Site 1 had had a fairly high proportion of medical staff in its initial intake, and the level of development in all associated fields had been proportionally faster than in the Hold. In particular they had been able to develop neuro-training techniques to enhance the mental abilities of their children to such a point that at least two in five were rudimentary telepaths. Of these, twelve percent were full telepaths able to communicate concepts and ideas at a distance, and the number was increasing with each generation. It was hardly surprising that the ESP research staff at the Keep were ecstatic when told about the developments at the Foundation, and a number of them began making plans for a visit in the near future.

If the construction of the Hold had been complex, then the construction of the Keep had been even more so, for starting from an excavation half a klick away, ostensibly a mining site, the construction team had driven a tunnel into Uluru, and then proceeded to hollow out much of the great rock, constructing seven levels totalling 280,000 square metres. At just over a klick in depth they had found an underground lake of warm slightly brackish water which had guaranteed their survival, serving as fuel for their TFR, heat, and of course as drinking water for the inhabitants. The construction had gone on, overcoming innumerable difficulties, and in the end, eighteen months later than at the Hold, the Keep had been declared open.

On the 244th day after leaving the Hold, the Gevcar crews sat in a loose semicircle facing the crowded auditorium, waiting for the applause which had greeted Richard Kreel's presentation to subside. To say that the great hall was crowded was an understatement, for it was unlikely that any additional person could have been squeezed in, and this in spite of the fact that the meeting was being broadcast on every view-wall and video set in the Keep. As Karel Houseman rose to his feet and stepped forward to the speaker's podium, all movement became stilled, as though the crowd was holding its collective breath.

'I cannot begin to express what I feel as I stand before you. This day is special for all of us who have come here from so far away, it marks the end of one era, and the beginning of a new one. For myself and for Sandy,' he paused to look over at her, and the warmth of the glance that flew between them was felt throughout the room, 'this day means more than I can tell you with words. We have travelled this Earth for fifty years in search of a dream, a dream that would help the world to rebuild. We have followed clue after clue, some of them led to dead ends, others to yet another step forward in the unravelling of the great puzzle. We have been scared, uplifted, filled with sorrow and with joy. We have lost good friends along the way, and made new ones too. There are so many things I could tell you about, probably more than you have time to listen to. Threejays over there,' pointing to where she sat off on his left, 'has written a journal of our search which will be available as soon as it can be proofed and downloaded. A long time ago, Sandy and I looked down on the Earth from space and saw that it was good, we also saw that it was being ruined by the greed, the hatred and the stupidity of man.' He stopped, taking a sip from the glass of water that had been placed beside him. 'Now the Hold and the Keep are together at last. Now more than ever we are absolutely certain that it is possible to rebuild. There will be those who believe that this is not possible, there will be the indifferent, who uncaring of the rest of humanity go about their small lives. There will also be those who fight tooth and nail against us because our success will mean the end of their savage ways. There will be hardships to be faced, battles to be fought.' Karel's back straightened, and his blue eyes burned from within his tanned face.

'I call upon you now to dedicate your future to life, I call upon you to fulfil the charter that was laid down fifty-four years ago by your Founders. You have been blessed with being born in this Survival Centre, now it is time to pay the debt to the generations of those who were not so lucky. Let us make a new beginning for a better world.'

The crowd seemed to rise as one to its feet, with the cheering of many voices swelling and growing as it spread from the room throughout the Keep, rising in pitch and intensity like a great wave that would sweep all before it, unstopping and unstoppable.

With the first light of the new dawn yet an hour away, Karel slipped out of the service airlock on Level C, emerging into a small natural cave, itself almost hidden from view by a fold in the brown rock face.

Following the ledge off to the east for a few hundred metres he reached an old footpath leading upwards. The ancient and heavily worn steps leading up to the flattened top of the massif were easy enough to follow in the light of the gibbous moon which looked down from low over the horizon, giving everything an eerie yellow glow. He moved easily, arms swinging loosely, hardly out of breath, enjoying the feeling of having a young healthy body again. The last few days had been hectic to say the least and he had been feeling edgy without quite understanding why. It was only when Sandy had gently suggested that he needed to be alone for a while, that he realized she had hit the nail on the head, yet another long-forgotten expression popping into his mind, and that that was exactly what he was missing. He had somehow and without looking for it become the leader of the all encompassing project of rebuilding the best of civilization, and the demands on his time were many. And so it was that in the chill of the early morning, long before most people in the Keep were awake, he had set out to climb to the top of the immense rock that had guarded its secret so well and for so long.

The only sound was the slight scuffing of his shoes on the rough surface, for the slight breeze, hardly enough to stir the thin tendrils of mist which floated insubstantially around, made no noise at all. Half an hour's steady climbing brought him to the end of the marked path and on to the roughly flat top of the rock which stretched off into the darkness. He wandered around for a few minutes until he came across a formation in which a natural depression had been carved by the seasons. Sitting down, his back resting on the slightly damp rock, he faced eastwards, eyes closed, letting his mantra run quietly through his mind, bringing him calm. Around him he could sense the immense emptiness of the desert, silent, yet not silent, for there is always life to be found if one listens carefully enough. Expanding his consciousness by steps as if reaching out into the night, he vaguely sensed the many thousands of souls in the rock beneath him, and then the vast almost empty land around them, and beyond that the all encompassing sea. As he sat there on Uluru he reached out and felt the finger-light touch of Leana's mind, a greeting from across the great ocean, with the warmth that accompanied all his meetings with her. 'We made it at last' his thought flowed to her, and through her he knew that Tante was talking to him. 'There was never any doubt Karel, you had to, as simple as that.'

Even with his eyes closed he could sense the lightening of the horizon, which was beginning to shift from the blackness of night into purple and from there on to the red of the coming day. As he sat, the image of the light grew brighter and changed in his mind and became the violent orange-yellow flame of a booster rocket which hurled the gleaming white shuttle into space, the vibration seeming to go on and on as the Earth dropped behind. And all of a sudden it came to him with absolute certainty that what he saw was not a memory, nor the past, but a glimpse of what still lay in store for him, though how Leana could possibly know that, he couldn't yet hope to understand.

Presently Captain Karel Houseman, late of the ESC, slipped into a dreamless sleep, a slight smile still creasing his lips, while the great red rock on which he sat raced forward into the light of a new dawn.

THE END